S0-AKI-436

NON SANZ DROICT.

The most excellent

Historie of the *Merchant* of *Venice*.

VVith the extreame crueltie of *Shylocke* the Iewe
towards the sayd Merchant, in cutting a iust pound
of his flesh: and the obtayning of *Portia*
by the choyse of three
chests.

As it hath beene diuers times acted by the Lord
Chamberlaine his Seruants.

Written by William Shakespeare.

AT LONDON,
Printed by *I. R.* for Thomas Heyes,
and are to be sold in Paules Church-yard, at the
signe of the Greene Dragon.
1600.

Title page of the earliest edition of *The Merchant of Venice*

William Shakespeare

The Merchant of Venice

With New and Updated Critical Essays and a Revised Bibliography

Edited by Kenneth Myrick

THE SIGNET CLASSICS SHAKESPEARE
General Editor: Sylvan Barnet

SIGNET CLASSICS

SIGNET CLASSICS
Published by New American Library, a division of
Penguin Group (USA) Inc., 375 Hudson Street,
New York, New York 10014, USA
Penguin Group (Canada), 10 Alcorn Avenue, Toronto,
Ontario M4V 3B2, Canada (a division of Pearson Penguin Canada Inc.)
Penguin Books Ltd., 80 Strand, London WC2R 0RL, England
Penguin Ireland, 25 St. Stephen's Green, Dublin 2,
Ireland (a division of Penguin Books Ltd.)
Penguin Group (Australia), 250 Camberwell Road, Camberwell, Victoria 3124,
Australia (a division of Pearson Australia Group Pty. Ltd.)
Penguin Books India Pvt. Ltd., 11 Community Centre, Panchsheel Park,
New Delhi - 110 017, India
Penguin Group (NZ), cnr Airborne and Rosedale Roads, Albany,
Auckland 1310, New Zealand (a division of Pearson New Zealand Ltd.)
Penguin Books (South Africa) (Pty.) Ltd., 24 Sturdee Avenue,
Rosebank, Johannesburg 2196, South Africa

Penguin Books Ltd., Registered Offices:
80 Strand, London WC2R 0RL, England

Published by Signet Classics, an imprint of New American Library, a division
of Penguin Group (USA) Inc. The Signet Classics edition of *The Merchant
of Venice* was first published in 1965, and an updated edition was published
in 1987.

First Signet Classics Printing (Second Revised Edition), April 1998
First Signet Classics Printing (Movie Tie-In Edition), December 2004
10 9 8 7 6 5 4 3 2 1

Copyright © Kenneth Myrick, 1965
Copyright © Sylvan Barnet, 1963, 1987, 1998
All rights reserved

SIGNET CLASSICS and logo are trademarks of Penguin Group (USA) Inc.

Library of Congress Catalog Card Number: 97-69247

Printed in the United States of America

Without limiting the rights under copyright reserved above, no part of this
publication may be reproduced, stored in or introduced into a retrieval system,
or transmitted, in any form, or by any means (electronic, mechanical, photocopy-
ing, recording, or otherwise), without the prior written permission of both the
copyright owner and the above publisher of this book.

If you purchased this book without a cover you should be aware that this book
is stolen property. It was reported as "unsold and destroyed" to the publisher
and neither the author nor the publisher has received any payment for this
"stripped book."

The scanning, uploading, and distribution of this book via the Internet or via
any other means without the permission of the publisher is illegal and punish-
able by law. Please purchase only authorized electronic editions, and do not
participate in or encourage electronic piracy of copyrighted materials. Your
support of the author's rights is appreciated.

Contents

Shakespeare: An Overview

Biographical Sketch

Between the record of his baptism in Stratford on 26 April 1564 and the record of his burial in Stratford on 25 April 1616, some forty official documents name Shakespeare, and many others name his parents, his children, and his grandchildren. Further, there are at least fifty literary references to him in the works of his contemporaries. More facts are known about William Shakespeare than about any other playwright of the period except Ben Jonson. The facts should, however, be distinguished from the legends. The latter, inevitably more engaging and better known, tell us that the Stratford boy killed a calf in high style, poached deer and rabbits, and was forced to flee to London, where he held horses outside a playhouse. These traditions are only traditions; they may be true, but no evidence supports them, and it is well to stick to the facts.

Mary Arden, the dramatist's mother, was the daughter of a substantial landowner; about 1557 she married John Shakespeare, a tanner, glove-maker, and trader in wool, grain, and other farm commodities. In 1557 John Shakespeare was a member of the council (the governing body of Stratford), in 1558 a constable of the borough, in 1561 one of the two town chamberlains, in 1565 an alderman (entitling him to the appellation of "Mr."), in 1568 high bailiff—the town's highest political office, equivalent to mayor. After 1577, for an unknown reason he drops out of local politics. What *is* known is that he had to mortgage his wife's property, and that he was involved in serious litigation.

The birthday of William Shakespeare, the third child and the eldest son of this locally prominent man, is unrecorded, but the Stratford parish register records that the infant was baptized on 26 April 1564. (It is quite possible that he was born on 23 April, but this date has probably been assigned by tradition because it is the date on which, fifty-two years later, he died, and perhaps because it is the feast day of St. George, patron saint of England.) The attendance records of the Stratford grammar school of the period are not extant, but it is reasonable to assume that the son of a prominent local official attended the free school—it had been established for the purpose of educating males precisely of his class—and received substantial training in Latin. The masters of the school from Shakespeare's seventh to fifteenth years held Oxford degrees; the Elizabethan curriculum excluded mathematics and the natural sciences but taught a good deal of Latin rhetoric, logic, and literature, including plays by Plautus, Terence, and Seneca.

On 27 November 1582 a marriage license was issued for the marriage of Shakespeare and Anne Hathaway, eight years his senior. The couple had a daughter, Susanna, in May 1583. Perhaps the marriage was necessary, but perhaps the couple had earlier engaged, in the presence of witnesses, in a formal "troth plight" which would render their children legitimate even if no further ceremony were performed. In February 1585, Anne Hathaway bore Shakespeare twins, Hamnet and Judith.

That Shakespeare was born is excellent; that he married and had children is pleasant; but that we know nothing about his departure from Stratford to London or about the beginning of his theatrical career is lamentable and must be admitted. We would gladly sacrifice details about his children's baptism for details about his earliest days in the theater. Perhaps the poaching episode is true (but it is first reported almost a century after Shakespeare's death), or perhaps he left Stratford to be a schoolmaster, as another tradition holds; perhaps he was moved (like Petruchio in *The Taming of the Shrew*) by

> Such wind as scatters young men through the world,
> To seek their fortunes farther than at home
> Where small experience grows.   (1.2.49–51)

In 1592, thanks to the cantankerousness of Robert Greene, we have our first reference, a snarling one, to Shakespeare as an actor and playwright. Greene, a graduate of St. John's College, Cambridge, had become a playwright and a pamphleteer in London, and in one of his pamphlets he warns three university-educated playwrights against an actor who has presumed to turn playwright:

> There is an upstart crow, beautified with our feathers, that with his *tiger's heart wrapped in a player's hide* supposes he is as well able to bombast out a blank verse as the best of you, and being an absolute Johannes-factotum [i.e., jack-of-all-trades] is in his own conceit the only Shake-scene in a country.

The reference to the player, as well as the allusion to Aesop's crow (who strutted in borrowed plumage, as an actor struts in fine words not his own), makes it clear that by this date Shakespeare had both acted and written. That Shakespeare is meant is indicated not only by *Shake-scene* but also by the parody of a line from one of Shakespeare's plays, *3 Henry VI*: "O, tiger's heart wrapped in a woman's hide" (1.4.137). If in 1592 Shakespeare was prominent enough to be attacked by an envious dramatist, he probably had served an apprenticeship in the theater for at least a few years.

In any case, although there are no extant references to Shakespeare between the record of the baptism of his twins in 1585 and Greene's hostile comment about "Shake-scene" in 1592, it is evident that during some of these "dark years" or "lost years" Shakespeare had acted and written. There are a number of subsequent references to him as an actor. Documents indicate that in 1598 he is a "principal comedian," in 1603 a "principal tragedian," in 1608 he is one of the "men players." (We do not have, however, any solid information about which roles he may have played; later traditions say he played Adam in *As You Like It* and the ghost in *Hamlet*, but nothing supports the assertions. Probably his role as dramatist came to supersede his role as actor.) The profession of actor was not for a gentleman, and it occasionally drew the scorn of university men like Greene who resented writing speeches for persons less educated than themselves, but it was respectable enough; players, if prosperous, were in effect members of the bourgeoisie, and there is nothing to suggest that Stratford considered William Shakespeare less than a solid citizen. When, in 1596, the Shakespeares were granted a coat of arms—i.e., the right to be considered gentlemen—the grant was made to Shakespeare's father, but probably William Shakespeare had arranged the matter on his own behalf. In subsequent transactions he is occasionally styled a gentleman.

Although in 1593 and 1594 Shakespeare published two narrative poems dedicated to the Earl of Southampton, *Venus and Adonis* and *The Rape of Lucrece*, and may well have written most or all of his sonnets in the middle nineties, Shakespeare's literary activity seems to have been almost entirely devoted to the theater. (It may be significant that the two narrative poems were written in years when the plague closed the theaters for several months.) In 1594 he was a charter member of a theatrical company called the Chamberlain's Men, which in 1603 became the royal company, the King's Men, making Shakespeare the king's playwright. Until he retired to Stratford (about 1611, apparently), he was with this remarkably stable company. From 1599 the company acted primarily at the Globe theater, in which Shakespeare held a one-tenth interest. Other Elizabethan dramatists are known to have acted, but no other is known also to have been entitled to a share of the profits.

Shakespeare's first eight published plays did not have his name on them, but this is not remarkable; the most popular play of the period, Thomas Kyd's *The Spanish Tragedy*, went through many editions without naming Kyd, and Kyd's authorship is known only because a book on the profession of acting happens to quote (and attribute to Kyd) some lines on the interest of Roman emperors in the drama. What is remarkable is that after 1598 Shakespeare's name commonly appears on printed plays—some of which are not his. Presumably his name was a drawing card, and publishers used it to attract potential buyers. Another indication of his popularity comes from Francis Meres, author of *Palladis Tamia: Wit's Treasury* (1598). In this anthology of snippets accompanied by an essay on literature, many playwrights are mentioned, but Shakespeare's name occurs more often than any other, and Shakespeare is the only playwright whose plays are listed.

From his acting, his play writing, and his share in a playhouse, Shakespeare seems to have made considerable money. He put it to work, making substantial investments in Stratford real estate. As early as 1597 he bought New Place, the second-largest house in Stratford. His family moved in soon afterward, and the house remained in the family until a granddaughter died in 1670. When Shakespeare made his will in 1616, less than a month before he died, he sought to leave his property intact to his descendants. Of small bequests to relatives and to friends (including three actors, Richard Burbage, John Heminges, and Henry Condell), that to his wife of the second-best bed has provoked the most comment. It has sometimes been taken as a sign of an unhappy marriage (other supposed signs are the apparently hasty marriage, his wife's seniority of eight years, and his residence in London without his family). Perhaps the second-best bed was the bed the couple had slept in, the best bed being reserved for visitors. In any case, had Shakespeare not excepted it, the bed would have gone (with the rest of his household possessions) to his daughter and her husband.

On 25 April 1616 Shakespeare was buried within the chancel of the church at Stratford. An unattractive monument to his memory, placed on a wall near the grave, says that he died on 23 April. Over the grave itself are the lines, perhaps by Shakespeare, that (more than his literary fame) have kept his bones undisturbed in the crowded burial ground where old bones were often dislodged to make way for new:

> Good friend, for Jesus' sake forbear
> To dig the dust enclosed here.
> Blessed be the man that spares these stones
> And cursed be he that moves my bones.

A Note on the Anti-Stratfordians, Especially Baconians and Oxfordians

Not until 1769—more than a hundred and fifty years after Shakespeare's death—is there any record of anyone expressing doubt about Shakespeare's authorship of the plays and poems. In 1769, however, Herbert Lawrence nominated Francis Bacon (1561–1626) in *The Life and Adventures of Common Sense*. Since then, at least two dozen other nominees have been offered, including Christopher Marlowe, Sir Walter Raleigh, Queen Elizabeth I, and Edward de Vere, 17th earl of Oxford. The impulse behind all anti-Stratfordian movements is the scarcely concealed snobbish opinion that "the man from Stratford" simply could not have written the plays because he was a country fellow without a university education and without access to high society. Anyone, the argument goes, who used so many legal terms, medical terms, nautical terms, and so forth, and who showed some familiarity with classical writing, must have attended a university, and anyone who knew so much about courtly elegance and courtly deceit must himself have moved among courtiers. The plays do indeed reveal an author whose interests were exceptionally broad, but specialists in any given field—law, medicine, arms and armor, and so on—soon find that the plays do not reveal deep knowledge in specialized matters; indeed, the playwright often gets technical details wrong.

The claim on behalf of Bacon, forgotten almost as soon as it was put forth in 1769, was independently reasserted by Joseph C. Hart in 1848. In 1856 it was reaffirmed by W. H. Smith in a book, and also by Delia Bacon in an article; in 1857 Delia Bacon published a book, arguing that Francis Bacon had directed a group of intellectuals who wrote the plays.

Francis Bacon's claim has largely faded, perhaps because it was advanced with such evident craziness by Ignatius Donnelly, who in *The Great Cryptogram* (1888) claimed to break a code in the plays that proved Bacon had written not only the plays attributed to Shakespeare but also other Renaissance works, for instance the plays of Christopher Marlowe and the essays of Montaigne.

Consider the last two lines of the Epilogue in *The Tempest*:

> As you from crimes would pardoned be,
> Let your indulgence set me free.

What was Shakespeare—sorry, Francis Bacon, Baron Verulam—*really* saying in these two lines? According to Baconians, the lines are an anagram reading, "Tempest of Francis Bacon, Lord Verulam; do ye ne'er divulge me, ye words." Ingenious, and it is a pity that in the quotation the letter *a* appears only twice in the cryptogram, whereas in the deciphered message it appears three times. Oh, no problem; just alter "Verulam" to "Verul'm" and it works out very nicely.

Most people understand that with sufficient ingenuity one can torture any text and find in it what one wishes. For instance: Did Shakespeare have a hand in the King James Version of the Bible? It was nearing completion in 1610, when Shakespeare was forty-six years old. If you look at the 46th Psalm and count forward for forty-six words, you will find the word *shake*. Now if you go to the end of the psalm and count backward forty-six words, you will find the word *spear*. Clear evidence, according to some, that Shakespeare slyly left his mark in the book.

Bacon's candidacy has largely been replaced in the twentieth century by the candidacy of Edward de Vere (1550–1604), 17th earl of Oxford. The basic ideas behind the Oxford theory, advanced at greatest length by Dorothy and Charlton Ogburn in *This Star of England* (1952, rev. 1955), a book of 1297 pages, and by Charlton Ogburn in *The Mysterious William Shakespeare* (1984), a book of 892 pages, are these: (1) The man from Stratford could not possibly have had the mental equipment and the experience to have written the plays—only a courtier could have written them; (2) Oxford had the requisite background (social position, education, years at Queen Elizabeth's court); (3) Oxford did not wish his authorship to be known for two basic reasons: writing for the public theater was a vulgar pursuit, and the plays show so much courtly and royal disreputable behavior that they would have compromised Oxford's position at court. Oxfordians offer countless details to support the claim. For example, Hamlet's phrase "that ever I was born to set it right" (1.5.89) barely conceals "E. Ver, I was born to set it right," an unambiguous announcement of de Vere's authorship, according to *This Star of England* (p. 654). A second example: Consider Ben

Jonson's poem entitled "To the Memory of My Beloved Master William Shakespeare," prefixed to the first collected edition of Shakespeare's plays in 1623. According to Oxfordians, when Jonson in this poem speaks of the author of the plays as the "swan of Avon," he is alluding not to William Shakespeare, who was born and died in Stratford-on-Avon and who throughout his adult life owned property there; rather, he is alluding to Oxford, who, the Ogburns say, used "William Shakespeare" as his pen name, and whose manor at Bilton was on the Avon River. Oxfordians do not offer any evidence that Oxford took a pen name, and they do not mention that Oxford had sold the manor in 1581, forty-two years before Jonson wrote his poem. Surely a reference to the Shakespeare who was born in Stratford, who had returned to Stratford, and who had died there only seven years before Jonson wrote the poem is more plausible. And exactly why Jonson, who elsewhere also spoke of Shakespeare as a playwright, and why Heminges and Condell, who had acted with Shakespeare for about twenty years, should speak of Shakespeare as the author in their dedication in the 1623 volume of collected plays is never adequately explained by Oxfordians. Either Jonson, Heminges and Condell, and numerous others were in on the conspiracy, or they were all duped—equally unlikely alternatives. Another difficulty in the Oxford theory is that Oxford died in 1604, and some of the plays are clearly indebted to works and events later than 1604. Among the Oxfordian responses are: At his death Oxford left some plays, and in later years these were touched up by hacks, who added the material that points to later dates. *The Tempest*, almost universally regarded as one of Shakespeare's greatest plays and pretty clearly dated to 1611, does indeed date from a period after the death of Oxford, but it is a crude piece of work that should not be included in the canon of works by Oxford.

The anti-Stratfordians, in addition to assuming that the author must have been a man of rank and a university man, usually assume two conspiracies: (1) a conspiracy in Elizabethan and Jacobean times, in which a surprisingly large number of persons connected with the theater knew that the actor Shakespeare did not write the plays attributed to him but for some reason or other pretended that he did; (2) a conspiracy of today's Stratfordians, the professors who teach Shakespeare in the colleges and universities, who are said to have a vested interest in preserving Shakespeare as the author of the plays they teach In fact, (1) it is inconceivable that the secret of Shakespeare's non-authorship could have been preserved by all of the people who supposedly were in on the conspiracy, and (2) academic fame awaits any scholar today who can disprove Shakespeare's authorship.

The Stratfordian case is convincing not only because hundreds or even thousands of anti-Stratford arguments—of the sort that say "ever I was born" has the secret double meaning "E. Ver, I was born"—add up to nothing at all but also because irrefutable evidence connects the man from Stratford with the London theater and with the authorship of particular plays. The anti-Stratfordians do not seem to understand that it is not enough to dismiss the Stratford case by saying that a fellow from the provinces simply couldn't have written the plays. Nor do they understand that it is not enough to dismiss all of the evidence connecting Shakespeare with the plays by asserting that it is perjured.

The Shakespeare Canon

We return to William Shakespeare. Thirty-seven plays as well as some nondramatic poems are generally held to constitute the Shakespeare canon, the body of authentic works. The exact dates of composition of most of the works are highly uncertain, but evidence of a starting point and/or of a final limiting point often provides a framework for informed guessing. For example, *Richard II* cannot be earlier than 1595, the publication date of some material to which it is indebted; *The Merchant of Venice* cannot be later than 1598, the year Francis Meres mentioned it. Sometimes arguments for a date hang on an alleged topical allusion, such as the lines about the unseasonable weather in *A Midsummer Night's Dream*, 2.1.81–117, but such an allusion, if indeed it is an allusion to an event in the real world, can be variously interpreted, and in any case there is always the possibility that a topical allusion was inserted years later, to bring the play up to date. (The issue of alterations in a text between the time that Shakespeare drafted it and the time that it was printed—alterations due to censorship or playhouse practice or Shakespeare's own second thoughts—will be discussed in "The Play Text as a Collaboration" later in this overview.) Dates are often attributed on the basis of style, and although conjectures about style usually rest on other conjectures (such as Shakespeare's development as a playwright, or the appropriateness of lines to character), sooner or later one must rely on one's literary sense. There is no documentary proof, for example, that *Othello* is not as early as *Romeo and Juliet*, but one feels that *Othello* is a later, more mature work, and because the first record of its performance is 1604, one is glad enough to set its composition at that date and not push it back into Shakespeare's early years. (*Romeo and Juliet* was first published in 1597, but evidence suggests that it was written a little earlier.) The following chronology, then, is indebted not only to facts but also to informed guesswork and sensitivity. The dates, necessarily imprecise for some works, indicate something like a scholarly consensus concerning the time of original composition. Some plays show evidence of later revision.

Plays. The first collected edition of Shakespeare, published in 1623, included thirty-six plays. These are all accepted as Shakespeare's, though for one of them, *Henry VIII*, he is thought to have had a collaborator. A thirty-seventh play, *Pericles*, published in 1609 and attributed to Shakespeare on the title page, is also widely accepted as being partly by Shakespeare even though it is not included in the 1623 volume. Still another play not in the 1623 volume, *The Two Noble Kinsmen*, was first published in 1634, with a title page attributing it to John Fletcher and Shakespeare. Probably most students of the subject now believe that Shakespeare did indeed have a hand in it. Of the remaining plays attributed at one time or another to Shakespeare, only one, *Edward III*, anonymously published in 1596, is now regarded by some scholars as a serious candidate. The prevailing opinion, however, is that this rather simple-minded play is not Shakespeare's; at most he may have revised some passages, chiefly scenes with the Countess of

Salisbury. We include *The Two Noble Kinsmen* but do not include *Edward III* in the following list.

1588–94	*The Comedy of Errors*
1588–94	*Love's Labor's Lost*
1589–91	*2 Henry VI*
1590–91	*3 Henry VI*
1589–92	*1 Henry VI*
1592–93	*Richard III*
1589–94	*Titus Andronicus*
1593–94	*The Taming of the Shrew*
1592–94	*The Two Gentlemen of Verona*
1594–96	*Romeo and Juliet*
1595	*Richard II*
1595–96	*A Midsummer Night's Dream*
1596–97	*King John*
1594–96	*The Merchant of Venice*
1596–97	*1 Henry IV*
1597	*The Merry Wives of Windsor*
1597–98	*2 Henry IV*
1598–99	*Much Ado About Nothing*
1598–99	*Henry V*
1599	*Julius Caesar*
1599–1600	*As You Like It*
1599–1600	*Twelfth Night*
1600–1601	*Hamlet*
1601–1602	*Troilus and Cressida*
1602–1604	*All's Well That Ends Well*
1603–1604	*Othello*
1604	*Measure for Measure*
1605–1606	*King Lear*
1605–1606	*Macbeth*
1606–1607	*Antony and Cleopatra*
1605–1608	*Timon of Athens*
1607–1608	*Coriolanus*
1607–1608	*Pericles*
1609–10	*Cymbeline*
1610–11	*The Winter's Tale*
1611	*The Tempest*

| 1612–13 | *Henry VIII* |
| 1613 | *The Two Noble Kinsmen* |

Poems. In 1989 Donald W. Foster published a book in which he argued that "A Funeral Elegy for Master William Peter," published in 1612, ascribed only to the initials W.S., *may* be by Shakespeare. Foster later published an article in a scholarly journal, *PMLA* 111 (1996), in which he asserted the claim more positively. The evidence begins with the initials, and includes the fact that the publisher and the printer of the elegy had published Shakespeare's *Sonnets* in 1609. But such facts add up to rather little, especially because no one has found any connection between Shakespeare and William Peter (an Oxford graduate about whom little is known, who was murdered at the age of twenty-nine). The argument is based chiefly on statistical examinations of word patterns, which are said to correlate with Shakespeare's known work. Despite such correlations, however, many readers feel that the poem does not sound like Shakespeare. True, Shakespeare has a great range of styles, but his work is consistently imaginative and interesting. Many readers find neither of these qualities in "A Funeral Elegy."

1592–93	*Venus and Adonis*
1593–94	*The Rape of Lucrece*
1593–1600	*Sonnets*
1600–1601	*The Phoenix and the Turtle*

Shakespeare's English

1. Spelling and Pronunciation. From the philologist's point of view, Shakespeare's English is modern English. It requires footnotes, but the inexperienced reader can comprehend substantial passages with very little help, whereas for the same reader Chaucer's Middle English is a foreign language. By the beginning of the fifteenth century the chief grammatical changes in English had taken place, and the final unaccented -*e* of Middle English had been lost (though it survives even today in spelling, as in *name*); during the fifteenth century the dialect of London, the commercial and political center, gradually displaced the provincial dialects, at least in writing; by the end of the century, printing had helped to regularize and stabilize the language, especially spelling. Elizabethan spelling may seem erratic to us (there were dozens of spellings of *Shakespeare*, and a simple word like *been* was also spelled *beene* and *bin*), but it had much in common with our spelling. Elizabethan spelling was conservative in that for the most part it reflected an older pronunciation (Middle English) rather than the sound of the language as it was then spoken, just as our spelling continues to reflect medieval pronunciation—most obviously in the now silent but formerly pronounced letters in a word such as *knight*. Elizabethan pronunciation, though not identical with ours, was much closer to ours than to that of the Middle Ages. Incidentally, though no one can be certain about what Elizabethan English sounded like, specialists tend to believe it was rather like the speech of a modern stage Irishman (*time* apparently was pronounced *toime*, *old* pronounced *awld*, *day* pronounced *die*, and *join* pronounced *jine*) and not at all like the Oxford speech that most of us think it was.

An awareness of the difference between our pronunciation and Shakespeare's is crucial in three areas—in accent, or number of syllables (many metrically regular lines may look irregular to us); in rhymes (which may not look like rhymes); and in puns (which may not look like puns). Examples will be useful. Some words that were at least on occasion stressed differently from today are *aspèct*, *còmplete*, *fòrlorn*, *revènue*, and *sepùlcher*. Words that sometimes had an additional syllable are *emp[e]ress*, *Hen[e]ry*, *mon[e]th*, and *villain* (three syllables, *vil-lay-in*). An additional syllable is often found in possessives, like *moon*'s (pronounced *moones*) and in words ending in -*tion* or -*sion*. Words that had one less syllable than they now have are *needle* (pronounced *neel*) and *violet* (pronounced *vilet*). Among rhymes now lost are *one* with *loan*, *love* with *prove*, *beast* with *jest*, *eat* with *great*. (In reading, trust your sense of metrics and your ear, more than your eye.) An example of a pun that has become obliterated by a change in pronunciation is Falstaff's reply to Prince Hal's "Come, tell us your reason" in *1 Henry IV*: "Give you a reason on compulsion? If reasons were as plentiful as blackberries, I would give no man a reason upon compulsion, I" (2.4.237–40). The *ea* in *reason* was pronounced rather like a long *a*, like the *ai* in *raisin*, hence the comparison with blackberries.

Puns are not merely attempts to be funny; like metaphors they often involve bringing into a meaningful relationship areas of experience normally seen as remote. In *2 Henry IV*, when Feeble is conscripted, he stoically says, "I care not. A man can die but once. We owe God a death" (3.2.242–43), punning on *debt*, which was the way *death* was pronounced. Here an enormously significant fact of life is put into simple commercial imagery, suggesting its commonplace quality. Shakespeare used the same pun earlier in *1 Henry IV*, when Prince Hal says to Falstaff, "Why, thou owest God a death," and Falstaff replies, " 'Tis not due yet: I would be loath to pay him before his day. What need I be so forward with him that calls not on me?" (5.1.126–29).

Sometimes the puns reveal a delightful playfulness; sometimes they reveal aggressiveness, as when, replying to Claudius's "But now, my cousin Hamlet, and my son," Hamlet says, "A little more than kin, and less than kind!" (1.2.64–65). These are Hamlet's first words in the play, and we already hear him warring verbally against Claudius. Hamlet's "less than kind" probably means (1) Hamlet is not of Claudius's family or nature, *kind* having the sense it still has in our word *mankind*; (2) Hamlet is not kindly (affectionately) disposed toward Claudius; (3) Claudius is not naturally (but rather unnaturally, in a legal sense incestuously) Hamlet's father. The puns evidently were not put in as sops to the groundlings; they are an important way of communicating a complex meaning.

2. *Vocabulary.* A conspicuous difficulty in reading Shakespeare is rooted in the fact that some of his words are no longer in common use—for example, words concerned with armor, astrology, clothing, coinage, hawking, horsemanship, law, medicine, sailing, and war. Shakespeare had a large vocabulary—something near thirty thousand words—but it was not so much a vocabulary of big words as a vocabulary drawn from a wide range of life, and it is partly

his ability to call upon a great body of concrete language that gives his plays the sense of being in close contact with life. When the right word did not already exist, he made it up. Among words thought to be his coinages are *accommodation, all-knowing, amazement, bare-faced, countless, dexterously, dislocate, dwindle, fancy-free, frugal, indistinguishable, lackluster, laughable, overawe, premeditated, sea change, star-crossed*. Among those that have not survived are the verb *convive*, meaning to feast together, and *smilet*, a little smile.

Less overtly troublesome than the technical words but more treacherous are the words that seem readily intelligible to us but whose Elizabethan meanings differ from their modern ones. When Horatio describes the Ghost as an "erring spirit," he is saying not that the ghost has sinned or made an error but that it is wandering. Here is a short list of some of the most common words in Shakespeare's plays that often (but not always) have a meaning other than their most usual modern meaning:

'a	he
abuse	deceive
accident	occurrence
advertise	inform
an, and	if
annoy	harm
appeal	accuse
artificial	skillful
brave	fine, splendid
censure	opinion
cheer	(1) face (2) frame of mind
chorus	a single person who comments on the events
closet	small private room
competitor	partner
conceit	idea, imagination
cousin	kinsman
cunning	skillful
disaster	evil astrological influence
doom	judgment
entertain	receive into service

envy	malice
event	outcome
excrement	outgrowth (of hair)
fact	evil deed
fancy	(1) love (2) imagination
fell	cruel
fellow	(1) companion (2) low person (often an insulting term if addressed to someone of approximately equal rank)
fond	foolish
free	(1) innocent (2) generous
glass	mirror
hap, haply	chance, by chance
head	army
humor	(1) mood (2) bodily fluid thought to control one's psychology
imp	child
intelligence	news
kind	natural, acting according to nature
let	hinder
lewd	base
mere(ly)	utter(ly)
modern	commonplace
natural	a fool, an idiot
naughty	(1) wicked (2) worthless
next	nearest
nice	(1) trivial (2) fussy
noise	music
policy	(1) prudence (2) stratagem
presently	immediately
prevent	anticipate
proper	handsome
prove	test
quick	alive
sad	serious
saw	proverb
secure	without care, incautious
silly	innocent

sensible	capable of being perceived by the senses
shrewd	sharp
so	provided that
starve	die
still	always
success	that which follows
tall	brave
tell	count
tonight	last night
wanton	playful, careless
watch	keep awake
will	lust
wink	close both eyes
wit	mind, intelligence

All glosses, of course, are mere approximations; sometimes one of Shakespeare's words may hover between an older meaning and a modern one, and as we have seen, his words often have multiple meanings.

3. Grammar. A few matters of grammar may be surveyed, though it should be noted at the outset that Shakespeare sometimes made up his own grammar. As E.A. Abbott says in *A Shakespearian Grammar,* "Almost any part of speech can be used as any other part of speech": a noun as a verb ("he childed as I fathered"); a verb as a noun ("She hath made compare"); or an adverb as an adjective ("a seldom pleasure"). There are hundreds, perhaps thousands, of such instances in the plays, many of which at first glance would not seem at all irregular and would trouble only a pedant. Here are a few broad matters.

Nouns: The Elizabethans thought the *-s* genitive ending for nouns (as in *man's*) derived from *his*; thus the line " 'gainst the count his galleys I did some service," for "the count's galleys."

Adjectives: By Shakespeare's time adjectives had lost the endings that once indicated gender, number, and case. About the only difference between Shakespeare's adjectives and ours is the use of the now redundant *more* or *most* with the comparative ("some more fitter place") or superlative

("This was the most unkindest cut of all"). Like double comparatives and double superlatives, double negatives were acceptable; Mercutio "will not budge for no man's pleasure."

Pronouns: The greatest change was in pronouns. In Middle English *thou, thy,* and *thee* were used among familiars and in speaking to children and inferiors; *ye, your,* and *you* were used in speaking to superiors (servants to masters, nobles to the king) or to equals with whom the speaker was not familiar. Increasingly the "polite" forms were used in all direct address, regardless of rank, and the accusative *you* displaced the nominative *ye.* Shakespeare sometimes uses *ye* instead of *you,* but even in Shakespeare's day *ye* was archaic, and it occurs mostly in rhetorical appeals.

Thou, thy, and *thee* were not completely displaced, however, and Shakespeare occasionally makes significant use of them, sometimes to connote familiarity or intimacy and sometimes to connote contempt. In *Twelfth Night* Sir Toby advises Sir Andrew to insult Cesario by addressing him as *thou:* "If thou thou'st him some thrice, it shall not be amiss" (3.2.46–47). In *Othello* when Brabantio is addressing an unidentified voice in the dark he says, "What are you?" (1.1.91), but when the voice identifies itself as the foolish suitor Roderigo, Brabantio uses the contemptuous form, saying, "I have charged thee not to haunt about my doors" (93). He uses this form for a while, but later in the scene, when he comes to regard Roderigo as an ally, he shifts back to the polite *you,* beginning in line 163, "What said she to you?" and on to the end of the scene. For reasons not yet satisfactorily explained, Elizabethans used *thou* in addresses to God—"O God, thy arm was here," the king says in *Henry V* (4.8.108)—and to supernatural characters such as ghosts and witches. A subtle variation occurs in *Hamlet.* When Hamlet first talks with the Ghost in 1.5, he uses *thou,* but when he sees the Ghost in his mother's room, in 3.4, he uses *you,* presumably because he is now convinced that the Ghost is not a counterfeit but is his father.

Perhaps the most unusual use of pronouns, from our point of view, is the neuter singular. In place of our *its, his* was often used, as in "How far that little candle throws *his* beams." But the use of a masculine pronoun for a neuter noun came to seem unnatural, and so *it* was used for the possessive as well as the nominative: "The hedge-sparrow fed the cuckoo so long / That it had it head bit off by it young." In the late sixteenth century the possessive form *its* developed, apparently by analogy with the *-s* ending used to indicate a genitive noun, as in *book*'s, but *its* was not yet common usage in Shakespeare's day. He seems to have used *its* only ten times, mostly in his later plays. Other usages, such as "you have seen Cassio and she together" or the substitution of *who* for *whom*, cause little problem even when noticed.

Verbs, Adverbs, and Prepositions: Verbs cause almost no difficulty: The third person singular present form commonly ends in *-s*, as in modern English (e.g., "He blesses"), but sometimes in *-eth* (Portia explains to Shylock that mercy "blesseth him that gives and him that takes"). Broadly speaking, the *-eth* ending was old-fashioned or dignified or "literary" rather than colloquial, except for the words *doth, hath,* and *saith*. The *-eth* ending (regularly used in the King James Bible, 1611) is very rare in Shakespeare's dramatic prose, though not surprisingly it occurs twice in the rather formal prose summary of the narrative poem *Lucrece*. Sometimes a plural subject, especially if it has collective force, takes a verb ending in *-s*, as in "My old bones aches." Some of our strong or irregular preterites (such as *broke*) have a different form in Shakespeare (*brake*); some verbs that now have a weak or regular preterite (such as *helped*) in Shakespeare have a strong or irregular preterite (*holp*). Some adverbs that today end in *-ly* were not inflected: "grievous sick," "wondrous strange." Finally, prepositions often are not the ones we expect: "We are such stuff as dreams are made on," "I have a king here to my flatterer."

Again, none of the differences (except meanings that have substantially changed or been lost) will cause much difficulty. But it must be confessed that for some elliptical passages there is no widespread agreement on meaning. Wise editors resist saying more than they know, and when they are uncertain they add a question mark to their gloss.

Shakespeare's Theater

In Shakespeare's infancy, Elizabethan actors performed wherever they could—in great halls, at court, in the courtyards of inns. These venues implied not only different audiences but also different playing conditions. The innyards must have made rather unsatisfactory theaters: on some days they were unavailable because carters bringing goods to London used them as depots; when available, they had to be rented from the innkeeper. In 1567, presumably to avoid such difficulties, and also to avoid regulation by the Common Council of London, which was not well disposed toward theatricals, one John Brayne, brother-in-law of the carpenter turned actor James Burbage, built the Red Lion in an eastern suburb of London. We know nothing about its shape or its capacity; we can say only that it may have been the first building in Europe constructed for the purpose of giving plays since the end of antiquity, a thousand years earlier. Even after the building of the Red Lion theatrical activity continued in London in makeshift circumstances, in marketplaces and inns, and always uneasily. In 1574 the Common Council required that plays and playing places in London be licensed because

> sundry great disorders and inconveniences have been found to ensue to this city by the inordinate haunting of great multitudes of people, specially youth, to plays, interludes, and shows, namely occasion of frays and quarrels, evil practices of incontinency in great inns having chambers and secret places adjoining to their open stages and galleries.

The Common Council ordered that innkeepers who wished licenses to hold performance put up a bond and make contributions to the poor.

The requirement that plays and innyard theaters be licensed, along with the other drawbacks of playing at inns and presumably along with the success of the Red Lion, led James Burbage to rent a plot of land northeast of the city walls, on property outside the jurisdiction of the city. Here he built England's second playhouse, called simply the Theatre. About all that is known of its construction is that it was wood. It soon had imitators, the most famous being the Globe (1599), essentially an amphitheater built across the Thames (again outside the city's jurisdiction), constructed with timbers of the Theatre, which had been dismantled when Burbage's lease ran out.

Admission to the theater was one penny, which allowed spectators to stand at the sides and front of the stage that jutted into the yard. An additional penny bought a seat in a covered part of the theater, and a third penny bought a more comfortable seat and a better location. It is notoriously difficult to translate prices into today's money, since some things that are inexpensive today would have been expensive in the past and vice versa—a pipeful of tobacco (imported, of course) cost a lot of money, about three pennies, and an orange (also imported) cost two or three times what a chicken cost—but perhaps we can get some idea of the low cost of the penny admission when we realize that a penny could also buy a pot of ale. An unskilled laborer made about five or sixpence a day, an artisan about twelve pence a day, and the hired actors (as opposed to the sharers in the company, such as Shakespeare) made about ten pence a performance. A printed play cost five or sixpence. Of course a visit to the theater (like a visit to a baseball game today) usually cost more than the admission since the spectator probably would also buy food and drink. Still, the low entrance fee meant that the theater was available to all except the very poorest people, rather as movies and most athletic events are today. Evidence indicates that the audience ranged from apprentices who somehow managed to scrape together the minimum entrance fee and to escape from their masters for a few hours, to prosperous members of the middle class and aristocrats who paid the additional fee for admission to the galleries. The exact proportion of men to women cannot be determined, but women of all classes certainly were present. Theaters were open every afternoon but Sundays for much of the year, except in times of plague, when they were closed because of fear of infection. By the way, no evidence suggests the presence of toilet facilities. Presumably the patrons relieved themselves by making a quick trip to the fields surrounding the playhouses.

There are four important sources of information about the

structure of Elizabethan public playhouses—drawings, a contract, recent excavations, and stage directions in the plays. Of drawings, only the so-called de Witt drawing (c. 1596) of the Swan—really his friend Aernout van Buchell's copy of Johannes de Witt's drawing—is of much significance. The drawing, the only extant representation of the interior of an Elizabethan theater, shows an amphitheater of three tiers, with a stage jutting from a wall into the yard or

Johannes de Witt, a Continental visitor to London, made a drawing of the Swan theater in about the year 1596. The original drawing is lost; this is Aernout van Buchell's copy of it.

center of the building. The tiers are roofed, and part of the stage is covered by a roof that projects from the rear and is supported at its front on two posts, but the groundlings, who paid a penny to stand in front of the stage or at its sides, were exposed to the sky. (Performances in such a playhouse were held only in the daytime; artificial illumination was not used.) At the rear of the stage are two massive doors; above the stage is a gallery.

The second major source of information, the contract for the Fortune (built in 1600), specifies that although the Globe (built in 1599) is to be the model, the Fortune is to be square, eighty feet outside and fifty-five inside. The stage is to be forty three feet broad, and is to extend into the middle of the yard, i.e., it is twenty-seven and a half feet deep.

The third source of information, the 1989 excavations of the Rose (built in 1587), indicate that the Rose was fourteen-sided, about seventy-two feet in diameter with an inner yard almost fifty feet in diameter. The stage at the Rose was about sixteen feet deep, thirty-seven feet wide at the rear, and twenty-seven feet wide downstage. The relatively small dimensions and the tapering stage, in contrast to the rectangular stage in the Swan drawing, surprised theater historians and have made them more cautious in generalizing about the Elizabethan theater. Excavations at the Globe have not yielded much information, though some historians believe that the fragmentary evidence suggests a larger theater, perhaps one hundred feet in diameter.

From the fourth chief source, stage directions in the plays, one learns that entrance to the stage was by the doors at the rear (*"Enter one citizen at one door, and another at the other"*). A curtain hanging across the doorway—or a curtain hanging between the two doorways—could provide a place where a character could conceal himself, as Polonius does, when he wishes to overhear the conversation between Hamlet and Gertrude. Similarly, withdrawing a curtain from the doorway could "discover" (reveal) a character or two. Such discovery scenes are very rare in Elizabethan drama, but a good example occurs in *The Tempest* (5.1.171), where a stage direction tells us, *"Here Prospero discovers Ferdinand and Miranda playing at chess."* There was also some sort of playing space "aloft" or "above" to represent, for instance, the top of a city's walls or a room above the street. Doubtless each theater had its own peculiarities, but perhaps we can talk about a "typical" Elizabethan theater if we realize that no theater need exactly fit the description, just as no mother is the average mother with 2.7 children.

This hypothetical theater is wooden, round, or polygonal (in *Henry V* Shakespeare calls it a "wooden *O*") capable of holding some eight hundred spectators who stood in the yard around the projecting elevated stage—these spectators were the "groundlings"—and some fifteen hundred additional spectators who sat in the three roofed galleries. The stage, protected by a "shadow" or "heavens" or roof, is entered from two doors; behind the doors is the "tiring house" (attiring house, i.e., dressing room), and above the stage is some sort of gallery that may sometimes hold spectators but can be used (for example) as the bedroom from which Romeo—according to a stage direction in one text—"goeth down." Some evidence suggests that a throne can be lowered onto the platform stage, perhaps from the "shadow"; certainly characters can descend from the stage through a trap or traps into the cellar or "hell." Sometimes this space beneath the stage accommodates a sound-effects man or musician (in *Antony and Cleopatra "music of the hautboys* [oboes] *is under the stage"*) or an actor (in *Hamlet* the *"Ghost cries under the stage"*). Most characters simply walk on and off through the doors, but because there is no curtain in front of the platform, corpses will have to be carried off (Hamlet obligingly clears the stage of Polonius's corpse, when he says, "I'll lug the guts into the neighbor room"). Other characters may have fallen at the rear, where a curtain on a doorway could be drawn to conceal them.

Such may have been the "public theater," so called because its inexpensive admission made it available to a wide range of the populace. Another kind of theater has been called the "private theater" because its much greater admission charge (sixpence versus the penny for general admission at the public theater) limited its audience to the wealthy or the prodigal. The private theater was basically a large room, entirely roofed and therefore artificially illuminated, with a stage at one end. The theaters thus were distinct in two ways: One was essentially an amphitheater that catered to the general public; the other was a hall that catered to the wealthy. In 1576 a hall theater was established in Blackfriars, a Dominican priory in London that had been suppressed in 1538 and confiscated by the Crown and thus was not under the city's jurisdiction. All the actors in this Blackfriars theater were boys about eight to thirteen years old (in the public theaters similar boys played female parts; a boy Lady Macbeth played to a man Macbeth). Near the end of this section on Shakespeare's theater we will talk at some length about possible implications in this convention of using boys to play female roles, but for the moment we should say that it doubtless accounts for the relative lack of female roles in Elizabethan drama. Thus, in *A Midsummer Night's Dream*, out of twenty-one named roles, only four are female; in *Hamlet*, out of twenty-four, only two (Gertrude and Ophelia) are female. Many of Shakespeare's characters have fathers but no mothers—for instance, King Lear's daughters. We need not bring in Freud to explain the disparity; a dramatic company had only a few boys in it.

To return to the private theaters, in some of which all of the performers were children—the "eyrie of . . . little eyases" (nest of unfledged hawks—2.2.347–48) which Rosencrantz mentions when he and Guildenstern talk with Hamlet. The theater in Blackfriars had a precarious existence, and ceased operations in 1584. In 1596 James Burbage, who had already made theatrical history by building the Theatre, began to construct a second Blackfriars theater. He died in 1597, and for several years this second Blackfriars theater was used by a troupe of boys, but in 1608 two of Burbage's sons and five other actors (including Shakespeare) became joint operators of the theater, using it in the winter when the open-air Globe was unsuitable. Perhaps such a smaller theater, roofed, artificially illuminated, and with a tradition of a wealthy audience, exerted an influence in Shakespeare's late plays.

Performances in the private theaters may well have had intermissions during which music was played, but in the public theaters the action was probably uninterrupted, flowing from scene to scene almost without a break. Actors would enter, speak, exit, and others would immediately enter and establish (if necessary) the new locale by a few properties and by words and gestures. To indicate that the scene took place at night, a player or two would carry a torch. Here are some samples of Shakespeare establishing the scene:

This is Illyria, lady.   (*Twelfth Night*, 1.2.2)

Well, this is the Forest of Arden.   (*As You Like It*, 2.4.14)

This castle has a pleasant seat; the air
Nimbly and sweetly recommends itself
Unto our gentle senses.   (*Macbeth*, 1.6.1–3)

The west yet glimmers with some streaks of day.
                                          (*Macbeth*, 3.3.5)

Sometimes a speech will go far beyond evoking the minimal setting of place and time, and will, so to speak, evoke the social world in which the characters move. For instance, early in the first scene of *The Merchant of Venice* Salerio suggests an explanation for Antonio's melancholy. (In the following passage, *pageants* are decorated wagons, floats, and *cursy* is the verb "to curtsy," or "to bow.")

Your mind is tossing on the ocean,
There where your argosies with portly sail—
Like signiors and rich burghers on the flood,
Or as it were the pageants of the sea—
Do overpeer the petty traffickers
That cursy to them, do them reverence,
As they fly by them with their woven wings.   (1.1.8–14)

Late in the nineteenth century, when Henry Irving produced the play with elaborate illusionistic sets, the first scene showed a ship moored in the harbor, with fruit vendors and dock laborers, in an effort to evoke the bustling and exotic life of Venice. But Shakespeare's words give us this exotic, rich world of commerce in his highly descriptive language when Salerio speaks of "argosies with portly sail" that fly with "woven wings"; equally important, through Salerio Shakespeare conveys a sense of the orderly, hierarchical society in which the lesser ships, "the petty traffickers," curtsy and thereby "do . . . reverence" to their superiors, the merchant prince's ships, which are "Like signiors and rich burghers."

On the other hand, it is a mistake to think that except for verbal pictures the Elizabethan stage was bare. Although Shakespeare's Chorus in *Henry V* calls the stage an "unworthy scaffold" (Prologue 1.10) and urges the spectators to "eke out our performance with your mind" (Prologue 3.35), there was considerable spectacle. The last act of *Macbeth*, for instance, has five stage directions calling for *"drum and colors,"* and another sort of appeal to the eye is indicated by the stage direction *"Enter Macduff, with Macbeth's head."* Some scenery and properties may have been substantial; doubtless a throne was used, but the pillars supporting the roof would have served for the trees on which Orlando pins his poems in *As You Like It*.

Having talked about the public theater—"this wooden *O*"—at some length, we should mention again that Shakespeare's plays were performed also in other locales. Alvin Kernan, in *Shakespeare, the King's Playwright: Theater in the Stuart Court 1603–1613* (1995) points out that "several of [Shakespeare's] plays contain brief theatrical performances, set always in a court or some noble house. When Shakespeare portrayed a theater, he did not, except for the choruses in *Henry V*, imagine a public theater" (p. 195). (Examples include episodes in *The Taming of the Shrew*, *A Midsummer Night's Dream*, *Hamlet*, and *The Tempest*.)

A Note on the Use of Boy Actors in Female Roles

Until fairly recently, scholars were content to mention that the convention existed; they sometimes also mentioned that it continued the medieval practice of using males in female roles, and that other theaters, notably in ancient Greece and in China and Japan, also used males in female roles. (In classical Noh drama in Japan, males still play the female roles.) Prudery may have been at the root of the academic failure to talk much about the use of boy actors, or maybe there really is not much more to say than that it was a convention of a male-centered culture (Stephen Greenblatt's view, in *Shakespearean Negotiations* [1988]). Further, the very nature of a convention is that it is not thought about: Hamlet is a Dane and Julius Caesar is a Roman, but in Shakespeare's plays they speak English, and we in the audience never give this odd fact a thought. Similarly, a character may speak in the presence of others and we understand, again without thinking about it, that he or she is not heard by the figures on the stage (the aside); a character alone on the stage may speak (the soliloquy), and we do not take the character to be unhinged; in a realistic (box) set, the fourth wall, which allows us to see what is going on, is miraculously missing. The no-nonsense view, then, is that the boy actor was an accepted convention, accepted unthinkingly—just as today we know that Kenneth Branagh is not Hamlet, Al Pacino is not Richard III, and Denzel Washington is not the Prince of Aragon. In this view, the audience takes the performer for the role, and that is that; such is the argument we now make for race-free casting, in which African-Americans and Asians can play roles of persons who lived in medieval Denmark and ancient Rome. But gender perhaps is different, at least today. It is a matter of abundant academic study: The Elizabethan theater is now sometimes called a transvestite theater, and we hear much about cross-dressing.

Shakespeare himself in a very few passages calls attention to the use of boys in female roles. At the end of *As You Like It* the boy who played Rosalind addresses the audience, and says, "O men, . . . if I were a woman, I would kiss as many of you as had beards that pleased me." But this is in the Epilogue; the plot is over, and the actor is stepping out of the play and into the audience's everyday world. A second reference to the practice of boys playing female roles occurs in *Antony and Cleopatra*, when Cleopatra imagines that she and Antony will be the subject of crude plays, her role being performed by a boy:

> The quick comedians
> Extemporally will stage us, and present
> Our Alexandrian revels: Antony
> Shall be brought drunken forth, and I shall see
> Some squeaking Cleopatra boy my greatness.   (5.2.216–20)

In a few other passages, Shakespeare is more indirect. For instance, in *Twelfth Night* Viola, played of course by a boy, disguises herself as a young man and seeks service in the house of a lord. She enlists the help of a Captain, and (by way of explaining away her voice and her beardlessness) says,

> I'll serve this duke
> Thou shalt present me as an eunuch to him.   (1.2.55–56)

In *Hamlet*, when the players arrive in 2.2, Hamlet jokes with the boy who plays a female role. The boy has grown since Hamlet last saw him: "By'r Lady, your ladyship is nearer to heaven than when I saw you last by the altitude of a chopine" (a lady's thick-soled shoe). He goes on: "Pray God your voice . . . be not cracked" (434–38).

Exactly how sexual, how erotic, this material was and is, is now much disputed. Again, the use of boys may have been unnoticed, or rather not thought about—an unexamined convention—by most or all spectators most of the time, perhaps *all* of the time, except when Shakespeare calls the convention to the attention of the audience, as in the passages just quoted. Still, an occasional bit seems to invite erotic thoughts. The clearest example is the name that Rosalind takes in *As You Like It*, Ganymede—the beautiful youth whom Zeus abducted. Did boys dressed to play female roles carry homoerotic appeal for straight men (Lisa Jardine's view, in *Still Harping on Daughters* [1983]), or for gay men, or for some or all women in the audience? Further, when the boy actor played a woman who (for the purposes of the plot) disguised herself as a male, as Rosalind, Viola, and Portia do—so we get a boy playing a woman playing a man—what sort of appeal was generated, and for what sort of spectator?

Some scholars have argued that the convention empowered women by letting female characters display a freedom unavailable in Renaissance patriarchal society; the convention, it is said, undermined rigid gender distinctions. In this view, the convention (along with plots in which female characters for a while disguised themselves as young men) allowed Shakespeare to say what some modern gender

critics say: Gender is a constructed role rather than a bio-
logical given, something we make, rather than a fixed binary
opposition of male and female (see Juliet Dusinberre, in
Shakespeare and the Nature of Women [1975]). On the other
hand, some scholars have maintained that the male disguise
assumed by some female characters serves only to reaffirm
traditional social distinctions since female characters who
don male garb (notably Portia in *The Merchant of Venice*
and Rosalind in *As You Like It*) return to their female garb
and at least implicitly (these critics say) reaffirm the status
quo. (For this last view, see Clara Claiborne Park, in an
essay in *The Woman's Part*, ed. Carolyn Ruth Swift Lenz et
al. [1980].) Perhaps no one answer is right for all plays; in
As You Like It cross-dressing empowers Rosalind, but in
Twelfth Night cross-dressing comically traps Viola.

Shakespeare's Dramatic Language: Costumes, Gestures and Silences; Prose and Poetry

Because Shakespeare was a dramatist, not merely a poet,
he worked not only with language but also with costume,
sound effects, gestures, and even silences. We have already
discussed some kinds of spectacle in the preceding section,
and now we will begin with other aspects of visual language;
a theater, after all, is literally a "place for seeing." Consider
the opening stage direction in *The Tempest*, the first play in
the first published collection of Shakespeare's plays: *"A
tempestuous noise of thunder and Lightning heard: Enter a
Ship-master, and a Boteswain."*

Costumes: What did that shipmaster and that boatswain
wear? Doubtless they wore something that identified them
as men of the sea. Not much is known about the costumes
that Elizabethan actors wore, but at least three points are
clear: (1) many of the costumes were splendid versions of
contemporary Elizabethan dress; (2) some attempts were
made to approximate the dress of certain occupations and of
antique or exotic characters such as Romans, Turks, and
Jews; (3) some costumes indicated that the wearer was

supernatural. Evidence for elaborate Elizabethan clothing can be found in the plays themselves and in contemporary comments about the "sumptuous" players who wore the discarded clothing of noblemen, as well as in account books that itemize such things as "a scarlet cloak with two broad gold laces, with gold buttons down the sides."

The attempts at approximation of the dress of certain occupations and nationalities also can be documented from the plays themselves, and it derives additional confirmation from a drawing of the first scene of Shakespeare's *Titus Andronicus*—the only extant Elizabethan picture of an identifiable episode in a play. (See pp. xxxviii–xxxix.) The drawing, probably done in 1594 or 1595, shows Queen Tamora pleading for mercy. She wears a somewhat medieval-looking robe and a crown; Titus wears a toga and a wreath, but two soldiers behind him wear costumes fairly close to Elizabethan dress. We do not know, however, if the drawing represents an actual stage production in the public theater, or perhaps a private production, or maybe only a reader's visualization of an episode. Further, there is some conflicting evidence: In *Julius Caesar* a reference is made to Caesar's doublet (a close-fitting jacket), which, if taken literally, suggests that even the protagonist did not wear Roman clothing; and certainly the lesser characters, who are said to wear hats, did not wear Roman garb.

It should be mentioned, too, that even ordinary clothing can be symbolic: Hamlet's "inky cloak," for example, sets him apart from the brightly dressed members of Claudius's court and symbolizes his mourning; the fresh clothes that are put on King Lear partly symbolize his return to sanity. Consider, too, the removal of disguises near the end of some plays. For instance, Rosalind in *As You Like It* and Portia and Nerissa in *The Merchant of Venice* remove their male attire, thus again becoming fully themselves.

Gestures and Silences: Gestures are an important part of a dramatist's language. King Lear kneels before his daughter Cordelia for a benediction (4.7.57–59), an act of humility that contrasts with his earlier speeches banishing her and that contrasts also with a comparable gesture, his ironic kneeling before Regan (2.4.153–55). Northumberland's failure to kneel before King Richard II (3.3.71–72) speaks volumes. As for silences, consider a moment in *Coriolanus*: Before the protagonist yields to his mother's entreaties (5.3.182), there is this stage direction: *"Holds her by the hand, silent."* Another example of "speech in dumbness" occurs in *Macbeth*, when Macduff learns that his wife and children have been murdered. He is silent at first, as Malcolm's speech indicates: "What, man! Ne'er pull your hat upon your brows. Give sorrow words" (4.3.208–09). (For a discussion of such moments, see Philip C. McGuire's *Speechless Dialect: Shakespeare's Open Silences* [1985].)

Of course when we think of Shakespeare's work, we think primarily of his language, both the poetry and the prose.

Prose: Although two of his plays (*Richard II* and *King John*) have no prose at all, about half the others have at least one quarter of the dialogue in prose, and some have notably more: *1 Henry IV* and *2 Henry IV*, about half; *As You Like It* and *Twelfth Night*, a little more than half; *Much Ado About Nothing*, more than three quarters; and *The Merry Wives of Windsor*, a little more than five sixths. We should remember that despite Molière's joke about M. Jourdain, who was amazed to learn that he spoke prose, most of us do not speak prose. Rather, we normally utter repetitive, shapeless, and often ungrammatical torrents; prose is something very different—a sort of literary imitation of speech at its most coherent.

Today we may think of prose as "natural" for drama; or even if we think that poetry is appropriate for high tragedy we may still think that prose is the right medium for comedy. Greek, Roman, and early English comedies, however, were written in verse. In fact, prose was not generally considered a literary medium in England until the late fifteenth century; Chaucer tells even his bawdy stories in verse. By the end of the 1580s, however, prose had established itself on the English comic stage. In tragedy, Marlowe made some use of prose, not simply in the speeches of clownish servants but even in the speech of a tragic hero, Doctor Faustus. Still, before Shakespeare, prose normally was used in the theater only for special circumstances: (1) letters and proclamations, to set them off from the poetic dialogue; (2) mad characters, to indicate that normal thinking has become disordered; and (3) low comedy, or speeches uttered by clowns even when they are not being comic. Shakespeare made use of these conventions, but he also went far beyond them. Sometimes he begins a scene in prose and then shifts into verse as the emotion is heightened; or conversely, he may shift from verse to prose when a speaker is lowering the emotional level, as when Brutus speaks in the Forum.

Shakespeare's prose usually is not prosaic. Hamlet's prose includes not only small talk with Rosencrantz and Guildenstern but also princely reflections on "What a piece of work is a man" (2.2.312). In conversation with Ophelia, he shifts from light talk in verse to a passionate prose denunciation of women (3.1.103), though the shift to prose here is perhaps also intended to suggest the possibility of madness. (Consult Brian Vickers, *The Artistry of Shakespeare's Prose* [1968].)

Poetry: Drama in rhyme in England goes back to the Middle Ages, but by Shakespeare's day rhyme no longer dominated poetic drama; a finer medium, blank verse (strictly speaking, unrhymed lines of ten syllables, with the stress on every second syllable) had been adopted. But before looking at unrhymed poetry, a few things should be said about the chief uses of rhyme in Shakespeare's plays. (1) A couplet (a pair of rhyming lines) is sometimes used to convey emotional heightening at the end of a blank verse speech; (2) characters sometimes speak a couplet as they leave the stage, suggesting closure; (3) except in the latest plays, scenes fairly often conclude with a couplet, and sometimes, as in *Richard II*, 2.1.145–46, the entrance of a new character within a scene is preceded by a couplet, which wraps up the earlier portion of that scene; (4) speeches of two characters occasionally are linked by rhyme, most notably in *Romeo and Juliet*, 1.5.95–108, where the lovers speak a sonnet between them; elsewhere a taunting reply occasionally rhymes with the

previous speaker's last line; (5) speeches with sententious
or gnomic remarks are sometimes in rhyme, as in the
duke's speech in *Othello* (1.3.199–206); (6) speeches of
sardonic mockery are sometimes in rhyme—for example,
Iago's speech on women in *Othello* (2.1.146–58)—and
they sometimes conclude with an emphatic couplet, as in
Bolingbroke's speech on comforting words in *Richard II*
(1.3.301–2); (7) some characters are associated with rhyme,
such as the fairies in *A Midsummer Night's Dream*; (8) in
the early plays, especially *The Comedy of Errors* and *The
Taming of the Shrew*, comic scenes that in later plays would
be in prose are in jingling rhymes; (9) prologues, choruses,
plays-within-the-play, inscriptions, vows, epilogues, and so
on are often in rhyme, and the songs in the plays are rhymed.

Neither prose nor rhyme immediately comes to mind
when we first think of Shakespeare's medium: It is blank
verse, unrhymed iambic pentameter. (In a mechanically
exact line there are five iambic feet. An iambic foot consists
of two syllables, the second accented, as in *away*; five feet
make a pentameter line. Thus, a strict line of iambic pentameter contains ten syllables, the even syllables being
stressed more heavily than the odd syllables. Fortunately,
Shakespeare usually varies the line somewhat.) The first
speech in *A Midsummer Night's Dream*, spoken by Duke
Theseus to his betrothed, is an example of blank verse:

> Now, fair Hippolyta, our nuptial hour
> Draws on apace. Four happy days bring in
> Another moon; but, O, methinks, how slow
> This old moon wanes! She lingers my desires,
> Like to a stepdame, or a dowager,
> Long withering out a young man's revenue.   (1.1.1–6)

As this passage shows, Shakespeare's blank verse is not
mechanically unvarying. Though the predominant foot is
the iamb (as in *apace* or *desires*), there are numerous varia-
tions. In the first line the stress can be placed on "fair," as the
regular metrical pattern suggests, but it is likely that "Now"
gets almost as much emphasis; probably in the second line
"Draws" is more heavily emphasized than "on," giving us a

trochee (a stressed syllable followed by an unstressed one); and in the fourth line each word in the phrase "This old moon wanes" is probably stressed fairly heavily, conveying by two spondees (two feet, each of two stresses) the oppressive tedium that Theseus feels.

In Shakespeare's early plays much of the blank verse is end-stopped (that is, it has a heavy pause at the end of each line), but he later developed the ability to write iambic pentameter verse paragraphs (rather than lines) that give the illusion of speech. His chief techniques are (1) enjambing, i.e., running the thought beyond the single line, as in the first three lines of the speech just quoted; (2) occasionally replacing an iamb with another foot; (3) varying the position of the chief pause (the caesura) within a line; (4) adding an occasional unstressed syllable at the end of a line, traditionally called a feminine ending; (5) and beginning or ending a speech with a half line.

Shakespeare's mature blank verse has much of the rhythmic flexibility of his prose; both the language, though richly figurative and sometimes dense, and the syntax seem natural. It is also often highly appropriate to a particular character. Consider, for instance, this speech from *Hamlet*, in which Claudius, King of Denmark ("the Dane"), speaks to Laertes:

> And now, Laertes, what's the news with you?
> You told us of some suit. What is't, Laertes?
> You cannot speak of reason to the Dane
> And lose your voice. What wouldst thou beg, Laertes,
> That shall not be my offer, not thy asking?   (1.2.42–46)

Notice the short sentences and the repetition of the name "Laertes," to whom the speech is addressed. Notice, too, the shift from the royal "us" in the second line to the more intimate "my" in the last line, and from "you" in the first three lines to the more intimate "thou" and "thy" in the last two lines. Claudius knows how to ingratiate himself with Laertes.

For a second example of the flexibility of Shakespeare's blank verse, consider a passage from *Macbeth*. Distressed by the doctor's inability to cure Lady Macbeth and by the imminent battle, Macbeth addresses some of his remarks to the doctor and others to the servant who is arming him. The entire speech, with its pauses, interruptions, and irresolution (in "Pull't off, I say," Macbeth orders the servant to remove the armor that the servant has been putting on him), catches Macbeth's disintegration. (In the first line, *physic* means "medicine," and in the fourth and fifth lines, *cast the water* means "analyze the urine.")

> Throw physic to the dogs, I'll none of it.
> Come, put mine armor on. Give me my staff.
> Seyton, send out.—Doctor, the thanes fly from me.—
> Come, sir, dispatch. If thou couldst, doctor, cast
> The water of my land, find her disease
> And purge it to a sound and pristine health,
> I would applaud thee to the very echo,
> That should applaud again.—Pull't off, I say.—
> What rhubarb, senna, or what purgative drug,
> Would scour these English hence? Hear'st thou of them?
>
> (5.3.47–56)

Blank verse, then, can be much more than unrhymed iambic pentameter, and even within a single play Shakespeare's blank verse often consists of several styles, depending on the speaker and on the speaker's emotion at the moment.

The Play Text as a Collaboration

Shakespeare's fellow dramatist Ben Jonson reported that the actors said of Shakespeare, "In his writing, whatsoever he penned, he never blotted out line," i.e., never crossed out material and revised his work while composing. None of Shakespeare's plays survives in manuscript (with the possible exception of a scene in *Sir Thomas More*), so we cannot fully evaluate the comment, but in a few instances the published work clearly shows that he revised his manuscript. Consider the following passage (shown here in facsimile) from the best early text of *Romeo and Juliet*, the Second Quarto (1599):

Ro. Would I were sleepe and peace so sweet to rest
The grey eyde morne smiles on the frowning night,
Checkring the Easterne Clouds with streaks of light,
And darknesse fleckted like a drunkard reeles,
From forth daies pathway, made by *Tytans* wheeles.
Hence will I to my ghostly Friers close cell,
His helpe to craue, and my deare hap to tell.

           Exit.

Enter Frier alone with a basket.   (night,
Fri. The grey-eyed morne smiles on the frowning
Checking the Easterne clowdes with streaks of light:
And fleckeld darknesse like a drunkard reeles,
From forth daies path, and *Titans* burning wheeles:
Now ere the sun aduance his burning eie,

Romeo rather elaborately tells us that the sun at dawn is
dispelling the night (morning is smiling, the eastern clouds
are checked with light, and the sun's chariot—Titan's
wheels—advances), and he will seek out his spiritual father,
the Friar. He exits and, oddly, the Friar enters and says pretty
much the same thing about the sun. Both speakers say that
"the gray-eyed morn smiles on the frowning night," but there
are small differences, perhaps having more to do with the
business of printing the book than with the author's
composition: For Romeo's "checkring," "fleckted," and
"pathway," we get the Friar's "checking," "fleckeld," and
"path." (Notice, by the way, the inconsistency in Elizabethan
spelling: Romeo's "clouds" become the Friar's "clowdes.")
    Both versions must have been in the printer's copy, and it
seems safe to assume that both were in Shakespeare's manuscript. He must have written one version—let's say he first
wrote Romeo's closing lines for this scene—and then he
decided, no, it's better to give this lyrical passage to the
Friar, as the opening of a new scene, but he neglected to
delete the first version. Editors must make a choice, and they
may feel that the reasonable thing to do is to print the text as
Shakespeare intended it. But how can we know what he
intended? Almost all modern editors delete the lines from

Romeo's speech, and retain the Friar's lines. They don't do this because they know Shakespeare's intention, however. They give the lines to the Friar because the first published version (1597) of *Romeo and Juliet* gives only the Friar's version, and this text (though in many ways inferior to the 1599 text) is thought to derive from the memory of some actors, that is, it is thought to represent a performance, not just a script. Maybe during the course of rehearsals Shakespeare—an actor as well as an author—unilaterally decided that the Friar should speak the lines; if so (remember that we don't know this to be a fact) his final intention was to give the speech to the Friar. Maybe, however, the actors talked it over and settled on the Friar, with or without Shakespeare's approval. On the other hand, despite the 1597 version, one might argue (if only weakly) on behalf of giving the lines to Romeo rather than to the Friar, thus: (1) Romeo's comment on the coming of the daylight emphasizes his separation from Juliet, and (2) the figurative language seems more appropriate to Romeo than to the Friar. Having said this, in the Signet edition we have decided in this instance to draw on the evidence provided by earlier text and to give the lines to the Friar, on the grounds that since Q1 reflects a production, in the theater (at least on one occasion) the lines were spoken by the Friar.

A playwright sold a script to a theatrical company. The script thus belonged to the company, not the author, and author and company alike must have regarded this script not as a literary work but as the basis for a play that the actors would create on the stage. We speak of Shakespeare as the author of the plays, but readers should bear in mind that the texts they read, even when derived from a single text, such as the First Folio (1623), are inevitably the collaborative work not simply of Shakespeare with his company—doubtless during rehearsals the actors would suggest alterations—but also with other forces of the age. One force was governmental censorship. In 1606 parliament passed "an Act to restrain abuses of players," prohibiting the utterance of oaths and the name of God. So where the earliest text of *Othello* gives us "By heaven" (3.3.106), the first Folio gives "Alas," presumably reflecting the compliance of stage practice with the law. Similarly, the 1623 version of *King Lear* omits the oath "Fut" (probably from "By God's foot") at 1.2.142, again presumably reflecting the line as it was spoken on the stage. Editors who seek to give the reader the play that Shakespeare initially conceived—the "authentic" play conceived by the solitary Shakespeare—probably will restore the missing oaths and references to God. Other editors, who see the play as a collaborative work, a construction made not only by Shakespeare but also by actors and compositors and even government censors, may claim that what counts is the play as it was actually performed. Such editors regard the censored text as legitimate, since it is the play that was (presumably) finally put on. A performed text, they argue, has more historical reality than a text produced by an editor who has sought to get at what Shakespeare initially wrote. In this view, the text of a play is rather like the script of a film; the script is not the film, and the play text is not the performed play. Even if we want to talk about the play that Shakespeare "intended," we will find ourselves talking about a script that he handed over to a company with the intention that it be implemented by actors. The "intended" play is the one that the actors—we might almost say "society"—would help to construct.

Further, it is now widely held that a play is also the work of readers and spectators, who do not simply receive meaning, but who create it when they respond to the play. This idea is fully in accord with contemporary post-structuralist critical thinking, notably Roland Barthes's "The Death of the Author," in *Image-Music-Text* (1977) and Michel Foucault's "What Is an Author?," in *The Foucault Reader* (1984). The gist of the idea is that an author is not an isolated genius; rather, authors are subject to the politics and other social structures of their age. A dramatist especially is a worker in a collaborative project, working most obviously with actors—parts may be written for particular actors—but working also with the audience. Consider the words of Samuel Johnson, written to be spoken by the actor David Garrick at the opening of a theater in 1747:

> The stage but echoes back the public voice;
> The drama's laws, the drama's patrons give,
> For we that live to please, must please to live.

The audience—the public taste as understood by the play-wright—helps to determine what the play is. Moreover, even members of the public who are not part of the playwright's immediate audience may exert an influence through censor-ship. We have already glanced at governmental censorship, but there are also other kinds. Take one of Shakespeare's most beloved characters, Falstaff, who appears in three of Shakespeare's plays, the two parts of *Henry IV* and *The Merry Wives of Windsor*. He appears with this name in the earliest printed version of the first of these plays, *1 Henry IV*, but we know that Shakespeare originally called him (after an historical figure) Sir John Oldcastle. Oldcastle appears in Shakespeare's source (partly reprinted in the Signet edition of *1 Henry IV*), and a trace of the name survives in Shake-speare's play, 1.2.43–44, where Prince Hal punningly addresses Falstaff as "my old lad of the castle." But for some reason—perhaps because the family of the historical Old-castle complained—Shakespeare had to change the name. In short, the play as we have it was (at least in this detail) sub-ject to some sort of censorship. If we think that a text should present what we take to be the author's intention, we probably will want to replace *Falstaff* with *Oldcastle*. But if we recognize that a play is a collaboration, we may welcome the change, even if it was forced on Shakespeare. Somehow *Falstaff*, with its hint of *false-staff*, i.e., inadequate prop, seems just right for this fat knight who, to our delight, enter-tains the young prince with untruths. We can go as far as saying that, at least so far as a play is concerned, an insis-tence on the author's original intention (even if we could know it) can sometimes impoverish the text.

The tiny example of Falstaff's name illustrates the point that the text we read is inevitably only a version—something in effect produced by the collaboration of the playwright with his actors, audiences, compositors, and editors—of a fluid text that Shakespeare once wrote, just as the *Hamlet* that we see on the screen starring Kenneth Branagh is not the *Hamlet* that Shakespeare saw in an open-air playhouse star-ring Richard Burbage. *Hamlet* itself, as we shall note in a moment, also exists in several versions. It is not surprising that there is now much talk about the *instability* of Shake-speare's texts.

Because he was not only a playwright but was also an actor and a shareholder in a theatrical company, Shakespeare probably was much involved with the translation of the play from a manuscript to a stage production. He may or may not have done some rewriting during rehearsals, and he may or may not have been happy with cuts that were made. Some plays, notably *Hamlet* and *King Lear*, are so long that it is most unlikely that the texts we read were acted in their entirety. Further, for both of these plays we have more than one early text that demands consideration. In *Hamlet*, the Second Quarto (1604) includes some two hundred lines not found in the Folio (1623). Among the passages missing from the Folio are two of Hamlet's reflective speeches, the "dram of evil" speech (1.4.13–38) and "How all occasions do inform against me" (4.4.32–66). Since the Folio has more numerous and often fuller stage directions, it certainly looks as though in the Folio we get a theatrical version of the play, a text whose cuts were probably made—this is only a hunch, of course—not because Shakespeare was changing his conception of Hamlet but because the playhouse demanded a modified play. (The problem is complicated, since the Folio not only cuts some of the Quarto but adds some material. Various explanations have been offered.)

Or take an example from *King Lear*. In the First and Second Quarto (1608, 1619), the final speech of the play is given to Albany, Lear's surviving son-in-law, but in the First Folio version (1623), the speech is given to Edgar. The Quarto version is in accord with tradition—usually the highest-ranking character in a tragedy speaks the final words. Why does the Folio give the speech to Edgar? One possible answer is this: The Folio version omits some of Albany's speeches in earlier scenes, so perhaps it was decided (by Shakespeare? by the players?) not to give the final lines to so pale a character. In fact, the discrepancies are so many between the two texts, that some scholars argue we do not simply have texts showing different theatrical productions. Rather, these scholars say, Shakespeare substantially revised the play, and we really have two versions of *King Lear* (and of *Othello* also, say some)—two different plays—not simply two texts, each of which is in some ways imperfect.

In this view, the 1608 version of *Lear* may derive from Shakespeare's manuscript, and the 1623 version may derive from his later revision. The Quartos have almost three hundred lines not in the Folio, and the Folio has about a hundred lines not in the Quartos. It used to be held that all the texts were imperfect in various ways and from various causes— some passages in the Quartos were thought to have been set from a manuscript that was not entirely legible, other passages were thought to have been set by a compositor who was new to setting plays, and still other passages were thought to have been provided by an actor who misremembered some of the lines. This traditional view held that an editor must draw on the Quartos and the Folio in order to get Shakespeare's "real" play. The new argument holds (although not without considerable strain) that we have two authentic plays, Shakespeare's early version (in the Quarto) and Shakespeare's—or his theatrical company's—revised version (in the Folio). Not only theatrical demands but also Shakespeare's own artistic sense, it is argued, called for extensive revisions. Even the titles vary: Q1 is called *True Chronicle Historie of the life and death of King Lear and his three Daughters*, whereas the Folio text is called *The Tragedie of King Lear*. To combine the two texts in order to produce what the editor thinks is the play that Shakespeare intended to write is, according to this view, to produce a text that is false to the history of the play. If the new view is correct, and we do have texts of two distinct versions of *Lear* rather than two imperfect versions of one play, it supports in a textual way the poststructuralist view that we cannot possibly have an unmediated vision of (in this case) a play by Shakespeare; we can only recognize a plurality of visions.

Editing Texts

Though eighteen of his plays were published during his lifetime, Shakespeare seems never to have supervised their publication. There is nothing unusual here; when a playwright sold a play to a theatrical company he surrendered his ownership to it. Normally a company would not publish the play, because to publish it meant to allow competitors to acquire the piece. Some plays did get published: Apparently hard-up actors sometimes pieced together a play for a publisher; sometimes a company in need of money sold a play; and sometimes a company allowed publication of a play that no longer drew audiences. That Shakespeare did not concern himself with publication is not remarkable; of his contemporaries, only Ben Jonson carefully supervised the publication of his own plays.

In 1623, seven years after Shakespeare's death, John Heminges and Henry Condell (two senior members of Shakespeare's company, who had worked with him for about twenty years) collected his plays—published and unpublished—into a large volume, of a kind called a folio. (A folio is a volume consisting of large sheets that have been folded once, each sheet thus making two leaves, or four pages. The size of the page of course depends on the size of the sheet—a folio can range in height from twelve to sixteen inches, and in width from eight to eleven; the pages in the 1623 edition of Shakespeare, commonly called the First Folio, are approximately thirteen inches tall and eight inches wide.) The eighteen plays published during Shakespeare's lifetime had been issued one play per volume in small formats called quartos. (Each sheet in a quarto has been folded twice, making four leaves, or eight pages, each page being about nine inches tall and seven inches wide, roughly the size of a large paperback.)

Heminges and Condell suggest in an address "To the great variety of readers" that the republished plays are presented in better form than in the quartos:

Before you were abused with diverse stolen and surreptitious copies, maimed and deformed by the frauds and stealths of injurious impostors that exposed them; even those, are now offered to your view cured and perfect of their limbs, and all the rest absolute in their numbers, as he [i.e., Shakespeare] conceived them.

There is a good deal of truth to this statement, but some of the quarto versions are better than others; some are in fact preferable to the Folio text.

Whoever was assigned to prepare the texts for publication

in the first Folio seems to have taken the job seriously and yet not to have performed it with uniform care. The sources of the texts seem to have been, in general, good unpublished copies or the best published copies. The first play in the collection, *The Tempest*, is divided into acts and scenes, has unusually full stage directions and descriptions of spectacle, and concludes with a list of the characters, but the editor was not able (or willing) to present all of the succeeding texts so fully dressed. Later texts occasionally show signs of carelessness: in one scene of *Much Ado About Nothing* the names of actors, instead of characters, appear as speech prefixes, as they had in the Quarto, which the Folio reprints; proofreading throughout the Folio is spotty and apparently was done without reference to the printer's copy; the pagination of *Hamlet* jumps from 156 to 257. Further, the proofreading was done while the presses continued to print, so that each play in each volume contains a mix of corrected and uncorrected pages.

Modern editors of Shakespeare must first select their copy; no problem if the play exists only in the Folio, but a considerable problem if the relationship between a Quarto and the Folio—or an early Quarto and a later one—is unclear. In the case of *Romeo and Juliet*, the First Quarto (Q1), published in 1597, is vastly inferior to the Second (Q2), published in 1599. The basis of Q1 apparently is a version put together from memory by some actors. Not surprisingly, it garbles many passages and is much shorter than Q2. On the other hand, occasionally Q1 makes better sense than Q2. For instance, near the end of the play, when the parents have assembled and learned of the deaths of Romeo and Juliet, in Q2 the Prince says (5.3.208–9),

Come, *Montague;* for thou art early vp
To see thy sonne and heire, now earling downe.

The last three words of this speech surely do not make sense, and many editors turn to Q1, which instead of "now earling downe" has "more early downe." Some modern editors take only "early" from Q1, and print "now early down"; others take "more early," and print "more early down." Further, Q1 (though, again, quite clearly a garbled and abbreviated text) includes some stage directions that are not found in Q2, and today many editors who base their text on Q2 are glad to add these stage directions, because the directions help to give us a sense of what the play looked like on Shakespeare's stage. Thus, in 4.3.58, after Juliet drinks the potion, Q1 gives us this stage direction, not in Q2: *"She falls upon her bed within the curtains."*

In short, an editor's decisions do not end with the choice of a single copy text. First of all, editors must reckon with Elizabethan spelling. If they are not producing a facsimile, they probably modernize the spelling, but ought they to preserve the old forms of words that apparently were pronounced quite unlike their modern forms—*lanthorn, alablaster*? If they preserve these forms are they really preserving Shakespeare's forms or perhaps those of a compositor in the printing house? What is one to do when one finds *lanthorn* and *lantern* in adjacent lines? (The editors of this series in general, but not invariably, assume that words should be spelled in their modern form, unless, for instance, a rhyme is involved.) Elizabethan punctuation, too, presents problems. For example, in the First Folio, the only text for the play, Macbeth rejects his wife's idea that he can wash the blood from his hand (2.2.60–62):

> No: this my Hand will rather
> The multitudinous Seas incarnardine,
> Making the Greene one, Red.

Obviously an editor will remove the superfluous capitals, and will probably alter the spelling to "incarnadine," but what about the comma before "Red"? If we retain the comma, Macbeth is calling the sea "the green one." If we drop the comma, Macbeth is saying that his bloody hand will make the sea ("the Green") *uniformly* red.

An editor will sometimes have to change more than spelling and punctuation. Macbeth says to his wife (1.7.46–47):

> I dare do all that may become a man,
> Who dares no more, is none.

For two centuries editors have agreed that the second line is unsatisfactory, and have emended "no" to "do": "Who dares do more is none." But when in the same play (4.2.21–22) Ross says that fearful persons

> Floate vpon a wilde and violent Sea
> Each way, and moue,

need we emend the passage? On the assumption that the compositor misread the manuscript, some editors emend "each way, and move" to "and move each way"; others emend "move" to "none" (i.e., "Each way and none"). Other editors, however, let the passage stand as in the original. The editors of the Signet Classic Shakespeare have restrained themselves from making abundant emendations. In their minds they hear Samuel Johnson on the dangers of emendation: "I have adopted the Roman sentiment, that it is more honorable to save a citizen than to kill an enemy." Some departures (in addition to spelling, punctuation, and lineation) from the copy text have of course been made, but the original readings are listed in a note following the play, so that readers can evaluate the changes for themselves.

Following tradition, the editors of the Signet Classic Shakespeare have prefaced each play with a list of characters, and throughout the play have regularized the names of the speakers. Thus, in our text of *Romeo and Juliet*, all speeches by Juliet's mother are prefixed "Lady Capulet," although the 1599 Quarto of the play, which provides our copy text, uses at various points seven speech tags for this one character: *Capu. Wi.* (i.e., Capulet's wife), *Ca. Wi., Wi., Wife, Old La.* (i.e., Old Lady), *La.,* and *Mo.* (i.e., Mother). Similarly, in *All's Well That Ends Well*, the character whom we regularly call "Countess" is in the Folio (the copy text) variously identified as *Mother, Countess, Old Countess, Lady,* and *Old Lady*. Admittedly there is some loss in regularizing, since the various prefixes may give us a hint of the way Shakespeare (or a scribe who copied Shakespeare's manuscript) was thinking of the character in a particular scene—for instance, as a mother, or as an old lady. But too much can be made of these differing prefixes, since the social relationships implied are *not* always relevant to the given scene.

We have also added line numbers and in many cases act and scene divisions as well as indications of locale at the beginning of scenes. The Folio divided most of the plays into acts and some into scenes. Early eighteenth-century editors increased the divisions. These divisions, which provide a convenient way of referring to passages in the plays, have been retained, but when not in the text chosen as the basis for the Signet Classic text they are enclosed within square brackets, [ ], to indicate that they are editorial additions. Similarly, though no play of Shakespeare's was equipped with indications of the locale at the heads of scene divisions, locales have here been added in square brackets for the convenience of readers, who lack the information that costumes, properties, gestures, and scenery afford to spectators. Spectators can tell at a glance they are in the throne room, but without an editorial indication the reader may be puzzled for a while. It should be mentioned, incidentally, that there are a few authentic stage directions—perhaps Shakespeare's, perhaps a prompter's—that suggest locales, such as *"Enter Brutus in his orchard,"* and *"They go up into the Senate house."* It is hoped that the bracketed additions in the Signet text will provide readers with the sort of help provided by these two authentic directions, but it is equally hoped that the reader will remember that the stage was not loaded with scenery.

Shakespeare on the Stage

Each volume in the Signet Classic Shakespeare includes a brief stage (and sometimes film) history of the play. When we read about earlier productions, we are likely to find them eccentric, obviously wrongheaded—for instance, Nahum Tate's version of *King Lear*, with a happy ending, which held the stage for about a century and a half, from the late seventeenth century until the end of the first quarter of the nineteenth. We see engravings of David Garrick, the greatest actor of the eighteenth century, in eighteenth-century garb

as King Lear, and we smile, thinking how absurd the production must have been. If we are more thoughtful, we say,
with the English novelist L. P. Hartley, "The past is a foreign
country; they do things differently there." But if the eighteenth-century staging is a foreign country, what of the plays
of the late sixteenth and seventeenth centuries? A foreign
language, a foreign theater, a foreign audience.

Probably all viewers of Shakespeare's plays, beginning
with Shakespeare himself, at times have been unhappy with
the plays on the stage. Consider three comments about production that we find in the plays themselves, which suggest
Shakespeare's concerns. The Chorus in *Henry V* complains
that the heroic story cannot possibly be adequately staged:

> But pardon, gentles all,
> The flat unraisèd spirits that hath dared
> On this unworthy scaffold to bring forth
> So great an object. Can this cockpit hold
> The vasty fields of France? Or may we cram
> Within this wooden *O* the very casques
> That did affright the air at Agincourt?
> . . . .
> Piece out our imperfections with your thoughts.
>
> (Prologue 1.8–14,23)

Second, here are a few sentences (which may or may not
represent Shakespeare's own views) from Hamlet's longish
lecture to the players:

> Speak the speech, I pray you, as I pronounced it to you, trippingly
> on the tongue. But if you mouth it, as many of our players do, I had
> as lief the town crier spoke my lines. . . . O, it offends me to the
> soul to hear a robustious periwig-pated fellow tear a passion to tat-
> ters, to very rags, to split the ears of the groundlings. . . . And let
> those that play your clowns speak no more than is set down for
> them, for there be of them that will themselves laugh, to set on
> some quantity of barren spectators to laugh too, though in the
> meantime some necessary question of the play be then to be con-
> sidered. That's villainous and shows a most pitiful ambition in the
> fool that uses it. (3.2.1–47)

Finally, we can quote again from the passage cited earlier in this introduction, concerning the boy actors who played the female roles. Cleopatra imagines with horror a theatrical version of her activities with Antony:

> The quick comedians
> Extemporally will stage us, and present
> Our Alexandrian revels: Antony
> Shall be brought drunken forth, and I shall see
> Some squeaking Cleopatra boy my greatness
> I' th' posture of a whore.
>
> (5.2.216–21)

It is impossible to know how much weight to put on such passages—perhaps Shakespeare was just being modest about his theater's abilities—but it is easy enough to think that he was unhappy with some aspects of Elizabethan production. Probably no production can fully satisfy a playwright, and for that matter, few productions can fully satisfy *us;* we regret this or that cut, this or that way of costuming the play, this or that bit of business.

One's first thought may be this: Why don't they just do "authentic" Shakespeare, "straight" Shakespeare, the play as Shakespeare wrote it? But as we read the plays—words written to be performed—it sometimes becomes clear that we do not know *how* to perform them. For instance, in *Antony and Cleopatra* Antony, the Roman general who has succumbed to Cleopatra and to Egyptian ways, says, "The nobleness of life / Is to do thus" (1.1.36–37). But what is "thus"? Does Antony at this point embrace Cleopatra? Does he embrace and kiss her? (There are, by the way, very few scenes of kissing on Shakespeare's stage, possibly because boys played the female roles.) Or does he make a sweeping gesture, indicating the Egyptian way of life?

This is not an isolated example; the plays are filled with lines that call for gestures, but we are not sure what the gestures should be. *Interpretation* is inevitable. Consider a passage in *Hamlet*. In 3.1, Polonius persuades his daughter, Ophelia, to talk to Hamlet while Polonius and Claudius eavesdrop. The two men conceal themselves, and Hamlet encounters Ophelia. At 3.1.131 Hamlet suddenly says to her, "Where's your father?" Why does Hamlet, apparently out of nowhere—they have not been talking about Polonius—ask this question? Is this an example of the "antic disposition" (fantastic behavior) that Hamlet earlier (1.5.172) had told Horatio and others—including us—he would display? That is, is the question about the whereabouts of her father a seemingly irrational one, like his earlier question (3.1.103) to Ophelia, "Ha, ha! Are you honest?" Or, on the other hand, has Hamlet (as in many productions) suddenly glimpsed Polonius's foot protruding from beneath a drapery at the rear? That is, does Hamlet ask the question because he has suddenly seen something suspicious and now is testing Ophelia? (By the way, in productions that do give Hamlet a physical cue, it is almost always Polonius rather than Claudius who provides the clue. This itself is an act of interpretation on the part of the director.) Or (a third possibility) does Hamlet get a clue from Ophelia, who inadvertently betrays the spies by nervously glancing at their place of hiding? This is the interpretation used in the BBC television version, where Ophelia glances in fear toward the hiding place just after Hamlet says "Why wouldst thou be a breeder of sinners?" (121–22). Hamlet, realizing that he is being observed, glances here and there *before* he asks "Where's your father?" The question thus is a climax to what he has been doing while speaking the preceding lines. Or (a fourth interpretation) does Hamlet suddenly, without the aid of any clue whatsoever, intuitively (insightfully, mysteriously, wonderfully) sense that someone is spying? Directors must decide, of course—and so must readers.

Recall, too, the preceding discussion of the texts of the plays, which argued that the texts—though they seem to be before us in permanent black on white—are unstable. The Signet text of *Hamlet*, which draws on the Second Quarto (1604) and the First Folio (1623) is considerably longer than any version staged in Shakespeare's time. Our version, even if spoken very briskly and played without any intermission, would take close to four hours, far beyond "the two hours' traffic of our stage" mentioned in the Prologue to *Romeo and Juliet*. (There are a few contemporary references to the duration of a play, but none mentions more than three hours.) Of Shakespeare's plays, only *The Comedy of Errors*, *Macbeth*, and *The Tempest* can be done in less than three hours without cutting. And even if we take a play that exists only in a short text, *Macbeth*, we cannot claim that we are experiencing the very play that Shakespeare conceived, partly because some of the Witches' songs almost surely are non-Shakespearean additions, and partly because we are not willing to watch the play performed without an intermission and with boys in the female roles.

Further, as the earlier discussion of costumes mentioned, the plays apparently were given chiefly in contemporary, that is, in Elizabethan dress. If today we give them in the costumes that Shakespeare probably saw, the plays seem not contemporary but curiously dated. Yet if we use our own dress, we find lines of dialogue that are at odds with what we see; we may feel that the language, so clearly not our own, is inappropriate coming out of people in today's dress. A common solution, incidentally, has been to set the plays in the nineteenth century, on the grounds that this attractively distances the plays (gives them a degree of foreignness, allowing for interesting costumes) and yet doesn't put them into a museum world of Elizabethan England.

Inevitably our productions are adaptations, *our* adaptations, and inevitably they will look dated, not in a century but in twenty years, or perhaps even in a decade. Still, we cannot escape from our own conceptions. As the director Peter Brook has said, in *The Empty Space* (1968):

> It is not only the hair-styles, costumes and make-ups that look dated. All the different elements of staging—the shorthands of behavior that stand for emotions; gestures, gesticulations and tones of voice—are all fluctuating on an invisible stock exchange all the time. . . . A living theatre that thinks it can stand aloof from anything as trivial as fashion will wilt. (p. 16)

As Brook indicates, it is through today's hairstyles, costumes, makeup, gestures, gesticulations, tones of voice—this includes our *conception* of earlier hairstyles, costumes, and so forth if we stage the play in a period other than our own—that we inevitably stage the plays.

It is a truism that every age invents its own Shakespeare, just as, for instance, every age has invented its own classical world. Our view of ancient Greece, a slave-holding society

in which even free Athenian women were severely circum-
scribed, does not much resemble the Victorians' view of
ancient Greece as a glorious democracy, just as, perhaps, our
view of Victorianism itself does not much resemble theirs.
We cannot claim that the Shakespeare on our stage is the
true Shakespeare, but in our stage productions we find a
Shakespeare that speaks to us, a Shakespeare that our ances-
tors doubtless did not know but one that seems to us to be the
true Shakespeare—at least for a while.

Our age is remarkable for the wide variety of kinds of
staging that it uses for Shakespeare, but one development
deserves special mention. This is the now common practice
of race-blind or color-blind or nontraditional casting, which
allows persons who are not white to play in Shakespeare.
Previously blacks performing in Shakespeare were limited
to a mere three roles, Othello, Aaron (in *Titus Andronicus*),
and the Prince of Morocco (in *The Merchant of Venice*),
and there were no roles at all for Asians. Indeed, African-
Americans rarely could play even one of these three roles,
since they were not welcome in white companies. Ira
Aldridge (c.1806–1867), a black actor of undoubted talent,
was forced to make his living by performing Shakespeare
in England and in Europe, where he could play not only
Othello but also—in whiteface—other tragic roles such as
King Lear. Paul Robeson (1898–1976) made theatrical history when he played Othello in London in 1930, and there
was some talk about bringing the production to the United
States, but there was more talk about whether American
audiences would tolerate the sight of a black man—a real
black man, not a white man in blackface—kissing and then
killing a white woman. The idea was tried out in summer
stock in 1942, the reviews were enthusiastic, and in the following year Robeson opened on Broadway in a production
that ran an astounding 296 performances. An occasional all-
black company sometimes performed Shakespeare's plays,
but otherwise blacks (and other minority members) were in
effect shut out from performing Shakespeare. Only since
about 1970 has it been common for nonwhites to play major
roles along with whites. Thus, in a 1996–97 production of
Antony and Cleopatra, a white Cleopatra, Vanessa Red-
grave, played opposite a black Antony, David Harewood.

Multiracial casting is now especially common at the New
York Shakespeare Festival, founded in 1954 by Joseph
Papp, and in England, where even siblings such as Claudio
and Isabella in *Measure for Measure* or Lear's three daughters may be of different races. Probably most viewers today
soon stop worrying about the lack of realism, and move
beyond the color of the performers' skin to the quality of the
performance.

Nontraditional casting is not only a matter of color or
race; it includes sex. In the past, occasionally a distinguished
woman of the theater has taken on a male role—Sarah Bern-
hardt (1844–1923) as Hamlet is perhaps the most famous
example—but such performances were widely regarded
as eccentric. Although today there have been some performances involving cross-dressing (a drag *As You Like It*
staged by the National Theatre in England in 1966 and in the
United States in 1974 has achieved considerable fame in
the annals of stage history), what is more interesting is the
casting of women in roles that traditionally are male but that
need not be. Thus, a 1993–94 English production of *Henry
V* used a woman—*not* cross-dressed—in the role of the governor of Harfleur. According to Peter Holland, who
reviewed the production in *Shakespeare Survey* 48 (1995),
"having a female Governor of Harfleur feminized the city
and provided a direct response to the horrendous threat of
rape and murder that Henry had offered, his language and
her body in direct connection and opposition" (p. 210). Ten
years from now the device may not play so effectively, but
today it speaks to us. Shakespeare, born in the Elizabethan
Age, has been dead nearly four hundred years, yet he is, as
Ben Jonson said, "not of an age but for all time." We must
understand, however, that he is "for all time" precisely
because each age finds in his abundance something for itself
and something of itself.

And here we come back to two issues discussed earlier in
this introduction—the instability of the text and, curiously,
the Bacon/Oxford heresy concerning the authorship of the
plays. *Of course* Shakespeare wrote the plays, and we should
daily fall on our knees to thank him for them—and yet there
is something to the idea that he is not their only author.
Every editor, every director and actor, and every reader to

some degree shapes them, too, for when we edit, direct, act, or read, we inevitably become Shakespeare's collaborator and re-create the plays. The plays, one might say, are so cunningly contrived that they guide our responses, tell us how we ought to feel, and make a mark on us, but (for better or for worse) we also make a mark on them.

—SYLVAN BARNET
Tufts University

Introduction

The Merchant of Venice is the earliest of three superb comedies in which Shakespeare has set a generous and clear-sighted woman in sharp contrast to a no less unusual, but markedly unsocial man. From beginning to end, Portia and Shylock—like Rosalind and Jaques in *As You Like It* and Viola and Malvolio in *Twelfth Night*—remain poles apart. It is significant that Portia in her greatest scene, and the two other heroines in nearly all of their scenes, are disguised as men. Only the audience and one confidante share their secret. Knowing it, the spectators naturally tend to center their interest in them and to view the play through their eyes. Portia, Rosalind, and Viola tend to overshadow their lovers, not because the men are not worthy of them, but because of their fascinating double roles.

On the Elizabethan stage, it was probably easier for Portia to take the leading role than it is in the modern theater, where Shylock is the central figure. For one thing, we are aware of the Holocaust and we can never witness anti-Semitism without immediately turning our sympathy to the victim. But putting this issue aside, we should also understand that in Shakespeare's company there was a better theatrical balance than in modern times, when the star actor tends to overshadow all the others. The lady's handicap is especially formidable when the star is, like Sir Henry Irving, both the manager of the theater and even the director of the troupe. Ellen Terry was at her best, she said, when she played against Irving, but she could not be the central figure of the play that Portia is meant to be. At times in the nineteenth century, Shylock so overshadowed everyone else that the beautiful final act was omitted entirely.

"*The Merchant of Venice* is a fairy tale," declared that

wise man of the theater, Harley Granville-Barker. We may think he made too much of this point, but he reminded us forcibly that the play is set in the realm of high romance. We cannot understand it in terms of modern realism. Strange and wonderful are the stories of the caskets, the pound of flesh, and the beautiful girl disguised as a wise young judge—not to mention the miser's daughter who blossoms into a delightful and virtuous lady, filled with the joy of life. We begin to sense this poetic atmosphere in the very first scene.

Act 1

1. Antonio and Bassanio

Antonio is not in the least the stodgy, smug, intolerant businessman that he is often supposed to be. A great merchant prince of the fabulous city of Venice, he sends out his splendid ships as far as Mexico and the Indies and shares his wealth with the needy and oppressed. In his quiet way, he—like Bassanio and Portia, Lorenzo and Jessica—is a figure of romance. His friends see poetry in his commercial ventures:

> your argosies with portly sail—
> Like signiors and rich burghers on the flood,
> Or as it were the pageants of the sea—
> Do overpeer the petty traffickers
> That cursy to them, do them reverence,
> As they fly by them with their woven wings.   (9–14)

His friends see also a great and ever-present danger. The modern merchant is often depicted as a type enjoying comfortable security. Salerio and Solanio, like people today when they think of the astronauts, are fascinated and appalled by the risks that Antonio takes. Yet he faces these constant dangers with a quiet mind. Shakespeare, like the medieval poets, could find romance in the old themes of love and battle; but with a poet's insight into men and affairs, he discovered it also in the merchant adventurer's commerce, in which, as in knightly times, danger went hand in hand with beauty and high achievement.

Antonio is admired and beloved for his good deeds. Yet Shakespeare has wisely given him a relatively passive role. If we felt his emotions too keenly, the scene of his trial would be too painful for comedy. His "sadness" contributes to this passiveness. One guess about the cause of his melancholy is that he fears Bassanio's approaching marriage will separate him from his friend. Another is that he is just in a strange mood. Antonio, however, is too generous to regret his friend's happy marriage, and the emphasis given to his mood suggests an important meaning.

Since perhaps 1965 or so, when gender criticism (a development of feminist criticism) began to take shape, some critics have argued that Antonio's melancholy is rooted in a homosexual attachment—perhaps repressed, perhaps expressed—to Bassanio. In stage productions influenced by this conception, Antonio may merely brighten visibly in Bassanio's presence, and be highly attentive to him, or he may express his interest more obviously, by touching him lovingly. For our age, such a sexual (more generally, a psychological) explanation seems to make sense, though Shakespeare's contemporaries might have seen the relationship not as sexual but as an example of male friendship, traditionally regarded (precisely because it supposedly was not sexual) as superior to heterosexual love.

Further, one can explain Antonio's melancholy in terms of the Elizabethan belief in presentiments. Shakespeare uses presentiments in many plays to foreshadow future events, especially dangers and misfortunes. It is somewhat analogous to the faith in extrasensory perception, which (though not shared by the present editor) is held by some of our very intelligent contemporaries. A striking parallel to Antonio's sadness is in *Richard II*, which was probably written just before *The Merchant of Venice*. In one scene the Queen's attendants are troubled about her sadness, a much more violent melancholy than Antonio's. Suddenly, after only a few moments, she hears the shocking news of Bolingbroke's rebellion, which is to bring about the dethronement and murder of her husband. She instantly recognizes the meaning of her presentiment. Antonio's unaccountable sadness is a less violent experience than the Queen's, apparently because the danger is more remote and because in the end he escapes it. But in kind, though not in degree, the two presentiments are alike.

Antonio's presentiment has an important dramatic function. It suggests to the audience some great danger of which he and his friends are totally unconscious. Thus it creates dramatic irony, quickens suspense, and awakens a warm concern for this modest and generous merchant prince, who is so much admired and beloved. In his next scene it also heightens our concern for him when he readily agrees to Shylock's apparently jovial suggestion that Antonio forfeit a pound of flesh if the three thousand ducats are not paid back on time.

Bassanio has sometimes been misunderstood even more seriously than Antonio—as a contemptible man of fashion who puts his friend's life in danger so that he can gamble on winning an heiress. His best qualities, as Professor Bernard Grebanier has remarked, have become increasingly rare in the last century and a half. He speaks with "an elegance which is innate and unconscious. . . . The miraculous thing is that . . . this patrician quality of the mind is united . . . with a manliness, an unaggressive virility of a kind to which the twentieth century is becoming totally a stranger." His first words about Portia,

In Belmont is a lady richly left,   (161)

do not mean that he wants to marry her for money, but that "there is good reason to promise the return of the loan" he is asking of his friend. His eloquent words about Portia herself assure us that his love for her is genuine.

As the play develops, we find Bassanio's friend, Gratiano, asking to go with him to Belmont. A loud extrovert, Gratiano "speaks an infinite deal of nothing, more than any man in all Venice," (1.1.114–15) and is the last person Bassanio would choose to accompany him on a delicate mission. But with a few very frank words of caution, he generously accedes to his friend's surprising request, without the slightest trace of irritation. At Belmont we see Bassanio not only as a delightful gentleman, but as a man of thought and insight as he meditates on which casket to choose. When he has won Portia, we like him for his overwhelming joy, his modesty, and his entire devotion to her.

The world of Bassanio and Antonio is not ours. Its values are chiefly those of a governing class—courage, justice, a high sense of honor, courtesy, learning, a love of beauty, compassion, and humility. (Not surprisingly, many recent productions, especially some inspired by a Marxist view of society, suggest that these apparent virtues are simply the tools by which a corrupt, hypocritical aristocracy disarms its opponents.) Lord Bassanio has the highest rank of anyone in the play except the Duke, yet he never shows even a trace of arrogance. Like Sir Philip Sidney, the most admired and beloved young Englishman of Shakespeare's time, Bassanio has lived beyond his means because of the position he occupies. For him, as for Sidney and Castiglione, life is at once an earnest task, an adventure, and a fine art. To Sidney, Shakespeare, and their contemporaries, the marriage of so fine a nobleman as Bassanio with a virtuous, gifted, humanely educated, and wholly delightful lady of wealth would be altogether fitting.

2. Portia

As for Portia, even most of Shylock's warmest partisans commonly find her irresistible in her early scenes, however they may dislike her way of defeating him in the court scene. Some, of course, grumble at her deft satire of her egregious parcel of wooers, and one critic can declare solemnly, "Portia herself, for some reason, is the least lovable of Shakespeare's comedy heroines." Harley Granville-Barker, who saw nearly all the characters with remarkable clarity, observed that the poet reveals Portia's character "to us mainly in little things, and lets us feel its whole happy virtue in the melody of her speech." Granville-Barker also points out that, hedged about as she is by her father's will in the early scenes, there is very little for her to do. However this may be, the strangeness of her situation captures our attention, and the naturalness of her thoughts and feelings leads us to identify ourselves at once with her cause and to sense the irony of her situation.

Although her father did not trust her to choose a husband for herself—this is a patriarchal society—yet, as her shrewd comments on her suitors reveal, few women ever had a keener insight into men's characters than she. Nevertheless, she does not really rebel against her father's will, and when she learns it has driven away six unwelcome suitors, she is amazed and delighted at the old man's foresight. Her filial piety meant more to the Elizabethans than to us—in their view, a patriarchal society was "natural"—but her quick feelings, her sense of responsibility, her wit and keen perception of the ridiculous belong to every age and make her one of the most magnetic of heroines.

Portia's most famous speech, memorized by generations of school children, is her praise of mercy, beginning "The quality of mercy is not strained" (4.1.183)—i.e., is not constrained, not forced. It is a notable speech, justly famous and it does Portia credit. And yet, like almost everything else in the play, it has its complexities. First, we should keep in mind that Portia delivers the speech in a particular situation: She is trying to save her husband's friend. The speech thus is not disinterested. Second, we may notice that once Shylock has been outwitted, Portia displays no mercy toward him, other than to advise him to beg mercy of the Duke (362). Perhaps we should not put too much weight on her failure to utter a merciful speech on behalf of Shylock, since what a character does is more important than what he or she does not do, but still, readers and viewers may feel that Portia, like Shylock, is complex.

3. Shylock and Antonio

Shylock. Three thousand ducats—well.
Bassanio. Ay, sir, for three months.
Shylock. For three months—well.   (1.3.1–3)

Shylock comes before us abruptly, with no previous hint that he exists. Antonio and Portia, in their first speeches, confide their thoughts and feelings to their friends. Bassanio, alone with Antonio, pours out his heart. But Shylock, from the first words he utters, is a strangely isolated figure, secretive and calculating, a miser with words. We begin to discover his real thoughts only when he utters them aside as Antonio enters. The hatred that he expresses so vehemently and his efforts later in the scene to appear as Antonio's cordial friend are in glaring contradiction.

Defenders of Shylock often argue that at first his offer of friendship is sincere, and that he never meant the forfeit of a pound of Antonio's flesh as anything but "a merry jest," until Jessica deserted him to elope with one of Antonio's Christian friends. This interpretation ignores the basic theatrical principle that every essential point must be clear to the entire audience. When a character in Shakespeare speaks aside to the audience, he always speaks his real thoughts. When Shylock says, as Antonio enters,

> If I can catch him once upon the hip,
> I will feed fat the ancient grudge I bear him,   (43–44)

we have no choice but to believe him.

E. E. Stoll's famous, though one-sided, interpretation of Shylock is indispensable for an understanding of Shylock's real character. Stoll demonstrates that the issue between the Jewish moneylender and the Christian merchant is not simply the taking of interest. It is the usurer's merciless exploitation of his victims. He is no mere banker, but a crafty and ruthless loan shark. The Tudor laws against usury stated an ideal and then compromised with the practical facts of trade. They outlawed any interest on any loan but imposed no penalty if the rate did not exceed ten percent. The typical usurer, however, found devious ways of exacting far more than the law allowed. His special victims were the inexperienced and the very needy—widows and orphans, and young gentlemen not yet possessed of their inheritance. For an original loan of a hundred pounds, the clever usurer might in a few years gain real estate worth five hundred or a thousand pounds, bringing his wretched debtor to beggary or death. The Elizabethan hatred of usury was sanctioned by Aristotle's theory that money cannot breed money; but far more important were the enormous interest rates and fraudulent contracts of clever scoundrels. Recognizing Shylock as a usurer, the Elizabethans must have been hostile to him, especially when they saw him plotting against Antonio's life.

Why does he hate this generous merchant? Antonio has denounced Shylock in public. He had loaned money to the usurer's victims, has charged them no interest at all and thus enabled many of them to escape total ruin. Although he has never till now either charged interest on a loan, or paid it, Antonio is ready to "break a custom" (61) rather than have his best friend risk losing Portia. For this, many critics, supposing the issue to involve one of Antonio's absolute principles, charge him with hypocrisy. But Antonio, as a man of affairs, is less interested in theory than in results. The charge would be valid only if he were exacting interest from a debtor. To rescue the usurer's victims, he has loaned them money at no interest. To enable Bassanio to win Portia, he will himself pay interest on a loan, rather than let his best friend lose his dearest hopes. In each case his concern is to bring generous aid to those in need.

While discussing the loan with Antonio, Shylock suddenly digresses and pours out one of his most eloquent and moving speeches. In the Rialto, he declares, in full view of crowds of merchants, Antonio has publicly disgraced him. He has called him dog, kicked him, and spat upon him. Some very intelligent readers have refused to believe these charges, but Antonio himself confirms them.

I am as like to call thee so again,
To spet on thee again, to spurn thee too.   (127–28)

It is a strange and shameful fact that for many centuries Christians held it to be proper to spit in a Jew's face on certain occasions. The idea goes back to the crucifixion, when (according to the Gospels) the Jews mocked Christ and spat upon him. Similarly, the horrible idea that the Jews had become a race accursed by God arose from their refusal to accept Jesus as the messiah. What Shakespeare's personal beliefs on these topics were, we cannot know. But we can talk about the effect of the speeches on viewers, and most viewers today would probably agree that the words Shakespeare gives Shylock seem designed to show us how it feels to be an outcast in a Christian society.

As a compassionate man, outraged by the usurer's inhumanity to his victims, Antonio is capable of the hot indignation evident in his answer to Shylock's charge. Today he might expose a dangerous public enemy by giving a television interview or presenting the facts to the prosecuting attorney. In Shakespeare's Venice, where the practice of usury seems to have been as inhuman as anywhere else, Antonio takes the kind of direct action that decent Americans sometimes took against an unscrupulous man in pioneer days on the frontier. Antonio deliberately insults the usurer, literally kicks him out of his place of business, does all he can to turn public opinion against him, and spends his own money to rescue Shylock's victims. Christ himself, though he preached the gospel of love, denounced the oppressors and hypocrites in public and whipped the money changers out of the temple. Antonio's just indignation is natural and understandable, and so is Shylock's bitter resentment. We begin to see Shylock as his own worst enemy, poisoned by greed and hate.

Acts 2 and 3

From the harsh but strangely compelling figure of Shylock, we turn immediately to Portia. In her scenes with Morocco and Aragon, she is a marvel of self-control and courtesy, although some of her speeches to them are edged with an irony that they never catch. Her whole future happiness is at stake, for neither Morocco nor Aragon can appreciate the best qualities of a Renaissance lady. Morocco is a warmhearted man of honor and courage who has the grace to think he may not deserve her. But there is something naive, almost barbaric, in his desire that his fate be decided by having his rivals and himself cut their flesh to see whose blood is the reddest. Morocco is one of only three black roles in Shakespeare; of the other two, one (Aaron, in *Titus Andronicus*) is a villain and the other (Othello) is a tragic hero. The Elizabethans, who did not distinguish between Moors and blacks, had at least three stereotypes (not entirely consistent) for blacks: They were villainous, they were especially given to passion, and they were unsophisticated. In *The Merchant of Venice*, however, Morocco is not so easily characterized. On the modern stage he is sometimes played as an absurd figure, given to ranting, but this is surely a mistake, if for no other reason than that a trivial Morocco, along with a trivial Aragon, inadvertently serves to diminish Bassanio, who in some degree is measured against them. Still, Morocco is evidently not worthy of Portia, who is highly endowed by nature and who has acquired the best culture of a remarkable society. She is also unfortunately endowed, however, with the race prejudice of her age (and ours?). Morocco's first line is "Mislike me not for my complexion"(2.1.1), but Portia will say, after he fails to choose the chest that contains her picture, "Let all of his complexion choose me so" (2.7.79). "Complexion" means "temperament" as well as color, but it does mean color, and we can wish she had not said this. Still, speaking of wishes, we can wish Morocco well, but we see that he is no mate for Portia. As for Aragon, he has the presumptuous pride that the Elizabethans attributed to Spaniards. He has also the naïveté to suppose that a man could actually deserve such a woman as Portia, and that he is that man. Most of Shakespeare's genuine lovers are, like Portia and Bassanio, humbled by their love.

One key to the meaning of a Shakespeare play is the way he directs our sympathies. In many of his masterpieces there is one person or more through whose eyes we are particularly invited to see the other characters and the events. In *Henry IV* it is chiefly Prince Hal, in *Hamlet* it is Horatio and Hamlet, in *Twelfth Night* it is Viola. Who is it in *The Merchant of Venice*?

In the opening scene, in which Antonio is the center of attention but at first does little, we see him as four of his friends do. In Shylock's first scene, many modern readers see him as he sees himself, but those who realize what a usurer actually was will look at him as Bassanio and Antonio do. Stoll, in a long analysis, argued that whenever we begin to sympathize with Shylock, his greed and hatred are emphasized. He accuses Antonio of disgracing him and then plots to kill him. He speaks kindly to his daughter as "Jessica, my girl," and instantly remembers his dream of moneybags (2.5.15, 18). He speaks of Launcelot as a kind "patch" (simpleton) but adds that he is "a huge feeder" (45). In one of his greatest scenes, he pours out a passionate defense of the Jewish people and a challenge to Christians to practice the mercy and humility that they profess (3.1.50–69); but he ends the speech on the note of revenge, arranging with Tubal at the end of the scene to meet him at the synagogue to plan the legalized murder of a generous Christian merchant.

Stoll makes an important point. But we can turn it around and show, on his own evidence, that in each of Shylock's scenes, except the briefest, he wins the sympathy of the audience for at least a few moments. When do we ever see the least touch of kindly feeling in Iago or Goneril? Shylock differs, too, from other Shakespearean villains—from Angelo in *Measure for Measure*, with whom he is often compared, and from Hamlet's uncle, King Claudius—in that these men are entirely conscious of their villainy. At the trial, Shylock can ask, apparently in all sincerity, "What judgment shall I dread, doing no wrong?" (4.1.89) The unique thing about Shylock is this strange sincerity. He can nurse the most diabolical passions and imagine he does no wrong.

Doubtless the Elizabethans laughed with Solanio and Salerio when they baited Shylock, for as Stoll has emphasized, a general audience in the theater will respond to the mood of the characters on stage. Yet we should not assume that these two friends of Antonio express more than a very small part of Shakespeare's attitude toward the Jew. These characters can scarcely be distinguished from one another, and we do not go to such people to find Shakespeare's whole meaning. Their function is chiefly to release the feelings of the audience or to tell us news. In the court scene, the jeers and imprecations of Gratiano provide a similar release. But Gratiano "speaks an infinite deal of nothing, more than any man in all Venice." The shallow comments of this excited extrovert contrast with the wisdom of Portia and the considered judgment of Antonio.

Throughout the play, Shakespeare has invited us to look at the other characters and the action through Portia's eyes, and to share her sympathies. One way he does this is in the skillful arrangement of contrasting scenes. He places Shylock's first scene between Portia's first and second, and her third just after Jessica's flight. Beginning with Portia's fourth scene (2.9), he alternates her scenes with Shylock's with almost exact regularity until their encounter in the courtroom. In this way the playwright silently draws ever more sharply the contrast between the usurer and the wise Renaissance lady, before either has any idea of the other's existence.

Our sympathies are never so strongly with Portia, or with Bassanio, as in the beautiful scene where he wins her, particularly in the tense moments while she watches him meditating on which casket to choose, and in the climax that brings them a happiness they can hardly express. When the sudden news comes of Antonio's catastrophic losses, Portia instantly offers her entire fortune to save her husband's friend of whom until now she has never heard. Like Bassanio and Antonio, she knows how to "give and hazard all she hath." In this scene of love and generous friendship, we see Portia at her best.

In the next scene we find Shylock at his worst, raging madly at Antonio and promising to take his life. It is his one scene in the play in which we can have no spark of sympathy for him, unless we believe (as is implied in some productions) that Shylock's rage is caused not by a hatred of Antonio as a competitor but by Jessica's desertion.

Shylock and Judaism

As we approach the court scene, we must face the question of Shakespeare's attitude toward the Jews. Stoll and some others believed he shared the hateful prejudice that had disgraced Christianity for over fifteen centuries. In 1935, Professor John W. Draper sharply challenged this view. "Shylock the Jew was merely exotic local color," he declared. "Shylock the usurer was a commentary on London life." The second statement is certainly true; there were many usurers in the great city, and their cruelty was notorious. The first statement is partly true. There were no Jews, or almost none, dwelling anywhere in Shakespeare's

London, unless we except the small band of a few hundred Portuguese who had converted from Judaism to Christianity. Shylock must have been an exotic figure to the Elizabethans.

His Judaism, however, is emphasized again and again. In Shylock the great virtues of the ancient Hebrews have often been corrupted into the nearest vices. Reverence for law has degenerated into legalism, loyalty to his own people into a vehement antipathy to Christians, practical sagacity into the love of money, a noble love of justice into a fanatical thirst for a revenge that excludes every thought of mercy. Yet until the climax of the court scene, Shylock is blindly unconscious of doing anything wrong. Here is no mere comic butt, no mere hypocrite and villain, but a warped and dangerous fanatic—sometimes comic, sometimes hateful—impervious to any normal appeal to common sense or natural kindness, but always strangely human. Something has poisoned this man, and apparently a whole people, originally splendidly endowed by nature.

Most modern readers find the source of the poison in Christian persecution. Shakespeare touches on this idea, especially in Shylock's great defense (3.1.55–63) of the humanity of the Jews. But his emphasis lies elsewhere. Shylock is fiercely conscious of his "sacred nation." He defends the iniquitous practice of usury by citing the Old Testament. As Christians had always said of the Jews from the days of St. Paul, he insists on the bare letter of the law and ignores the spirit. He goes to the synagogue to plan Antonio's death. In the court scene he declares solemnly he has "an oath in heaven" that he will cut the pound of flesh from Antonio. Earlier we see momentarily a better side of his Judaism, in his memory of his wife's first gift. It is obvious, nevertheless, that Shakespeare has many times connected Shylock's worst qualities with the Hebrew religion.

So hateful is this idea to us that we must be very certain just what it meant to Shakespeare. The prejudice is not at all the Nazi's hatred of the Jew's blood and supposed race, for Jessica is "a daughter to his blood" but—and this *but* is very important—not to "his manners," i.e., his moral values and actions. The hostility is directed against Shylock's code of ethics and the religion that is assumed to be its source.

How could the humane and clear-sighted Shakespeare ever have taken such a view of one of the world's great religions? Perhaps we can most easily understand his view if we remember the attitude toward Puritans that is held today by some humane but not well-informed people. Without examining the facts with an open mind, they see the Puritans as narrow zealots or even hypocrites, who—like Shylock—despised beauty and merrymaking, loved money, and looked down with contempt on their less sanctified neighbors. Although these people think of themselves as enlightened and tolerant, they regard the Puritan religion as a fanaticism—a perverted view of life which warped a man's mind, chilled his sympathies, and poisoned his relations with all who did not share the special outlook of the chosen few. One can see how this picture developed, but impartial historians know it to be, on the whole, distorted and unjust.

The analogy with Judaism is very close, for the Puritans' emphasis on the Old Testament made them the most Hebraic of Christian groups. In Elizabeth's reign, even men of large minds and generous sympathies could regard the Jewish faith very much as many of our contemporaries regard Puritanism. For centuries Christians had been taught almost universally that the ancient religion of Israel had degenerated into a narrow fanaticism, teaching a pedantic adherence to the mere letter of the law and ignoring the spirit. "The letter killeth but the spirit giveth life," wrote St. Paul in *II Corinthians*. As a Christian scholar of our time, James Parkes, wrote: "The inadequacy of the law . . . was [the Church Fathers'] continual accusation against the Jews." Parkes also observed that our English word *law* is no adequate equivalent for the original word in the Hebrew text, *Torah*:

> The written law was . . . the basis of *Torah,* but *Torah* itself was the complete revelation of the holy community or nation through which the individual in every act could fulfill the purpose of God in his creation.

Between this lofty Hebrew concept and the Christian idea of the divine mercy which at once fulfills and transcends the law, there is no irreconcilable conflict.

The Trial

The scene of Antonio's trial surpasses almost anything Shakespeare had written previously in both range and power. The sustained clash of wills, the battle of ideas, the variety of characterization, the prolonged suspense (relieved now and then by touches of comedy), the deepening irony, and the stunning reversal of fortune when Portia finally turns Shylock's own weapon against himself—all these reveal the hand of a great craftsman and the inspiration of a master poet.

Often in the nineteenth century, and sometimes in the twentieth, this scene has been interpreted as "The Tragedy of Shylock." Stoll interpreted it as harsh comedy. After the reversal of fortune, he says, "The Jew's very words are echoed by Portia and Gratiano as they jeer, and at every turn that justice takes ... there are now peals and shouts of laughter." Neither interpretation—Shylock as tragic hero of Shylock as comic butt—does justice to Shakespeare's sane and compassionate view.

In the first place, though everyone else is appalled at Shylock's cruelty, he himself is here a figure of real dignity. The mad fierceness of his last two scenes is gone. As he addresses the Duke, his language is eloquent, and his strange reasoning is cogent. Confident in the justice of his cause, he regards Gratiano's bitter curse with amused indifference. To the Duke and Portia he shows a courteous respect. Up to the sudden reversal of his fortunes, he treats her with admiration and genuine friendliness. In one sense, we see him at his best in this scene. With some exceptions, his bearing in more than half the scene is that of a civilized man of affairs. The contrast between his manner and his fanatical purpose heightens the effect. He is a shrewd and persuasive advocate in his astounding case. When the Duke makes a powerful appeal that he show "human gentleness and love," Shylock defends with powerful logic his right to take Antonio's life.

Duke. How shalt thou hope for mercy, rend'ring none?
Shylock. What judgment shall I dread, doing no wrong?
(4.1.88–89)

The tension of the scene mounts steadily, but Shakespeare skillfully breaks it now and then. Just before Bellario's messenger (Nerissa) comes in, we are deeply moved by the selfless friendship of Bassanio and Antonio, as each insists that he should die for the other. Then the sight of Nerissa trying, without quite perfect success, to act the part of an experienced law clerk brings a hint of comedy. As spectators we need not laugh, but all will feel a slight lessening of tension. When Shylock takes the occasion to whet his knife on his sole, the grotesque act brings us still nearer to comedy.

Portia enters dressed as a judge and gets quickly down to business. By adopting male dress, a woman can enter the male world of Venice—chiefly a place of commerce and law, in contrast to Belmont, chiefly a place of music and love—and can in fact excel the men. It is not an exaggeration to say that in this play cross-dressing calls into doubt the traditional idea that women are essentially weaker than men.

Portia begins by granting that Shylock's procedure cannot be attacked under the law:

> *Portia.* Then must the Jew be merciful.
> *Shylock.* On what compulsion must I?   (181–82)

The question reveals how tightly his moral code is bound to the letter of the law. What it forbids he will never do. But he can neither give nor forgive. Portia, in a speech that almost sums up the meaning of the play, explains that mercy must be an entirely free gift (183–201). It blesses the giver and the receiver alike. To show mercy is the privilege of kings, of God himself. But if Shylock insists on the letter of the law, sentence must be given against the merchant. Then comes Portia's quiet masterstroke.

> Tarry a little; there is something else.
> This bond doth give thee here no jot of blood.   (304–5)

Stunned as he is, Shylock tries to accept the previous offer of thrice the bond. But having refused it, he now has no claim on it or even on the bare principal. The law has yet another hold on him. He, an alien, has plotted against a citizen's life. All his vast wealth is forfeit, half to Antonio, half to the state, and his life lies "in the mercy of the Duke only."

Portia has appealed in vain to reason, to charity, and to self-interest. Now she has turned the letter of the law against Shylock. He has been guilty of the mad presumption that the Greeks called *hubris*. For him this sudden blow is a profound psychological shock. No longer can he boast he does no wrong. *By his own code,* the letter of the law, he knows he is guilty of a deadly crime. Stunned and broken, he kneels before the Duke.

The strict court of Venice understands mercy as well as justice. Justice demands that the offender be punished, be forced to make amends to the injured party, and be restrained from doing further harm. Mercy draws a distinction between a crime willed and a crime enacted. As the prince of Christian humanists, Erasmus, says of charity, mercy requires that the Christian "be an enemy only to vice. Let him kill the Turk, but save the man." Let Portia and the Duke kill his fanaticism, but save the man.

Can we honestly say that he receives mercy? By the mere letter of the law he receives it abundantly. He now owns not a penny's worth of property, and his life is forfeit. The Duke instantly pardons him his life, but Shylock is ready to die. It is now Antonio's opportunity to show mercy. Under the law, one half of Shylock's wealth is now Antonio's, the other half the state's. Following a hint of the Duke's, the merchant proposes, first, that the half which is the state's be restored conditionally to Shylock. Second, he offers to use his own half as a permanent loan without interest, and at the Jew's death to give it outright to Jessica and Lorenzo. He imposes two conditions: first, that the young couple shall receive all Shylock's property at his death; second, that he immediately become a Christian.

In view of Shylock's own cruelty to his luckless debtors, these terms would seem to us both just and merciful, were it not for the forced conversion. This we are bound to resent if we think of the Hebrew faith only as it really is. But if we see it as it had been misunderstood by Christians for over fifteen centuries, we can appropriate the words of Edmund Burke (written with no reference to Judaism) to describe their view of it as "an uncouth, pernicious, and degrading superstition."

The forced conversion of Shylock is an attempt (however loathsome it must seem to us) to free Shylock from his barbarism and to bring him into an allegedly humane society. It is noteworthy that Antonio, the Duke, and Portia never show any hatred of Shylock. In their view he is being saved from himself. Still, a modern viewer can hardly avoid thinking that the Portia who spoke so eloquently of mercy when she was seeking to persuade Shylock to spare Antonio now says nothing about mercy.

Fulfillment

The final scene at Portia's estate will seem irrelevant and bitterly ironical to those who still regard Shylock as a victim of Christian bigotry. To others it will be something very different. A good man has been saved from death. A greatly gifted but fanatic and dangerous man has begun to see life in an altogether new way. Now, in the peace and the magical beauty of the evening, Lorenzo and Jessica are recalling famous lovers of the past. Their earnest mood, broken by playful teasing, Lorenzo's poetic nature as revealed in his words about the music of the spheres, the entrance of Portia and Nerissa, happy in a work of redemption fully achieved—all this suggests powerfully the happy harmony of life at its best. Gratiano's sudden quarrel with Nerissa and the women's harmless teasing of the men about the rings they gave away bring us back to ordinary life and to the mood of comedy. Portia's news that three of Antonio's argosies

Are richly come to harbor suddenly,   (5.1.277)

and her good news also for Jessica and Lorenzo give promise of long happiness for them. Gratiano's final speech, with its bawdy pun on Nerissa's ring (vulva), brings a laugh from the audience. But Gratiano is easily the most vulgar character in the play. Can we let him establish the final mood of the play? There is the question of exactly how a director—*The Merchant of Venice* was meant to be performed, not read—will handle the final exit of Gratiano and the others. In particular, a director must decide whether or not Antonio will stand apart from the three pairs of lovers. If Antonio does stand apart, he will cast a shadow over what otherwise seems to be a festive occasion. How directors have handled the final exit is discussed at length in Robert Smallwood's essay, reprinted on pages 156–59 of this book.

—KENNETH MYRICK
Tufts University

The Merchant of Venice

[Dramatis Personae

The Duke of Venice
The Prince of Morocco } suitors to Portia
The Prince of Aragon
Antonio, a merchant of Venice
Bassanio, his friend, suitor to Portia
Gratiano
Salerio } friends to Antonio and Bassanio
Solanio
Lorenzo, in love with Jessica
Shylock, a Jew
Tubal, a Jew, his friend
Launcelot Gobbo, a clown, servant to Shylock
Old Gobbo, father to Launcelot
Leonardo, servant to Bassanio
Balthasar
Stephano } servants to Portia
Portia, an heiress
Nerissa, her waiting woman
Jessica, daughter to Shylock
Magnificoes of Venice, Officers of the court of justice,
    Jailer, Servants, and other Attendants

Scene: Venice and Belmont]

The Merchant of Venice

[ACT 1

Scene 1. *Venice. A street.*]

Enter Antonio, Salerio, and Solanio.

Antonio. In sooth I know not why I am so sad.°1
  It wearies me, you say it wearies you;
  But how I caught it, found it, or came by it,
  What stuff 'tis made of, whereof it is born,
  I am to learn;°   5
  And such a want-wit° sadness° makes of me
  That I have much ado to know myself.

Salerio. Your mind is tossing on the ocean,°
  There where your argosies° with portly° sail—
  Like signiors and rich burghers on the flood,   10
  Or as it were the pageants° of the sea—
  Do overpeer the petty traffickers
  That cursy° to them, do them reverence,
  As they fly by them with their woven wings.

Solanio. Believe me, sir, had I such venture° forth,   15
  The better part of my affections would

---

1 The degree sign (°) indicates a footnote, which is keyed to the text by line number. Text references are printed in **boldface** type; the annotation follows in roman type.
1.1.1 **sad** sober, depressed **5 am to learn** need to learn, cannot guess (the incomplete line indicates a short pause) 6 **want-wit** dull fellow 6 **sadness** depression 8 **ocean** (pronounced "ó-ce-an") 9 **argosies** great merchant ships 9 **portly** stately 11 **pageants** floats, splendidly decorated wagons in the shape of castles, dragons, etc. 13 **cursy** curtsy, bow 15 **venture** unpredictable enterprise

Be with my hopes abroad. I should be still°
Plucking the grass to know where sits the wind,
Peering in maps for ports and piers and roads;°
20 And every object that might make me fear
Misfortune to my ventures, out of doubt
Would make me sad.

Salerio.   My wind cooling my broth
Would blow me to an ague° when I thought
What harm a wind too great might do at sea.
25 I should not see the sandy hourglass run
But I should think of shallows and of flats,
And see my wealthy *Andrew*° docked in sand,
Vailing° her high top lower than her ribs
To kiss her burial. Should I go to church
30 And see the holy edifice of stone
And not bethink me straight of dangerous rocks,
Which touching but my gentle° vessel's side
Would scatter all her spices on the stream,
Enrobe the roaring waters with my silks—
35 And in a word, but even now worth this,°
And now worth nothing?° Shall I have the thought
To think on this, and shall I lack the thought
That such a thing bechanced° would make me sad?
But tell me not! I know Antonio
40 Is sad to think upon his merchandise.

Antonio. Believe me, no. I thank my fortune for it,
My ventures are not in one bottom° trusted,
Nor to one place; nor is my whole estate
Upon the fortune of this present year.
45 Therefore my merchandise makes me not sad.

Solanio. Why then you are in love.

Antonio.   Fie, fie!

Solanio. Not in love neither? Then let us say you are sad

17 **still** always   19 **roads** harbors   23 **ague** trembling fit   27 **Andrew** the name of a ship   28 **Vailing** lowering, in recognition of a superior   32 **gentle** noble and gentle; hence, splendid and frail   35, 36 **this, nothing** (spoken with an emphatic gesture)   38 **bechanced** should it happen   42 **bottom** ship

Because you are not merry; and 'twere as easy
For you to laugh and leap, and say you are merry
Because you are not sad. Now by two-headed Janus,°   *50*
Nature hath framed strange° fellows in her time:
Some that will evermore peep through their eyes
And laugh like parrots at a bagpiper,
And other of such vinegar aspect
That they'll not show their teeth in way of smile   *55*
Though Nestor° swear the jest be laughable.

　　Enter Bassanio, Lorenzo, and Gratiano.

Here comes Bassanio, your most noble kinsman,
Gratiano, and Lorenzo. Fare ye well;
We leave you now with better company.

Salerio. I would have stayed till I had made you merry,   *60*
If worthier friends had not prevented° me.

Antonio. Your worth is very dear in my regard.
I take it your own business calls on you,
And you embrace th' occasion to depart.

Salerio. Good morrow, my good lords.   *65*

Bassanio. Good signiors both, when shall we laugh? Say,
　　when?
You grow exceeding strange;° must it be so?

Salerio. We'll make our leisures to attend on yours.
　　　　　　　　　Exeunt Salerio and Solanio.

Lorenzo. My Lord Bassanio, since you have found
　　Antonio,
We two will leave you; but at dinner time   *70*
I pray you have in mind where we must meet.

Bassanio. I will not fail you.

Gratiano. You look not well, Signior Antonio.

50 **two-headed Janus** Roman god of entrances and hence of all begin-
nings; depicted with two faces, one cheerful, one sad, symbolizing the
uncertainty of the future (Solanio suggests that Antonio is as strange a
figure as Janus)   51 **strange** marvelously queer   56 **Nestor** the oldest
and most venerable Greek leader in the Trojan War; a type of gravity and
wisdom   61 **prevented** forestalled   67 **strange** distant

You have too much respect upon° the world;
75 They lose it that do buy it with much care.
Believe me, you are marvelously changed.

Antonio. I hold the world but as the world, Gratiano—
A stage, where every man must play a part,
And mine a sad one.

Gratiano.   Let me play the fool!
80 With mirth and laughter let old wrinkles come,
And let my liver° rather heat with wine
Than my heart cool with mortifying groans.°
Why should a man whose blood is warm within
Sit like his grandsire, cut in alabaster?
85 Sleep when he wakes? And creep into the jaundice°
By being peevish? I tell thee what, Antonio—
I love thee, and 'tis my love that speaks—
There are a sort of men whose visages
Do cream and mantle° like a standing pond,
90 And do a willful stillness entertain°
With purpose to be dressed in an opinion°
Of wisdom, gravity, profound conceit,°
As who should say, "I am Sir Oracle,°
And when I ope my lips, let no dog bark!"
95 O my Antonio, I do know of these
That therefore only are reputed wise
For saying nothing; when I am very sure
If they should speak, would almost dam° those ears,
Which hearing them would call their brothers fools.
100 I'll tell thee more of this another time.

74 **respect upon** regard for 81 **liver** one of the supposed seats of the
passions 82 **mortifying groans** groans supposed to deaden vitality
(by drawing blood from the heart) 85 **jaundice** disease thought to
be caused by peevishness 89 **cream and mantle** become impassive
like thick cream on a bowl of milk, or a mantle of scum on a pond
90 **entertain** assume 91 **opinion** reputation (as in line 102) 92 **profound conceit** power of forming profound conceptions 93 **I am Sir
Oracle** i.e., I am as wise as a Greek oracle (inspired by the gods)
98 **dam** (often emended to "damn," and probably a pun: If these silent
and reputedly wise men ever did speak, the abundance of their foolish
words would not only dam up the ears of the listeners, but also make the
listeners call the formerly silent men fools, and thus bring on the listeners the penalty of damnation which is pronounced on all who apply
this term to a brother-man. See Matthew 5:22)

But fish not with this melancholy bait
For this fool gudgeon,° this opinion.
Come, good Lorenzo. Fare ye well awhile;
I'll end my exhortation after dinner.

Lorenzo. Well, we will leave you then till dinner time. 105
I must be one of these same dumb wise men,
For Gratiano never lets me speak.

Gratiano. Well, keep me company but two years moe,°
Thou shalt not know the sound of thine own tongue.

Antonio. Fare you well; I'll grow a talker for this gear.° 110

Gratiano. Thanks i' faith; for silence is only commend-
able
In a neat's tongue° dried and a maid not vendible.°
Exeunt [Gratiano and Lorenzo].

Antonio. Is that anything now?

Bassanio. Gratiano speaks an infinite deal of nothing,
more than any man in all Venice. His reasons are as 115
two grains of wheat hid in two bushels of chaff: you
shall seek all day ere you find them, and when you
have them they are not worth the search.

Antonio. Well, tell me now, what lady is the same
To whom you swore a secret pilgrimage 120
That you today promised to tell me of?

Bassanio. 'Tis not unknown to you, Antonio,
How much I have disabled mine estate,
By something° showing a more swelling port°
Than my faint means would grant continuance.° 125
Nor do I now make moan to be abridged°

101–02.**But . . . gudgeon** don't cultivate melancholy to gain a reputation for silent wisdom, for the judgment of the multitude is stupid ("gudgeon" = proverbially foolish fish) 108 **moe** more ("moe" is the old
positive form of which "more" was the comparative) 110 **gear** stuff (a
mild jest, showing that Gratiano has cheered Antonio for a moment)
112 **neat's tongue** beef tongue 112 **vendible** salable, i.e., marriageable 124 **something** somewhat 124 **swelling port** impressive style
of living 125 **grant continuance** allow me to continue 126 **abridged**
cut down

From such a noble rate;° but my chief care
Is to come fairly off from the great debts
Wherein my time, something too prodigal,°
130 Hath left me gaged.° To you, Antonio,
I owe the most in money and in love,
And from your love I have a warranty
To unburden all my plots and purposes
How to get clear of all the debts I owe.

135 *Antonio.* I pray you, good Bassanio, let me know it,
And if it stand as you yourself still° do,
Within the eye of honor, be assured
My purse, my person, my extremest means
Lie all unlocked to your occasions.°

140 *Bassanio.* In my schooldays, when I had lost one shaft°
I shot his fellow° of the selfsame flight°
The selfsame way, with more advisèd° watch,
To find the other forth; and by adventuring both
I oft found both. I urge this childhood proof°
145 Because what follows is pure innocence.°
I owe you much, and like a willful youth°
That which I owe is lost; but if you please
To shoot another arrow that self way
Which you did shoot the first, I do not doubt,
150 As I will watch the aim, or° to find both,
Or bring your latter hazard° back again
And thankfully rest debtor for the first.

Antonio. You know me well, and herein spend but time
To wind about my love with circumstance;°
155 And out of doubt you do me now more wrong
In making question of my uttermost

---

127 **rate** scale   129 **my time, something too prodigal** the lavish way
I spent my time   130 **gaged** pledged   136 **still** always   139 **occasions**
needs   140 **shaft** arrow   141 **fellow** duplicate   141 **selfsame flight**
identical in size and in the feathers   142 **advisèd** considered   144 **proof**
experience   145 **pure innocence** childlike sincerity   146 **like a willful
youth** i.e., like one who neglected sound advice and learned by making
mistakes   150 **or** either   151 **hazard** thing risked   154 **To wind ...
circumstance** to approach my love circuitously with elaborate talk

Than if you had made waste of all I have.
Then do but say to me what I should do
That in your knowledge may by me be done,
And I am prest unto it.° Therefore speak.   *160*

Bassanio. In Belmont is a lady richly left;°
And she is fair and, fairer than that word,
Of wondrous virtues.° Sometimes from her eyes
I did receive fair speechless messages.
Her name is Portia, nothing undervalued   *165*
To° Cato's daughter, Brutus' Portia;°
Nor is the wide world ignorant of her worth,
For the four winds blow in from every coast
Renownèd suitors, and her sunny locks
Hang on her temples like a golden fleece,   *170*
Which makes her seat° of Belmont Colchos' strond,°
And many Jasons come in quest of her.
O my Antonio, had I but the means
To hold a rival place with one of them,
I have a mind presages me° such thrift°   *175*
That I should questionless be fortunate!

Antonio. Thou know'st that all my fortunes are at sea;
Neither have I money, nor commodity°
To raise a present sum. Therefore go forth;
Try what my credit can in Venice do.   *180*
That shall be racked° even to the uttermost
To furnish thee to Belmont, to fair Portia.
Go presently° inquire, and so will I,
Where money is; and I no question make
To have it of my trust or for my sake.°   *Exeunt.*   *185*

---

160 **prest unto it** ready to aid you in it (from Latin *praesto,* at hand,
ready)   161 **richly left** left rich   163 **virtues** powers and gifts (a more
inclusive word than today)   165–66 **nothing undervalued/To** of no
less value than   166 **Brutus' Portia** famed for her intellectual gifts, her
resolution, and her wifely devotion (see *Julius Caesar,* 2.1. 233–308)
171 **seat** estate   171 **Colchos' strond** the shore east of the Black Sea
where Jason won the Golden Fleece   175 **a mind presages me** a presentiment that foretells me   175 **thrift** thriving, success   178 **commodity** merchandise   181 **racked** stretched to the point of torture (as
on the rack)   183 **presently** instantly   185 **of my trust or for my sake**
on my credit or on the basis of friendship

[Scene 2. *Belmont. Portia's house.*]

Enter Portia with her waiting woman, Nerissa.

Portia. By my troth,° Nerissa, my little body is aweary
of this great world.

Nerissa. You would be, sweet madam, if your miseries
were in the same abundance as your good fortunes
are; and yet for aught I see, they are as sick that sur-
feit° with too much as they that starve with nothing.
It is no mean° happiness, therefore, to be seated in
the mean;° superfluity comes sooner by° white hairs,
but competency° lives longer.

Portia. Good sentences,° and well pronounced.

Nerissa. They would be better if well followed.

Portia. If to do were as easy to know what were good
to do, chapels had been° churches, and poor men's
cottages princes' palaces. It is a good divine that follows his own instructions; I can easier teach twenty
what were good to be done, than to be one of the
twenty to follow mine own teaching. The brain may
devise laws for the blood,° but a hot temper° leaps
o'er a cold decree;° such a hare is madness the youth
to skip o'er the meshes° of good counsel the cripple.
But this reasoning is not in the fashion° to choose me
a husband. O me, the word "choose"! I may neither
choose who I would nor refuse who I dislike, so is
the will of a living daughter curbed by the will° of

5

10

15

20

1.2.1 **troth** faith   5–6 **surfeit** are overfed, glutted   7, 8 **mean** (1)
slight (2) golden mean   8 **comes sooner by** acquires sooner   9 **com-
petency** a modest but comfortable fortune   10 **sentences** sententious
maxims   13 **had been** would have been   18 **blood** passion   18 **hot
temper** ardent temperament   19 **cold decree** decision made in cold
judgment   20 **meshes** nets for catching small creatures   21 **in the
fashion** of the sort   24 **will . . . will** wish . . . last will and testament

a dead father. Is it not hard, Nerissa, that I cannot   25
choose one, nor refuse none?°

Nerissa. Your father was ever virtuous, and holy men
at their death have good inspirations. Therefore the
lott'ry that he hath devised in these three chests of
gold, silver, and lead, whereof who chooses his mean-   30
ing chooses you, will no doubt never be chosen by
any rightly but one who you shall rightly love. But
what warmth is there in your affection towards any of
these princely suitors that are already come?

Portia. I pray thee overname them; and as thou namest   35
them I will describe them, and according to my description level at my affection.

Nerissa. First, there is the Neapolitan prince.

Portia. Ay, that's a colt indeed, for he doth nothing but
talk of his horse, and he makes it a great appropri-   40
ation to his own good parts° that he can shoe him
himself. I am much afeard my lady his mother
played false with a smith.

Nerissa. Then is there the County° Palatine.

Portia. He doth nothing but frown—as who should say,   45
"And° you will not have me, choose!" He hears
merry tales and smiles not; I fear he will prove the
weeping philosopher° when he grows old, being so
full of unmannerly sadness° in his youth. I had
rather be married to a death's-head with a bone in   50
his mouth than to either of these. God defend me
from these two!

Nerissa. How say you by the French lord, Monsieur Le
Bon?

Portia. God made him, and therefore let him pass for a   55
man. In truth, I know it is a sin to be a mocker, but

26 **refuse none** refuse any   40–41 **appropriation . . . parts** personal
accomplishment added to his talents   44 **County** Count   46 **And** if
47–48 **the weeping philosopher** i.e., another Heraclitus   49 **unmannerly sadness** unbecoming seriousness

he! Why, he hath a horse better than the Neapolitan's,
a better bad habit of frowning than the Count Palatine; he is every man in no man. If a throstle° sing,
60 he falls straight a-cap'ring; he will fence with his own
shadow. If I should° marry him, I should° marry
twenty husbands. If he would despise me, I would
forgive him; for if he love me to madness, I shall
never requite him.

65 *Nerissa.* What say you then to Falconbridge, the young
baron of England?

Portia. You know I say nothing to him, for he understands not me, nor I him. He hath neither Latin,
French, nor Italian; and you will come into the court
70 and swear that I have a poor pennyworth in the English. He is a proper° man's picture, but alas, who can
converse with a dumbshow? How oddly he is suited!
I think he bought his doublet° in Italy, his round
hose° in France, his bonnet in Germany, and his be-
75 havior everywhere.

Nerissa. What think you of the Scottish lord, his neighbor?

Portia. That he hath a neighborly charity in him, for he
borrowed a box of the ear of the Englishman and
80 swore he would pay him again when he was able. I
think the Frenchman° became his surety and sealed
under for another.

Nerissa. How like you the young German,° the Duke of
Saxony's nephew?

85 *Portia.* Very vilely in the morning when he is sober, and
most vilely in the afternoon when he is drunk. When
he is best he is a little worse than a man, and when he

59 **throstle** song thrush   61 **should ... should** were to ... would be
obliged to   71 **proper** handsome   73 **doublet** upper garment, cor-
responding to the modern coat   73–74 **round hose** lower garment,
combining the functions of breeches and stockings   76–81 **Scottish
lord ... Frenchman** (an allusion to the French promises of aid to the
Scots against the English, promises that were often broken)   83 **German** (Germans were proverbially heavy drinkers)

is worst he is little better than a beast.° And the worst
fall that ever fell, I hope I shall make shift° to go
without him.　　　　　　　　　　　　　　　　　　　*90*

Nerissa. If he should offer to choose, and choose the
right casket, you should refuse to perform your
father's will if you should refuse to accept him.

Portia. Therefore, for fear of the worst, I pray thee set
a deep glass of Rhenish wine on the contrary casket,　*95*
for if the devil be within and that temptation without,
I know he will choose it. I will do anything, Nerissa,
ere I will be married to a sponge.

Nerissa. You need not fear, lady, the having any of these
lords. They have acquainted me with their determi-　*100*
nations; which is indeed to return to their home, and
to trouble you with no more suit, unless you may be
won by some other sort° than your father's imposition,° depending on the caskets.

Portia. If I live to be as old as Sibylla,° I will die as　*105*
chaste as Diana unless I be obtained by the manner
of my father's will. I am glad this parcel of wooers
are so reasonable, for there is not one among them but
I dote on his very absence; and I pray God grant them
a fair departure.　　　　　　　　　　　　　　　　*110*

Nerissa. Do you not remember, lady, in your father's
time, a Venetian, a scholar and a soldier, that came
hither in company of the Marquis of Montferrat?

Portia. Yes, yes, it was Bassanio!—as I think, so was he
called.　　　　　　　　　　　　　　　　　　　　*115*

Nerissa. True, madam. He, of all the men that ever my
foolish eyes looked upon, was the best deserving a
fair lady.

87–88 **best ... beast** (a pun, "beast" being pronounced almost like
"best." Such quibbles were not necessarily comic, but were considered
clever and interesting)　89 **make shift** find a way　103 **sort** manner
103–04 **imposition** command　105 **Sibylla** the Cumean Sibyl (Apollo
promised her as many years of life as were the grains of sand she was
holding in her hand)

Portia. I remember him well, and I remember him
120   worthy of thy praise.

Enter a Servingman.

How now? What news?

Servingman. The four strangers° seek for you, madam,
to take their leave; and there is a forerunner come
from a fifth, the Prince of Morocco, who brings word
125   the Prince his master will be here tonight.

Portia. If I could bid the fifth welcome with so good
heart as I can bid the other four farewell, I should
be glad of his approach. If he have the condition of a
saint and the complexion of a devil, I had rather he
130   should shrive me than wive me. Come, Nerissa. Sirrah,° go before. Whiles we shut the gate upon one
wooer, another knocks at the door.   *Exeunt.*

[Scene 3. *Venice. A public place.*]

Enter Bassanio with Shylock the Jew.

Shylock. Three thousand ducats—well.

Bassanio. Ay, sir, for three months.

Shylock. For three months—well.

Bassanio. For the which, as I told you, Antonio shall be
5   bound.°

Shylock. Antonio shall become bound—well.

122 **four strangers** (apparently Shakespeare originally described four
suitors, then added two more, and forgot to change "four" to "six")
130–31 **Sirrah** (a regular form of address to a social inferior. Portia
speaks to the servant)   1.3.5 **bound** under legal obligation as cosigner
of the bond

Bassanio. May° you stead° me? Will you pleasure me? Shall I know your answer?

Shylock. Three thousand ducats for three months, and Antonio bound.   *10*

Bassanio. Your answer to that.

Shylock. Antonio is a good man.°

Bassanio. Have you heard any imputation to the contrary?

Shylock. Ho no, no, no, no! My meaning in saying he is   *15*
a good man, is to have you understand me that he is
sufficient.° Yet his means are in supposition:° he hath
an argosy bound to Tripolis, another to the Indies; I
understand, moreover, upon the Rialto,° he hath a
third at Mexico, a fourth for England—and other   *20*
ventures he hath, squand'red abroad. But ships are
but boards, sailors but men; there be land rats and
water rats, water thieves and land thieves—I mean
pirates°—and then there is the peril of waters, winds,
and rocks. The man is, notwithstanding, sufficient.   *25*
Three thousand ducats—I think I may take his bond.

Bassanio. Be assured you may.

Shylock. I will be assured I may. And that I may be assured, I will bethink me. May I speak with Antonio?

Bassanio. If it please you to dine with us.   *30*

Shylock. Yes, to smell pork, to eat of the habitation
which your prophet the Nazarite° conjured the devil
into! I will buy with you, sell with you, talk with you,
walk with you, and so following; but I will not eat
with you, drink with you, nor pray with you. What   *35*
news on the Rialto? Who is he comes here?

7 **May** can   7 **stead** be of service to   12 **good man** good business risk
(Bassanio takes the word as referring to moral character)   17 **sufficient**
adequate, responsible   17 **in supposition** doubtful   19 **Rialto** famous
bridge in Venice, the center of commercial activity   24 **pirates** (pronounced "pi-rats," with quibble on "rats")   32 **the Nazarite** Christ (the
allusion is to the episode in Mark 5:1–13, Luke 8:26–33)

Enter Antonio.

Bassanio. This is Signior Antonio.

Shylock. [*Aside*] How like a fawning publican° he
    looks.
    I hate him for° he is a Christian;
40   But more, for that in low simplicity
    He lends out money gratis, and brings down
    The rate of usance° here with us in Venice.
    If I can catch him once upon the hip,°
    I will feed fat the ancient grudge I bear him.
45   He hates our sacred nation, and he rails,
    Even there where merchants most do congregate,
    On me, my bargains, and my well-won thrift,°
    Which he calls interest. Cursèd be my tribe
    If I forgive him.

Bassanio.   Shylock, do you hear?

50   *Shylock.* I am debating of my present store,°
    And by the near guess of my memory
    I cannot instantly raise up the gross°
    Of full three thousand ducats. What of that?
    Tubal, a wealthy Hebrew of my tribe,
55   Will furnish me. But soft,° how many months
    Do you desire? [*To Antonio*] Rest you fair, good
    signior!
    Your worship was the last man in our mouths.

Antonio. Shylock, albeit I neither lend nor borrow
    By taking nor by giving of excess,
60   Yet to supply the ripe wants of my friend,
    I'll break a custom. [*To Bassanio*] Is he yet pos-
    sessed°
    How much ye would?°

---

38 **publican** (sometimes glossed as a Roman tax-gatherer, as in Matthew 11:17, Luke 18:10, and sometimes as an Elizabethan innkeeper.
Perhaps Shylock uses it as an inexact but bitter term of reproach)
39 **for** because   42 **usance** interest   43 **upon the hip** at a disadvan-
tage (a term in wrestling)   47 **thrift** prosperity   50 **present store**
stock of ready money   52 **gross** whole amount   55 **soft** hold, stay
61 **possessed** apprised   62 **would** desire

Shylock.   Ay, ay, three thousand ducats.

Antonio. And for three months.

Shylock. I had forgot—three months, you told me   60
so. Well then, your bond. And let me see—but hear you: 65
Methoughts° you said you neither lend nor borrow
Upon advantage.°

Antonio.   I do never use it.

Shylock. When Jacob° grazed his uncle Laban's
    sheep—
    This Jacob from our holy Abram was,
    As his wise mother wrought in his behalf,   70
    The third possessor; ay, he was the third—

Antonio. And what of him? Did he take interest?

Shylock. No, not take interest   not as you would say
    Directly int'rest. Mark what Jacob did:
    When Laban and himself were compremised°   75
    That all the eanlings which were streaked and pied
    Should fall as Jacob's hire, the ewes being rank
    In end of autumn turnèd to the rams;
    And when the work of generation was
    Between these woolly breeders in the act,   80
    The skillful shepherd pilled° me° certain wands,
    And in the doing of the deed of kind°
    He stuck them up before the fulsome ewes,
    Who then conceiving, did in eaning° time
    Fall parti-colored lambs, and those were Jacob's.   85
    This was a way to thrive, and he was blest;
    And thrift is blessing if men steal it not.

Antonio. This was a venture,° sir, that Jacob served for,
    A thing not in his power to bring to pass,
    But swayed and fashioned by the hand of heaven.   90
    Was this inserted to make interest good?
    Or is your gold and silver ewes and rams?

---

66 **Methoughts** it seemed to me   67 **advantage** interest   68 **Jacob**
(see Genesis 30:25–43; 31:1–13)   75 **were compremised** had reached
an agreement   81 **pilled** stripped   81 **me** (the ethical dative)   82 **kind**
nature   84 **eaning** lambing   88 **venture** unpredictable enterprise

Shylock. I cannot tell; I make it breed as fast.
　　But note me, signior—

Antonio. 　　　　　　　Mark you this, Bassanio,
95　The devil can cite Scripture for his purpose.
　　An evil soul producing holy witness
　　Is like a villain with a smiling cheek,
　　A goodly° apple rotten at the heart.
　　O what a goodly outside falsehood hath!

Shylock. Three thousand ducats—'tis a good round
100　sum.
　　Three months from twelve—then let me see, the
　　rate—

Antonio. Well, Shylock, shall we be beholding° to you?

Shylock. Signior Antonio, many a time and oft
　　In the Rialto you have rated° me
105　About my moneys and my usances.
　　Still° have I borne it with a patient shrug,
　　For suff'rance° is the badge of all our tribe.
　　You call me misbeliever, cutthroat dog,
　　And spet upon my Jewish gaberdine,°
110　And all for use of that which is mine own.
　　Well then, it now appears you need my help.
　　Go to, then.° You come to me and you say,
　　"Shylock, we would have moneys"—you say so,
　　You that did void your rheum° upon my beard
115　And foot me as you spurn a stranger cur
　　Over your threshold! Moneys is your suit.
　　What should I say to you? Should I not say,
　　"Hath a dog money? Is it possible
　　A cur can lend three thousand ducats?" Or
120　Shall I bend low, and in a bondman's key,
　　With bated breath, and whisp'ring humbleness,
　　Say this:

---

98 **goodly** fine-appearing　102 **beholding** beholden, obligated　104 **rated** berated, reviled　106 **Still** always　107 **suff'rance** long-suffering　109 **gaberdine** the distinctive gown or mantle of the Jews　112 **Go to, then** (an exclamation suggesting annoyance) · 114 **rheum** spittle

"Fair sir, you spet on me on Wednesday last,
You spurned me such a day, another time
You called me dog; and for these courtesies   *125*
I'll lend you thus much moneys"?

Antonio. I am as like to call thee so again,
To spet on thee again, to spurn thee too.
If thou wilt lend this money, lend it not
As to thy friends—for when did friendship take   *130*
A breed for barren metal° of his friend?—
But lend it rather to thine enemy,
Who if he break,° thou mayst with better face
Exact the penalty.

Shylock.   Why look you, how you storm!
I would be friends with you, and have your love,   *135*
Forget the shames that you have stained me with,
Supply your present wants, and take no doit°
Of usance for my moneys; and you'll not hear me.
This is kind° I offer.

Bassanio. This were kindness.

Shylock.   This kindness will I show: *140*
Go with me to a notary; seal me there
Your single° bond, and, in a merry sport,
If you repay me not on such a day,
In such a place, such sum or sums as are
Expressed in the condition, let the forfeit   *145*
Be nominated for an equal pound
Of your fair flesh, to be cut off and taken
In what part of your body pleaseth me.

Antonio. Content, in faith. I'll seal to such a bond,
And say there is much kindness° in the Jew.   *150*

Bassanio. You shall not seal to such a bond for me!
I'll rather dwell in my necessity.

---

131 **breed for barren metal** interest (Aristotelian doctrine held that
money, unlike living things, cannot reproduce)   133 **break** become
insolvent   137 **doit** tiny Dutch coin, valued at one-eighth of an English
penny   139 **kind** kind and natural (in contrast to usurious dealings)
142 **single** without further security   150 **kindness** natural friendliness

Antonio. Why fear not, man; I will not forfeit it.
    Within these two months—that's a month before
155 This bond expires—I do expect return
    Of thrice three times the value of this bond.

Shylock. O father Abram, what these Christians are,
    Whose own hard dealings teaches them suspect
    The thoughts of others! Pray you tell me this:
160 If he should break his day,° what should I gain
    By the exaction of the forfeiture?
    A pound of man's flesh taken from a man
    Is not so estimable, profitable neither,
    As flesh of muttons, beefs, or goats. I say
165 To buy his favor I extend this friendship.
    If he will take it, so; if not, adieu.°
    And for my love I pray you wrong me not.°

Antonio. Yes, Shylock, I will seal unto this bond.

Shylock. Then meet me forthwith at the notary's;
170 Give him direction for this merry bond,
    And I will go and purse the ducats straight,
    See to my house, left in the fearful° guard
    Of an unthrifty knave,° and presently°
    I'll be with you.   *Exit.*

Antonio.   Hie thee, gentle Jew.°
175 The Hebrew will turn Christian; he grows kind.

Bassanio. I like not fair terms and a villain's mind.

Antonio. Come on. In this there can be no dismay;
    My ships come home a month before the day.
                                Exeunt.

---

160 **break his day** break his promise to pay on the due date   166 **adieu** (probably the word has the original meaning, "I commend you to God")   167 **And ... wrong me not** i.e., and for the friendship I have shown you, please don't misjudge me in the future   172 **fearful** hazardous   173 **unthrifty knave** careless youngster   173 **presently** instantly   174 **gentle Jew** courteous Jew (with a pun on "gentile")

[ACT 2

Scene 1. *Belmont. Portia's house.*]

*[Flourish of cornets.] Enter [the Prince of]
Morocco, a tawny Moor all in white, and three or
four Followers accordingly, with Portia, Nerissa,
and their Train.*

Morocco. Mislike me not for my complexion,
  The shadowed° livery° of the burnished sun,
  To whom I am a neighbor and near bred.
  Bring me the fairest creature northward born,
  Where Phoebus'° fire scarce thaws the icicles,   *5*
  And let us make incision° for your love
  To prove whose blood is reddest, his or mine.
  I tell thee, lady, this aspect° of mine
  Hath feared the valiant.° By my love I swear,
  The best-regarded virgins of our clime   *10*
  Have loved it too. I would not change this hue,
  Except to steal your thoughts, my gentle queen.

Portia. In terms of choice° I am not solely led
  By nice° direction of a maiden's eyes.
  Besides, the lott'ry of my destiny   *15*

2.1.2 **shadowed** dark   2 **livery** uniform for a king's or nobleman's
retainers   5 **Phoebus'** the sun-god's   6 **make incision** cut our flesh
8 **aspect** (pronounced "a-spèct")   9 **feared the valiant** caused the valiant
to fear   13 **In terms of choice** with respect to my choice   14 **nice**
fastidious

Bars me the right of voluntary choosing.
But if my father had not scanted° me,
And hedged me by his wit° to yield myself
His wife who wins me by that means I told you,
20　Yourself, renownèd Prince, then stood as fair
As any comer I have looked on yet
For my affection.

Morocco.　　　　Even for that I thank you.
Therefore I pray you lead me to the caskets
To try my fortune. By this scimitar,
25　That slew the Sophy,° and a Persian prince
That won three fields of Sultan Solyman,
I would o'erstare° the sternest eyes that look,
Outbrave the heart most daring on the earth,
Pluck the young sucking cubs from the she-bear,
30　Yea, mock the lion when 'a° roars for prey,
To win thee, lady. But alas the while,
If Hercules and Lichas° play at dice
Which is the better man, the greater throw
May turn by fortune from the weaker hand.
35　So is Alcides° beaten by his page,
And so may I, blind Fortune leading me,
Miss that which one unworthier may attain,
And die with grieving.

Portia.　　　　　You must take your chance,
And either not attempt to choose at all,
40　Or swear before you choose, if you choose wrong
Never to speak to lady afterward
In way of marriage. Therefore be advised.°

Morocco. Nor will not.° Come, bring me unto my
chance.

Portia. First, forward to the temple; after dinner
Your hazard shall be made.

---

17 **scanted** limited ｜ 18 **hedged me by his wit** fenced me in by his
clever intellect　25 **Sophy** Shah of Persia　27 **o'erstare** outstare　30 **'a**
he　32 **Lichas** Hercules' page　35 **Alcides** Hercules　42 **be advised**
consider well　43 **Nor will not** nor will I (ever woo another for my wife)

Morocco.   Good fortune, then,   45
  To make me blest or cursèd'st among men!
                    [*Flourish of cornets.*] *Exeunt.*

          [Scene 2. *Venice. A street.*]

     Enter [*Launcelot Gobbo,*] *the Clown, alone.*

Launcelot. Certainly my conscience will serve me to
  run from this Jew my master. The fiend is at
  mine elbow and tempts me, saying to me, "Gobbo,
  Launcelot Gobbo, good Launcelot," or "good
  Gobbo," or "good Launcelot Gobbo—use your   5
  legs, take the start, run away." My conscience says,
  "No. Take heed, honest Launcelot; take heed,
  honest Gobbo," or as aforesaid, "honest Launcelot
  Gobbo, do not run; scorn running with thy heels."°
  Well, the most courageous fiend bids me pack.   10
  "Fia!"° says the fiend; "away!" says the fiend. "For
  the heavens,° rouse up a brave mind," says the
  fiend, "and run." Well, my conscience hanging about
  the neck of my heart says very wisely to me, "My
  honest friend Launcelot, being an honest man's   15
  son"—or rather an honest woman's son, for indeed
  my father did something smack, something grow
  to, he had a kind of taste°—Well, my conscience
  says, "Launcelot, budge not." "Budge," says the
  fiend. "Budge not," says my conscience. "Con-   20
  science," say I, "you counsel well." "Fiend," say I,
  "you counsel well." To be ruled by my conscience,

2.2.9 **scorn running with thy heels** (1) scorn to run away with your feet
(2) scorn utterly to run   11 **Fia!** (from Italian *via,* away)   11–12 **For
the heavens** by heaven, or for heaven's sake (in either case a grotesque
thing for the fiend to say)   17–18 **did something smack . . . had a kind
of taste** (both phrases indicate a tendency to vice)

I should stay with the Jew my master who (God
bless the mark!)° is a kind of devil; and to run away
25   from the Jew, I should be ruled by the fiend who,
saving your reverence, is the devil himself. Certainly
the Jew is the very devil incarnation;° and in my
conscience, my conscience is but a kind of hard conscience to offer to counsel me to stay with the Jew.
30   The fiend gives the more friendly counsel. I will run,
fiend; my heels are at your commandment, I will
run.

Enter Old Gobbo with a basket.

Gobbo. Master young man, you, I pray you, which is
the way to Master Jew's?

35   *Launcelot.* [*Aside*] O heavens, this is my true-begotten
father who, being more than sand-blind,° high-
gravel-blind,° knows me not. I will try confusions
with him.

Gobbo. Master young gentleman, I pray you, which is
40   the way to Master Jew's?

Launcelot. Turn up on your right hand at the next
turning, but at the next turning of all, on your left;
marry,° at the very next turning turn of no hand,
but turn down indirectly to the Jew's house.

45   *Gobbo.* Be God's sonties,° 'twill be a hard way to hit!
Can you tell me whether one Launcelot that dwells
with him, dwell with him or no?

Launcelot. Talk you of young Master Launcelot?
[*Aside*] Mark me now! Now will I raise the
50   waters.°—Talk you of young Master Launcelot?

23–24 **God bless the mark!** (used, like "saving your reverence" in line
26, to avert a bad omen)   27 **incarnation** (blunder for "incarnate")
36 **sand-blind** dull of sight   36–37 **high-gravel-blind** (Launcelot's
comic superlative for "sand-blind")   43 **marry** (a mild interjection,
originally an oath, by the Virgin Mary)   45 **Be God's sonties** by God's
little saints   49–50 **raise the waters** rouse a storm of emotion (a nautical metaphor?)

Gobbo. No master,° sir, but a poor man's son. His father, though I say't, is an honest exceeding poor man and, God be thanked, well to live.°

Launcelot. Well, let his father be what 'a will, we talk of young Master Launcelot.   55

Gobbo. Your worship's friend,° and Launcelot, sir.

Launcelot. But I pray you, ergo° old man, ergo I beseech you, talk you of young Master Launcelot?

Gobbo. Of Launcelot, an't° please your mastership.

Launcelot. Ergo, Master Launcelot. Talk not of Master   60
Launcelot, father, for the young gentleman, according to Fates and Destinies and such odd sayings, the Sisters Three and such branches of learning, is indeed deceased, or as you would say in plain terms, gone to heaven.   65

Gobbo. Marry, God forbid! The boy was the very staff of my age, my very prop.

Launcelot. [*Aside*] Do I look like a cudgel or a hovel-post, a staff, or a prop?° Do you know me, father?°

Gobbo. Alack the day, I know you not, young gentle-   70
man, but I pray you tell me, is my boy—God rest his soul—alive or dead?

Launcelot. Do you not know me, father?°

Gobbo. Alack, sir, I am sand-blind! I know you not.

Launcelot. Nay, indeed if you had your eyes you might   75
fail of the knowing me. It is a wise father that knows his own child. Well, old man, I will tell you news of your son. [*Kneels, with his back to his father.*] Give me your blessing. Truth will come to light; murder

51 **No master** (as a servant, Launcelot has no claim to the title of master)   52–53 **exceeding . . . to live** poverty-stricken and well-to-do   56 **Your worship's friend** (he politely insists on his son's humble status)   57 **ergo** therefore   59 **an't** if it   68–69 **Do I . . . a prop?** (spoken directly to the audience)   69, 73 **father** (a term of courtesy often used by the young to the old, without implying blood relationship)

80 cannot be hid long—a man's son may, but in the
end truth will out.

Gobbo. Pray you, sir, stand up. I am sure you are not
Launcelot, my boy.

Launcelot. Pray you let's have no more fooling about
85 it, but give me your blessing. I am Launcelot—your
boy that was, your son that is, your child that
shall be.

Gobbo. I cannot think you are my son.

Launcelot. I know not what I shall think of that; but
90 I am Launcelot, the Jew's man, and I am sure
Margery your wife is my mother.

Gobbo. Her name is Margery indeed! I'll be sworn, if
thou be Launcelot thou art mine own flesh and
blood. Lord worshipped might he be, what a beard°
95 hast thou got! Thou hast got more hair on thy chin
than Dobbin my fill-horse° has on his tail.

Launcelot. [*Rises*] It should seem then that Dobbin's
tail grows backward. I am sure he had more hair of
his tail than I have of my face when I last saw him.

100 *Gobbo.* Lord, how art thou changed! How dost thou
and thy master agree? I have brought him a present.
How 'gree you now?

Launcelot. Well, well; but for mine own part, as I have
set up my rest° to run away, so I will not rest till I
105 have run some ground. My master's a very Jew. Give
him a present? Give him a halter!° I am famished
in his service; you may tell° every finger I have with
my ribs. Father, I am glad you are come. Give me
your present to one Master Bassanio, who indeed
110 gives rare new liveries. If I serve not him I will run

94 **beard** (the sand-blind father places his hand on his son's head, and
mistakes Launcelot's fashionable long hair for a huge beard)   96 **fill-
horse** cart horse   104 **set up my rest** wagered all (with word play on
"rest" and "run")   106 **halter** hangman's noose   107 **tell** count

as far as God has any ground. O rare fortune, here
comes the man. To him, father, for I am a Jew if
I serve the Jew any longer.

*Enter Bassanio, with [Leonardo and] a Follower
or two.*

Bassanio. You may do so, but let it be so hasted that
supper be ready at the farthest by five of the clock.   *115*
See these letters delivered, put the liveries to making,
and desire Gratiano to come anon° to my lodging.
                              [*Exit one of his men.*]

Launcelot. To him, father!

Gobbo. God bless your worship!

Bassanio. Gramercy.° Wouldst thou aught with me?   *120*

Gobbo. Here's my son, sir, a poor boy—

Launcelot. Not a poor boy, sir, but the rich Jew's man,
that would, sir, as my father shall specify—

Gobbo. He hath a great infection,° sir, as one would
say, to serve—   *125*

Launcelot. Indeed, the short and the long is, I serve
the Jew, and have a desire, as my father shall
specify—

Gobbo. His master and he, saving your worship's reverence, are scarce cater-cousins.°   *130*

Launcelot. To be brief, the very truth is that the Jew,
having done me wrong, doth cause me, as my father,
being I hope an old man, shall frutify° unto you—

Gobbo. I have here a dish of doves that I would bestow
upon your worship, and my suit is—   *135*

---

117 **anon** straightway   120 **Gramercy** many thanks (French *grand
merci*)   124 **infection** (Gobbo's mistake for "affection," i.e., liking)
130 **cater-cousins** great friends   133 **frutify** (for "fructify," a blunder
for a word like "signify")

Launcelot. In very brief, the suit is impertinent° to myself, as your worship shall know by this honest old
man, and though I say it, though old man, yet poor
man, my father.

140 *Bassanio.* One speak for both. What would you?

Launcelot. Serve you, sir.

Gobbo. That is the very defect° of the matter, sir.

Bassanio. I know thee well; thou hast obtained thy suit.
Shylock thy master spoke with me this day,
145 And hath preferred° thee, if it be preferment
To leave a rich Jew's service to become
The follower of so poor a gentleman.

Launcelot. The old proverb° is very well parted between my master Shylock and you, sir. You have
150 the grace of God, sir, and he hath enough.

Bassanio. Thou speak'st it well. Go, father, with thy
son;
Take leave of thy old master and inquire
My lodging out. [*To a Servant*] Give him a livery
More guarded° than his fellows'. See it done.

155 *Launcelot.* Father, in. I cannot get a service; no! I have
ne'er a tongue in my head! Well! [*Studies his palm.*]
If any man in Italy have a fairer table° which doth
offer to swear upon a book—I shall have good fortune! Go to, here's a simple line of life. Here's a
160 small trifle of wives. Alas, fifteen wives is nothing;
eleven widows and nine maids is a simple coming-in
for one man. And then to scape drowning thrice,
and to be in peril of my life with the edge of a feather-
bed! Here are simple scapes.° Well, if Fortune be a
165 woman, she's a good wench for this gear.° Father,

---

136 **impertinent** (for "pertinent")   142 **defect** (for "effect")   145 **pre-
ferred** recommended for a higher position   148 **proverb** (such as, "He
that hath the grace of God hath enough")   154 **guarded** ornamented
157 **table** palm   164 **scapes** escapes   165 **gear** business, i.e., the good
fortune that he pretends to read in his palm

come. I'll take my leave of the Jew in the twinkling.
        Exit Clown [*Launcelot, with Old Gobbo*].

Bassanio. I pray thee, good Leonardo, think on this:
    These things being bought and orderly bestowed,
    Return in haste, for I do feast tonight
    My best-esteemed acquaintance. Hie thee, go.   *170*

Leonardo. My best endeavors shall be done herein.

                Enter Gratiano.

Gratiano. Where's your master?

Leonardo.   Yonder, sir, he walks.
                        Exit Leonardo.

Gratiano. Signior Bassanio!

Bassanio. Gratiano!

Gratiano. I have suit to you.

Bassanio.   You have obtained it!   *175*

Gratiano. You must not deny me. I must go with you
    to Belmont.

Bassanio. Why then you must. But hear thee, Gratiano:
    Thou art too wild, too rude, and bold of voice—
    Parts that become thee happily enough
    And in such eyes as ours appear not faults;   *180*
    But where thou art not known—why, there they
        show
    Something too liberal.° Pray thee take pain
    To allay with some cold drops of modesty
    Thy skipping spirit, lest through thy wild behavior
    I be misconst'red° in the place I go to,   *185*
    And lose my hopes.

Gratiano.   Signior Bassanio, hear me:
    If I do not put on a sober habit,°
    Talk with respect, and swear but now and then,

---

182 **liberal** free (a kind word to describe Gratiano!)   185 **misconst'red**
misconstrued   187 **habit** (1) bearing (2) garment

Wear prayer books in my pocket, look demurely—
190 Nay more, while grace is saying hood mine eyes
Thus with my hat, and sigh and say Amen,
Use all the observance of civility°
Like one well studied in a sad ostent°
To please his grandam, never trust me more.

195 *Bassanio.* Well, we shall see your bearing.

Gratiano. Nay, but I bar tonight. You shall not gauge
        me
By what we do tonight.

Bassanio.   No, that were pity.
I would entreat you rather to put on
Your boldest suit of mirth, for we have friends
200 That purpose merriment. But fare you well;
I have some business.

Gratiano. And I must to Lorenzo and the rest,
But we will visit you at supper time.   *Exeunt.*

[Scene 3. *Venice. Shylock's house.*]

Enter Jessica and [Launcelot] the Clown.

Jessica. I am sorry thou wilt leave my father so;
Our house is hell, and thou a merry devil
Didst rob it of some taste of tediousness.
But fare thee well; there is a ducat for thee.
5 And, Launcelot, soon at supper shalt thou see
Lorenzo, who is thy new master's guest.
Give him this letter; do it secretly.
And so farewell. I would not have my father
See me in talk with thee.

192 **civility** civilized behavior   193 **sad ostent** sober and earnest
appearance

Launcelot. Adieu!° Tears exhibit° my tongue. Most   10
   beautiful pagan, most sweet Jew, if a Christian do
   not play the knave and get thee, I am much deceived.° But adieu! These foolish drops do something drown my manly spirit. Adieu!

Jessica. Farewell, good Launcelot.   *[Exit Launcelot.]*   15
   Alack, what heinous sin is it in me
   To be ashamed to be my father's child!
   But though I am a daughter to his blood,
   I am not to his manners. O Lorenzo,
   If thou keep promise, I shall end this strife,   20
   Become a Christian and thy loving wife!   *Exit.*

[Scene 4. *Venice. A street.*]

  Enter Gratiano, Lorenzo, Salerio, and Solanio.

Lorenzo. Nay, we will slink away in supper time,
   Disguise us at my lodging, and return
   All in an hour.

Gratiano. We have not made good preparation.

Salerio. We have not spoke us yet of torchbearers.°   5

Solanio. 'Tis vile, unless it may be quaintly ordered,°
   And better in my mind not undertook.

Lorenzo. 'Tis now but four of clock. We have two
   hours
   To furnish us.

2.3.10 **Adieu** (perhaps not merely "good-bye," but "I commend you to
God")   10 **exhibit** (for "inhibit")   11–13 **if a ... deceived** (perhaps
Launcelot is giving a hint of what happens in 2.5, but perhaps "do"
should be emended to "did," and "get" should be understood in the sense
of "beget")   2.4.5 **spoke us yet of torchbearers** talked about getting
torchbearers (who were regularly used in this sort of street festivity)
6 **quaintly ordered** artfully arranged

Enter Launcelot [with a letter].

Friend Launcelot, what's the news?

10 *Launcelot.* And it shall please you to break up° this,
it shall seem to signify.

Lorenzo. I know the hand. In faith, 'tis a fair hand,
And whiter than the paper it° writ on
Is the fair hand that writ.

Gratiano.   Love-news, in faith!

15 *Launcelot.* By your leave, sir.

Lorenzo. Whither goest thou?

Launcelot. Marry, sir, to bid° my old master the Jew
to sup tonight with my new master the Christian.

Lorenzo. Hold here, take this. [*Gives money.*] Tell
gentle° Jessica
20 I will not fail her. Speak it privately.
                              Exit Clown [Launcelot].
Go, gentlemen;
Will you prepare you for this masque tonight?
I am provided of a torchbearer.

Salerio. Ay marry, I'll be gone about it straight.

Solanio. And so will I.

25 *Lorenzo.*   Meet me and Gratiano
At Gratiano's lodging some hour hence.

Salerio. 'Tis good we do so.   *Exit [with Solanio].*

Gratiano. Was not that letter from fair Jessica?

Lorenzo. I must needs tell thee all. She hath directed
30 How I shall take her from her father's house,
What gold and jewels she is furnished with,
What page's suit she hath in readiness.
If e'er the Jew her father come to heaven,

10 **break up** open   13 **it** i.e., the hand   17 **bid** ask   19, 34 **gentle**
charming and possessed of all attributes of a lady (with a pun on "gentile," as elsewhere)

It will be for his gentle daughter's sake;
And never dare misfortune cross her foot,°   35
Unless she do it under this excuse,
That she is issue to a faithless° Jew.
Come, go with me; peruse this as thou goest.
Fair Jessica shall be my torchbearer.°
                              Exit [*with Gratiano*].

[*Scene 5. Venice. Before Shylock's house.*]

Enter [*Shylock the*] *Jew and* [*Launcelot,*] *his man
that was the Clown.*

Shylock. Well, thou shalt see, thy eyes shall be thy
    judge,
The difference of old Shylock and Bassanio.—
What,° Jessica!—Thou shalt not gormandize
As thou hast done with me.—What, Jessica!—
And sleep, and snore, and rend apparel out.—   5
Why, Jessica, I say!

Launcelot.   Why, Jessica!

Shylock. Who bids thee call? I do not bid thee call.

Launcelot. Your worship was wont to tell me I could
    do nothing without bidding.

                    Enter Jessica.

Jessica. Call you? What is your will?   10

Shylock. I am bid forth to supper, Jessica.
There are my keys. But wherefore should I go?
I am not bid for love—they flatter me.
But yet I'll go in hate, to feed upon
The prodigal Christian. Jessica my girl,   15

35 **cross her foot** cross her path   37 **faithless** lacking the Christian
faith   39 **torchbearer** i.e., disguised as a page   2.5.3 **What** (exclamation of impatience, like "Why" in line 6)

Look to my house. I am right loath to go.
There is some ill a-brewing towards my rest,
For I did dream of moneybags tonight.°

Launcelot. I beseech you, sir, go. My young master
20   doth expect your reproach.°

Shylock. So do I his.

Launcelot. And they have conspired together. I will
not say you shall see a masque, but if you do, then
it was not for nothing that my nose fell a-bleeding
25   on Black Monday° last at six o'clock i' th' morning,
falling out that year on Ash Wednesday was four
year in th' afternoon.°

Shylock. What, are there masques? Hear you me,
Jessica:
Lock up my doors; and when you hear the drum
30   And the vile squealing of the wry-necked fife,°
Clamber not you up to the casements then,
Nor thrust your head into the public street
To gaze on Christian fools with varnished faces;°
But stop my house's ears—I mean my casements;
35   Let not the sound of shallow fopp'ry enter
My sober house. By Jacob's staff I swear
I have no mind of feasting forth tonight;
But I will go. Go you before me, sirrah.
Say I will come.

Launcelot.   I will go before, sir.
40   Mistress, look out at window for all this:
There will come a Christian by
Will be worth a Jewess' eye.   *[Exit.]*

18 **tonight** last night (the premonition is serious for Shylock, comic
for the audience)   20 **reproach** (Launcelot's word for "approach")
25 **Black Monday** Easter Monday   26–27 **falling . . . afternoon**
(apparently Launcelot means "four years ago on Ash Wednesday," but
he may be intentionally talking nonsense)   30 **wry-necked fife** fife-
player with neck twisted to one side (the mouthpiece of the Elizabethan
fife was set at an angle, and these words are therefore sometimes taken
to mean the instrument; but Shylock would be less scornful of the instrument than of the gay fool with his neck at a crazy angle)   33 **varnished
faces** painted masks (Shylock no doubt puns on "varnished" in the sense
of "insincere")

Shylock. What says that fool of Hagar's offspring,° ha?

Jessica. His words were "Farewell, mistress"—nothing
  else.

Shylock. The patch° is kind enough, but a huge feeder,   45
  Snail-slow in profit,° and he sleeps by day
  More than the wildcat. Drones hive not with me;
  Therefore I part with him, and part with him
  To one that I would have him help to waste
  His borrowed purse. Well, Jessica, go in;   50
  Perhaps I will return immediately.
  Do as I bid you, shut doors after you.
  Fast bind, fast find,
  A proverb never stale in thrifty mind.   *Exit.*

Jessica. Farewell; and if my fortune be not crost,   55
  I have a father, you a daughter, lost.   *Exit.*

[*Scene 6. Venice. Before Shylock's house.*]

Enter the Masquers, Gratiano and Salerio.

Gratiano. This is the penthouse° under which Lorenzo
  Desired us to make stand.

Salerio.   His hour is almost past.

Gratiano. And it is marvel he outdwells his hour,
  For lovers ever run before the clock.

Salerio. O ten times faster Venus' pigeons° fly   5
  To seal love's bonds new-made, than they are wont
  To keep obligèd faith° unforfeited!

43 **Hagar's offspring** Ishmael, son of Abraham by the servant Hagar
(mother and son were cast out by Abraham after Isaac's birth)   45 **patch**
fool   46 **in profit** in any profitable activity   2.6.1 **penthouse** shelter
formed by a projecting roof   5 **Venus' pigeons** (they drew her chariot)
7 **obligèd faith** faith pledged (in marriage)

Gratiano. That ever holds. Who riseth from a feast
 With that keen appetite that he sits down?
10 Where is the horse that doth untread again
 His tedious measures° with the unbated fire
 That he did pace them first? All things that are
 Are with more spirit chasèd than enjoyed.
 How like a younger° or a prodigal
15 The scarfèd° bark puts from her native bay,
 Hugged and embracèd by the strumpet wind!
 How like the prodigal doth she return,
 With over-weathered° ribs and ragged sails,
 Lean, rent, and beggared by the strumpet wind!

     Enter Lorenzo.

20 *Salerio.* Here comes Lorenzo: more of this hereafter.

Lorenzo. Sweet friends, your patience for my long
 abode.°
 Not I but my affairs have made you wait.
 When you shall please to play the thieves for wives,
 I'll watch as long for you then. Approach;
25 Here dwells my father Jew. Ho, who's within?

   [*Enter*] *Jessica above* [*in boy's clothes*].

Jessica. Who are you? Tell me for more certainty,
 Albeit I'll swear that I do know your tongue.

Lorenzo. Lorenzo, and thy love.

Jessica. Lorenzo certain, and my love indeed,
30 For who love I so much? And now who knows
 But you, Lorenzo, whether I am yours?

Lorenzo. Heaven and thy thoughts are witness that
 thou art.

Jessica. Here, catch this casket; it is worth the pains.
 I am glad 'tis night, you° do not look on me,

11 **measures** paces   14 **younger** younger son   15 **scarfèd** decorated
with scarfs (i.e., flags and streamers)   18 **over-weathered** long exposed
to stormy weather   21 **abode** delay   34 **'tis night, you** (an ellipsis,
"and" being understood

For I am much ashamed of my exchange.°   35
But love is blind, and lovers cannot see
The pretty follies that themselves commit;
For if they could, Cupid himself would blush
To see me thus transformèd to a boy.

Lorenzo. Descend, for you must be my torchbearer.   40

Jessica. What, must I hold a candle to my shames?
They in themselves, good sooth, are too too light.°
Why, 'tis an office of discovery,° love,
And I should be obscured.

Lorenzo.   So are you, sweet,
Even in the lovely garnish° of a boy.   45
But come at once;
For the close° night doth play the runaway,
And we are stayed for at Bassanio's feast.

Jessica. I will make fast the doors and gild myself
With some moe° ducats, and be with you straight.   50
                                [*Exit above.*]

Gratiano. Now by my hood, a gentle° and no Jew!

Lorenzo. Beshrow° me but I love her heartily!
For she is wise, if I can judge of her,
And fair she is, if that mine eyes be true,
And true she is, as she hath proved herself;   55
And therefore, like herself, wise, fair, and true,
Shall she be placèd in my constant soul.

                Enter Jessica [*below*].

What, art thou come? On, gentlemen, away!
Our masquing mates by this time for us stay.
                Exit [*with Jessica and Salerio*].

                Enter Antonio.

Antonio. Who's there?   60

___

35 **exchange** i.e., of clothes   42 **light** immodest (with a pun)   43 **office of discovery** task in which my disguise will be revealed   45 **garnish** pleasing attire   47 **close** secret   50 **moe** more   51 **gentle** refined lady (with the usual pun on "gentile")   52 **Beshrow** (a light word for "curse")

Gratiano. Signior Antonio?

Antonio. Fie, fie, Gratiano, where are all the rest?
　'Tis nine o'clock, our friends all stay for you.
　No masque tonight. The wind is come about;
65　Bassanio presently° will go aboard.
　I have sent twenty out to seek for you.

Gratiano. I am glad on't. I desire no more delight.
　Than to be under sail and gone tonight.　　*Exeunt.*

[Scene 7. *Belmont. Portia's house.*]

[*Flourish of cornets.*] *Enter Portia with Morocco
and both their Trains.*

Portia. Go, draw aside the curtains and discover°
　The several caskets to this noble Prince.
　Now make your choice.

Morocco. This first, of gold, who this inscription bears,
　"Who chooseth me shall gain what many men
5　　desire."
　The second, silver, which this promise carries,
　"Who chooseth me shall get as much as he deserves."
　This third, dull lead, with warning all as blunt,°
　"Who chooseth me must give and hazard all he
　　hath."
10　How shall I know if I do choose the right?

Portia. The one of them contains my picture, Prince.
　If you choose that, then I am yours withal.

Morocco. Some god direct my judgment! Let me see—

65 **presently** at this present moment 2.7.1 **discover** reveal 8 **as blunt** as blunt as the lead is dull (with quibbles on "blunt" in the senses of "abrupt in speech and manner" and of "not sharp," and on "dull" in the senses of "not sharp" and "not shining")

I will survey th' inscriptions back again.
What says this leaden casket?   15
"Who chooseth me must give and hazard all he
   hath."
Must give—for what? For lead! Hazard for lead?
This casket threatens; men that hazard all
Do it in hope of fair advantages.
A golden mind stoops not to shows of dross;   20
I'll then nor give nor hazard aught for lead.
What says the silver with her virgin hue?
"Who chooseth me shall get as much as he deserves."
As much as he deserves? Pause there, Morocco,
And weigh thy value with an even hand: 25
If thou be'st rated by thy estimation,°
Thou dost deserve enough, and yet enough
May not extend so far as to the lady;
And yet to be afeard of my deserving
Were but a weak disabling° of myself.   30
As much as I deserve? Why that's the lady!
I do in birth deserve her, and in fortunes,
In graces, and in qualities of breeding;
But more than these, in love I do deserve.
What if I strayed no farther, but chose here?   35
Let's see once more this saying graved in gold:
"Who chooseth me shall gain what many men
   desire."
Why that's the lady! All the world desires her;
From the four corners of the earth they come
To kiss this shrine, this mortal breathing saint.   40
The Hyrcanian deserts° and the vasty wilds
Of wide Arabia are as throughfares now
For princes to come view fair Portia.
The watery kingdom, whose ambitious head
Spets in the face of heaven, is no bar   45
To stop the foreign spirits, but they come
As o'er a brook to see fair Portia.
One of these three contains her heavenly picture.
Is't like that lead contains her? 'Twere damnation

26 **estimation** reputation   30 **disabling** undervaluing   41 **Hyrcanian deserts** Persian deserts (famous for savage beasts)

50 To think so base a thought; it were too gross°
   To rib her cerecloth° in the obscure° grave.
   Or shall I think in silver she's immured,
   Being ten times undervalued to tried gold?
   O sinful thought! Never so rich a gem
55 Was set in worse than gold. They have in England
   A coin that bears the figure of an angel
   Stampèd in gold—but that's insculped° upon;
   But here an angel° in a golden bed
   Lies all within. Deliver me the key.
60 Here do I choose, and thrive I as I may!

Portia. There, take it, Prince; and if my form lie there,
   Then I am yours.   [*He opens the golden casket.*]

Morocco.   O hell! What have we here?
   A carrion Death,° within whose empty eye
   There is a written scroll! I'll read the writing.
65   "All that glisters is not gold;°
       Often have you heard that told.
       Many a man his life hath sold
       But my outside to behold;
       Gilded tombs do worms infold.
70   Had you been as wise as bold,
       Young in limbs, in judgment old,
       Your answer had not been inscrolled.°
       Fare you well, your suit is cold."
   Cold indeed, and labor lost.
75 Then farewell heat, and welcome frost!
   Portia, adieu. I have too grieved a heart
   To take a tedious leave. Thus losers part.
               Exit [*with his Train. Flourish of cornets*].

Portia. A gentle° riddance. Draw the curtains, go.
   Let all of his complexion° choose me so.   *Exeunt.*

---

50 **it were too gross** lead would be too coarse (bodies of wealthy
persons were often encased in lead)   51 **cerecloth** waxed embalming
cloth   51 **obscure** (accent on first syllable)   57 **insculped** sculptured
58 **angel** i.e., Portia's picture   63 **Death** death's head   65 **All . . . gold**
(proverbial)   72 **inscrolled** written on the scroll   78 **gentle** well-bred
79 **complexion** temperament (not merely coloring)

[Scene 8. *Venice. A street.*]

Enter Salerio and Solanio.

Salerio. Why, man, I saw Bassanio under sail;
　　With him is Gratiano gone along,
　　And in their ship I am sure Lorenzo is not.

Solanio. The villain° Jew with outcries raised the Duke,
　　Who went with him to search Bassanio's ship.　　　　5

Salerio. He came too late, the ship was under sail.
　　But there the Duke was given to understand
　　That in a gondola were seen together
　　Lorenzo and his amorous Jessica.
　　Besides, Antonio certified the Duke　　　　　　　　10
　　They were not with Bassanio in his ship.

Solanio. I never heard a passion° so confused,
　　So strange, outrageous, and so variable
　　As the dog Jew did utter in the streets:
　　"My daughter! O my ducats! O my daughter!　　　15
　　Fled with a Christian! O my Christian ducats!
　　Justice! The law! My ducats and my daughter!
　　A sealèd bag, two sealèd bags of ducats,
　　Of double ducats, stol'n from me by my daughter!
　　And jewels—two stones, two rich and precious
　　　　stones,　　　　　　　　　　　　　　　　　　20
　　Stol'n by my daughter! Justice! Find the girl!
　　She hath the stones upon her, and the ducats!"

Salerio. Why, all the boys in Venice follow him,
　　Crying his stones, his daughter, and his ducats.

Solanio. Let good Antonio look he keep his day,°　　25
　　Or he shall pay for this.

2.8.4 **villain** low-bred fellow (not scoundrel; a vaguer term than today)
12 **passion** emotional outburst   25 **keep his day** pay on the exact day
appointed

Salerio.   Marry, well rememb'red.
I reasoned° with a Frenchman yesterday,
Who told me, in the narrow seas° that part
The French and English there miscarrièd
30   A vessel of our country richly fraught.°
I thought upon Antonio when he told me,
And wished in silence that it were not his.

Solanio. You were best to tell Antonio what you hear.
Yet do not suddenly, for it may grieve him.

35   *Salerio.* A kinder gentleman treads not the earth.
I saw Bassanio and Antonio part.
Bassanio told him he would make some speed
Of his return; he answered, "Do not so.
Slubber° not business for my sake, Bassanio,
40   But stay the very riping of the time;
And for the Jew's bond which he hath of me,
Let it not enter in your mind of love.°
Be merry, and employ your chiefest thoughts
To courtship and such fair ostents° of love
45   As shall conveniently become you there."
And even there, his eye being big with tears,
Turning his face, he put his hand behind him,
And with affection wondrous sensible°
He wrung Bassanio's hand; and so they parted.

50   *Solanio.* I think he only loves the world for him.
I pray thee let us go and find him out,
And quicken his embracèd heaviness°
With some delight or other.

Salerio.   Do we so.   *Exeunt.*

---

27 **reasoned** talked   28 **narrow seas** English Channel   30 **fraught**
freighted   39 **Slubber** hurry over in a slovenly way   42 **mind of love**
loving thoughts (probably about both Antonio and Portia)   44 **ostents**
shows, expressions   48 **affection wondrous sensible** wonderfully strong
emotion   52 **quicken his embracèd heaviness** lighten the gloom
which he has embraced

[*Scene 9. Belmont. Portia's house.*]

Enter Nerissa and a Servitor.

Nerissa. Quick, quick I pray thee, draw the curtain
    straight.°
    The Prince of Aragon hath ta'en his oath,
    And comes to his election° presently.°
    [*Flourish of cornets.*] *Enter Aragon, his Train, and
    Portia.*

Portia. Behold, there stand the caskets, noble Prince.
    If you choose that wherein I am contained,   5
    Straight shall our nuptial rites be solemnized;
    But if you fail, without more speech, my lord,
    You must be gone from hence immediately.

Aragon. I am enjoined by oath to observe three things:
    First, never to unfold to any one   10
    Which casket 'twas I chose; next, if I fail
    Of the right casket, never in my life
    To woo a maid in way of marriage;
    Lastly, if I do fail in fortune of my choice,
    Immediately to leave you and be gone.   15

Portia. To these injunctions everyone doth swear
    That comes to hazard for my worthless self.

Aragon. And so° have I addressed me.° Fortune now
    To my heart's hope! Gold, silver, and base lead.
    "Who chooseth me must give and hazard all he hath."   20
    You shall look fairer ere I give or hazard.
    What says the golden chest? Ha, let me see!
    "Who chooseth me shall gain what many men desire."

2.9.1 **straight** at once   3 **election** choice   3 **presently** at this present
moment, instantly   18 **so** on these terms   18 **have I addressed me** I
have addressed myself (to this affair)

What many men desire—that "many" may be meant
25   By° the fool multitude that choose by show,
Not learning more than the fond° eye doth teach,
Which pries not to th' interior, but like the martlet°
Builds in the weather on the outward wall,
Even in the force and road of casualty.°
30   I will not choose what many men desire,
Because I will not jump with° common spirits
And rank me with the barbarous multitudes.
Why then, to thee, thou silver treasure house!
Tell me once more what title thou dost bear.
35   "Who chooseth me shall get as much as he deserves."
And well said too, for who shall go about
To cozen° fortune, and be honorable
Without the stamp of merit? Let none presume
To wear an undeservèd dignity.
40   O that estates, degrees,° and offices°
Were not derived corruptly, and that clear honor
Were purchased by the merit of the wearer!
How many then should cover° that stand bare!
How many be commanded that command;
45   How much low peasantry would then be gleanèd°
From the true seed of honor!° And how much honor
Picked from the chaff and ruin of the times
To be varnished.° Well, but to my choice.
"Who chooseth me shall get as much as he deserves."
50   I will assume desert. Give me a key for this,
And instantly unlock my fortunes here.

                    [*He opens the silver casket.*]

Portia. Too long a pause for that which you find there.°

---

25 **By** with regard to   26 **fond** foolish   27 **martlet** martin, a bird
29 **in . . . casualty** exposed to the tyrannic force of mischance and
lying in the open road   31 **jump with** accord with   37 **cozen** cheat
40 **degrees** ranks   40 **offices** official positions   43 **cover** wear hats, in
sign of authority   45 **gleanèd** picked out, as in gleaning grain (cf. line
47, "Picked from the chaff")   46 **seed of honor** descendants of ancient
nobility   48 **To be new varnished** to have the luster of their family
restored   52 **Too . . . there** (probably an aside)

Aragon. What's here? The portrait of a blinking idiot
     Presenting me a schedule!° I will read it.
     How much unlike art thou to Portia!   55
     How much unlike my hopes and my deservings!
     "Who chooseth me shall have as much as he
          deserves."
     Did I deserve no more than a fool's head?
     Is that my prize? Are my deserts no better?

Portia. To offend and judge are distinct offices,   60
     And of opposèd natures.°

Aragon.   What is here?
               "The fire° seven times tried this;°
               Seven times tried that judgment is
               That did never choose amiss.
               Some there be that shadow's kiss;   65
               Such have but a shadow's bliss.
               There be fools alive iwis,°
               Silvered o'er,° and so was this.
               Take what wife you will to bed,
               I° will ever be your head.   70
               So be gone; you are sped."°
     Still more fool I shall appear
     By the time I linger here.
     With one fool's head I came to woo,
     But I go away with two.   75
     Sweet, adieu. I'll keep my oath,
     Patiently to bear my wroath.°   [*Exit with his Train.*]

Portia. Thus hath the candle singed the moth.
     O these deliberate fools! When they do choose,
     They have the wisdom by their wit° to lose.   80

Nerissa. The ancient saying is no heresy:
     Hanging and wiving goes by destiny.

Portia. Come draw the curtain, Nerissa.

54 **schedule** scroll   60–61 **To offend . . . natures** the offender is not to
judge himself   62 **fire** (pronounced fí-er)   62 **this** i.e., the silver of the
casket   67 **iwis** certainly   68 **Silvered o'er** i.e., with the gray hair usually associated with wisdom   70 **I** "the blinking idiot" of line 53   71 **you
are sped** you have achieved your fortune   77 **wroath** heavy lot (?)
80 **wit** cleverness

Enter Messenger.

Messenger. Where is my lady?

Portia.   Here. What would my lord?°

85 *Messenger.* Madam, there is alighted at your gate
        A young Venetian, one that comes before
        To signify th' approaching of his lord,
        From whom he bringeth sensible regrets,°
        To wit, besides commends and courteous breath,
90   Gifts of rich value. Yet I have not seen°
        So likely° an ambassador of love.
        A day in April never came so sweet
        To show how costly° summer was at hand,
        As this forespurrer° comes before his lord.

95 *Portia.* No more, I pray thee. I am half afeard
        Thou wilt say anon he is some kin to thee,
        Thou spend'st such high-day wit° in praising him.
        Come, come, Nerissa, for I long to see
        Quick Cupid's post° that comes so mannerly.

100 *Nerissa.* Bassanio, Lord Love,° if thy will it be!

                                        Exeunt.

84 **What would my lord?** (a gay, jesting retort to the messenger's "my
lady")   88 **sensible regrets** a quibble: greetings (1) expressing strong
feeling, and (2) conveying tangible gifts   90 **yet I have not seen** not yet
have I seen   91 **likely** promising   93 **costly** rich, plenteous   94 **fore-
spurrer** advance messenger (one who spurs his horse ahead of his party)
97 **high-day wit** imagination befitting a festive occasion   99 **post** messenger   100 **Lord Love** god of love

[ACT 3

Scene 1. *Venice. A street.*]

[Enter] Solanio and Salerio.

Solanio. Now what news on the Rialto?

Salerio. Why, yet it lives there unchecked° that Antonio
hath a ship of rich lading wracked on the narrow
seas°—the Goodwins° I think they call the place—
a very dangerous flat, and fatal, where the carcasses   5
of many a tall ship lie buried as they say, if my gos-
sip° Report be an honest woman of her word.

Solanio. I would she were as lying a gossip in that, as
ever knapped° ginger or made her neighbors believe
she wept for the death of a third husband. But it is   10
true, without any slips of prolixity° or crossing the
plain highway of talk,° that the good Antonio, the
honest Antonio—O that I had a title good enough to
keep his name company!—

Salerio. Come, the full stop.°   15

Solanio. Ha, what sayest thou? Why the end is, he hath
lost a ship.

Salerio. I would it might prove the end of his losses.

3.1.2 **it lives there unchecked** it is reported without dispute   3–4 **narrow
seas** English Channel   4 **Goodwins** Goodwin Sands, a shoal   6–7 **gossip** talkative comrade   9 **knapped** snapped, bit   11 **slips of prolixity**
long-winded lies   11–12 **crossing . . . talk** going counter to honest
speech   15 **Come, the full stop** come to the end of your sentence

47

Solanio. Let me say Amen betimes,° lest the devil cross
20   my prayer, for here he comes in the likeness of a Jew.

Enter Shylock.

How now, Shylock? What news among the merchants?

Shylock. You knew, none so well, none so well as you,
of my daughter's flight.

25   *Salerio.* That's certain. I for my part knew the tailor that
made the wings she flew withal.

Solanio. And Shylock for his own part knew the bird
was fledge,° and then it is the complexion° of them
all to leave the dam.

30   *Shylock.* She is damned for it.

Salerio. That's certain, if the devil may be her judge.

Shylock. My own flesh and blood to rebel!

Solanio. Out upon it, old carrion! Rebels it° at these
years?

35   *Shylock.* I say my daughter is my flesh and my blood.

Salerio. There is more difference between thy flesh and
hers than between jet and ivory, more between your
bloods than there is between red wine and Rhenish.
But tell us, do you hear whether Antonio have had
40   any loss at sea or no?

Shylock. There I have another bad match! A bankrout,° a prodigal, who dare scarce show his head on
the Rialto, a beggar that was used to come so smug°
upon the mart! Let him look to his bond. He was
45   wont to call me usurer. Let him look to his bond. He
was wont to lend money for a Christian cursy.° Let
him look to his bond.

---

19 **betimes** promptly   28 **fledge** feathered, able to fly   28 **complexion**
natural disposition   33 **Rebels it** (a contemptuous pun on "flesh and
blood" in the sense of fleshly desire)   41–42 **bankrout** bankrupt
43 **smug** well-groomed   46 **cursy** courtesy

Salerio. Why, I am sure if he forfeit thou wilt not take
his flesh. What's that good for?

Shylock. To bait fish withal. If it will feed nothing else, 50
it will feed my revenge. He hath disgraced me, and
hind'red me half a million, laughed at my losses,
mocked at my gains, scorned my nation, thwarted
my bargains, cooled my friends, heated mine enemies—and what's his reason? I am a Jew. Hath not 55
a Jew eyes? Hath not a Jew hands, organs, dimensions,° senses, affections,° passions?—fed with the
same food, hurt with the same weapons, subject to
the same diseases, healed by the same means, warmed
and cooled by the same winter and summer as a 60
Christian is? If you prick us, do we not bleed? If you
tickle us, do we not laugh? If you poison us, do we
not die? And if you wrong us, shall we not revenge?
If we are like you in the rest, we will resemble you in
that. If a Jew wrong a Christian, what is his humil- 65
ity?° Revenge! If a Christian wrong a Jew, what
should his sufferance be by Christian example? Why
revenge! The villainy you teach me I will execute, and
it shall go hard but I will better the instruction.

Enter a Man from Antonio.

[*Man.*] Gentlemen, my master Antonio is at his house, 70
and desires to speak with you both.

Salerio. We have been up and down to seek him.

Enter Tubal.

Solanio. Here comes another of the tribe. A third cannot be matched, unless the devil himself turn Jew.
Exeunt Gentlemen [*Solanio, Salerio, and Man*].

Shylock. How now, Tubal! What news from Genoa? 75
Hast thou found my daughter?

56–57 **dimensions** limbs, features, etc.   57 **affections** feelings
65–66 **what is his humility?** what does his Christian humility amount
to?

Tubal. I often came where I did hear of her, but cannot find her.

Shylock. Why there, there, there, there! A diamond
80 gone cost me two thousand ducats in Frankford! The
curse never fell upon our nation till now; I never felt
it till now. Two thousand ducats in that, and other
precious, precious jewels. I would my daughter were
dead at my foot, and the jewels in her ear! Would she
85 were hearsed at my foot, and the ducats in her coffin!
No news of them? Why, so! And I know not what's
spent in the search. Why thou loss upon loss—the
thief gone with so much, and so much to find the
thief!—and no satisfaction, no revenge, nor no ill
90 luck stirring but what lights o' my shoulders, no sighs
but o' my breathing, no tears but o' my shedding.

Tubal. Yes, other men have ill luck too. Antonio, as I
heard in Genoa—

Shylock. What, what, what? Ill luck, ill luck?

95 *Tubal.* Hath an argosy cast away coming from Tripolis.

Shylock. I thank God, I thank God! Is it true, is it true?

Tubal. I spoke with some of the sailors that escaped the
wrack.

Shylock. I thank thee, good Tubal. Good news, good
100 news! Ha, ha! Heard in Genoa?

Tubal. Your daughter spent in Genoa, as I heard, one
night fourscore ducats.

Shylock. Thou stick'st a dagger in me. I shall never see
my gold again. Fourscore ducats at a sitting, fourscore
105 ducats!

Tubal. There came divers of Antonio's creditors in my
company to Venice that swear he cannot choose but
break.°

108 **break** go bankrupt

Shylock. I am very glad of it. I'll plague him; I'll torture
him. I am glad of it.   *110*

Tubal. One of them showed me a ring that he had of
your daughter for a monkey.

Shylock. Out upon her! Thou torturest me, Tubal. It
was my turquoise; I had it of Leah° when I was a
bachelor. I would not have given it for a wilderness *115*
of monkeys.

Tubal. But Antonio is certainly undone.

Shylock. Nay, that's true, that's very true. Go, Tubal,
fee me an officer;° bespeak° him a fortnight before.
I will have the heart of him if he forfeit, for were he *120*
out of Venice I can make what merchandise° I will.
Go, Tubal, and meet me at our synagogue; go, good
Tubal; at our synagogue, Tubal.   *Exeunt.*

[Scene 2. *Belmont. Portia's house.*]

Enter Bassanio, Portia, Gratiano, [*Nerissa,*] *and
all their Trains.*

Portia. I pray you tarry; pause a day or two
    Before you hazard, for in choosing wrong
    I lose your company. Therefore forbear awhile.
    There's something tells me (but it is not love)
    I would not lose you; and you know yourself   *5*
    Hate counsels not in such a quality.°
    But lest you should not understand me well—
    And yet a maiden hath no tongue but thought—
    I would detain you here some month or two
    Before you venture for me. I could teach you   *10*

114 **Leah** Shylock's wife   119 **officer** (to arrest Antonio)   119 **bespeak**
engage   121 **merchandise** wealth   3.2.6 **in such a quality** in such a
manner of speech as I am using to you

How to choose right, but then I am forsworn.
So will I never be. So may you miss me.
But if you do, you'll make me wish a sin—
That I had been forsworn. Beshrow° your eyes!
15   They have o'erlooked° me and divided me;
One half of me is yours, the other half yours—
Mine own I would say; but if mine then yours,
And so all yours! O these naughty° times
Puts bars between the owners and their rights!
20   And so, though yours, not yours. Prove it so,°
Let fortune go to hell for it, not I.
I speak too long, but 'tis to peize° the time,
To eche° it and to draw it out in length,
To stay you from election.

Bassanio.   Let me choose,
25   For as I am, I live upon the rack.°

Portia. Upon the rack, Bassanio? Then confess
What treason there is mingled with your love.°

Bassanio. None but that ugly treason of mistrust,
Which makes me fear th' enjoying of my love.
30   There may as well be amity and life
'Tween snow and fire, as treason and my love.

Portia. Ay, but I fear you speak upon the rack,
Where men enforcèd° do speak anything.

Bassanio. Promise me life, and I'll confess the truth.

Portia. Well then, confess and live.

35   *Bassanio.*   Confess and love
Had been the very sum of my confession!
O happy torment, when my torturer
Doth teach me answers for deliverance.°

14 **Beshrow** curse (but a playful word)   15 **o'erlooked** bewitched
18 **naughty** wicked   20 **Prove it so** if it should prove so   22 **peize**
weigh down, hence retard   23 **eche** eke out, i.e., lengthen   25 **rack**
instrument of torture, on which the body was pulled with great force,
often breaking the joints; used to force confessions, especially in trials
for treason   27 **What treason . . . love** (spoken playfully)   33 **enforcèd**
compelled (by torture)   38 **answers for deliverance** answers to free
me from torture

But let me to my fortune and the caskets.

Portia. Away then! I am locked in one of them;   40
If you do love me, you will find me out.
Nerissa and the rest, stand all aloof.
Let music sound while he doth make his choice;
Then if he lose he makes a swanlike end,°
Fading in music. That the comparison   45
May stand more proper, my eye shall be the stream
And wat'ry deathbed for him. He may win;
And what is music then? Then music is
Even as the flourish° when true subjects bow
To a new-crownèd monarch. Such it is   50
As are those dulcet sounds in break of day,
That creep into the dreaming bridegroom's ear
And summon him to marriage. Now he goes,
With no less presence,° but with much more love,
Than young Alcides,° when he did redeem   55
The virgin tribute° paid by howling Troy
To the sea monster. I stand for sacrifice;
The rest aloof are the Dardanian wives,
With blearèd visages come forth to view
The issue of th' exploit. Go, Hercules!   60
Live thou,° I live. With much, much more dismay°
I view the fight than thou that mak'st the fray.°

*A song the whilst Bassanio comments on the
caskets to himself.*

Tell me where is fancy° bred,
Or in the heart, or in the head?
How begot, how nourishèd?   65
    Reply, reply.
It is engend'red in the eyes,

---

44 **swanlike end** an end like the swan's (who was supposed never
to sing until it sang enchantingly at its death)   49 **flourish** fanfare of
trumpets   54 **presence** noble bearing   55 **Alcides** Hercules   56 **virgin
tribute** Hesione, Priam's sister, who was offered as a divine sacrifice to
be devoured by a sea monster; Hercules slew the monster and saved her
61 **Live thou** if thou live   61 **dismay** alarm and terror   62 **fray** com-
bat   63 **fancy** love based only on the senses, especially the sight

With gazing fed, and fancy dies
In the cradle where it lies.
70　　　　Let us all ring fancy's knell.
I'll begin it—Ding, dong, bell.
All.　　　　Ding, dong, bell.

Bassanio. So° may the outward shows be least
　　themselves;°
The world is still° deceived with ornament.
75 In law, what plea so tainted and corrupt,
But being seasoned with a gracious voice,
Obscures the show of evil? In religion,
What damnèd error but some sober brow
Will bless it, and approve it with a text,°
80 Hiding the grossness with fair ornament?
There is no vice so simple but assumes
Some mark of virtue on his outward parts.
How many cowards whose hearts are all as false
As stairs of sand, wear yet upon their chins
85 The beards of Hercules and frowning Mars,
Who inward searched, have livers white as milk!°
And these assume but valor's excrement°
To render them redoubted.° Look on beauty,
And you shall see 'tis purchased by the weight,
90 Which therein works a miracle in nature,
Making them lightest° that wear most of it:
So are those crispèd° snaky golden locks,
Which maketh such wanton° gambols with the wind
Upon supposèd fairness, often known
95 To be the dowry° of a second head,
The skull that bred them in the sepulcher.
Thus ornament is but the guilèd° shore
To a most dangerous sea, the beauteous scarf

---

73 **So** thus　73 **least themselves** least like what they really are　74 **still**
continually　79 **approve it with a text** prove it by a biblical text
86 **livers white as milk** (a pale liver supposedly caused cowardice)
87 **excrement** excrescence, outer appearance　88 **redoubted** dreaded
91 **lightest** (a pun on "light" in the sense of unchaste)　92 **crispèd** curled
93 **wanton** playful　95 **dowry** gift of property, i.e., hair from a dead
person's head　97 **guilèd** full of guile, treacherous

Veiling an Indian° beauty; in a word,
The seeming truth which cunning times put on   *100*
To entrap the wisest. Therefore then, thou gaudy
    gold,
Hard food for Midas, I will none of thee;
Nor none of thee, thou pale and common drudge°
'Tween man and man. But thou, thou meager° lead
Which rather threaten'st than dost promise aught,   *105*
Thy paleness moves me more than eloquence;
And here choose I. Joy be the consequence!

Portia. [*Aside*] How all the other passions fleet to air,
    As doubtful thoughts, and rash-embraced despair,
    And shudd'ring fear, and green-eyed jealousy.   *110*
    O love, be moderate, allay thy ecstasy,
    In measure rain thy joy, scant° this excess!
    I feel too much thy blessing. Make it less
    For fear I surfeit.°

Bassanio. [*Opening the leaden casket*] What find I here?
    Fair Portia's counterfeit!° What demigod°   *115*
    Hath come so near creation? Move these eyes?
    Or whether, riding on the balls of mine,°
    Seem they in motion? Here are severed lips
    Parted with sugar breath; so sweet a bar°
    Should sunder such sweet friends.° Here in her hairs   *120*
    The painter plays the spider, and hath woven
    A golden mesh t' entrap the hearts of men
    Faster° than gnats in cobwebs. But her eyes—
    How could he see to do them? Having made one,
    Methinks it should have power to steal both his   *125*
    And leave itself unfurnished.° Yet look how far

99 **Indian** East Indian, hence dusky   103 **pale and common drudge**
pale hack worker, i.e., silver   104 **meager** poverty-stricken, of slight
value   112 **scant** lessen   114 **surfeit** grow sick with too much, i.e., too
much joy   115 **counterfeit** image   115 **demigod** i.e., half-divine painter
117 **the balls of mine** my eyeballs   119 **so sweet a bar** i.e., Portia's
breath   120 **sweet friends** i.e., her lips   123 **Faster** tighter   126 **unfurnished** not provided with its mate (since the picture of the first eye has
taken away both of the painter's eyes)

The substance° of my praise doth wrong this shadow°
In underprizing it, so far this shadow
Doth limp behind the substance. Here's the scroll,
130   The continent and summary° of my fortune.

          "You that choose not by the view
          Chance as fair,° and choose as true.
          Since this fortune falls to you,
          Be content and seek no new.
135   If you be well pleased with this
          And hold your fortune for your bliss,
          Turn you where your lady is,
          And claim her with a loving kiss."

A gentle° scroll. Fair lady, by your leave.
          [*Kisses her.*]
140   I come by note,° to give and to receive.
Like one of two contending in a prize,°
That thinks he hath done well in people's eyes,
Hearing applause and universal shout,
Giddy in spirit, still gazing in a doubt
145   Whether those peals of praise be his° or no—
So, thrice-fair lady, stand I even so,
As doubtful whether what I see be true,
Until confirmed, signed, ratified by you.

Portia. You see me, Lord Bassanio, where I stand,
150   Such as I am. Though for myself alone
I would not be ambitious in my wish
To wish myself much better, yet for you
I would be trebled twenty times myself,
A thousand times more fair, ten thousand times more
    rich,
155   That only to stand high in your account,°
I might in virtues, beauties, livings,° friends,

127, 129 **The substance** Portia herself   127, 128 **this shadow** her picture   130 **The continent and summary** that which contains and sums
up   132 **Chance as fair** have as fair fortune   139 **gentle** courteous,
well-bred   140 **by note** according to instructions (in lines 137–38)
141 **prize** contest for a prize, as in a tournament   145 **his** intended for
him   155 **account** esteem, regard   156 **livings** possessions

Exceed account.° But the full sum of me
Is sum of something — which, to term in gross,°
Is an unlessoned girl, unschooled, unpracticed;
Happy in this, she is not yet so old   160
But she may learn; happier than this,
She is not bred so dull but she can learn;
Happiest of all, is that her gentle spirit
Commits itself to yours to be directed,   .
As from her lord, her governor, her king.   165
Myself, and what is mine, to you and yours
Is now converted.° But now° I was the lord
Of this fair mansion, master of my servants,
Queen o'er myself; and even now, but now,
This house, these servants, and this same myself   170
Are yours, my lord's. I give them with this ring,
Which when you part from, lose, or give away,
Let it presage° the ruin of your love
And be my vantage to exclaim on° you.

Bassanio. Madam, you have bereft me of all words.   175
Only my blood speaks to you in my veins,
And there is such confusion in my powers
As, after some oration fairly spoke
By a belovèd prince,° there doth appear
Among the buzzing pleasèd multitude;   180
Where every something being blent together
Turns to a wild of nothing, save of joy
Expressed and not expressed. But when this ring
Parts from this finger, then parts life from hence!
O then be bold to say Bassanio's dead!   185

Nerissa. My lord and lady, it is now our time,
That have stood by and seen our wishes prosper,
To cry "good joy." Good joy, my lord and lady!

---

157 **account** computation   158 **term in gross** describe in broad terms
167 **converted** changed, i.e., made yours   167 **But now** only now
173 **presage** foretell   174 **vantage to exclaim on** opportunity to, cry
out against (lines 173–74 spoken playfully)   179 **prince** (a feminine as
well as a masculine noun; hence suitably applied to Portia)

Gratiano. My Lord Bassanio, and my gentle lady,
190   I wish you all the joy that you can wish—
      For I am sure you can wish none from° me;
      And when your honors mean to solemnize
      The bargain of your faith, I do beseech you
      Even at that time I may be married too.

195 *Bassanio.* With all my heart, so° thou canst get a wife.

Gratiano. I thank your lordship, you have got me one.
      My eyes, my lord, can look as swift as yours:
      You saw the mistress, I beheld the maid.
      You loved, I loved; for intermission°
200   No more pertains to me, my lord, than you.
      Your fortune stood upon the caskets there,
      And so did mine too, as the matter falls;
      For wooing here until I sweat again,°
      And swearing till my very roof° was dry
205   With oaths of love, at last—if promise last°—
      I got a promise of this fair one here
      To have her love, provided that your fortune
      Achieved her mistress.

Portia.   Is this true, Nerissa?

Nerissa. Madam, it is, so you stand pleased withal.

210 *Bassanio.* And do you, Gratiano, mean good faith?

Gratiano. Yes, faith, my lord.

Bassanio. Our feast shall be much honored in your
      marriage.

Gratiano. We'll play with them the first boy for a
      thousand ducats.

215 *Nerissa.* What, and stake down?°

Gratiano. No, we shall ne'er win at that sport, and stake
      down.

---

191 **from** away from   195 **so** provided   199 **intermission** pausing
203 **again** i.e., again and again   204 **roof** roof of the mouth   205 **if
promise last** if her promise holds   215 **stake down** a betting term
(with an off-color pun)

But who comes here? Lorenzo and his infidel!°
What, and my old Venetian friend Salerio!

*Enter Lorenzo, Jessica, and Salerio, a Messenger
from Venice.*

Bassanio. Lorenzo and Salerio, welcome hither,   220
   If that the youth of my new int'rest° here
   Have power to bid you welcome. By your leave,
   I bid my very friends and countrymen,
   Sweet Portia, welcome.

Portia.   So do I, my lord.   225
   They are entirely welcome.

Lorenzo. I thank your honor. For my part, my lord,
   My purpose was not to have seen you here,
   But meeting with Salerio by the way,
   He did entreat me past all saying nay
   To come with him along.

Salerio.   I did, my lord,   230
   And I have reason for it. Signior Antonio
   Commends him to you.°   [*Gives Bassanio a letter.*]

Bassanio.   Ere I ope his letter,
   I pray you tell me how my good friend doth.

Salerio. Not sick, my lord, unless it be in mind,
   Nor well, unless in mind. His letter there   235
   Will show you his estate.°   *Open the letter.*

Gratiano. Nerissa, cheer yond stranger; bid her
      welcome.
   Your hand, Salerio. What's the news from Venice?
   How doth that royal merchant,° good Antonio?
   I know he will be glad of our success;   240
   We are the Jasons, we have won the Fleece.

----

218 **infidel** one who lacks the true faith (Gratiano applies the term playfully to Jessica; cf. 2.6.51)   221 **int'rest** claim   232 **Commends him
to you** sends you his best wishes   236 **estate** state, condition   239 **royal
merchant** merchant prince

Salerio. I would you had won the fleece° that he hath
lost!

Portia. There are some shrowd° contents in yond same
    paper
    That steals the color from Bassanio's cheek:
245 Some dear friend dead, else nothing in the world
    Could turn so much the constitution
    Of any constant man. What, worse and worse?
    With leave, Bassanio—I am half yourself,
    And I must freely have the half of anything
    That this same paper brings you.

250 *Bassanio.*   O sweet Portia,
    Here are a few of the unpleasant'st words
    That ever blotted paper! Gentle lady,
    When I did first impart my love to you,
    I freely told you all the wealth I had
255 Ran in my veins—I was a gentleman.
    And then I told you true; and yet, dear lady,
    Rating myself at nothing, you shall see
    How much I was a braggart. When I told you
    My state° was nothing, I should then have told you
260 That I was worse than nothing; for indeed
    I have engaged° myself to a dear friend,
    Engaged my friend to his mere° enemy
    To feed my means. Here is a letter, lady,
    The paper as the body of my friend,
265 And every word in it a gaping wound
    Issuing lifeblood. But is it true, Salerio?
    Hath all his ventures failed? What, not one hit?
    From Tripolis, from Mexico and England,
    From Lisbon, Barbary, and India,
270 And not one vessel scape the dreadful touch
    Of merchant-marring rocks?

Salerio.   Not one, my lord.
    Besides, it should appear that if he had
    The present° money to discharge° the Jew,

242 **fleece** (pun on "fleets")   243 **shrowd** evil, grievous; literally "cursed"
259 **state** estate, fortune   261 **engaged** pledged   262 **mere** absolute
273 **present** ready   273 **discharge** pay

He would not take it. Never did I know
A creature that did bear the shape of man   275
So keen and greedy to confound° a man.
He plies the Duke at morning and at night,
And doth impeach the freedom of the state°
If they deny him justice. Twenty merchants,
The Duke himself, and the magnificoes   280
Of greatest port° have all persuaded with him,
But none can drive him from the envious° plea
Of forfeiture, of justice, and his bond.

Jessica. When I was with him, I have heard him swear
To Tubal and to Chus, his countrymen,   285
That he would rather have Antonio's flesh
Than twenty times the value of the sum
That he did owe him; and I know, my lord,
If law, authority, and power deny not,
It will go hard with poor Antonio.   290

Portia. Is it your dear friend that is thus in trouble?

Bassanio. The dearest friend to me, the kindest man,
The best-conditioned° and unwearied spirit
In doing courtesies, and one in whom
The ancient Roman honor more appears   295
Than any that draws breath in Italy.

Portia. What sum owes he the Jew?

Bassanio. For me, three thousand ducats.

Portia.   What, no more?
Pay him six thousand, and deface° the bond.
Double six thousand and then treble that,   300
Before a friend of this description
Shall lose a hair through Bassanio's fault.
First go with me to church and call me wife,
And then away to Venice to your friend!
For never shall you lie by Portia's side   305

276 **confound** ruin, destroy   278 **impeach . . . state** charge that Venice
is no free state   280–81 **magnificoes/Of greatest port** nobles of highest
dignity   282 **envious** malignant   293 **The best-conditioned** of the best
disposition   299 **deface** destroy

With an unquiet soul. You shall have gold
To pay the petty debt twenty times over;
When it is paid, bring your true friend along.
My maid Nerissa and myself meantime
310   Will live as maids and widows. Come away!
For you shall hence° upon your wedding day.
Bid your friends welcome, show a merry cheer;
Since you are dear bought, I will love you dear.
But let me hear the letter of your friend.

315   [*Bassanio.* (*Reads*)] "Sweet Bassanio, my ships have
all miscarried, my creditors grow cruel, my estate is
very low, my bond to the Jew is forfeit. And since in
paying it, it is impossible I should live, all debts are
cleared between you and I if I might but see you at
320   my death. Notwithstanding, use your pleasure. If
your love do not persuade you to come, let not my
letter."

Portia. O love, dispatch all business and be gone!

Bassanio. Since I have your good leave to go away,
325   I will make haste; but till I come again
No bed shall e'er be guilty of my stay,
Nor rest be interposer 'twixt us twain.   *Exeunt.*

[Scene 3. *Venice. A street.*]

Enter [*Shylock*] *the Jew and Solanio and Antonio
and the Jailer.*

Shylock. Jailer, look to him. Tell not me of mercy.
This is the fool that lent out money gratis.
Jailer, look to him.

Antonio.   Hear me yet, good Shylock.

Shylock. I'll have my bond! Speak not against my bond!

311 **shall hence** must go hence

I have sworn an oath that I will have my bond.   5
Thou call'dst me dog before thou hadst a cause,
But since I am a dog, beware my fangs.
The Duke shall grant me justice. I do wonder,
Thou naughty° jailer, that thou art so fond°
To come abroad with him at his request.   10

Antonio. I pray thee hear me speak.

Shylock. I'll have my bond. I will not hear thee speak.
I'll have my bond, and therefore speak no more.
I'll not be made a soft and dull-eyed fool,
To shake the head, relent, and sigh, and yield   15
To Christian intercessors. Follow not.
I'll have no speaking; I will have my bond.

Exit Jew.

Solanio. It is the most impenetrable cur
That ever kept° with men.

Antonio.   Let him alone;
I'll follow him no more with bootless° prayers.   20
He seeks my life. His reason well I know:
I oft delivered from his forfeitures°
Many that have at times made moan to me.
Therefore he hates me.

Solanio.   I am sure the Duke
Will never grant this forfeiture to hold.   25

Antonio. The Duke cannot deny the course of law;
For the commodity° that strangers° have
With us in Venice, if it be denied,
Will much impeach the justice of the state,
Since that the trade and profit of the city   30
Consisteth of all nations. Therefore go.
These griefs° and losses have so bated° me
That I shall hardly spare a pound of flesh
Tomorrow to my bloody creditor.

3.3.9 **naughty** wicked   9 **fond** foolish   19 **kept** dwelt   20 **bootless**
unavailing   22 **forfeitures** penalties that he could have legally exacted
27 **commodity** commercial advantage   27 **strangers** foreigners   32 **griefs**
pains   32 **bated** reduced

35   Well, jailer, on. Pray God Bassanio come
      To see me pay his debt, and then I care not!   *Exeunt.*

      [Scene 4. *Belmont. Portia's house.*]

      Enter Portia, Nerissa, Lorenzo, Jessica, and
          [*Balthasar,*] *a Man of Portia's.*

      Lorenzo. Madam, although I speak it in your presence,
          You have a noble and a true conceit°
          Of godlike amity,° which appears most strongly
          In bearing thus the absence of your lord.
5   But if you knew to whom you show this honor,
          How true a gentleman you send relief,
          How dear a lover° of my lord your husband,
          I know you would be prouder of the work
          Than customary bounty can enforce you.°

10   *Portia.* I never did repent for doing good,
          Nor shall not now; for in companions
          That do converse and waste° the time together,
          Whose souls do bear an egal° yoke of love,
          There must be needs a like proportion
15   Of lineaments, of manners, and of spirit;
          Which makes me think that this Antonio,
          Being the bosom lover of my lord,
          Must needs be like my lord. If it be so,
          How little is the cost I have bestowed
20   In purchasing° the semblance° of my soul
          From out the state of hellish cruelty!
          This comes too near the praising of myself;

3.4.2 **conceit** idea, conception 3 **amity** friendship 7 **lover** friend
8–9 **prouder . . . you** prouder of this action than even your habitual
kindness can make you 12 **converse and waste** associate and spend
13 **egal** equal 20 **purchasing** gaining 20 **semblance** likeness (Portia
refers to the old idea that a genuine friend or lover is a second self.
Antonio is like Bassanio, and therefore like Portia)

Therefore no more of it. Hear other things:
Lorenzo, I commit into your hands
The husbandry° and manage of my house,   25
Until my lord's return. For mine own part,
I have toward heaven breathed a secret vow
To live in prayer and contemplation,
Only attended by Nerissa here,
Until her husband and my lord's return.   30
There is a monast'ry two miles off,
And there we will abide. I do desire you
Not to deny this imposition,°
The which my love and some necessity
Now lays upon you.

Lorenzo.   Madam, with all my heart;   35
I shall obey you in all fair commands.

Portia. My people do already know my mind,
And will acknowledge you and Jessica
In place of Lord Bassanio and myself.
So fare you well till we shall meet again.   40

Lorenzo. Fair thoughts and happy hours attend on you!

Jessica. I wish your ladyship all heart's content.

Portia. I thank you for your wish, and am well pleased
To wish it back on you. Fare you well, Jessica.
                    Exeunt [*Jessica and Lorenzo*].
Now, Balthasar,   45
As I have ever found thee honest-true,
So let me find thee still. Take this same letter,
And use thou all th' endeavor of a man
In speed to Padua. See thou render this
Into my cousin's hands, Doctor Bellario;   50
And look what° notes and garments he doth give
    thee
Bring them, I pray thee, with imagined speed°
Unto the tranect,° to the common ferry

---

25 **husbandry** care   33 **imposition** task that I impose   51 **look what**
whatever   52 **imagined speed** speed of imagination   53 **tranect** ferry

Which trades to Venice. Waste no time in words
55   But get thee gone. I shall be there before thee.

Balthasar. Madam, I go with all convenient speed.°
                                 [*Exit.*]

Portia. Come on, Nerissa; I have work in hand
  That you yet know not of. We'll see our husbands
  Before they think of us.

Nerissa.   Shall they see us?

60 *Portia.* They shall, Nerissa, but in such a habit°
  That they shall think we are accomplishèd°
  With that we lack. I'll hold thee any wager,
  When we are both accoutered like young men,
  I'll prove the prettier° fellow of the two,
65   And wear my dagger with the braver grace,°
  And speak between the change of man and boy
  With a reed° voice, and turn two mincing steps
  Into a manly stride, and speak of frays
  Like a fine bragging youth; and tell quaint° lies,
70   How honorable ladies sought my love,
  Which I denying, they fell sick and died—
  I could not do withal!° Then I'll repent,
  And wish, for all that,° that I had not killed them.
  And twenty of these puny lies I'll tell,
75   That men shall swear I have discontinued school
  Above a twelvemonth. I have within my mind
  A thousand raw tricks of these bragging Jacks,°
  Which I will practice.

Nerissa.   Why, shall we turn to° men?

Portia. Fie, what a question's that,
80   If thou wert near a lewd° interpreter!

---

56 **convenient speed** speed suited (to this emergency)   60 **habit** garment, i.e., men's clothes   61 **accomplishèd** provided   64 **prettier** more dashing   65 **braver grace** finer masculine grace   67 **reed** high or squeaky, like the sound of a reed pipe   69 **quaint** clever and elaborate   72 **I could not do withal** I could not help it   73 **for all that** in spite of that   77 **Jacks** fellows   78 **turn to** turn into (with an off-color pun; cf. 1.3.78)   80 **lewd** bad

But come, I'll tell thee all my whole device
When I am in my coach, which stays for us
At the park gate; and therefore haste away,
For we must measure twenty miles today.   *Exeunt.*

[*Scene 5. Belmont. A garden.*]

Enter [Launcelot the] Clown and Jessica.

Launcelot. Yes truly; for look you, the sins of the father
are to be laid upon the children.° Therefore, I promise you I fear you.° I was always plain with you, and
so now I speak my agitation° of the matter. Therefore be o' good cheer, for truly I think you are   5
damned. There is but one hope in it that can do you
any good, and that is but a kind of bastard hope
neither.

Jessica. And what hope is that, I pray thee?

Launcelot. Marry, you may partly hope that your fa-   10
ther got you not—that you are not the Jew's daughter.

Jessica. That were a kind of bastard hope indeed! So°
the sins of my mother should be visited upon me.

Launcelot. Truly then, I fear you are damned both by
father and mother. Thus when I shun Scylla your   15
father, I fall into Charybdis your mother. Well, you
are gone both ways.

Jessica. I shall be saved by my husband.° He hath
made me a Christian.

Launcelot. Truly, the more to blame he! We were   20

3.5.1–2 **sins . . . children** (see Exodus 20:5)   3 **fear you** fear for you
4 **agitation** (blunder for "cogitation")   12 **So** thus   18 **saved by my
husband** (see 1 Corinthians 7:14)

Christians enow° before,° e'en as many as could well
live one by another.° This making of Christians will
raise the price of hogs; if we grow all to be pork-
eaters, we shall not shortly have a rasher° on the
25   coals for money.

Enter Lorenzo.

Jessica. I'll tell my husband, Launcelot, what you say.
Here he comes.

Lorenzo. I shall grow jealous° of you shortly, Launcelot, if you thus get my wife into corners.

30   *Jessica.* Nay, you need not fear us, Lorenzo. Launcelot
and I are out.° He tells me flatly there's no mercy
for me in heaven because I am a Jew's daughter; and
he says you are no good member of the commonwealth, for in converting Jews to Christians you raise
35   the price of pork.

Lorenzo. [*To Launcelot*] I shall answer that better to the
commonwealth than you can the getting up of
the Negro's belly. The Moor° is with child by you,
Launcelot!

40   *Launcelot.* It is much that the Moor should be more
than reason; but if she be less than an honest° woman, she is indeed more than I took her for.

Lorenzo. How every fool can play upon the word! I
think the best grace° of wit will shortly turn into
45   silence, and discourse grow commendable in none
only but parrots. Go in, sirrah; bid them prepare for
dinner.

Launcelot. That is done, sir. They have all stomachs.

---

21 **enow** enough   21 **before** before you turned Christian   22 **one by
another** one off another   24 **rasher** slice of bacon   28 **jealous** jealous
31 **out** at odds   38 **Moor** (pronounced "more"; hence Launcelot quibbles
on "much," "more," and "Moor")   41 **honest** chaste   44 **grace** virtue

Lorenzo. Goodly Lord, what a wit-snapper are you!
Then bid them prepare dinner.   50

Launcelot. That is done too, sir. Only "cover"° is the
word.

Lorenzo. Will you cover then, sir?

Launcelot. Not so, sir, neither! I know my duty.

Lorenzo. Yet more quarreling with occasion!° Wilt   55
thou show the whole wealth of thy wit in an instant?
I pray thee understand a plain man in his plain
meaning: go to my fellows, bid them cover the table,
serve in the meat, and we will come in to dinner.

Launcelot. For the table,° sir, it shall be served in; for   60
the meat, sir, it shall be covered;° for your coming
in to dinner, sir, why let it be as humors and con-
ceits° shall govern.   *Exit Clown* [*Launcelot*].

Lorenzo. O dear discretion,° how his words are suited!°
The fool hath planted in his memory   65
An army of good words; and I do know
A many° fools that stand in better place,
Garnished° like him, that for a tricksy word
Defy the matter.° How cheer'st thou,° Jessica?
And now, good sweet, say thy opinion—   70
How dost thou like the Lord Bassanio's wife?

Jessica. Past all expressing. It is very meet
The Lord Bassanio live an upright life,
For having such a blessing in his lady,
He finds the joys of heaven here on earth;   75
And if on earth he do not merit it,

51 **cover** cover the table (Launcelot proceeds to quibble on "cover" in
the sense of "wear a hat")   55 **quarreling with occasion** caviling at
every opportunity   60 **table** (1) the piece of furniture (2) the meal
61 **covered** i.e., to be kept hot   62–63 **humors and conceits** fancies
and notions   64 **dear discretion** precious common sense   64 **suited**
fitted together (?) dressed up (?)   67 **A many** (an old idiom for a large
number)   68 **Garnished** decked out   69 **the matter** good sense
69 **How cheer'st thou** how is it with thee (the implication is that he
kisses her)

In reason he should never come to heaven.
Why, if two gods should play some heavenly match
And on the wager lay° two earthly women,
And Portia one, there must be something else°
Pawned with the other, for the poor rude world
Hath not her fellow.

Lorenzo.   Even such a husband
Hast thou of me as she is for a wife.

Jessica. Nay, but ask my opinion too of that!

Lorenzo. I will anon. First let us go to dinner.

Jessica. Nay, let me praise you while I have a stomach.°

Lorenzo. No, pray thee, let it serve for table-talk;
Then howsome'er° thou speak'st, 'mong other things
I shall digest it.

Jessica.   Well, I'll set you forth.°
                              Exit [with Lorenzo].

---

79 **lay** stake   80 **something else** i.e., to make the wager fair   86 **stomach** (a pun on "desire" [to praise you] and an "appetite" for dinner) 88 **howsome'er** however   89 **I'll set you forth** I'll give a fine account of you

[ACT 4

Scene 1. *Venice. A court of justice.*]

Enter the Duke, the Magnificoes, Antonio,
Bassanio, [Salerio,] and Gratiano [with others].

Duke. What,° is Antonio here?

Antonio. Ready, so please your Grace.

Duke. I am sorry for thee. Thou art come to answer
A stony adversary, an inhuman wretch,
Uncapable of pity, void and empty   5
From any dram° of mercy.

Antonio.   I have heard
Your Grace hath ta'en great pains to qualify°
His rigorous course; but since he stands obdurate,
And that no lawful means can carry me
Out of his envy's reach,° I do oppose   10
My patience to his fury, and am armed
To suffer with a quietness of spirit
The very tyranny and rage° of his.

Duke. Go one, and call the Jew into the court.

Salerio. He is ready at the door; he comes, my lord.   15

4.1.1 **What** why (interjection) 6 **dram** mite, drop (literally an eighth
of an ounce) 7 **qualify** moderate 10 **his envy's reach** the reach of
his malignant hate 13 **tyranny and rage** savagery and passion
71

Enter Shylock.

Duke. Make room, and let him stand before our° face.
　　Shylock, the world thinks, and I think so too,
　　That thou but leadest this fashion of thy malice
　　To the last hour of act; and then 'tis thought
20　　Thou'lt show thy mercy and remorse° more strange°
　　Than is thy strange° apparent cruelty;
　　And where thou now exacts the penalty,
　　Which is a pound of this poor merchant's flesh,
　　Thou wilt not only loose° the forfeiture,
25　　But touched with human gentleness and love,
　　Forgive a moiety° of the principal,
　　Glancing an eye of pity on his losses,
　　That have of late so huddled on his back—
　　Enow° to press a royal merchant° down
30　　And pluck commiseration of his state
　　From brassy bosoms and rough hearts of flint,
　　From stubborn Turks and Tartars never trained
　　To offices of tender courtesy.
　　We all expect° a gentle° answer, Jew.

Shylock. I have possessed° your Grace of what I
35　　purpose,
　　And by our holy Sabbath have I sworn
　　To have the due and forfeit of my bond.
　　If you deny it, let the danger light
　　Upon your charter and your city's freedom!°
40　　You'll ask me why I rather choose to have
　　A weight of carrion flesh than to receive
　　Three thousand ducats. I'll not answer that,
　　But say it is my humor. Is it answered?
　　What if my house be troubled with a rat,
45　　And I be pleased to give ten thousand ducats

---

16 **our** (the royal "we," appropriate in giving an order, but in the next
line the Duke uses "I," the informal singular, suited for a personal appeal
to Shylock's feelings)　20 **remorse** compassion　20 **strange** wonderful　21 **strange** astonishing　24 **loose** release　26 **moiety** portion
29 **Enow** enough　29 **royal merchant** merchant prince　34 **expect**
await　34 **gentle** befitting a gentleman　35 **possessed** informed
38–39 **danger . . . freedom** (cf. 3.3.27–31)

To have it baned?° What, are you answered yet?
Some men there are love not a gaping pig,°
Some that are mad if they behold a cat,
And others, when the bagpipe sings i' th' nose,
Cannot contain their urine; for affection,°   50
Master of passion,° sways it to the mood
Of what it likes or loathes. Now for your answer:
As there is no firm reason to be rend'red
Why he cannot abide a gaping pig,
Why he a harmless necessary cat,   55
Why he° a woollen bagpipe, but of force°
Must yield to such inevitable shame°
As to offend, himself being offended;
So can I give no reason, nor I will not,
More than a lodged° hate and a certain° loathing   60
I bear Antonio, that I follow thus
A losing suit against him. Are you answered?

Bassanio. This is no answer, thou unfeeling man,
To excuse the current of thy cruelty!

Shylock. I am not bound° to please thee with my
answers.   65

Bassanio. Do all men kill the things they do not love?

Shylock. Hates any man the thing he would not kill?

Bassanio. Every offense is not a hate at first.

Shylock. What, wouldst thou have a serpent sting thee
twice?

Antonio. I pray you think you question° with the Jew.   70
You may as well go stand upon the beach

---

46 **baned** poisoned   47 **gaping pig** young roast pig, often served with
fruit in its open mouth (Shylock invokes the old theory of natural
antipathy to explain his hatred of Antonio, thus concealing the
real cause; cf. 1.3.39–42)   50 **affection** natural sympathy or antipathy
51 **passion** powerful emotion   54–56 **he ... he ... he** (pronounced
with heavy emphasis; this man ... that man ... another)   56 **of force**
of necessity, against his will   57 **shame** (as in line 50, above)   60 **lodged**
fixed   60 **certain** assured, steadfast   65 **bound** bound by law   70 **think
you question** remember you argue

And bid the main flood bate his° usual height;
You may as well use question with the wolf,
Why he hath made the ewe bleat for the lamb;
75   You may as well forbid the mountain pines
To wag their high tops and to make no noise
When they are fretten° with the gusts of heaven;
You may as well do anything most hard
As seek to soften that—than which what's harder?—
80   His Jewish heart. Therefore I do beseech you
Make no moe offers, use no farther means,
But with all brief and plain conveniency°
Let me have judgment, and the Jew his will.

Bassanio. For thy three thousand ducats here is six.

85   *Shylock.* If every ducat in six thousand ducats
Were in six parts, and every part a ducat,
I would not draw° them. I would have my bond.

Duke. How shalt thou hope for mercy, rend'ring none?

Shylock. What judgment shall I dread, doing no wrong?
90   You have among you many a purchased slave,
Which like your asses and your dogs and mules
You use in abject and in slavish parts,°
Because you bought them. Shall I say to you,
"Let them be free! Marry them to your heirs!
95   Why sweat they under burdens? Let their beds
Be made as soft as yours, and let their palates
Be seasoned with such viands"? You will answer,
"The slaves are ours." So do I answer you:
The pound of flesh which I demand of him
100   Is dearly bought, is mine, and I will have it.
If you deny me, fie upon your law!
There is no force in the decrees of Venice.
I stand for judgment. Answer; shall I have it?

Duke. Upon my power I may dismiss this court
105   Unless Bellario, a learned doctor

---

72 **main flood bate his** ocean at high tide reduce its   77 **fretten** fretted
82 **brief and plain conveniency** suitable brevity and directness   87 **draw**
take   92 **parts** duties

Whom I have sent for to determine this,
Come here today.

Salerio.   My lord, here stays without
A messenger with letters from the doctor,
New come from Padua.

Duke. Bring us the letters. Call the messenger.   *110*

Bassanio. Good cheer, Antonio! What, man, courage
     yet!
The Jew shall have my flesh, blood, bones, and all,
Ere thou shalt lose for me one drop of blood.

Antonio. I am a tainted wether° of the flock,
Meetest° for death. The weakest kind of fruit   *115*
Drops earliest to the ground, and so let me.
You cannot better be employed, Bassanio,
Than to live still, and write mine epitaph.

     Enter Nerissa [dressed like a Lawyer's Clerk].

Duke. Came you from Padua, from Bellario?

Nerissa. From both, my lord. Bellario greets your
     Grace.   [*Presents a letter.*]   *120*

Bassanio. Why dost thou whet thy knife so earnestly?

Shylock. To cut the forfeiture from that bankrout there.

Gratiano. Not on thy sole, but on thy soul, harsh Jew,
Thou mak'st thy knife keen; but no metal can—
No, not the hangman's° ax—bear° half the keenness   *125*
Of thy sharp envy.° Can no prayers pierce thee?

Shylock. No, none that thou hast wit enough to make.

Gratiano. O be thou damned, inexecrable° dog,
And for thy life let justice be accused!°
Thou almost mak'st me waver in my faith,   *130*

114 **tainted wether** infected ram   115 **Meetest** fittest   125 **hangman's**
executioner's   125 **bear** have   126 **envy** malignant hate   128 **inexe-
crable** most execrable, detestable   129 **And ... accused** (a much
debated line. Probably, "Let justice be accused because you have been
allowed to live so long")

To hold opinion with Pythagoras°
That souls of animals infuse themselves
Into the trunks of men. Thy currish spirit
Governed a wolf who, hanged for human slaughter,°
135   Even from the gallows did his fell° soul fleet,
And whilst thou layest in thy unhallowed dam,°
Infused itself in thee; for thy desires
Are wolvish, bloody, starved, and ravenous.

Shylock. Till thou canst rail the seal from off my bond,
140   Thou but offend'st thy lungs to speak so loud.
Repair thy wit, good youth, or it will fall
To cureless ruin.° I stand here for law.

Duke. This letter from Bellario doth commend
A young and learned doctor to our court.
Where is he?

145   *Nerissa.*   He attendeth here hard by
To know your answer whether you'll admit him.

Duke. With all my heart. Some three or four of you
Go give him courteous conduct to this place.
Meantime the court shall hear Bellario's letter.

150   [*Clerk. (Reads)*] "Your Grace shall understand that at
the receipt of your letter I am very sick; but in the
instant that your messenger came, in loving visita-
tion was with me a young doctor of Rome. His name
is Balthasar. I acquainted him with the cause in
155   controversy between the Jew and Antonio the
merchant. We turned o'er many books together.
He is furnished with my opinion which, bettered
with his own learning, the greatness whereof I cannot enough commend, comes with him at my impor-
160   tunity to fill up° your Grace's request in my stead.

---

131 **Pythagoras** Greek philosopher of the 6th century B.C. who taught
the doctrine of the transmigration of souls   134 **hanged for human
slaughter** (wolves, dogs, and other animals were sometimes hanged for
killing or attacking people; hence the phrase "hangdog look")   135 **fell**
fierce   136 **dam** mother of an animal, here a she-wolf   141–42 **fall/To
cureless ruin** i.e., like a house too long out of repair   160 **fill up** satisfy

I beseech you let his lack of years be no impediment
to let° him lack a reverend estimation, for I never
knew so young a body with so old a head. I leave
him to your gracious acceptance, whose trial° shall
better publish his commendation."   165

*Enter Portia for Balthasar, [dressed like a Doctor
of Laws].*

Duke. You hear the learn'd Bellario, what he writes;
And here, I take it, is the doctor come.
Give me your hand. Come you from old Bellario?

Portia. I did, my lord.

Duke.   You are welcome; take your place.
Are you acquainted with the difference°   170
That holds this present question° in the court?

Portia. I am informèd throughly° of the cause.°
Which is the merchant here? And which the Jew?

Duke. Antonio and old Shylock, both stand forth.

Portia. Is your name Shylock?

Shylock.   Shylock is my name.   175

Portia. Of a strange° nature is the suit you follow,
Yet in such rule that° the Venetian law
Cannot impugn you as you do proceed.
[*To Antonio*] You stand within his danger,° do you
not?

Antonio. Ay, so he says.

Portia.   Do you confess the bond?   180

Antonio. I do.

Portia.   Then must the Jew be merciful.

---

162 **to let** to cause 164 **trial** conduct when brought to the test
170 **difference** dispute 171 **question** case under judicial examination
172 **throughly** thoroughly 172 **cause** case 176 **strange** astonishing
177 **in such rule that** within the rule so that 179 **danger** power to harm

Shylock. On what compulsion must I? Tell me that.

Portia. The quality of mercy is not strained;°
    It droppeth as the gentle rain from heaven
185   Upon the place beneath. It is twice blest;
    It blesseth him that gives and him that takes.
    'Tis mightiest in the mightiest; it becomes
    The thronèd monarch better than his crown.
    His scepter shows the force of temporal power,
190   The attribute to awe and majesty,
    Wherein doth sit the dread and fear of kings;
    But mercy is above this scept'red sway;
    It is enthronèd in the hearts of kings,
    It is an attribute to God himself,
195   And earthly power doth then show likest God's
    When mercy seasons justice. Therefore, Jew,
    Though justice be thy plea, consider this:
    That, in the course of justice, none of us
    Should see salvation.° We do pray for mercy,
200   And that same prayer doth teach us all to render
    The deeds of mercy. I have spoke thus much
    To mitigate the justice of thy plea;
    Which if thou follow, this strict court of Venice
    Must needs give sentence 'gainst the merchant there.

205 *Shylock.* My deeds upon my head! I crave the law,
    The penalty and forfeit of my bond.

Portia. Is he not able to discharge the money?

Bassanio. Yes, here I tender it for him in the court,
    Yea, twice° the sum. If that will not suffice,
210   I will be bound to pay it ten times o'er
    On forfeit of my hands, my head, my heart.

183 **strained** constrained, compelled   198–99 **That . . . salvation** (referring to the doctrine that God can justly condemn every man, since none is free of sin)   209 **twice** (in lines 226 and 233 "thrice" the money has been offered, and editors therefore commonly emend "twice" to "thrice," on the assumption that here the compositor misread the manuscript. But in line 84 the offered amount is indeed double—six thousand ducats for three thousand—and therefore emendation to "thrice" still leaves an inconsistency, unless the point is that as Bassanio's fears for Antonio grow, he raises the offer)

If this will not suffice, it must appear
That malice bears down truth. And I beseech you,
Wrest once the law to your authority.°
To do a great right, do a little wrong,　　　　*215*
And curb this cruel devil of his will.

Portia. It must not be. There is no power in Venice
Can alter a decree establishèd.
'Twill be recorded for a precedent,
And many an error by the same example　　　　*220*
Will rush into the state. It cannot be.

Shylock. A Daniel come to judgment!° Yea, a Daniel!
O wise young judge, how I do honor thee!

Portia. I pray you let me look upon the bond.

Shylock. Here 'tis, most reverend Doctor, here it is.　　*225*

Portia. Shylock, there's thrice thy money off'red thee.

Shylock. An oath, an oath! I have an oath in heaven;
Shall I lay perjury upon my soul?
No, not for Venice!

Portia.　　　　　　　　Why, this bond is forfeit;
And lawfully by this the Jew may claim　　　　*230*
A pound of flesh, to be by him cut off
Nearest the merchant's heart. Be merciful.
Take thrice thy money; bid me tear the bond.

Shylock. When it is paid, according to the tenure.°
It doth appear you are a worthy judge;　　　　*235*
You know the law, your exposition
Hath been most sound. I charge you by the law,
Whereof you are a well-deserving pillar,
Proceed to judgment. By my soul I swear
There is no power in the tongue of man　　　　*240*
To alter me. I stay° here on my bond.

---

214 **Wrest . . . authority** for once twist the law a little and subject it to
your authority　222 **A Daniel come to judgment** the young biblical
hero who secured justice for Susannah (See Apocrypha, Susannah: 42–64)
234 **tenure** conditions　241 **stay** take my stand

Antonio. Most heartily I do beseech the court
 To give the judgment.

Portia.   Why then, thus it is:
 You must prepare your bosom for his knife—

245 *Shylock.* O noble judge! O excellent young man!

Portia. For the intent and purpose of the law
 Hath full relation to° the penalty,
 Which here appeareth due upon the bond.

Shylock. 'Tis very true. O wise and upright judge!
250 How much more elder art thou than thy looks!

Portia. Therefore lay bare your bosom.

Shylock.   Ay, his breast—
 So says the bond, doth it not, noble judge?
 "Nearest his heart"; those are the very words.

Portia. It is so. Are there balance° here to weigh
 The flesh?

255 *Shylock.*   I have them ready.

Portia. Have by some surgeon, Shylock, on your
 charge,°
 To stop his wounds, lest he do bleed to death.

Shylock. Is it so nominated in the bond?

Portia. It is not so expressed, but what of that?
260 'Twere good you do so much for charity.

Shylock. I cannot find it; 'tis not in the bond.

Portia. You, merchant, have you anything to say?

Antonio. But little. I am armed and well prepared.
 Give me your hand, Bassanio; fare you well.
265 Grieve not that I am fall'n to this for you,
 For herein Fortune shows herself more kind
 Than is her custom: it is still her use°

247 **Hath full relation to** is related inseparably to 254 **balance** (plural)
scales 256 **on your charge** at your expense 267 **still her use** ever
her custom

To let the wretched man outlive his wealth,
To view with hollow eye and wrinkled brow
An age of poverty; from which ling'ring penance   *270*
Of such misery doth she cut me off.
Commend me to your honorable wife.
Tell her the process° of Antonio's end,
Say how I loved you, speak me fair in death;
And when the tale is told, bid her be judge   *275*
Whether Bassanio had not once a love.°
Repent but you° that you shall lose your friend,
And he repents not° that he pays your debt;
For if the Jew do cut but deep enough,
I'll pay it instantly with all my heart.°   *280*

Bassanio. Antonio, I am married to a wife
Which is as dear to me as life itself;
But life itself, my wife, and all the world
Are not with me esteemed above thy life.
I would lose all, ay sacrifice them all   *285*
Here to this devil, to deliver you.

Portia. Your wife would give you little thanks for that
If she were by to hear you make the offer.

Gratiano. I have a wife who I protest I love.
I would she were in heaven, so she could   *290*
Entreat some power to change this currish Jew.

Nerissa. 'Tis well you offer it behind her back;
The wish would make else an unquiet house.

Shylock. These be the Christian husbands! I have a
    daughter;
Would any of the stock of Barabbas°   *295*
Had been her husband, rather than a Christian!
We trifle time. I pray thee pursue sentence.

273 **process** whole story   276 **love** friend (with a quibble on "love," in
the sense of "lover")   277 **Repent but you** if you but feel sorrow
278 **And he repents not** then he regrets not   280 **with all my heart** (a
quibble on "heart" in the senses of soul and of the physical organ)
295 **Barabbas** (1) the thief freed by Pilate when the people demanded
that Christ be crucified (2) the name of the villainous hero in Marlowe's
The Jew of Malta

Portia. A pound of that same merchant's flesh is thine.
The court awards it, and the law doth give it—

300 *Shylock.* Most rightful judge!

Portia. And you must cut this flesh from off his breast.
The law allows it, and the court awards it.

Shylock. Most learned judge! A sentence! Come, prepare!

Portia. Tarry a little; there is something else.
305 This bond doth give thee here no jot of blood;
The words expressly are "a pound of flesh."
Take then thy bond, take thou thy pound of flesh;
But in the cutting it, if thou dost shed
One drop of Christian blood, thy lands and goods
310 Are by the laws of Venice confiscate
Unto the state of Venice.

Gratiano. O upright judge! Mark, Jew. O learned
judge!

Shylock. Is that the law?

Portia.   Thyself shalt see the act;
For, as thou urgest justice, be assured
315 Thou shalt have justice more than thou desir'st.

Gratiano. O learned judge! Mark, Jew. A learned
judge!

Shylock. I take this offer then. Pay the bond thrice
And let the Christian go.

Bassanio.   Here is the money.

Portia. Soft!
320 The Jew shall have all justice. Soft, no haste;
He shall have nothing but the penalty.

Gratiano. O Jew! An upright judge, a learnèd judge!

Portia. Therefore prepare thee to cut off the flesh.
Shed thou no blood, nor cut thou less nor more
325 But just a pound of flesh. If thou tak'st more

Or less than a just° pound, be it but so much
As makes it light or heavy in the substance°
Or the division° of the twentieth part
Of one poor scruple°—nay, if the scale do turn
But in the estimation° of a hair—						*330*
Thou diest, and all thy goods are confiscate.

Gratiano. A second Daniel! A Daniel, Jew!
Now, infidel, I have you on the hip!

Portia. Why doth the Jew pause? Take thy forfeiture.

Shylock. Give me my principal, and let me go.				*335*

Bassanio. I have it ready for thee; here it is.

Portia. He hath refused it in the open court.
He shall have merely justice and his bond.

Gratiano. A Daniel still say I, a second Daniel!
I thank thee, Jew, for teaching me that word.				*340*

Shylock. Shall I not have barely my principal?

Portia. Thou shalt have nothing but the forfeiture,
To be so taken at thy peril, Jew.

Shylock. Why, then the devil give him good of it!
I'll stay no longer question.°

Portia.				Tarry, Jew!				*345*
The law hath yet another hold on you.
It is enacted in the laws of Venice,
If it be proved against an alien
That by direct or indirect attempts
He seek the life of any citizen,						*350*
The party 'gainst the which he doth contrive
Shall seize° one half his goods; the other half
Comes to the privy coffer° of the state;
And the offender's life lies in the mercy
Of the Duke only, 'gainst all other voice.					*355*

---

326 **just**	exact	327 **substance**	amount	328 **division**	portion
328–29 **twentieth ... scruple** i.e., one grain	330 **estimation** value
345 **stay no longer question** remain for no more talk	352 **seize** take
possession of	353 **privy coffer** equivalent to the British Privy Purse,
money provided for the monarch's own use

In which predicament° I say thou stand'st,
For it appears by manifest proceeding
That indirectly, and directly too,
Thou hast contrived against the very life
360 Of the defendant, and thou hast incurred
The danger formerly by me rehearsed.°
Down therefore, and beg mercy of the Duke.

Gratiano. Beg that thou mayst have leave to hang
          thyself!
And yet, thy wealth being forfeit to the state,
365 Thou hast not left the value of a cord;
Therefore thou must be hanged at the state's charge.

Duke. That thou shalt see the difference of our spirit,
I pardon thee thy life before thou ask it.
For° half thy wealth, it is Antonio's;
370 The other half comes to the general state,
Which humbleness may drive unto a fine.°

Portia. Ay, for the state, not for Antonio.

Shylock. Nay, take my life and all! Pardon not that!
You take my house, when you do take the prop
375 That doth sustain my house. You take my life
When you do take the means whereby I live.

Portia. What mercy can you render him, Antonio?

Gratiano. A halter gratis! Nothing else, for God's sake!

Antonio. So please my lord the Duke and all the court
380 To quit° the fine for one half of his goods,
I am content; so° he will let me have
The other half in use,° to render it
Upon his death unto the gentleman
That lately stole his daughter.
385 Two things provided more: that for this favor
He presently° become a Christian;
The other, that he do record a gift

---

356 predicament situation   **361 rehearsed** cited   **369 For** as for   **371
may drive unto a fine** may persuade me to reduce to a fine   **380 quit** remit
381 so provided   **382 in use** in trust, to use in his business   **386 presently**
instantly

Here in the court of all he dies possessed
Unto his son Lorenzo and his daughter.

Duke. He shall do this, or else I do recant°   390
The pardon that I late pronouncèd here.

Portia. Art thou contented, Jew? What dost thou say?

Shylock. I am content.

Portia.   Clerk, draw a deed of gift.

Shylock. I pray you give me leave to go from hence.
I am not well. Send the deed after me,   395
And I will sign it.

Duke.   Get thee gone, but do it.

Gratiano. In christ'ning shalt thou have two godfathers.
Had I been judge, thou shouldst have had ten
    more°—
To bring thee to the gallows, not to the font.
                    Exit [*Shylock*].

Duke. Sir, I entreat you home with me to dinner.   400

Portia. I humbly do desire your Grace of pardon.
I must away this night toward Padua,
And it is meet I presently set forth.

Duke. I am sorry that your leisure serves you not.°
Antonio, gratify° this gentleman,   405
For in my mind you are much bound to him.
                    Exit Duke and his Train.

Bassanio. Most worthy gentleman, I and my friend
Have by your wisdom been this day acquitted
Of grievous penalties, in lieu whereof,°
Three thousand ducats due unto the Jew   410
We freely cope° your courteous pains withal.

---

390 **recant** retract   398° **ten more** i.e., to make a jury of twelve
404 **serves you not** is not sufficient for you   405 **gratify** show your
gratitude to   409 **in lieu whereof** in return for   411 **We freely cope** of
our own frée will we requite

    Antonio. And stand indebted, over and above,
      In love and service to you evermore.

415 *Portia.* He is well paid that is well satisfied,
      And I, delivering you, am satisfied,
      And therein do account myself well paid;
      My mind was never yet more mercenary.
      I pray you know me when we meet again.
      I wish you well, and so I take my leave.

420 *Bassanio.* Dear sir, of force I must attempt you further.
      Take some remembrance of us as a tribute,
      Not as fee. Grant me two things, I pray you—
      Not to deny me, and to pardon me.

    Portia. You press me far, and therefore I will yield.
425   Give me your gloves; I'll wear them for your sake.
                [*Bassanio takes off his gloves.*]
      And for your love I'll take this ring from you.
      Do not draw back your hand; I'll take no more,
      And you in love° shall not deny me this.

    Bassanio. This ring, good sir, alas, it is a trifle!
430   I will not shame myself to give you this.

    Portia. I will have nothing else but only this,
      And now methinks I have a mind to it.

    Bassanio. There's more depends on this than on the
      value.°
      The dearest ring in Venice will I give you,
435   And find it out by proclamation.
      Only for this, I pray you pardon me.°

    Portia. I see, sir, you are liberal in offers.
      You taught me first to beg, and now methinks
      You teach me how a beggar should be answered.

440 *Bassanio.* Good sir, this ring was given me by my wife,
      And when she put it on she made me vow
      That I should neither sell nor give nor lose it.

428 in love in your good will to me   **433 the value** the ring's value
436 Only . . . pardon me only as for this ring, I beg you to excuse me

Portia. That 'scuse serves many men to save their gifts.
    And if your wife be not a madwoman,
    And know how well I have deserved this ring,   *445*
    She would not hold out enemy forever
    For giving it to me. Well, peace be with you!
                        Exeunt [Portia and Nerissa].

Antonio. My Lord Bassanio, let him have the ring.
    Let his deservings, and my love withal,
    Be valued 'gainst your wife's commandement.°   *450*

Bassanio. Go, Gratiano, run and overtake him;
    Give him the ring, and bring him if thou canst
    Unto Antonio's house. Away, make haste!
                        Exit Gratiano.
    Come, you and I will thither presently,
    And in the morning early will we both   *455*
    Fly toward Belmont. Come, Antonio.   *Exeunt.*

               [Scene 2. *Venice. A street.*]

    Enter [Portia and] Nerissa, [disguised as before].

Portia. Inquire the Jew's house out, give him this deed,°
    And let him sign it. We'll away tonight
    And be a day before our husbands home.
    This deed will be well welcome to Lorenzo.

               Enter Gratiano.

Gratiano. Fair sir, you are well o'erta'en.   *5*
    My Lord Bassanio upon more advice°
    Hath sent you here this ring, and doth entreat
    Your company at dinner.

Portia.   That cannot be.

---

450 **commandement** (four syllables)   4.2.1 **this deed** the deed of gift
for Lorenzo and Jessica   6 **upon more advice** on further consideration

His ring I do accept most thankfully,
10   And so I pray you tell him. Furthermore,
I pray you show my youth old Shylock's house.

Gratiano. That will I do.

Nerissa.   Sir, I would speak with you.
[*Aside to Portia*] I'll see if I can get my husband's
     ring,
Which I did make him swear to keep forever.

Portia. [*Aside to Nerissa*] Thou mayst, I warrant. We
15   shall have old swearing°
That they did give the rings away to men;
But we'll outface them, and outswear them too.
Away, make haste! Thou know'st where I will tarry.

Nerissa. Come, good sir, will you show me to this
     house?   [*Exeunt.*]

15 **old swearing** a lot of hard swearing

[ACT 5

Scene 1. *Belmont. A garden before Portia's house.*]

Enter Lorenzo and Jessica.

Lorenzo. The moon shines bright. In such a night as
    this,
  When the sweet wind did gently kiss the trees
  And they did make no noise, in such a night
  Troilus° methinks mounted the Troyan walls,
  And sighed his soul toward the Grecian tents   5
  Where Cressid° lay that night.

Jessica.   In such a night
  Did Thisbe° fearfully o'ertrip the dew,
  And saw the lion's shadow ere himself,
  And ran dismayed away.

Lorenzo.   In such a night
  Stood Dido° with a willow° in her hand   10
  Upon the wild sea banks, and waft° her love
  To come again to Carthage.

5.1.1–23 (the lovers' playful contest in verse-making belongs to a type
of poetic dialogue as old as Virgil's *Eclogues*)   4 **Troilus** hero of
Chaucer's *Troilus and Cressida* and of Shakespeare's play of the same
title; a type of the faithful lover   6 **Cressid** Cressida, a type of the faithless woman   7 **Thisbe** heroine of the tragic tale of *Pyramus and Thisbe*
in Ovid's *Metamorphoses*   10 **Dido** Queen of Carthage whom Aeneas
loved but abandoned at the call of duty   10 **willow** proverbially associated with forsaken love   11 **waft** waved (with the willow branch)

Jessica.   In such a night
Medea° gathered the enchanted herbs
That did renew old Aeson.°

Lorenzo.   In such a night
15   Did Jessica steal° from the wealthy Jew,
And with an unthrift love° did run from Venice
As far as Belmont.

Jessica.   In such a night
Did young Lorenzo swear he loved her well,
Stealing her soul with many vows of faith,
And ne'er a true one.

20 *Lorenzo.*   In such a night
Did pretty Jessica, like a little shrow,°
Slander her love, and he forgave it her.

Jessica. I would out-night you, did nobody come;
But hark, I hear the footing of a man.

              Enter [Stephano,] a Messenger.

25 *Lorenzo.* Who comes so fast in silence of the night?

Messenger. A friend.

Lorenzo. A friend? What friend? Your name I pray
you, friend.

Messenger. Stephano is my name, and I bring word
My mistress will before the break of day
30   Be here at Belmont. She doth stray about
By holy crosses° where she kneels and prays
For happy wedlock hours.

Lorenzo.   Who comes with her?

Messenger. None but a holy hermit and her maid.
I pray you, is my master yet returned?

13 **Medea** princess and sorceress who helped Jason to obtain the Golden
Fleece, and later was deserted by him   14 **Aeson** father of Jason,
restored to youth by Medea   15 **steal** (a pun) steal money, steal away
16 **unthrift love** (a pun) a love which disregards wealth, and a lover
without wealth   21 **shrow** shrew   31 **holy crosses** (a common sight in
Renaissance Italy; used to mark shrines on hilltops, beside roads, etc.)

Lorenzo. He is not, nor we have not heard from him.   *35*
    But go we in, I pray thee, Jessica,
    And ceremoniously let us prepare
    Some welcome for the mistress of the house.

             Enter [Launcelot, the] Clown.

Launcelot. Sola,° sola! Wo ha! Ho sola, sola!

Lorenzo. Who calls?   *40*

Launcelot. Sola! Did you see Master Lorenzo and
    Mistress Lorenzo? sola, sola!

Lorenzo. Leave holloaing, man! Here.

Launcelot. Sola! Where? Where?

Lorenzo. Here!   *45*

Launcelot. Tell him there's a post come from my
    master, with his horn full of good news.° My master
    will be here ere morning.   *[Exit.]*

Lorenzo. Sweet soul, let's in, and there expect° their
    coming.
    And yet no matter; why should we go in?   *50*
    My friend Stephano, signify, I pray you,
    Within the house, your mistress is at hand,
    And bring your music forth into the air.
                     [Exit Stephano.]
    How sweet the moonlight sleeps upon this bank!
    Here will we sit and let the sounds of music   *55*
    Creep in our ears; soft stillness and the night
    Become° the touches° of sweet harmony.
    Sit, Jessica. Look how the floor of heaven
    Is thick inlaid with patens° of bright gold.
    There's not the smallest orb which thou behold'st   *60*
    But in his motion like an angel sings,

---

39 **Sola** (Launcelot imitates a courier's horn)   47 **horn full of good news**
(Launcelot puns on the cornucopia, "the horn of plenty")   49 **expect** await
57 **Become** befit   57, 67 **touches** notes produced by touching the strings
or stops of a musical instrument   59 **patens** tiles

Still quiring° to the young-eyed cherubins;
Such harmony is in immortal souls,
But whilst this muddy vesture of decay°
65   Doth grossly close it in, we cannot hear it.

[*Enter Musicians.*]

Come ho, and wake Diana° with a hymn!
With sweetest touches pierce your mistress' ear
And draw her home with music.   *Play music.*

Jessica. I am never merry when I hear sweet music.

70   *Lorenzo.* The reason is, your spirits are attentive.
For do but note a wild and wanton° herd
Or race of youthful and unhandled colts
Fetching mad bounds, bellowing and neighing loud,
Which is the hot condition° of their blood:
75   If they but hear perchance a trumpet sound,
Or any air of music touch their ears,
You shall perceive them make a mutual stand,°
Their savage eyes turned to a modest gaze
By the sweet power of music. Therefore the poet
80   Did feign that Orpheus° drew trees, stones, and
         floods;
Since naught so stockish,° hard, and full of rage°
But music for the time doth change his nature.
The man that hath no music in himself,
Nor is not moved with concord of sweet sounds,
85   Is fit for treasons, stratagems, and spoils;°
The motions° of his spirit are dull as night,
And his affections° dark as Erebus.°
Let no such man be trusted. Mark the music.

62 **quiring** making music (a reference to the music of the spheres. It was thought that the harmonious movement of the spheres, in Ptolemaic astronomy, produced a heavenly music inaudible to human ears) 64 **muddy vesture of decay** earthy garment subject to decay, i.e., the body   66 **Diana** goddess of the moon and of chastity   71 **wanton** frolicsome, untrained   74 **hot condition** impetuous nature   77 **make a mutual stand** stand still by common consent   80 **Orpheus** famous legendary Greek poet and musician   81 **stockish** blockish, dull   81 **rage** passion   85 **spoils** plundering   86 **motions** inward promptings   87 **affections** emotions   87 **Erebus** the dark underworld of the Greeks

Enter Portia and Nerissa.

Portia. That light we see is burning in my hall;
How far that little candle throws his beams!   *90*
So shines a good deed in a naughty° world.

Nerissa. When the moon shone we did not see the
candle.

Portia. So doth the greater glory dim the less.
A substitute° shines brightly as a king
Until a king be by, and then his state   *95*
Empties itself,° as doth an inland brook
Into the main of waters.° Music, hark!

Nerissa. It is your music, madam, of the house.

Portia. Nothing is good, I see, without respect;°
Methinks it sounds much sweeter than by day.   *100*

Nerissa. Silence bestows that virtue on it, madam.

Portia. The crow doth sing as sweetly as the lark
When neither is attended;° and I think
The nightingale, if she should sing by day
When every goose is cackling, would be thought   *105*
No better a musician than the wren.
How many things by season, seasoned are
To their right praise and true perfection!°
Peace! [*Music ceases*.] How the° moon sleeps with
Endymion,°
And would not be awaked.°

Lorenzo.   That is the voice,   *110*
Or I am much deceived, of Portia.

---

91 **naughty** evil   94 **substitute** deputy   95–96 **his state/Empties itself**
i.e., his own glory merges into the king's   97 **main of waters** ocean
99 **without respect** without reference to circumstances   103 **attended**
heeded   107–08 **by season . . . perfection** by the right occasion are made
ready to receive their fitting praise and attain their full perfection
109 **Peace! How the** (the quarto reads "Peace, how the"; editors often
emend to "Peace, ho! The")   109 **Endymion** a handsome shepherd,
beloved of Diana   109–10 **Peace . . . awaked** addressed to the musicians

Portia. He knows me as the blind man knows the
    cuckoo,
  By the bad voice.

Lorenzo.   Dear lady, welcome home.

Portia. We have been praying for our husbands' welfare,
115   Which speed we hope the better for our words.
  Are they returned?

Lorenzo.   Madam, they are not yet,
  But there is come a messenger before
  To signify their coming.

Portia.   Go in, Nerissa.
  Give order to my servants that they take
120 No note at all of our being absent hence—
  Nor you, Lorenzo—Jessica, nor you.

                       [*A tucket° sounds.*]

Lorenzo. Your husband is at hand; I hear his trumpet.
  We are no telltales, madam; fear you not.

Portia. This night methinks is but the daylight sick;
125 It looks a little paler. 'Tis a day
  Such as the day is when the sun is hid.

Enter Bassanio, Antonio, Gratiano, and their Followers.

Bassanio. We should hold day with the Antipodes,°
  If you would walk in absence of the sun.

Portia. Let me give light,° but let me not be light,
130 For a light wife doth make a heavy° husband,
  And never be Bassanio so for me.
  But God sort all!° You are welcome home, my lord.

Bassanio. I thank you, madam. Give welcome to my
    friend.

---

121 s.d. **tucket** trumpet call (Bassanio, like every nobleman, had his
individual tucket)   127 **Antipodes** dwellers on the opposite side of the
earth   129, 130 **light, heavy** (Portia quibbles on "light" in the senses of
radiance, unchaste, and of little weight, and on "heavy" in the senses
of weighty and despondent, weighed down with trouble)   132 **God
sort all** let God ordain all according to his wisdom

This is the man, this is Antonio,
To whom I am so infinitely bound.   135

Portia. You should in all sense° be much bound to him,
For, as I hear, he was much bound for you.

Antonio. No more than I am well acquitted of.°

Portia. Sir, you are very welcome to our house.
It must appear in other ways than words;   140
Therefore I scant this breathing courtesy.°

Gratiano. [*To Nerissa*] By yonder moon I swear you do
   me wrong!
In faith, I gave it to the judge's clerk.
Would he were gelt° that had it, for my part,°
Since you do take it, love, so much at heart.   145

Portia. A quarrel, ho, already! What's the matter?

Gratiano. About a hoop of gold, a paltry ring
That she did give me, whose posy° was
For all the world like cutler's poetry
Upon a knife, "Love me, and leave me not."   150

Nerissa. What° talk you of the posy or the value?
You swore to me when I did give it you
That you would wear it till your hour of death,
And that it should lie with you in your grave.
Though not for me,° yet for your vehement oaths,   155
You should have been respective° and have kept it.
Gave it a judge's clerk! No, God's my judge,
The clerk will ne'er wear hair on's face that had it!

Gratiano. He will, and if he live to be a man.

Nerissa. Ay, if a woman live to be a man.   160

Gratiano. Now by this hand, I gave it to a youth,
A kind of boy, a little scrubbèd° boy

136 **in all sense** (1) in all reason (2) in all senses   138 **acquitted of** freed
from   141 **breathing courtesy** courtesy that is only breath, i.e., words
144 **gelt** castrated   144 **for my part** so far as I care   148 **posy** (a con-
traction of "poesy," i.e., "poetry") motto (inscribed on a ring)   151 **What**
why   155 **Though not for me** if not for my sake   156 **respective**
regardful, heedful   162 **scrubbèd** stunted

No higher than thyself, the judge's clerk,
A prating boy that begged it as a fee.
165 I could not for my heart deny it him.

Portia. You were to blame—I must be plain with you—
To part so slightly with your wife's first gift,
A thing stuck on with oaths upon your finger,
And so riveted with faith unto your flesh.
170 I gave my love a ring, and made him swear
Never to part with it; and here he stands.
I dare be sworn for him he would not leave it°
Nor pluck it from his finger, for the wealth
That the world masters.° Now in faith, Gratiano,
175 You give your wife too unkind° a cause of grief.
And, 'twere to me, I should be mad° at it.

Bassanio. [*Aside*] Why, I were best to cut my left hand
     off
And swear I lost the ring defending it.

Gratiano. My Lord Bassanio gave his ring away
180 Unto the judge that begged it, and indeed
Deserved it too; and then the boy, his clerk
That took some pains in writing, he begged mine;
And neither man nor master would take aught
But the two rings.

Portia.   What ring gave you, my lord?
185 Not that, I hope, which you received of me.

Bassanio. If I could add a lie unto a fault,°
I would deny it; but you see my finger
Hath not the ring upon it—it is gone.

Portia. Even so void is your false heart of truth.
190 By heaven, I will ne'er come in your bed
Until I see the ring!

Nerissa.   Nor I in yours
Till I again see mine!

---

172 **leave it** let it go   174 **masters** possesses   175 **unkind** unnaturally cruel   176 **mad** in a frenzy   186 **fault** faulty act

Bassanio.   Sweet Portia,
  If you did know to whom I gave the ring,
  If you did know for whom I gave the ring,
  And would conceive for what° I gave the ring,   195
  And how unwillingly I left the ring
  When naught would be accepted but the ring,
  You would abate the strength of your displeasure.

Portia. If you had known the virtue of the ring,
  Or half her worthiness that gave the ring,   200
  Or your own honor to contain° the ring,
  You would not then have parted with the ring.
  What man is there so much unreasonable,
  If you had pleased to have defended it
  With any terms of zeal,° wanted the modesty   205
  To urge the thing held as a ceremony?°
  Nerissa teaches me what to believe;
  I'll die for't but some woman had the ring!

Bassanio. No, by my honor, madam! By my soul
  No woman had it, but a civil doctor,°   210
  Which did refuse three thousand ducats of me
  And begged the ring, the which I did deny him,
  And suffered him to go displeased away,
  Even he that had held up the very life
  Of my dear friend. What should I say, sweet lady?   215
  I was enforced to send it after him.
  I was beset with shame and courtesy.°
  My honor would not let ingratitude
  So much besmear it. Pardon me, good lady!
  For by these blessèd candles of the night,   220
  Had you been there, I think you would have begged
  The ring of me to give the worthy doctor.

Portia. Let not that doctor e'er come near my house.

195 **conceive for what** form a conception of why   201 **honor to contain** honorable duty to retain   205 **terms of zeal** ardent language 205–06 **wanted . . . ceremony** would have been so lacking in modesty as to urge a claim on the thing you were keeping as a hallowed symbol 210 **civil doctor** doctor of civil law   217 **beset with shame and courtesy** assailed by feelings of shame and the obligations of courtesy

Since he hath got the jewel that I loved,
225   And that which you did swear to keep for me,
I will become as liberal° as you;
I'll not deny him anything I have,
No, not my body nor my husband's bed.
Know him I shall, I am well sure of it.
230   Lie not a night from home. Watch me like Argus.°
If you do not, if I be left alone—
Now by mine honor which is yet mine own,
I'll have that doctor for mine bedfellow.

Nerissa. And I his clerk. Therefore be well advised°
235   How you do leave me to mine own protection.

Gratiano. Well, do you so. Let not me take° him then!
For if I do, I'll mar the young clerk's pen.°

Antonio. I am th' unhappy subject of these quarrels.

Portia. Sir, grieve not you; you are welcome not with-
standing.

240 *Bassanio.* Portia, forgive me this enforcèd wrong,°
And in the hearing of these many friends
I swear to thee, even by thine own fair eyes,
Wherein I see myself—

Portia.   Mark you but that!
In both my eyes he doubly sees himself,
245   In each eye one. Swear by your double self,°
And there's an oath of credit.°

Bassanio.   Nay, but hear me.
Pardon this fault, and by my soul I swear
I never more will break an oath with thee.

Antonio. I once did lend my body for his wealth,°
250   Which but for him that had your husband's ring

226 **liberal** (1) licentious (2) generous   230 **Argus** a monstrous giant
of Greek myth, with a hundred eyes; a type of never-failing watchful-
ness   234 **be well advised** be very careful   236 **take** get hold of
237 **pen** (double entendre)   240 **this enforcèd wrong** this wrong I was
forced to commit   245 **double self** a quibble (1) twofold image (2)
double-dealing character   246 **oath of credit** oath to be believed (spoken
in irony)   249 **wealth** welfare

Had quite miscarried. I dare be bound again,
My soul upon the forfeit, that your lord
Will never more break faith advisedly.°

Portia. Then you shall be his surety. Give him this,
And bid him keep it better than the other.   255

Antonio. Here, Lord Bassanio. Swear to keep this ring.

Bassanio. By heaven, it is the same I gave the doctor!

Portia. I had it of him. Pardon me, Bassanio,
For by this ring the doctor lay with me.

Nerissa. And pardon me, my gentle Gratiano,   260
For that same scrubbèd boy, the doctor's clerk,
In lieu of° this, last night did lie with me.

Gratiano. Why, this is like the mending of highways
In summer, where the ways are fair enough.
What, are we cuckolds° ere we have deserved it?   265

Portia. Speak not so grossly. You are all amazed.°
Here is a letter; read it at your leisure.
It comes from Padua from Bellario.
There you shall find that Portia was the doctor,
Nerissa there her clerk. Lorenzo here   270
Shall witness I set forth as soon as you,
And even but now returned. I have not yet
Entered my house. Antonio, you are welcome,
And I have better news in store for you
Than you expect. Unseal this letter soon;   275
There you shall find three of your argosies
Are richly come to harbor suddenly.
You shall not know by what strange° accident
I chancèd on this letter.

Antonio.   I am dumb!

Bassanio. Were you the doctor, and I knew you not?   280

---

253 **advisedly** deliberately   262 **In lieu of** in return for   265 **cuckolds**
husbands of faithless wives   266 **amazed** utterly bewildered; literally,
entangled in a maze or labyrinth   278 **strange** astonishing

Gratiano. Were you the clerk that is to make me
    cuckold?

Nerissa. Ay, but the clerk that never means to do it,
    Unless he live until he be a man.

Bassanio. Sweet Doctor, you shall be my bedfellow.
285   When I am absent, then lie with my wife.

Antonio. Sweet lady, you have given me life and living!
    For here I read for certain that my ships
    Are safely come to road.°

Portia.   How now, Lorenzo?
    My clerk hath some good comforts too for you.

290 *Nerissa.* Ay, and I'll give them him without a fee.
    There do I give to you and Jessica
    From the rich Jew, a special deed of gift,
    After his death, of all he dies possessed of.

Lorenzo. Fair ladies, you drop manna in the way
    Of starvèd people.°

295 *Portia.*   It is almost morning,
    And yet I am sure you are not satisfied
    Of these events at full.° Let us go in,
    And charge us there upon° inter'gatories,°
    And we will answer all things faithfully.

300 *Gratiano.* Let it be so. The first inter'gatory
    That my Nerissa shall be sworn on° is,
    Whether till the next night she had rather stay,
    Or go to bed now, being two hours to day.
    But were the day come, I should wish it dark
305   Till I were couching with the doctor's clerk.
    Well, while I live I'll fear no other thing
    So sore, as keeping safe Nerissa's ring.   *Exeunt.*

FINIS

288 **road** anchorage   295 **starvèd people** (Lorenzo, though of good
social position, was, like Bassanio, far from rich)   296–97 **not satisfied
. . . full** not fully satisfied how these events came to pass   298 **charge us
there upon** load us with questions   298 **inter'gatories** interrogatories,
i.e., questions formally drawn up to be put to a defendant or witness and
answered under oath   301 **sworn on** sworn to under oath

Textual Note

The exact date of the play's composition is uncertain, but the play was in existence in 1598, when Francis Meres mentioned it in *Palladis Tamia*, and it may have been written as early as 1596, if the reference to the ship *Andrew* in 1.1.27 is indebted—as has been conjectured—to news of the capture of the Spanish ship *St. Andrew* in the Cádiz expedition. In 1598 and in 1600 the play was entered in the Stationers' Register. It was first published in a quarto (Q1) in 1600. The interesting part of the title page runs thus: "The most excellent/ Historie of the Merchant/ of Venice./ With the extreame crueltie of Shylocke the Iewe/ towards the sayd Merchant, in cutting a iust pound/ of his flesh: and the obtayning of Portia/ by the choyse of three/ chests./ As it hath beene diuers times acted by the Lord/ Chamberlaine his Seruants./ Written by William Shakespeare." The absence of some necessary stage directions (e.g., entrances of some characters who later speak) suggests that the copy for this quarto could not have been a promptbook. Conversely, there are some bits of evidence that suggest the copy was very close to Shakespeare's manuscript; for example, such a stage direction as "Enter Portia for Balthazar" seems to reflect an author's conception of his action. But plays that are commonly thought to be printed from Shakespeare's manuscript usually have some confusions in them, the result of a somewhat illegible manuscript, and *The Merchant* lacks such confusions. Probably, then, the printer's copy for the first quarto was a scribe's careful and clean copy of the manuscript—but, of course, it is unwise to be dogmatic about such matters.

In 1619 a second quarto (Q2) appeared, falsely dated 1600. Q2 was based on Q1, and though it corrects some palpable errors in Q1, Q2 has no independent authority. In 1623 the play was again reprinted, in the First Folio, again from Q1. And again, of course, there are some slight departures from Q1, ranging from misprints to the addition of some interesting stage directions that doubtless reflect playhouse practice. The most notable are directions calling for the flourishing of cornets.

Q1, then, the only authoritative text, and the source of all others, serves as the basis for the present edition, but some changes have been made. Solanio, Salarino, and Salerio have, as in most modern editions, been reduced to Solanio and Salerio. (Possibly Shakespeare began with three such characters in mind, but as he worked he apparently found he could make do with two, and Salarino disappeared. The name Salarino—which in Q1 occurs in stage directions at 1.1; 2.4, 6, 7; 3.1—in this edition is replaced by Salerio. Salarino is a diminutive of Salerio, and it is possible that Shakespeare did not intend them to be distinct. In any case, the name Salerio must stay, because it appears in the dialogue as well as in the stage directions.) Spelling and punctuation have been modernized, and speech prefixes have been regularized (e.g., we give "Shylock," though Q1 varies between "Shylock," "Shy.," and "Iew"). Act divisions, first introduced in the Folio, are given, and for ease of reference, the scene divisions established by the Globe edition are given. These additions, like necessary stage directions that are not found in Q1, are enclosed in square brackets. A superfluous stage direction ("*Enter Tubal,*" at 3.1.74) has been deleted, the positions of a few stage directions are slightly altered, and obvious typographical errors have been corrected. Other departures from Q1 are listed below, the adopted reading given first, in *italic* type, the rejected reading in roman type. If the adopted reading comes from Q2 or F, that fact is indicated.

1.1.27 *docked* docks   113 *Is* It is

1.2.59 *throstle* Trassell

2.1.s.d. *Morocco* Morochus   35 *page* rage

2.2.99 *last* [Q2] lost

2.7.69 *tombs* timber

2.8.39 *Slubber* [Q2, F] slumber

3.1.100 *Hoard* heere

3.2.67 eyes [F] eye   81 *vice* voyce

3.1.s.d. *Solanio* Salerio

3.4.49 *Padua* Mantua   50 *cousin's* [Q2, F] cosin   81 *my* [Q2, F] my my

3.5.21 *e'en* [Q2, F] in   27 *comes*. come?   77 *merit it* meane it, it   84 *a wife* [F] wife

4.1.30 *his state* [Q2, F] this states   31 *flint* [Q2] flints   51 *Master* Maisters
74 *bleat* [F] bleake   75 *mountain* [F] mountaine of   100 *is mine* as mine
229 *No, not* [Q2] Not not   396 *Gratiano* [Q2, F] Shy [lock]

5.1.41–42 *Master Lorenzo and Mistress Lorenzo*? M. Lorenzo, & M. Lorenzo
49 *Sweet soul* [concludes Launcelot's speech]   51 *Stephano* [Q2] Stephen
87 *Erebus* [F] Terebus   152 *it you* [Q2, F] you

A Note on the Sources of
The Merchant of Venice

Some of Shakespeare's plays are close to their sources, and it is useful and often illuminating to see how he departs from Plutarch or Holinshed, Greene or Lodge. But no known work can be the only source for *The Merchant of Venice*. Apparently Shakespeare combined a number of sources, all of which repay careful study.

If he drew chiefly on a single source, it may have been a play called *The Jew*, which Stephen Gosson mentioned favorably in 1579, in his *School of Abuse*, and which he said showed "the greediness of worldly choosers" and the "bloody minds of usurers." Some scholars believe that the term "worldly choosers" shows that the casket story (in which worldly-minded suitors are discomfited by choosing the gold or silver casket) has been combined with the story of the usurer and the pound of flesh. Yet the word "greediness" seems less appropriate to suitors than to usurers. In any case, *The Jew* is not extant, and speculation about Shakespeare's debt to it is idle.

Of extant works, *Il Pecorone* (The Dunce), an Italian collection of prose tales by an author who calls himself Ser Giovanni Fiorentino, is the most relevant. The first tale of the fourth day concerns the Lady of Belmonte, a widow who demands that each traveler seek to possess her; if he does, she will wed him, but if he fails, all his goods are forfeit. Giannetto voyages to Belmonte twice; twice he is drugged and therefore fails and loses his goods. His godfather then borrows from a Jewish usurer and furnishes him for a third voyage. (Giannetto has lied, telling his godfather that the goods were lost in shipwrecks.) This time Giannetto—

warned by the Lady's maid—is successful. There follows the usurer's demand for the overdue money, the cleverness of the lawyer, the Lady in disguise (as in Shakespeare), and the business of the ring.

There is no indubitable proof that Shakespeare borrowed directly from *Il Pecorone*. He could have found the tale of the pound of flesh in other works, such as Alexander Silvayne's *The Orator* and Anthony Munday's *Zelauto*. It seems more than possible, however, that Shakespeare read *Il Pecorone* either in a translation or in Italian—a language which, with his good knowledge of Latin, he might very easily have acquired.

If he read it in one language or another, probably his most notable changes are the alteration of the indecent test imposed on the wooer, the addition of the usurer's daughter, and the omission of the wooer's incredibly long forgetfulness of his benefactor's danger, together with the ennoblement of all the leading characters.

The story of the caskets comes ultimately from Oriental folklore. Shakespeare's immediate source is believed to be an English version of the *Gesta Romanorum*, a collection of medieval Latin tales, translated into English in 1577 and "bettered" by the same translator in 1595. Possibly the author of the old play *The Jew* is responsible for joining the casket plot to the bond plot, but we know little about that play; Shakespeare may have been the first to combine the two stories.

Finally, it should be mentioned that Shakespeare's play about Christians and a Jew must owe something to Marlowe's *The Jew of Malta*, and also to the trial, in 1594, of Dr. Roderigo Lopez, the converted Portuguese Jew who, though very probably innocent, was convicted and executed on the charge of plotting to poison Queen Elizabeth I. In *The Jew of Malta*, Shakespeare would have found a Jew who is a scoundrel but is, at certain moments, a really human figure wronged by the Christians around him. Shylock's daughter Jessica may owe something to Marlowe's Abigail, who loves a Christian, but both Abigail and her beloved are killed, whereas Jessica escapes into a happy marriage with Lorenzo. In the Lopez trial, Shakespeare would have found the usual depiction of the murderous Jew.

Geoffrey Bullough, in the first volume of his *Narrative and Dramatic Sources of Shakespeare*, has brought together selections from Silvayne's *The Orator*, Anthony Munday's *Zelauto*, and *Il Pecorone*. To anyone who browses through this material, it is clear enough that Shakespeare did not invent the chief episodes of his play. It is no less clear that the remarkable characterizations, the moral tone, the poetry, and probably the deft interweaving of the various strands of the plot are the work of a great dramatic poet.

Commentaries

NICHOLAS ROWE

From The Works of Mr. William Shakespear

In *Twelfth Night* there is something singularly ridiculous and pleasant in the fantastical steward Malvolio. . . . Petruchio, in *The Taming of the Shrew,* is an uncommon piece of humor. . . . To these I might add that incomparable character of Shylock the Jew, in *The Merchant of Venice;* but though we have seen that play received and acted as a comedy, and the part of the Jew performed by an excellent comedian, yet I cannot but think it was designed tragically by the author. There appears in it such a deadly spirit of revenge, such a savage fierceness and fellness, and such a bloody designation of cruelty and mischief, as cannot agree either with the style or characters of comedy. The play itself, take it all together, seems to me to be one of the most finished of any of Shakespear's. The tale, indeed, in that part relating to the caskets, and the extravagant and unusual kind of bond given by Antonio, is a little too much removed from the rules of probability: but taking the fact for granted, we must allow it to be very beautifully written. There is something in the friendship of Antonio to Bassanio very great, generous, and tender. The whole fourth act, supposing, as I said, the fact to be probable, is extremely fine. But there are two passages that deserve a particular notice. The first is what Portia says in praise of mercy, and the other on the power of music. [1709]

WILLIAM HAZLITT

From Characters of Shakespear's Plays

This is a play that in spite of the change of manners and prejudices still holds undisputed possession of the stage. Shakespear's malignant has outlived Mr. Cumberland's benevolent Jew. In proportion as Shylock has ceased to be a popular bugbear, "baited with the rabble's curse," he becomes a half-favorite with the philosophical part of the audience, who are disposed to think that Jewish revenge is at least as good as Christian injuries. Shylock is *a good hater*; "a man no less sinned against than sinning." If he carries his revenge too far, yet he has strong grounds for "the lodged hate he bears Anthonio," which he explains with equal force of eloquence and reason. He seems the depositary of the vengeance of his race; and though the long habit of brooding over daily insults and injuries has crusted over his temper with inveterate misanthropy, and hardened him against the contempt of mankind, this adds but little to the triumphant pretensions of his enemies. There is a strong, quick, and deep sense of justice mixed up with the gall and bitterness of his resentment. The constant apprehension of being burnt alive, plundered, banished, reviled, and trampled on, might be supposed to sour the most forbearing nature, and to take something from that "milk of human kindness," with which his persecutors contemplated his indignities. The desire of revenge is almost inseparable from the sense of wrong; and we can hardly help sympathizing with the proud spirit, hid beneath his "Jewish gaberdine," stung to madness by

From *Characters of Shakespear's Plays* by William Hazlitt, 2nd ed. (London: Taylor & Hessey, 1818).

repeated undeserved provocations, and laboring to throw off the load of obloquy and oppression heaped upon him and all his tribe by one desperate act of "lawful" revenge, till the ferociousness of the means by which he is to execute his purpose, and the pertinacity with which he adheres to it, turn us against him; but even at last, when disappointed of the sanguinary revenge with which he had glutted his hopes, and exposed to beggary and contempt by the letter of the law on which he had insisted with so little remorse, we pity him, and think him hardly dealt with by his judges. In all his answers and retorts upon his adversaries, he has the best not only of the argument but of the question, reasoning on their own principles and practice. They are so far from allowing of any measure of equal dealing, of common justice or humanity between themselves and the Jew, that even when they come to ask a favor of him, and Shylock reminds them that "on such a day they spit upon him, another spurned him, another called him dog, and for these curtesies request he'll lend them so much monies"—Anthonio, his old enemy, instead of any acknowledgment of the shrewdness and justice of his remonstrance, which would have been preposterous in a respectable Catholic merchant in those times, threatens him with a repetition of the same treatment—

"I am as like to call thee so again,
    To spit on thee again, to spurn thee too."

After this, the appeal to the Jew's mercy, as if there were any common principle of right and wrong between them, is the rankest hypocrisy, or the blindest prejudice; and the Jew's answer to one of Anthonio's friends, who asks him what his pound of forfeit flesh is good for, is irresistible—

"To bait fish withal; if it will feed nothing else, it will feed my revenge. He hath disgrac'd me, and hinder'd me of half a million, laughed at my losses, mock'd at my gains, scorn'd my nation, thwarted my bargains, cool'd my friends, heated mine enemies; and what's his reason? I am a Jew. Hath not a Jew eyes; hath not a Jew hands, organs, dimensions, senses, affections, passions; fed with the same food, hurt with the same weapons, subject to the same diseases, healed by the same means, warmed and cooled by the same winter and summer that a Christian is? If you prick us, do we not bleed? If you tickle us, do we not laugh? If you poison us, do we not die? And if you wrong us, shall we not revenge? If we are like you in the rest, we will resemble you in that. If a Jew wrong a Christian, what is his humility? revenge. If a Christian wrong a Jew, what should his sufferance be by Christian example? why revenge. The villainy you teach me I will execute, and it shall go hard but I will better the instruction."

The whole of the trial scene, both before and after the entrance of Portia, is a masterpiece of dramatic skill. The legal acuteness, the passionate declamations, the sound maxims of jurisprudence, the wit and irony interspersed in it, the fluctuations of hope and fear in the different persons, and the completeness and suddenness of the catastrophe, cannot be surpassed. Shylock, who is his own counsel, defends himself well, and is triumphant on all the general topics that are urged against him, and only fails through a legal flaw. Take the following as an instance—

> "*Shylock.* What judgment shall I dread, doing no wrong?
>   You have among you many a purchas'd slave,
>   Which like your asses, and your dogs, and mules,
>   You use in abject and in slavish part,
>   Because you bought them:—shall I say to you,
>   Let them be free, marry them to your heirs?
>   Why sweat they under burdens? let their beds
>   Be made as soft as yours, and let their palates
>   Be season'd with such viands? you will answer,
>   The slaves are ours:—so do I answer you:
>   The pound of flesh, which I demand of him,
>   Is dearly bought, is mine, and I will have it:
>   If you deny me, fie upon your law!
>   There is no force in the decrees of Venice:
>   I stand for judgment: answer; shall I have it?"

The keenness of his revenge awakes all his faculties; and he beats back all opposition to his purpose, whether grave or gay, whether of wit or argument, with an equal degree of earnestness and self-possession. His character is displayed as distinctly in other less prominent parts of the play, and we may collect from a few sentences the history of his life—his descent and origin, his thrift and domestic economy, his affection for his daughter, whom he loves next to his wealth, his courtship and his first present to Leah, his wife! "I would not have parted with it" (the ring which he first gave her) "for a wilderness of monkies!" What a fine Hebraism is implied in this expression!

Portia is not a very great favorite with us; neither are we in love with her maid, Nerissa. Portia has a certain degree of affection and pedantry about her, which is very unusual in Shakespear's women, but which perhaps was a proper qualification for the office of a "civil doctor," which she undertakes and executes so successfully. The speech about Mercy is very well; but there are a thousand finer ones in Shakespear. We do not admire the scene of the caskets: and object entirely to the Black Prince, Morocchius. We should like Jessica better if she had not deceived and robbed her father, and Lorenzo, if he had not married a Jewess, though he thinks he has a right to wrong a Jew. The dialogue between this newly-married couple by moonlight, beginning "On such a night," etc., is a collection of classical elegancies. Launcelot, the Jew's man, is an honest fellow. The dilemma in which he describes himself placed between his "conscience and the fiend," the one of which advises him to run away from his master's service and the other to stay in it, is exquisitely humorous.

Gratiano is a very admirable subordinate character. He is the jester of the piece: yet one speech of his, in his own defense, contains a whole volume of wisdom.

"*Anthonio.* I hold the world but as the world, Gratiano,
    A stage, where every one must play his part;
    And mine a sad one.
  Gratiano. Let me play the fool:
    With mirth and laughter let old wrinkles come;
    And let my liver rather heat with wine,
    Than my heart cool with mortifying groans.
    Why should a man, whose blood is warm within,
    Sit like his grandsire cut in alabaster?
    Sleep when he wakes? and creep into the jaundice
    By being peevish? I tell thee what, Anthonio—

I love thee, and it is my love that speaks;—
There are a sort of men, whose visages
Do cream and mantle like a standing pond:
And do a wilful stillness entertain,
With purpose to be drest in an opinion
Of wisdom, gravity, profound conceit;
As who should say, *I am Sir Oracle,*
And when I ope my lips, let no dog bark!
O, my Anthonio, I do know of these,
That therefore only are reputed wise,
For saying nothing; who, I am very sure,
If they should speak, would almost damn those ears,
Which hearing them, would call their brothers, fools.
I'll tell thee more of this another time:
But fish not with this melancholy bait,
For this fool's gudgeon, this opinion."

Gratiano's speech on the philosophy of love, and the effect of habit in taking off the force of passion, is as full of spirit and good sense. The graceful winding up of this play in the fifth act, after the tragic business is despatched, is one of the happiest instances of Shakespear's knowledge of the principles of the drama. We do not mean the pretended quarrel between Portia and Nerissa and their husbands about the rings, which is amusing enough, but the conversation just before and after the return of Portia to her own house, beginning "How sweet the moonlight sleeps upon this bank," and ending "Peace! how the moon sleeps with Endymion, and would not be awaked." There is a number of beautiful thoughts crowded into that short space, and linked together by the most natural transitions.

When we first went to see Mr. Kean in Shylock, we expected to see, what we had been used to see, a decrepit old man, bent with age and ugly with mental deformity, grinning with deadly malice, with the venom of his heart congealed in the expression of his countenance, sullen, morose, gloomy, inflexible, brooding over one idea, that of his hatred, and fixed on one unalterable purpose, that of his revenge. We were disappointed, because we had taken our idea from other actors, not from the play. There is no proof there that Shylock is old, but a single line, "Bassanio and *old*

Shylock, both stand forth"—which does not imply that he is infirm with age—and the circumstance that he has a daughter marriageable, which does not imply that he is old at all. It would be too much to say that his body should be made crooked and deformed to answer to his mind, which is bowed down and warped with prejudices and passion. That he has but one idea is not true; he has more ideas than any other person in the piece; and if he is intense and inveterate in the pursuit of his purpose, he shows the utmost elasticity, vigor, and presence of mind, in the means of attaining it. But so rooted was our habitual impression of the part from seeing it caricatured in the representation, that it was only from a careful perusal of the play itself that we saw our error. The stage is not in general the best place to study our author's characters in. It is too often filled with traditional commonplace conceptions of the part, handed down from sire to son, and suited to the taste of *the great vulgar and the small*—" 'Tis an unweeded garden: things rank and gross do merely gender in it!" If a man of genius comes once in an age to clear away the rubbish, to make it fruitful and wholesome, they cry, " 'Tis a bad school: it may be like nature, it may be like Shakespear, but it is not like us." Admirable critics!

ANONYMOUS

Henry Irving's Shylock

The production by Mr. Irving at the Lyceum of *The Merchant of Venice* was eagerly expected and had a double source of certain attraction. The beauties of Miss Ellen Terry's Portia were already known; those of Mr. Irving's Shylock had to be discovered. The character of Shylock has given food for much discussion. It is well known that modern interpretations of the part have differed entirely from those given by the actors who, before the days of Macklin, treated the part from the point of view of the most grotesque comedy; and a good many people have told us how Shakspeare intended it to be treated. Mr. Hawkins, in the current number of the *Theatre* magazine, has argued very ingeniously and interestingly, from the fact that *The Merchant of Venice* appeared during the excitement caused by the iniquities of the Jew physician, Rodrigo Lopez, that the play was intended by its author as "a plea for toleration towards the Jews." The theory is well worked out and hangs well enough together, since it is admitted that, supposing this to have been Shakspeare's intention, his position as a manager, bound to please his public, hampered him in its execution. But we have always been of opinion that theorizing as to Shakspeare's intentions and the meanings of his characters, however interesting it may be as an exercise of ingenuity, has little practical import. It will hardly seem probable that Shakspeare was in the habit of sitting down with a set purpose to teach certain moral lessons by means

From *The Saturday Review*, 8 November 1879.

116

of certain characters, to be rendered in certain definite ways; and yet one might infer from the work of commentators that this was the case. No manager or play-writer could believe that any part would ever be given in precisely the same way by any two actors, except so far as it might be done by servile imitation; and, indeed, to make this possible would involve a degradation of character to caricature. Such a broad rule as that Shylock ought not to be played as a low-comedy part, or that Lear ought not to be from beginning to end a driveling idiot, may of course be laid down; but one has surely no more right to expect an actor to execute a part in the way imagined to be right by commentators than to demand that a painter should seize just this or that aspect of a great historical subject. The enthusiasm aroused by Mr. Irving's Shylock, even in those who find his rendering of the character differ from their view of it, goes, however, to prove that, as has been suggested, an elaborate analysis of Shakspeare's characters made from studying the text is valuable chiefly as a mental exercise.

Mr. Irving presents Shylock as a picturesque figure, with an air as of a man feeling the bitterness of oppression, and conscious of his own superiority in all but circumstance to the oppressor—a feeling which is finely indicated when, in talk with Antonio, he touches the Christian merchant, and, seeing the action resented, bows deprecatingly, with an affectation of deep humility. He dwells with concentrated bitterness on the expressions of hatred to Antonio in the speech beginning "How like a fawning publican he looks"; and here, in the implacable determination of "If I can catch him once upon the hip, I will feed fat the ancient grudge I bear him," we have the prologue, as it were, to the intense revengefulness of the last scene. It may be noted that since the first night Mr. Irving's performance has gained in leading up consistently to its climax—as consistently, that is, as is possible in the case of a human creature worked on by mixed emotions which sometimes baffle scrutiny. The point which on the first night seemed most striking to many people in the general scope of the actor's representation was that his Shylock was intended to be, before all things, dignified, and it was thought that his acting in the scene when he bewails the loss of his daughter and his ducats was at variance with the rest of the performance. It would perhaps be neither easy nor desirable to make Shylock altogether digni-fied at this point; but it is not the less true that Mr. Irving has improved the rendering of this scene, and, with it, the whole value of his representation.

To return, however, to Mr. Irving's first scene, we may note specially the bitterness of subdued scorn in the speech beginning "Signior Antonio, many a time and oft in the Rialto you have rated me," and the diabolical mockery of good humor with which he proposes the "merry bond." In the next scene in which the Jew appears we have again his hatred and desire for revenge marked strongly in the resolu-tion to go forth to supper "in hate, to feed upon the prodigal Christian," and to part with Launcelot "to one that I would have him help to waste his borrowed purse"; and at the end of the act Mr. Irving has introduced a singularly fine touch of invention. Lorenzo has fled with his stolen bride and her stolen money, and a crowd of masquers has crossed the stage and disappeared over the picturesque bridge with laugh-ter and music. Then Shylock is seen, lantern in hand, advancing, bent in thought; and, as he comes close to his robbed and deserted house, the curtain falls. The effect, however, would, to our thinking, be doubled if the curtain had not fallen for a moment and been raised again just before this appearance of Shylock—if the masquers had disap-peared in sight of the audience, and the sounds of revelry had died away in the distance. It may be conjectured that the dropping of the curtain signifies the interval of time which might naturally elapse between the elopement and Shy-lock's return; but this is, we think, needless. Mr. Irving, in the scene already referred to of the third act, is now less vehement than might have been expected; the Jew's passion seems to have exhausted him, but is not for that the less intense in itself. He is overweighted with trouble, and the delivery of the words "no ill luck stirring, but what lights o' my shoulders; no sighs, but o' my breathing; no tears, but o' my shedding," is charged with the pathos of the heaviest grief, and it may be the importance given by the actor's feeling and art to this passage which makes one think that less than its due value is given to the following passage about Leah's ring.

It is, however, in the fourth act, as is fitting, that the actor's complete triumph is attained, and in this there seems to us no room for anything but admiration. From the moment of his entrance to that of his finding his revenge torn from him he is the very incarnation of deadly, resistless hatred. While he listens to the Duke's speech in mitigation he has the horrible stillness and fascination of the rattlesnake. When he answers, his speech is that of a man possessed of his purpose, coldly tenacious of his rights. His object has been gained, and the passion which has been concentrated on it will not deign to waste itself in supporting a position that is unassailable. His scorn of Gratiano's railings seems bitter from habit, and not because he is one whit moved by them. There is something appalling in his aspect when he stands waiting for the long desired moment with the knife in one hand and the scales in the other, and his pointing to the bond with the knife as he asks, "Is it so nominated in the bond?" is admirably conceived and executed. When the moment of defeat arrives it strikes him like lightning, but its effect, like that of his expected triumph, is so powerful that it cannot find expression in any accustomed use of gesture or attitude. He is still in his despair as in his victory; but it is the stillness of one suffering instead of threatening death. Where he before inspired terror, he cannot now but command respect for the very awfulness of his downthrow. He leaves the court with a dignity that seems the true expression of his belief in his nation and himself. His mind is occupied with greater matters than the light jeers of Gratiano, and to these jeers he replies with three slow downward movements of the head, which are infinitely expressive of his acceptance of that which has befallen him and of his power to bear himself nobly under its weight. "Gratiano speaks an infinite deal of nothing," and what he says at this moment seems empty indeed when answered with this silent eloquence. Nothing could be finer than Mr. Irving's acting at this point, which is the climax of a scene the power and imagination of which can scarcely be rivaled.

The striking excellences of Miss Ellen Terry's Portia are, if anything, bettered by being transferred to a larger stage than that on which they were first presented to a London audience. Every changing phase of the part is rendered with the highest instinct and art, and every change seems natural and easy. The tenderness; the love so fine that it finds no check to open acknowledgment; the wit, the dignity; and in the last scene the desire to be merciful and to inspire mercy, giving way to a just and overwhelming wrath, and followed again by the natural playfulness of the lady who is not the less a great lady because she indulges it, are alike rendered with a skill that one must call perfect. As feats of acting the assumption to Nerissa of a bragging youth's manner, and the exit in the trial scene are specially remarkable; but it is needless to point out in detail the patent beauties of a performance with which we can find no fault.

ELMER EDGAR STOLL

From Shylock

As much as fifteen years ago[1] Professor Wendell expressed the opinion, which Professor Matthews has of late reasserted, that Shylock was rightly represented on the stage in Shakespeare's time as a comic character, and rightly in our time as sympathetically human; but the dramatist's intention he left in the dark. . . .

The dramatist's intention—that, I must believe, together with his success or failure in fulfilling it, is the only matter of importance. . . .

Only now and then have critics frankly denied it, and declared that the purpose of the author has only an historical interest. That way, they seem to see, if not madness, chaos lies. For thus a work of art means anything, everything—that is, nothing—and what is the use of discussing it? . . .

The puzzle whether *The Merchant of Venice* is not meant for tragedy . . . is cleared up when, as Professor Baker suggests, we forget Sir Henry Irving's acting, and remember that the title—and the hero—is not the "Jew of Venice" as he would lead us to suppose. . . .

Hero or not, Shylock is given a villain's due. His is the heaviest penalty to be found in all the pound of flesh

From *Shakespeare Studies* by E. E. Stoll (New York: The Macmillan Company, 1927). Grateful acknowledgment is made to Mrs. Doris Franklin for permission to reprint these excerpts.
[1]This essay was written in 1911. The editor has abbreviated it and deleted the footnotes citing abundant authorities. The remaining footnotes have been renumbered [editor's note].

stories, including that in *Il Pecorone,* which served as a model for the play . . . —impoverishment, sentence of death, and an outrage done to his faith from which Jews were guarded even by decrees of German emperors and Roman pontiffs. . . . We know that the poet is not with Shylock, for on that point, in this play as in every other, the impartial, inscrutable poet leaves little or nothing to suggestion or surmise. As is his custom elsewhere, by the comments of the good characters, by the methods pursued in the disposition of scenes, and by the downright avowals of soliloquy, he constantly sets us right.

As for the first of these artifices, all the people who come in contact with Shylock except Tubal—among them being those of his own house, his servant and his daughter—have a word or two to say on the subject of his character, and never a good one. And in the same breath they spend on Bassanio and Antonio, his enemies, nothing but words of praise. . . .

As for the second artifice, the ordering of the scenes is such as to enforce this contrast. . . . Launcelot and Jessica, in separate scenes, are introduced before Shylock reaches home, that, hearing their story, we may side with them, and, when the old curmudgeon appears, may be moved to laughter as he complains of Launcelot's gormandizing, sleeping, and rending apparel out. . . . Still more conspicuous is this care when Shylock laments over his daughter and his ducats. Lest then by any chance a stupid or tenderhearted audience should not laugh but grieve, Solanio reports his outcries—in part word for word—two scenes in advance, as matter of mirth to himself and all the boys in Venice. . . .

As for the third artifice, that a sleepy audience may not make the mistake of the cautious critic and take the villain for the hero, Shakespeare is at pains to label the villain by an aside at the moment the hero appears on the boards:

> I hate him for he is a Christian,
> But more for that in low simplicity
> He lends out money gratis, and brings down
> The rate of usance here with us in Venice.

Those are his motives, later confessed repeatedly;[2] and either one brands him a villain more unmistakably in that day, as we shall see, than in ours. . . .

Only twice does Shakespeare seem to follow Shylock's pleadings and reasonings with any sympathy—"Hath a dog money?" in the first scene in which he appears, and "Hath not a Jew eyes"? in the third act—but a bit too much has been made of this. Either plea ends in such fashion as to alienate the audience. To Shylock's reproaches the admirable Antonio, "one of the gentlest and humblest of all the men in Shakespeare's theater" [i.e., dramas], praised and honored by everyone but Shylock, retorts, secure in his virtue, that he is just as like to spit on him and spurn him again. And Shylock's celebrated justification of his race runs headlong into a justification of his villainy: "The villainy which you teach me I will execute, and it shall go hard but I will better the instruction." "Hath not a Jew eyes?" and he proceeds to show that your Jew is no less than a man, and as such has a right, not to respect or compassion, as the critics for a century have had it, but to revenge. Neither large nor lofty are his claims. . . .

By all the devices, then, of Shakespeare's dramaturgy Shylock is proclaimed, as by the triple repetition of a crier, to be the villain, though a comic villain or butt. Nor does the poet let pass any of the prejudices of that day which might heighten this impression. A miser, a moneylender, a Jew— all three had from time immemorial been objects of popular detestation and ridicule, whether in life or on the stage. The union of them in one person is in Shakespeare's time the rule . . .: to the popular imagination a moneylender was a sordid miser with a hooked nose. So it is in the acknowledged prototype of Shylock, Marlowe's "bottle-nosed" monster, Barabas, the Jew of Malta. . . .

In the Elizabethan drama and character-writing, then, the Jew is both moneylender and miser, a villain who hankers after the Christian's blood, a gross egoist, even an atheist (though charged with dealings with the devil), and at the same time a butt, a hook-nosed niggard. And a similar spirit of rude caricature and boisterous burlesque, with even less

[2]1.3.39f.; 3.1.51.; 3.2. 2, 22f. [Stoll's note condensed].

of characterization, prevails, we have seen, in the treatment
of the Jew in early popular drama on the Continent. Such is
the soil from which the figure of Shylock grew; for almost
everything in Shakespeare is a growth, and strikes root deep
in the present and in the past, in stage tradition and in the life
about him.

The tradition having been examined, it now remains to
examine the opinions, or antipathies, of the time—a sorry
tale to tell. Critics have wondered at the knowledge of
Jewish character displayed by Shakespeare; but Sir Sidney
Lee some years since[3] showed that although banished from
England in 1290, and not readmitted until the latter days of
Cromwell, Jews were then not unknown. "Store of Jewes we
have in England," to quote *The Wandering Jew Telling Fortunes to Englishmen* (1640); "a few in Court, many in the
Citty, more in the Countrey." In 1594, shortly before *The
Merchant of Venice* was written, one of these Jews at court
made something of a stir. Lopez, the Queen's physician, was
tried for conspiracy against her life. Sir Sidney Lee has
shown the bitterness of feeling which it provoked, and the
weight that was given to the fact that the offender was a Jew
by prosecutor, judges, and people. "The perjured and murderous Jewish doctor," cried Coke, "is worse than Judas
himself"; and "of a religious profession," he said again, "fit
for any execrable undertaking." Even his judges spoke of
him as "that vile Jew." Though no longer a Jew by faith,
when he protested from the scaffold that "he loved the
Queen as he loved Jesus Christ," such words "from a man of
the Jewish profession," says Camden, were "heard not
without laughter"; and "He is a Jew!" men cried aloud as the
breath passed from his body. "And what's his reason?" asks
Shylock in the play; "I am a Jew!"
Of itself this incident is enough to show that although

---

[3]*Gentleman's Magazine,* 1880, p. 187 f.; *Academy,* 14 May 1887; *Transactions of New Shakespeare Society,* 1888. Commonly they followed the trade
of old-clothes dealer, it appears from a passage quoted by Sir Sidney Lee from
Every Woman in her Humour (1609) and from Rowley's *Search for Money,*
p. 15—as both now and in the days of St. Jerome. Creizenach quotes Hey-
wood's *Challenge for Beauty* (1635) on their character: "Your English Jewes,
they'le buy and sell their fathers, prostrate their wives, and make money of
their own children, the male stewes can witnesse that." (*Works,* vol. v, 26.)

there was by no means a Jewish peril in Shakespeare's day,
the race-hatred of Angevin times had not burned out. Race-
hatred, indeed, or the desire to profit by it, may have
prompted the writing of this play, that Shakespeare's company might in the present excitement compete with
Henslowe's in their *Jew of Malta.* Even the Reformation, in
England as in Germany, had done little to quench it: only the
later Puritans felt any relentings towards the chosen race.
Hebrews of the Hebrews themselves, it was small wonder.
The visionaries, the Fifth Monarchy men, the Root-and-
Branch men, often looked almost kindly upon the Jews as
they made the Jewish Sabbath henceforth and for ever the
British Sabbath, contemplated surrounding Cromwell with a
Sanhedrim of seventy councillors, and urged on Parliament
the establishing of the *Torah* as the law of the realm. But the
nation as a whole was not so minded; with it race-hatred
went deeper than religion. Cromwell admitted the Jews in
1655; but it had to be, as Graetz remarks, by the back door,
for the Commission designated to sit upon the measure was
under the necessity of being admonished and dissolved like
Parliament itself. Prynne, who for his own faith had lost his
ears, wrote what was, measured by his own professional dis-
senter's standard, a *Short Demurrer,* in two parts, in which,
like Luther a century before him, he raked up all the charges
against the Jews that had ever been made, including usury,
coining, cheating and oppression, crucifixion of children,
blasphemy and sacrilege, malice towards man and God, the
murder of Christ, obstinacy and hardness of heart. "Do not I
hate them, O Lord, that hate thee?" he cries, with none to
contradict him, in his zeal; "I hate them with a perfect
hatred." And others there were like him, as appears from the
petition to Parliament of Robert Rich, surnamed Mordecai,
in 1653, on behalf of the Jews of England, Scotland, and Ireland: "Ever since 1648, it was hoped that persecution for
conscience' sake would cease and truth and mercy take its
place, but contrary thereto, these three last years hundreds in
England have been cast into dungeons and prisons, some
have perished, and others endured whippings, stonings, and
spoilings of goods for matters concerning their law and conscience," etc. Even after these persecutions had, under
Cromwell's iron hand, been allayed, and the Jews admitted

to the rights of worship, it was upon a precarious basis. The doors of the first synagogue were threefold and double-locked. In 1660, a remonstrance upon their usurious and fraudulent practices was made by the Lord Mayor and Aldermen to the King, praying for the imposition on them of special taxes, seizure of their personal property, and banishment for residence without a license. Even after the Revolution, in 1689, a bill specially to tax the Jews was introduced into Parliament.

Such were the disabilities under which the Jews labored for a century after Shakespeare's day. What is the recorded opinion of his contemporaries? Coke, Solicitor-General, is comprehensible in abusing Lopez, but he is hardly so as, no longer Solicitor but a jurist, ex-Chief Justice of the King's Bench, he abuses the Jews in his *Institutes of the Laws of England.* "Odious," he calls them in his commentary on the *Statute De Judaismo,* "both to God and man";—"these cruel Jews, wicked and wretched men." Bishop Joseph Hall, writing to Samuel Burton, Archdeacon of Gloucester, in 1607, rejoices that "our church is well rid of that accursed nation, whom yet Rome harbors . . . while instead of spitting at, or that their Neapolitan correction whereof Gratian speaks, the Pope solemnly receives at their hands that Bible which they at once approve and overthrow." He hates Rome for her tolerance and indulgence, forsooth. "The subtlest and most subdolous people," writes James Howell in 1633 to Lord Clifford; "the most hateful race of men." Jeremy Taylor thinks it is a wonder how the anger of God is gone out upon that miserable people. And Robert South, the greatest preacher in England a century after Shakespeare's death, declares, in a long and virulent passage, that it was appointed as the bitterest humiliation of Christ's life on earth that he should be born of the race of the Jews, "the most sordid and degenerate upon the earth." "And to this very day," he continues, "how much are they disgusted in all those kingdoms and dominions where they are dispersed! They are like dung upon the face of the earth; and that not so much for their being scattered as for being so offensive." Nor is it a legal or theological prejudice merely. Popular literature, like the drama, is, as we have already seen, imbued with it; and dozens of ballads, like *Hugh of Lincoln* and *Gernutus*, still handed it down orally from generation to generation. Enlightenment prevailed not against it.... Frightful persecutions, the Jew-burnings, which at times of great emotional exaltation or depression raged through Europe in the thirteenth and fourteenth centuries, were almost always popular movements, not instigated or directed by the church; and princes, kings, emperors, popes like Clement VI, even fanatics like Saint Bernard, the Dominicans and the Franciscans, had, time and again, to interpose between the Jews and the violence of the mob. Converts fared little better than the faithful. And it was not the priest-ridden countries but those which first attained to a consciousness of national unity—England, France, Spain— as Wellhausen has shown, that expelled the Jews from their borders. In Italy, hard by the papal throne, they enjoyed greater security. In England, in the twentieth year of Henry III, the inhabitants of Southampton petitioned the king for a like privilege with the men of Newcastle, that no Jew should dwell amongst them, and Parliament granted Edward I a fifteenth in return for the favor of expelling the Jewish community as a whole. If, then, the hatred of Jews is at bottom a racial and social, rather than a religious, prejudice, and not Protestantism, not even the free thought of the Renaissance, but only Puritan fanaticism, late in the seventeenth century, availed, in any measure, to dispel it, why should we refuse to recognize it in Shakespeare, who, more than any other poet, reflected the settled prejudices and passions of his race?

To the Middle Ages, in the dearth of Jews and contemporary references to Jews in Elizabethan England, we must turn for illustration—but medieval is the sentiment of this comedy. Most readers and critics nowadays resent the despoiling of Shylock at the end. Indeed, where is there another instance of a villain in a Shakespearean comedy, with such cause for his villainy, coming off so ill? But even a century later, as we have seen, a sense of justice did not keep the government from the consideration of measures of confiscation and extra taxation; and all the European history of the Jewish race for a thousand years before is made up of such measures, put, without consideration, into effect. In the

days of Titus, and afterwards in every nation and princi-
pality of Europe, they were *servi cameroe*; and, in return
for the slight protection they thus received, they were pil-
laged and plundered, legally or illegally. Of his Jews every
feudatory-in-chief spoke as of his serfs or his hounds; and he
sold them, or bought them, or mortgaged them, or, like
William Rufus waxed furious in defense of them, according
to his needs. The king took possession of all the real property of which a Jew was seized, in case of his "death, out-
lawry, or departure hence" (or, in some parts of Europe, as
soon, apparently, as he was known to have purchased it);
and, in defiance of the fourth Lateran Council, of all property whatsoever, as the fruits of usury, on his conversion.
"Judæus vero nihil proprium habere potest," says Bracton
(and the principle prevailed far beyond the Channel); *"quia
quidquid acquirit non sibi acquirit sed regi, quia non vivunt
sibi ipsis sed aliis, et sic aliis acquirunt et non sibi ipsis."*
"They are doomed to perpetual servitude," writes Saint
Thomas Aquinas, "and the lords of the earth may use their
goods as their own." "The curse of the Patriarch rests upon
the descendants of Ham," declared in 1851 the Supreme
Court of Georgia, with reference to another subject race;
"the Negro and his master are but fulfilling a divine appoint-
ment." A medieval sentiment, but alive in Shakespeare's
day and not totally extinct in our own.

Nor were men content with injustice that was legal. . . .
We do not forget that Shylock was also a usurer. Dr.
Honigmann, who is one of them that interpret *The Merchant
of Venice* as a plea for toleration, says that in Shakespeare's
day the word did not carry with it any stigma. Never, surely,
was opinion more mistaken. By laws civil and ecclesiastical,
usury—that is, the exaction of interest of any sort—was a
crime. With expanding trade and manufacture the practice
was widening, but was by no one approved in principle. By
37 Henry VIII, cap. ix, the old laws against usury are, indeed,
abolished, and a rate of ten percent is indirectly legalized by
the fixing of severe penalties for any rate higher; but the
practice is condemned, and classed with corrupt bargains. . . . In 1552, however, by *6 Edward VI, cap. xx,* the act
of Henry VIII is annulled . . . and severe penalties are
enacted against any usury whatever, "forasmuch as Usurie is

by the word of God utterly prohibited, as a vyce most odyous and detestable. . . ." In 1570, by *13 Elizabeth, cap. viii, 6 Edward VI* is annulled and *37 Henry VIII* reenacted, but "foreasmuch as all Usurie, being forbydden by the Law of God is synne and detestable," it ordains that even interest at ten percent or under is forfeitable. . . . It is expressly provided that all offenders shall "also be punished and corrected according to the ecclesiastical laws heretofore made against usury." . . .

[By another and earlier law of Elizabeth's reign, usury is one of the five crimes for which an offender may be subject to excommunication.]

Shylock was both moneylender and Jew. In him are embodied two of the deepest and most widely prevalent social antipathies of two thousand years, prevalent still, but in Shakespeare's day sanctioned by the teachings of religion besides. All that was religious in them Shakespeare probably shared like any other easygoing churchman; but all that was popular and of the people was part and parcel of his breath and blood. . . .

Those who will have it that Shylock, though bad, was made so, do violence to Shakespeare in two different ways. In the first place, they have recourse to an all-pervading irony. Antonio, gentlest and humblest of Shakespeare's heroes, kicking and spitting at Jews and thrusting salvation down their throats,— such, they say, is the spectacle of race-hatred pointed at by the poet. And those others who will have it that Shylock is a noble spirit brought to shame, carry the irony still further, into the characterization of Antonio and his friends. He, not Shylock, is the caricature: his virtues are but affectations and shams; his friends are parasites, spendthrifts, and fribbles! They make no effort to raise the three thousand ducats to save him, they do not even provide him with a surgeon against his need.[4] That is, nothing is what it seems; a comedy ending in moonlight blandishments

---

[4]These are only cases of neglect, which in Shakespeare abound. But as I have said elsewhere, only the positive counts, or else the negative made as prominent as the positive. On the stage—particularly the popular and Shakespearean stage—it is what a man does, not what he leaves undone, that makes the character; on the stage there are, so to speak, no sins of omission.

and badinage is a tragedy, and the play written for the cus-
tomers of the Globe flies over their honest heads to the peaks
of nineteenth-century criticism. Irony is surely unthinkable
unless the author intends it, and here not the slightest trace
of such an intention appears. Moreover, a play of Shakespeare's is self-contained; the irony is within it, so to speak,
not underneath it. There is irony in the appearance of
Banquo at the moment when Macbeth presumes hypocriti-
cally to wish for his presence at the feast; or, more obviously
still, in the fulfilment of the Witches' riddling oracles; but
there is no irony, as we have seen, such as Mr. Yeats discovers in the success of Henry V and the failure of Richard
II. There is irony in the situation of a king so powerful
reduced to a state so pitiful, before he has "shook off the
regal thoughts wherewith he reigned"; but Shakespeare does
not dream that to fail and be a Richard is better than to suc-
ceed and be a Henry—or an Antonio. He knows not the way
of thinking which lightly sets the judgment of the world
aside, nor the ways of modern artistic expression, which
almost withholds the purport of the higher judgment from
the world. No abysmal irony undermines his solid sense and
straightforward meaning. Shylock is indeed condemned; Sir
Henry Irving took no counsel of the poet when he made his
exit from the ducal palace in pathetic triumph.

Nor is Jessica treated with malice, in mockery or irony, as,
having forsaken him and robbed him and never since given
him a regretful or pitying thought, she now revels in jest
and sentiment, in moonlight and melody, at Belmont. . . .
Signior Croce may be horrified at Jessica as was Rousseau
at the unfilial Cléante; but just as sympathy at the theater traditionally is for the debtor and against the moneylender, so
it is for the amorous son or eloping daughter and against the
hard-hearted, stingy father. Thus it had been on the stage
since the days of Plautus; cheating the old man was both
sport for the slave and relief for the son's necessities. Either
consideration gave pleasure in the comic theater. It is not
ideal justice—that is not the business of comedy. . . .

In the second place, they do violence to Shakespeare, as
Mr. Hudson observes, in representing Shylock as the product
of his environment. The thoughts of men had hardly begun
to run in such channels; the ancient rigors of retribution held

fast; men still believed in heaven and hell, in villains and heroes. Though in Shakespeare there is little of George Eliot's moral austerity, as brought to bear on Tito Melema, for instance, Mr. Yeats errs, I think, in the opinion that his plays are, like all great literature, "written in the spirit of the Forgiveness of Sin." Macbeth is not forgiven, nor is Othello. Richard III and Iago were damned even in the making. Though the shortcomings of Falstaff, Bardolph, Pistol, and Nym serve a while as food for mirth, Shakespeare is in full accord with Henry V as he casts his fellows out of his company and out of his mind, to meet their end, maybe, in the brothel or on the gallows. And he is in full accord with Portia and the Duke in the judgment scene. Except in comedy, he has not the spirit of forgiveness which, like Uncle Toby's towards the Devil, comes of mere kindness of heart; and neither in comedy nor in tragedy has he the forgiveness of our psychological and social drama and novel, where both villains and heroes are no more, which comes of fullness of knowledge. Thus he deals with poverty, the hard-hearted, greasy, foul-smelling, ignorant and ungrateful multitude, for which he so often utters his aversion; and thus he deals with the kindred subject of heredity. If a scoundrel is a bastard, or is mean of birth, the fact is not viewed as an extenuating circumstance, but is turned to a reproach. It may in a sense explain his depravity, but never explain it away. It sets the seal upon it. It confirms the prejudice that there is a difference between noble blood and that of low degree. So, though our hearts are softened by Shylock's recital of the indignities he has suffered, the hearts of the Elizabethans, by a simpler way of thinking, are hardened. It confirms the prejudice that there is a difference betwixt Christian and Jew. The Fathers, Protestant theologians like Luther, seventeenth-century lawyers like Coke and Prynne, review the pitiful story of the Jews in Europe grimly, with at best a momentary and furtive pathos. It proves their notion of the curse. . . .

With this conventionality in mind [i.e., that the underdog deserves his fate] we may approach the final question, whether villain and [comic] butt as Shylock is, he may not also be, as Professor Schelling thinks, a pathetic creation. As we have seen, he speaks of Shylock as "semi-humorous," a character in whom there is a grotesqueness bordering on laughter and a pathos bordering on tears. The union of butt and villain is common in Shakespeare's day, as old indeed as the stupid devils of the miracle-plays; and the union of villain and droll goes back to the cleverer devils, and the devils of Dante and medieval painting, and underlies the characterization of most of the villains—Aaron and Iago, for instance—in Shakespearean and Elizabethan drama. But villain, butt, and pathetic figure, all in one, is a thing difficult to conceive. . . .

Before, then, we take up this question whether Shylock is also pathetic, we must consider some fundamental principles, too much ignored: (1) That the interpretation of literature—and of drama even more—is, as we have seen, mainly a study in emphasis. (2) That much comedy skirts the confines of tragedy, and what keeps it comedy is emphasis, or a conventional "isolation," as Monsieur Bergson has called it. (3) That comedy follows without question the manners and prejudices of the time. (4) That in the Shylock scenes there is so large an element of formal external comic technique that it is impossible to consider Shylock only "semi-humorous," in part pathetic. . . .

On the third principle we have been touching already. . . . This Rousseau pointed out long ago, and Monsieur Bergson has made it still clearer. The comic character is "*insocial,*" out of harmony with his social environment; and the spectator is kept "*insensible,*" unsympathetic—there, as Monsieur Bergson says, are two prerequisites. . . .

Now, in London there was no such refined society, or highly unified, organized, and sensitive social consciousness, as in Paris at the time of Molière, or in Athens at the time of Aristophanes; and Shakespeare, by temperament, was not a satirist; but nevertheless the comic spirit and method of all three dramatists had something in common, and the less refined the social consciousness, the more vindictive it is if aroused. Shakespeare's comedies are of course romantic, sentimental, and fanciful; but this contrast of low life with high life is one of his sources of comic effect as well; and honest but humble folk in *A Midsummer Night's*

Dream, Much Ado, As You Like It, and *The Winter's Tale* are made almost unbelievably stupid and ridiculous, while those who in vanity aspire to rise above their appointed place and station, like Justice Shallow and Malvolio, are cheated or made the victims of a ruthless practical joke. Sir Toby, Maria, and the Clown sport with Malvolio while he howls in torment; and Autolycus, to the delight of himself and the audience, fleeces simple, trusting souls who have no fault save their rusticity. . . . But the most remarkable prejudice brought to bear for a comic effect in Shakespeare, is (as, from what has been said, might have been expected) not one which arises out of the *beau monde* at all but out of the people, society in the largest sense. It is the prejudice against Jew, miser, usurer. In each of these roles singly Shylock could not but be a purely repellent or comic figure on the stage because he was an object of derision in the street, indeed by tradition was on the stage as a comic figure already established; and in these roles combined and united, not in a tragedy, but in a comedy, how could he possibly be thought pathetic at all?

. . . We here approach the last principle—the situation has been hedged about with the most explicitly comic technique and apparatus. . . . Here, quite apart from the social and racial prejudices . . . are the comic devices of repetition and inversion, as well as others less easily designated.

By repetition I mean, as in chapter IV, not the repetition of words or phrases at happy junctures . . . but the repetition of a *motif*, as in the daughter-ducats dialogue with Tubal, and in this case it takes the form of alternation:

Tubal. One of them showed me a ring that he had of your daughter for a monkey.

Shylock. Out upon her. Thou torturest me, Tubal. It was my turquoise; I had it of Leah when I was a bachelor. I would not have given it for a wilderness of monkeys.

This, most critics assert, the great historian [Creizenach] of the drama almost alone dissenting, is pathos: it is not the ducats behind the turquoise ("a diamond gone, cost me two thousand ducats in Frankfort!") but the thought of Leah that wrings his heart. "What a fine Hebraism is implied in this expression!" cries Hazlitt. "He has so deep a veneration for his dead wife," says Hawkins, with impenetrable gravity, "that a wilderness of monkeys would not compensate for the loss of the ring she had given him in youth." More Elizabethan fun running to waste! . . . Now he shrieks in grief for his ducats or his daughter, now in glee at Antonio's ruin. In his rage at the trading of a turquoise for a monkey, he blurts out, true to his native instincts, "not for a wilderness of monkeys!" and the Elizabethan audience, as well as some few readers today, have the heart—or the want of it—to think the valuation funny. . . .

Wrenched from the context, there are phrases, even sentences, that may, indeed, seem pathetic. But Shakespeare, as soon as Tubal enters, lets Shylock strike up the tune of "my daughter—my ducats," and, adhering to the method of comic alternation throughout the scene, plays the familiar dramatic trick of taking the audience in for a moment and of then clapping upon the seemingly pathetic sentiment a cynical, selfish, or simply incongruous one:

> Two thousand ducats in that; and other precious, precious jewels. I would my daughter were dead at my foot—and the jewels in her ear! Would she were hears'd at my foot—and the ducats in her coffin.

. . . The pathos is a pretense, a moment's illusion; the laughter alone is real. Nor is it restrained—it is nothing less than a roar. . . .

Then there is inversion, the tables turned. . . . The trial scene is an example. . . .

Professor Baker holds that Shakespeare evinces a sense of dramatic values in presenting Shylock's disappointment as tragic in his own eyes, amusing in Gratiano's. How is the tragic value presented? By the miser and usurer's prostrate prayer to the Duke to take his life if he would take his wealth, or by the plea that he is not well? The biter bitten, is the gibe cast at him at the end of *Il Pecorone*; and that, exactly, is the spirit of the scene. . . . Shylock's disappointment is tragic to

him, but good care is taken that it shall not be to us. Shakespeare is less intent on values than on the conduct and direction of our sympathies through the scene. This he manages
both by the action and the comment. The scene is a rise and
a fall, a triumph turned into a defeat, an apparent tragedy
into a comedy; and the defeat is made to repeat the stages of
the triumph so as to bring home to us the fact—the comic
fact—of retribution. When fortune turns, almost all the steps
of the ladder whereby Shylock with scales and knife had
climbed to clutch the fruit of revenge he must now descend
empty-handed and in bitterness; and what had been offered
to him and refused by him, he is now, when he demands it
again, refused. With the course of the action the comment is
in perfect accord and unison, marking and signalizing the
stages of Shylock's fall. The outcries against the Jew and his
stony heart, of the Duke, Bassanio, and Gratiano—protested
against by Antonio as futile—give place to the jeers of Gratiano and the irony of the fair judge. Gratiano is not the only
one to crow. "Thou shalt have justice, more than thou
desir'st—Soft! The Jew shall have all justice—Why doth
the Jew pause? Take thy forfeiture—Tarry, Jew; the law
hath yet another hold on you—Art thou contented, Jew?
What dost thou say?" Aimed at Shylock as he pleads and
squirms, these words fall from lips which had a moment
before extolled the heavenly qualities of mercy! But for
more than the meager mercy which Shylock is shown there
is neither time nor place, the crowing fits the latter part of the
action as perfectly as the indignant comment had fitted the
earlier, and we must equally accept it or divest the scene of
meaning and sense. The Jew's very words are echoed by
Portia and Gratiano as they jeer, and at every turn that the
course of justice takes (welcomed by Shylock, while it was
in his favor, with hoarse cries of gloating and triumph) there
are now peals and shouts of laughter, such laughter as arises
when Tartuffe the hypocrite is caught by Orgon—*"un rire se
lève de tous les coins de la salle, un rire de vengeance si vous
voulez, un rire amer, un rire violent."* The running fire
assails him to the very moment—and beyond it—that Shylock says he is not well, and staggers out, amid Gratiano's
jeers touching his baptism, to provoke in the audience the

laughter of triumph and vengeance in his own day and bring tears to their eyes in ours. How can we here for a moment sympathize with Shylock unless at the same time we indignantly turn, not only against Gratiano, but against Portia, the Duke, and all Venice as well?

LINDA BAMBER

The Avoidance of Choice:
A Woman's Privilege

The one woman in the comedies whose marriage actually does involve a betrayal of her father is Jessica. Two things, however, distinguish her choice from that of the women in the tragedies: first, it is so lightheartedly made that we hardly perceive it as a choice; and second, Shylock is such a villain that we rarely take his feelings into account. The following exchange is illustrative of both Jessica's insouciance and the general assumption in *The Merchant of Venice* that Shylock is a dreadful person:

> *Launcelot.* . . . look you, the sins of the father are to be laid upon the children. . . . you may partly hope that your father got you not—that you are not the Jew's daughter.
> *Jessica.* That were a kind of bastard hope indeed! So the sins of my mother should be visited upon me.
> *Launcelot.* Truly then, I fear you are damned both by father and mother. Thus when I shun Scylla your father, I fall into Charybdis your mother. Well, you are gone both ways.
>
> (3.5.1–18)

In this fantasy the betrayal of Shylock is pushed back a generation from Jessica to her mother; Jessica is thoroughly

From *Comic Women, Tragic Men* by Linda Bamber. (Stanford, Calif.: Stanford University Press, 1982), pp. 117–20.

justified in her desertion of her father; and the whole issue is cheerfully dismissed in Jessica's last remark: "I shall be saved by my husband. He hath made me a Christian" (19–20). In this exchange heavy themes are orchestrated very lightly; salvation and damnation are subjects for witty repartee. Similarly, the theme of the betrayed father is so lightheartedly developed as to defuse anxieties even as it provokes them.

Furthermore, Shylock and Jessica are not the only father and daughter in the play. They are only the father and daughter appropriate to Venice, to realism, to the world of hard choices. The late Duke of Belmont and Portia present the Belmont version of the father-daughter theme. Portia's father has left a will that would seem to require her to choose between love and family loyalty. But whereas Jessica actually makes such a choice, Portia is spared the trouble of doing so. Her will *happens* to coincide with the terms of her father's will. . . . Jessica's betrayal of Shylock is balanced by the happy outcome of Portia's obedience to her father's will.

How are we to understand the feminine avoidance of choice in Shakespeare's comedies? On the one hand it may seem to depotentiate the women; the comic heroine may seem a masculine wish-fulfillment, an Other who may be loved at no risk to the Self. But on the other hand, the avoidance of choice is a positive gift and a comic prerogative. In the world of comedy the barriers are lowered between our alternatives, and it is the characters who take advantage of the situation that appeal to us most. In *A Midsummer Night's Dream,* for instance, the barrier is temporarily lowered between the world of reality and the world of the imagination. Bottom appeals to us because he moves with such aplomb between the real and the fantastic, stepping over the barriers as if they were not there. This is what we long to do in comedy: *not* to choose between competing worlds but to move between them with Bottom's stupendous calm. In tragedy, of course, the situation is different. In tragedy our alternatives are mutually exclusive, and characters who refuse to choose between them write themselves out of the story. Octavia and Ophelia, for instance, are much reduced by their failures to choose between men—Antony and

Caesar in Octavia's case, and Hamlet and Polonius in Ophelia's. In tragedy we reserve our admiration for those who face their choices squarely, like Cordelia and Desdemona. But in comedy we are attracted to characters who minister to our sense of freedom from choice, and it is no coincidence that these characters are often women. It is the feminine Other who is most at home in the alternative world; the male Self, as we shall see, is less than brilliant in this setting. Bottom is an exception, a male character whose presence dissolves all oppositions; but Bottom is hardly a male Self. His unconsciousness (not to say stupidity) makes him Other to the reader just as his lack of social status makes him Other to the Athenian lovers. When the feminine Other represents the avoidance of choice she does so more consciously than Bottom—although not necessarily more appealingly.

In *The Merchant of Venice,* for instance, Portia spares us the choice between love and law, Belmont and Venice, stepping Bottomlike over the barriers between the two worlds. Just as Bottom goes from being a real tinker to being an imaginary ass-headed creature, Portia goes from being a Belmont heiress to being a Venetian judge. But Bottom is at home in the world of the fantastic because he refuses to dwell on its differences from ordinary life. Portia, on the other hand, is at home in Venice because she knows exactly what the differences are between this public world and the world she has come from. She is perfectly conscious of the choices that face us in this play; she is merely confident that they need not be made.

In this play, general philosophical choices arise from specific choices made by the male hero, Bassanio. Bassanio is faced with a conflict between his concern for his friend and his own desire to marry Portia. He chooses Portia, allows Antonio to become bound to Shylock, and is about to suffer the consequences when Portia sweeps into Venice and saves him from them. At the same time she saves *us* from the philosophical choice between love and law. Because of her, we do not have to choose between our desire for social order and our desire to see our representative excused from society's bargains. On the one hand,

> The duke cannot deny the course of law;
> For the commodity that strangers have
> With us in Venice, if it be denied,
> Will much impeach the justice of the state,
> Since that the trade and profit of the city
> Consisteth of all nations.

(3.3.26–31)

In other words, it will be bad for business, bad for all our business, if Antonio is let off from his bond. But on the other hand, Antonio is a good man, a dear friend, and does not deserve to die at Shylock's hands. The conflict is absolute; when Portia arrives from Belmont it simply melts away. The course of law is upheld *and* Antonio is saved; because of the comic heroine we can have things both ways.

In Shakespearean comedy the successful avoidance of choice is a feminine prerogative, and the men are burdened with a graceless tendency to choose. During Antonio's trial, for instance, Bassanio blunders into this strange speech:

> Antonio, I am married to a wife
> Which is as dear to me as life itself;
> But life itself, my wife, and all the world
> Are not with me esteemed above thy life.
> I would lose all, ay sacrifice them all,
> Here to this devil, to deliver you.

(4.1.281–86)

In a passion to show his friendship for Antonio, Bassanio offers up his love for Portia, gratuitously creating a conflict between the two. No one has demanded the sacrifice of Portia, nor is it clear how it could possibly be of any help. Portia, in disguise as Bellario, is understandably annoyed to hear her husband say these lines. She tells him coolly, "Your wife would give you little thanks for that / If she were by to hear you make the offer." In mock revenge, Portia later pretends to have sacrificed Bassanio to a figure from his own public life: "Pardon me, Bassanio, / For by this ring the doctor lay with me" (5.1.258–59). Of course, Portia herself is the "doctor." As Bellario she demands the ring from Bassanio; as Portia she produces the ring to prove her own infidelity. The point is Bassanio's failure to be two things at once as Portia has been. Since he has betrayed her by choosing between love and friendship, she pretends to have betrayed him by choosing between men. The contrast is striking between the two characters at this moment. Bassanio seems heavy, puzzled, slightly unfit for the world of comedy; he has chosen Portia over Antonio, Antonio over Portia, and now he wants Portia again. Each time he has clumsily identified himself with a single desire. Portia, on the other hand, is talented and desirous as both a woman and a man, Bassanio's wife and, as it were, his lawyer. It is the feminine Other who can avoid choice in comedy, who can perform alternative identities, who can move gracefully between worlds that the hero finds mutually exclusive. The male Self seems tainted in the world of comedy by the lingering necessity to choose. He expects to be one thing only, like a tragic hero; in comedy we are blessedly free to be this and then that, or both at once.

In the courtroom scene, Bassanio fabricates a conflict where none exists; but the comic hero's choice is not always unnecessary. The typical choice faced by the hero in comedy is the one between love and friendship, between a woman and a man. But with the exception of *A Midsummer Night's Dream,* no play deals with a conflict for women between friendship and love. The final word on female friendship comes in *The Merry Wives of Windsor* when Mr. Ford derides the intimacy between Mrs. Page and his wife. Mr. Ford tells Mrs. Page, "I think if your husbands were dead, you two would marry," and Mrs. Page snaps back, "Be sure of that—two other husbands" (3.2.13–15). Marriage is marriage; friendship is friendship. The feminine Other is confident she may simultaneously enjoy relationships that may be mutually exclusive for the male Self.

ALEXANDER LEGGATT

The Fourth and Fifth Acts

[Portia's] disguise gives her, like Julia, a masculine freedom of action. But at first she comes to Venice speaking the accents of Belmont, conditioned by the world of easy wealth she has always known. She opposes the free bounty of mercy to Shylock's had demand for justice:

> The quality of mercy is not strained;
> It droppeth as the gentle rain from heaven
> Upon the place beneath. (4.1.183–85)

But the result of this plea is the most serious instance yet of the device by which a speech is addressed to an uncomprehending listener. Portia speaks of God, heaven and, at the lowest level, of throned monarchs. But Shylock is resolutely a creature of the earth. The most detailed reference he has made to his own tradition is a story of copulating rams. When he speaks of our common humanity, it is in physical terms: "If you prick us, do we not bleed? If you tickle us, do we not laugh?" (3.1.61–2). He seeks even his revenge in the most crudely physical terms. Portia's speech on mercy has an easy flow, but its images are somewhat disembodied.[1] Shylock, as is frequently remarked, hoards his words,[2] but his language is as concrete as the scraping sound of the knife on his shoe, and he illustrates his arguments with pungent coarseness:

From *Shakespeare's Comedy of Love* by Alexander Leggatt. (London: Methuen, 1974), pp. 137–50.
[1]See Clifford Leech, *The Dramatist's Experience* (London, 1970), pp. 158–59.
[2]See Mark Van Doren, *Shakespeare* (New York, 1939), p. 101; and Theodore Weiss, *The Breath of Clowns and Kings* (London, 1971), p. 126.

Some men there are love not a gaping pig;
Some that are mad if they behold a cat;
And others, when the bagpipe sings i'th' nose,
Cannot contain their urine. . . .   (4.1.47–50)

Portia and Shylock speak with utterly opposing voices; there
can be no meeting of minds between them. Her plea for mercy
may have won the hearts of the anthologists, but for all the
effect it has on Shylock she might as well not have spoken. He
cannot be cracked from outside, for his implacable "humor,"
as he himself describes it (4.1.43), is its own justification, a
closed circle of logic—"Hates any man the thing he would not
kill?" (57)—to which no other standard is relevant.

Portia, like Bassanio, must now answer a riddle: she must
enter the mind of her adversary, just as Bassanio entered the
mind of her dead father and saw the inner logic of the casket
game. According to Thomas Marc Parrott, "In Portia's decision we see the triumph of the spirit over the letter, of equity
over legalism."[3] We see, I think, something more painful
and alarming than that. When her appeal to mercy fails,
Portia begins to test Shylock, as the caskets had tested her
unwanted suitors. In a series of exchanges she establishes
that he will not take the money, that he has no surgeon by
to stanch the blood (" 'tis not in the bond"—261), and that
he does have the balances to weigh the flesh: in short, that he
takes his bond logically and literally, as Morocco and
Arragon took the casket mottoes logically and literally. Very
well, then: there is one piece of logic he has overlooked. She
will use the letter to defeat the letter. When she gives her
judgment there is a new tone in her voice, a cold remorseless
logic, with a leaden thump on the key words:

This bond doth give thee here no jot of blood:
The words expressly are "a pound of flesh."
Take then thy bond, take thou thy pound of flesh;
But, in the cutting of it, if thou dost shed
One drop of Christian blood, thy lands and goods
Are, by the laws of Venice, confiscate
Unto the state of Venice.   (305–11)

[3]*Shakespearean Comedy* (New York, 1949), p. 139.

She follows up her argument in detail, releasing one by one the full terrors of the law that Shylock had invoked, playing Shylock's own game with a deadly thoroughness that is more than a little alarming. She does in a more purposeful way what Gratiano does more shallowly by flinging Shylock's own words back at him. She leaves it to Gratiano to show triumph, and to the Duke and Antonio to show mercy: she reserves for herself only the impersonal accents of the law. In place of the flowing bounty of her earlier speeches we hear, at the climax of her argument, the hard command: "Down, therefore, and beg mercy of the Duke" (362). Mercy no longer flows freely: it has to be begged, as Shylock made Antonio and his friends beg. As Bassanio entered and understood the conventions of Belmont, Portia has now entered and understood the special conventions of Shylock's mind, the diabolical game of "justice." And she destroys Shylock with the weapon most fatal to convention—parody.

But—apart from the strange moment when Shylock first proposed the bond—we had not previously thought of Venice as a particularly conventionalized world, certainly not when compared with Belmont. It seemed, if less congenial, more natural and realistic. In this respect, however, the balance of the play has now shifted: Venice, in the trial scene, has become a formal world where a simple dramatic issue is at stake. As in the earlier Belmont scenes, a riddle must be solved. We still hear a wide range of voices, from the tense authority of the Duke to the savagery of Gratiano, but the speed and fluidity are gone, and the sense of busy traffic is stilled as a single crucial issue is decided. The enclosure of the action in the court—something new for the Venetian scenes—adds to this effect. Belmont, on the other hand, has acquired a more open and natural dramatic idiom in the immediately preceding scenes, beginning with the arrival of the messengers from Venice. Portia's preparations for her journey have some of the haste and bustle of Bassanio's preparations in the earlier scenes:

> Take this same letter,
> And use thou all th'endeavor of a man
> In speed to Padua; see thou render this
> Into my cousin's hands, Doctor Bellario;

And look what notes and garments he doth give thee,
Bring them, I pray thee, with imagined speed
Unto the traject, to the common ferry
Which trades to Venice.   (3.4.47–54)

And just before the trial we have that casual, inconsequential scene with Lorenzo, Jessica and Lancelot. Lancelot's jokes, the preparations for dinner, the seemingly irrelevant detail of the Moor's pregnancy (and where did *she* come from, by the way?)—all these combine to suggest a natural world, going about its independent business, far from the passions of the courtroom.

There may also be, in that scene, some ironic foreshadowing of the trial. Lancelot's complaint that "This making of Christians will raise the price of hogs" (3.5.22) may refer forward to Shylock, as well as backward to Jessica. More important, some of Lancelot's joking depends on the excessively literal interpretation of words. Lorenzo remarks,

              I do know
A many fools that stand in better place,
Garnished like him, that for a tricksy word
Defy the matter.   (66–69)

This is followed immediately by Jessica's praise of Portia; yet we will soon see Portia play Lancelot's game in a far more serious way. These touches, light though they are, may have a slight distancing effect if we can remember them in the trial scene itself, since they place some of the key motifs of that scene in a context that trivializes them. But there is a more daring effect, right at the heart of the trial scene. Portia has just told Antonio to prepare for death, and he and Bassanio are taking a last farewell. The crisis is nearly upon us, when we hear the following:

Bassanio. Antonio, I am married to a wife
    Which is as dear to me as life itself;
    But life itself, my wife, and all the world
    Are not with me esteemed above thy life;
    I would lose all, ay, sacrifice them all

Here to this devil, to deliver you.
Portia. Your wife would give you little thanks for that,
  If she were by to hear you make the offer.
Gratiano. I have a wife who I protest I love;
  I would she were in heaven, so she could
  Entreat some power to change this currish Jew.
Nerissa. 'Tis well you offer it behind her back;
  The wish would make else an unquiet house.
Shylock. (*Aside*) These be the Christian husbands! I have a
    daughter—
  Would any of the stock of Barrabas
  Had been her husband, rather than a Christian!

                                              (4.1.281–95)

Like Salerio's arrival in Belmont, this exchange jolts us out
of our involvement with the immediate business of the
scene, and forces us to see it in a larger context. But here the
effect is reversed: we are pulled away from the suffering of
the courtroom and reminded of the more comic world of
love. As Bassanio speaks, his earnest manner is compromised by our growing realization of the irony of his making
the offer in Portia's presence. The effect of his speech
hovers between serious concern and laughter; but in the
comic symmetry of the following exchanges, and the wry
abruptness of the women's replies (especially Nerissa's),
the balance quickly tilts toward laughter. Even Shylock
makes a joke of it, though his joke is more bitter and takes
us back eventually to the serious business of the scene. The
defeat of Shylock comes only a few lines later; but this passage has already put us at a slight distance from the trial, and
lessened (though not destroyed) the seriousness of our
involvement with it, by reminding us that there is a world
elsewhere.

  It is as well that the trial is thus slightly distanced and conventionalized: it helps us to remember that Portia, in out-
Shylocking Shylock, is adopting a necessary but temporary
role, not showing us her true face. There is something not
only unclean but unreal about the trial, both in Shylock's
demand and in the manner of his defeat. At the heart of the
casket game is human reality, reassuringly ordinary and
familiar. There is, in the grimmer game that Shylock plays,

human reality of a different kind, his deep need for vengeance on Antonio; but to satisfy that need he depends on an
impersonal, logical principle, which is no respector of persons, and which can be used just as easily against Shylock as
for him. Portia, in her grim parody of Shylock, shows us
what "justice" really looks like when it is taken to its logical
conclusion. It is a mad obsession with precision:

> if thou tak'st more
> Or less than a just pound—be it but so much
> As makes it light or heavy in the substance,
> Or the division of the twentieth part
> Of one poor scruple; nay, if the scale do turn
> But in the estimation of a hair—
> Thou diest, and all thy goods are confiscate.

> (325–31)

The freeflowing generosity of Portia's normal speech—
"Pay him six thousand, and deface the bond; / Double six
thousand, and then treble that" (3.2.301–2)—is sharply reversed, and becomes an obsession with increasingly minute
measurement. This is more truly fantastic than anything in
the Belmont scenes: like some of the more unsettling fan-
tasies of Lewis Carroll, it shows what happens when logical
principles are set to work without the restraints of humanity
and common sense. If we are to emerge from the play with
any feeling of reassurance at all, we need to feel—as I think
we do—that this mad trial is not a final vision of human
reality.

All the same, Shylock's hate is real enough, however fantastic the manner in which he has tried to satisfy it. And that
hate has merely been defeated, not dissipated. The mercy
shown him by the Duke and Antonio makes no more impression on him than Portia's abstract appeal had done. Moreover, while Shylock can be ordered off the stage, he remains
an immovable part of the play's vision: he is too vigorous
and convincing a figure to be brushed aside with a wave of
the hand, like Egeus, and quickly forgotten. In fact, we need
to remember him if the final scene is to have its full effect. I
have already remarked on the exclusiveness—indeed, the
privateness—of the comic finale, and I think the vision of

harmony it offers is carefully and deliberately restricted. It is right that it should be so, for the play as a whole has shown an uncomfortable world where hate breeds easily and where even love makes painful demands.

Toward the end of *Love's Labor's Lost* and *A Midsummer Night's Dream* there were passages in which the play's central vision was stated in objective terms, apart from the immediate concerns of the characters: the songs of Spring and Winter, an image of mutability, and the description of Theseus's hounds, an image of harmony. At the start of Act 5 of *The Merchant of Venice*, there is a similar but longer and more elaborate passage. It may seem odd at first glance that Lorenzo and Jessica, so unsatisfying as purely romantic lovers, should be chosen to deliver a rhapsody on the beauty of the night, the music of the spheres and the power of harmony. But that is just the point. In their scene at Belmont just before the trial, they have established a special conversational technique by which, while praising the perfections of others, they joke about their own distance from perfection. Jessica says of Portia:

> Why, if two gods should play some heavenly match,
> And on the wager lay two earthly women,
> And Portia one, there must be something else
> Pawned with the other; for the poor rude world
> Hath not her fellow.
> *Lorenzo.*　　　　　　　Even such a husband
> Hast thou of me as she is for a wife.
> *Jessica.* Nay, but ask my opinion too of that.
> *Lorenzo.* I will anon; first let us go to dinner.
> *Jessica.* Nay, let me praise you while I have a stomach.

(3.5.78–86)

As soon as they discuss themselves, they become chatty and ironic. And through the opening passage of Act 5 they teasingly set themselves against higher, unattainable ideals. Their first exchange, on tragic stories of love, is patterned and graceful, but its very patterning makes those tragic tales seem remote. The passage thus creates a comic exorcism of the tragic side of love, recalling the technique of *A Midsummer Night's Dream* (in fact one of the tales is that of

Pyramus and Thisbe). Then, using the same patterned dialogue (and burlesquing it in the process) they descend from these high, remote tales of sorrow and infidelity to a joking accusation of infidelity here and now:

> Lorenzo.   In such a night
> Did Jessica steal from the wealthy Jew,
> And with an unthrift love did run from Venice,
> As far as Belmont.
> Jessica.   In such a night
> Did young Lorenzo swear he loved her well,
> Stealing her soul, with many vows of faith,
> And ne'er a true one.
> Lorenzo.   In such a night
> Did pretty Jessica, like a little shrew,
> Slander her love, and he forgave it her.
> Jessica. I would out-night you, did no body come;
> But, hark, I hear the footing of a man.
>
> (5.1.14–24)

The pattern is mocked, and then broken. As in the depiction of Portia's three suitors, we descend from the remote and exotic to the immediate and human—though here the descent is not so much reassuring as sharply comic. There can be a sadness, too, in this descent: Lorenzo's next meditation, on the music of the spheres, is less stylized, more earnest in tone and admits the imperfections of the here and now with deeper regret:

> Such harmony is in immortal souls,
> But whilst this muddy vesture of decay
> Doth grossly close it in, we cannot hear it.   (6.63–5)

When comedy measures itself against the world of tragedy it can mock it easily enough, for its own vision is essentially different. But beyond tragedy is the vision of permanent, immutable harmony—a vision that is closer to comedy's own concerns; and here there is a deeper sadness in measuring the distance between two imperfect human lovers and the principle of love that orders the universe.

That is as much as Lorenzo and Jessica can give us; but they have seen in Portia a vision of perfection in human terms. And when Portia herself enters the argument is taken one step further:

Portia. That light we see is burning in my hall.
  How far that little candle throws his beams!
  So shines a good deed in a naughty world.
Nerissa. When the moon shone, we did not see the candle.
Portia. So doth the greater glory dim the less:
  A substitute shines brightly as a king
  Until a king be by, and then his state
  Empties itself, as doth an inland brook
  Into the main of waters. Music! hark!
Nerissa. It is your music, madam, of the house.
Portia. Nothing is good, I see, without respect;
  Methinks it sounds much sweeter than by day.
Nerissa. Silence bestows that virtue on it, madam.
Portia. The crow doth sing as sweetly as the lark
  When neither is attended; and I think
  The nightingale, if she should sing by day,
  When every goose is cackling, would be thought
  No better a musician than the wren.
  How many things by season season'd are
  To their right praise and true perfection!

                                                   (89–108)

The importance of context, so vital a part of Shakespeare's comic technique, is here argued explicitly by one of his characters. Context can be used in a variety of ways; but here Portia's argument is that placing too great a beauty against a lesser one, measuring ourselves against standards that are too high, is unjustly belittling, and may blind us to the real beauty of the lesser light. If we concentrate on each experience for its merits, we may find beauty even from the most unlikely sources. (The merry owl of *Love's Labor's Lost* was mildly surprising; here we are asked to think of a sweetly-singing crow!) The argument is confirmed by the atmosphere of the scene as a whole, in which constant references to the beauty of the night and the charm of the music combine to create an image of the harmony that can be achieved even in the fallen world.

This passage, with its hard-won but steady idealism, is still generalized; indeed we may feel that it achieves its confidence only by keeping off the problems of the characters themselves; and the more boisterous, bawdy fun of the ring sequence may seem like a descent to crude realities, away from the vision of harmony. But the ideal is not totally disembodied. It is centered on Portia, the figure of the greatest range and authority in the play: the candle shines from her house; it is her music that sounds. And I suspect that in the ring sequence Portia is applying her attitude of acceptance to the most difficult unresolved dilemma remaining in the play—the conflicting loyalties of Bassanio. The ring embodies those conflicting loyalties: it is Portia's wedding ring, given away at Antonio's insistence, as a sign that his gratitude for his friend's safety outweighs his wife's command:

> My Lord Bassanio, let him have the ring.
> Let his deservings, and my love withal,
> Be valued 'gainst your wife's commandment.   (4.1.448–50)

The conflicting demands on Bassanio have been at the bottom of the most striking moments of dislocation in the play, when Salerio brought Antonio's letter to Belmont, and when Portia and Nerissa spoke up for themselves as wives, at the crisis of the trial scene. The whole idea of obligation has been a painful one, conveyed in images of bodily torture:

> Here is a letter, lady,
> The paper as the body of my friend,
> And every word in it a gaping wound
> Issuing life-blood.   (3.2.263–6)

The image is rooted in Antonio's grisly debt to Shylock, incurred in serving Bassanio—who wishes at one point that he could repay the debt in similar terms: "The Jew shall have my flesh, blood, bones and all, / Ere thou shalt lose for me one drop of blood" (4.1.112–13). The same imagery is used when Portia lectures Gratiano for having given away his ring, which, she says, was "riveted with faith unto your flesh" (5.1.169). Bassanio, not liking the turn of the conversation, exclaims aside "Why, I were best to cut my left hand off, / And swear I lost the ring defending it" (117-8). But here the tone is lighter; and throughout the final scene we are made to see the comic side of Bassanio's dilemma. The dialogue is patterned and repetitive, Gratiano and Nerissa add their usual comic symmetry, and when the women claim to have slept with the youths who had the rings, the laughter becomes broad and earthy. As we saw in the trial scene, there was always a comic potential in the conflicting demands on Bassanio, and when he is finally made to face that conflict, a comic idiom is used. There are one or two hints of serious feeling, as in Bassanio's pained recollection, "I was beset with shame and courtesy" (5.1.217), but for the most part the technique is that of the lovers' quarrel in *A Midsummer Night's Dream*, keeping us at a distance from the pain of the dilemma by emphasizing the neatness of its pattern.[4]

We know, too, that Bassanio's dilemma, so far as it is represented by the giving of the ring, is more apparent than real. He gave Portia's ring to Portia, and the revelation of this provides a neat comic resolution. Without wishing to be too solemn about it, one may suggest that the solution to the comic problem points to a way of resolving the deeper emotional dilemma: there is no final contradiction between Bassanio's ties with Portia and his ties with Antonio. It is the capacity to love that matters, and love can extend itself beyond a single person. This was suggested earlier in the play, when Portia saw her obligation to Antonio (whom she had never seen) as an extension of her love for Bassanio. Being close friends, she argued, the two men must be similar:

[4]In Terry Hands's production for the Royal Shakespeare Company in 1971, an attempt was made to present the ring sequence as a serious emotional dilemma (for example, when Bassanio parted with the ring, Portia burst into tears). But all through the last scene, there was a distinct feeling that the actors were fighting the natural rhythm of the dialogue, and I think the experiment, interesting though it was, demonstrated that the normal comic reading, which usually works so well, is in fact the right one.

Which makes me think that this Antonio,
Being the bosom lover of my lord,
Must needs be like my lord. If it be so,
How little is the cost I have bestowed
In purchasing the semblance of my soul
From out the state of hellish cruelty!   (3.4.16–21)

In the final scene, it is Antonio who gives the ring back to
Bassanio, suggesting, emblematically, that he has a share in
their happiness.[5] In this way, a personal, emotional dilemma
is transformed into a comic plot design, lightened and conventionalized; and in the process its pain is dissipated and it
becomes an occasion for happiness. Portia's general idea of
seeking happiness in the here and now, even in the most
unlikely places, is here applied in practice.

But we are also aware, I think, that happiness can be
drawn out of such a situation only if its implications are
carefully limited. Antonio's quiet manner in the final
scene—"I am th'unhappy subject of these quarrels"
(5.1.238)—does not suggest a joyful acceptance of his
role in the emblematic pattern of harmony. The sexual
joking of Gratiano's final speech narrows the implications
of love to the two pairs of lovers going off to bed, and
Antonio can have no part in this. The restoration of his
galleys is an event so mysterious and remote that it carries
no emotional weight to match the very real anxiety of his
earlier losses:

Portia. . . . Unseal this letter soon;
   There you shall find three of your argosies
   Are richly come to harbor suddenly.
   You shall not know by what strange accident
   I chanced on this letter.
Antonio.   I am dumb.   (275–79)

---

[5]See Hyman, "The Rival Lovers," *Shakespeare Quarterly 21* (1970): 113. At
the end of Sonnet 42 a similar solution is proposed to the love triangle: "But
here's the joy: my friend and I are one; / Sweet flattery! then she loves but me
alone." But here the solution is presented with obvious irony, as a rhetorical
trick that carries no real consolation.

There is no direct statement that Antonio is still unhappy, though an actor can suggest this.[6] But the stage is dominated by four lovers (six, if we count Lorenzo and Jessica), and he is the odd man out. Moreover, the satisfactions he is given are so conventionalized that we cannot be sure how much weight they carry in personal terms—very little, if we are to judge by his reticent manner: the character seems a little detached from the conventional pattern in which he is placed. As in *A Midsummer Night's Dream*, the harmony of the comic ending must be achieved by selection; Portia's speeches about finding beauty by shutting out distractions have suggested as much. But while in the other play we were only *told* what had been left out, here we are shown. The play includes many characters—notably Shylock—who have no part in the final scene. Antonio is on stage, but his involvement is limited and his share in the lovers' harmony is dubious. And the comic stylization of the ring sequence, though it functions effectively on its own terms, involves a narrowing of the play's stylistic and emotional range. In short, the play has shown a larger world than it can finally bring into harmony. This sense of instability is reflected in the dramatic idiom. The play's ultimate gamble, I have suggested, is to combine conventionalized action with human reality, naturalistically conceived. This combination produces shifting, unpredictable results, from the trust in convention in the casket scenes to the distaste of the trial scene, in which the conventionalized action suggests an unhealthy narrowing of vision. In the end Shakespeare pulls back from some of the new territory he has explored: the ring sequence, with its patterned teams of lovers, recalls *Love's Labor's Lost* and *A Midsummer Night's Dream* in its comically stylized presentation of the games of romantic love. It presents, in a now familiar way, an image of order coming from apparent disorder: it is a standard comic ending. But such an ending is itself a convention, and in *The Merchant of Venice* that convention, for all its power, is allowed only a limited success in bringing order out of an

---

[6]Tyrone Guthrie's production at Stratford, Ontario, in 1955 ended with Antonio alone on stage, still holding the letter with the news of his galleys. As the lights faded, he let the paper fall.

intractable world. The security the lovers attain is, like the candle that shines from Portia's house, "a good deed in a naughty world," an area of private happiness for those who can achieve it. The gamble of wedding complex characters to formalized action is exciting, but the combination is too volatile to allow more than a limited sense of harmony at the end.

ROBERT SMALLWOOD

The End of *The Merchant of Venice*:
Four Versions

"Exeunt" says the Folio (and the Quarto) text at the end of *The Merchant of Venice*: please, director, just get these seven principal players—and any attendants your budget has allowed you to afford (of late, in my observation, usually none)—off the stage. The method of removing them is up to the director, for the text offers absolutely nothing beyond the one word "Exeunt." And this single example is explanation enough of why a "director," in one guise or another, will always be necessary, for someone has to make the decision. In making it, of course, it has to be borne in mind that six of the seven are three pairs of lovers (Portia and Bassanio, Nerissa and Gratiano, and Jessica and Lorenzo), at least one of whom, but by implication the others, are leaving to go to bed to consummate a marriage which took place in Act 3 but which was then left unconsummated because of urgent business in a Venetian court of law. The seventh person is Antonio, who opened the play speculating on the reasons for a state of sadness which has still not, at least textually, been explained. Earlier generations of "producers," or of actor-managers (if they were not playing Shylock and had allowed the play to run beyond his Act 4 exit), would have lowered a curtain on a final "tableau"; and a modern director might, perhaps, similarly "freeze" the scene before a final blackout.

From *Shakespeare: An Illustrated Stage History,* ed. Jonathan Bate and Russell Jackson. New York: Oxford University Press, 1996. By permission of Oxford University Press. The title of this extract is the editor's.

But a tableau or a freeze requires the placing of the actors in some series of relationships, so hardly avoids decision-making. The usual method nowadays is to obey the direction and get the actors off the stage. A simultaneous mass exit is of course possible (though I have never seen it); but since some of the participants in the exit are heading for the marriage bed such a suggestion of a group experience in the offing would not be as decision-evading as might at first seem to be the case. Every recent production in my experience has made firm conceptual choices here that bring to a final point interpretative themes pursued through the play. Let us consider a selection of them.

The solution to the problem offered most commonly in recent productions is the one adopted by Terry Hands at Stratford in 1971. As the play ended the three pairs of lovers left the stage in turn, hand in hand, in their vivid and beautiful costumes, blues, whites, oranges. Portia and Bassanio moved off last and Antonio was left alone, pale and serious, in his black suit, his unanswered, undeclared love for Bassanio thwarted. Our last image was of him caught in a narrow spotlight in a solitariness that somehow recalled the loneliness of Shylock's exit at the end of the preceding scene. And as the lights went down a melancholy note on a horn was heard—the sound of the shofar that marks the end of the Day of Atonement for those who knew it, but for the majority of audiences, I suspect, just a sound in keeping with the seriousness of the moment. The production throughout had concerned itself with the isolation of Shylock and Antonio, and it pressed its point home at the close.

When John Barton directed the play in Edwardian costume at the Other Place in 1978 there was no such barrier to the gracious, easy friendship of Antonio and Bassanio, no suggestion of any connection between the elegant, easy-going Antonio of David Bradley and the shiny-suited, obsequious, nub end–saving Shylock of Patrick Stewart. When the time came to get three pairs of lovers and Antonio off the stage, therefore, Gratiano and Nerissa and Lorenzo and Jessica made their exits first, leaving Portia, Bassanio, and Antonio on stage. To celebrate the legal victory (and the weddings), champagne had been served for the return to

Belmont, and at the end Antonio refilled three glasses, drank
a final toast to Portia and Bassanio, and walked briskly from
the stage, leaving them to make their departure slowly, hand
in hand, as the sound of the dawn chorus of birds began.

Neither of these productions may be accused of distorting
the play, of not allowing it to "speak for itself," for both had
most meticulously observed all the information provided by
the text—and in the process had found quite opposite meanings in the play's closing moments, and thence in the piece
as a whole. At Stratford in 1984 John Caird, too, did what
was required of him by the text when he took his seven
actors off the stage, the two minor pairs of lovers first, then
Portia taking Bassanio's arm and seeming about to turn
upstage past an Antonio who had throughout been a dark,
gloomy, unknowable presence. But as she passed him, in a
moment of remorse, or compassion, something possessed
her to take his arm too, and the three of them left together.
As they did, and the lights went down, the thought popped
alarmingly into one's head: "He'll be there for breakfast. . . .
And I bet he'll stay a month," the idea of "love me, love my
friend" that had pervaded the play thus brooding over its
final moments. And still all the director had done was to take
seven actors off the stage.

Bill Alexander likewise used the final "Exeunt" to press
home the concerns of his production of *The Merchant of
Venice* at Stratford in 1987. The basic theme and motive of
the production was the damage to human community
inflicted by religious hatred: a Star of David and a Madonna
and Child, crudely painted on the back wall of the set, were
alternately lit according to which side was in the ascen-
dancy; menacing figures lurked in the shadows when
Antonio and Bassanio visited Shylock in the ghetto, and
when Shylock ventured to the Rialto he was jostled and
goaded by Salerio and Solanio; in the trial scene rival sup-
porters bayed at each other across the court room, and as
Shylock prepared to cut the flesh the Christians intoned
prayers in Latin and Shylock recited a Hebrew ritual, with
Antonio tied to a spar of wood, arms akimbo (giving
offence, the RSC's mailbag suggested, to members of both
religious communities in the audience). When it came to the

end of the play this idea of religious antagonism was pushed to the final blackout: in a scene of much extrovert heterosexual love play between Portia and Bassanio (and Nerissa and Gratiano), clearly intended to humiliate Antonio and to press home the hopelessness of his overt homosexual love for Bassanio, one noticed that Lorenzo and Jessica were not indulging in the same enthusiastic preparations for bedtime. Their relationship, indeed, had clearly soured by the time they arrived in Belmont in Act 3, Jessica finding herself in a no-man's-land between her apostasy to the faith of her birth and the racial and religious prejudice she encountered as Lorenzo's wife. (Gratiano's "cheer yond stranger" (3.2.237), for example, uttered with patronizing contempt, was met by a shrug of inactivity from Nerissa.) At the end, as the lovers rushed off to bed and Lorenzo drifted off after them, Jessica was left on stage with Antonio. She was looking around for something she had lost, and suddenly one saw that Antonio had found it: It was the little cruciform necklace that Lorenzo had given her as a betrothal gift, symbol of her new (though more recently rather tarnished) love, or of her apostasy, as one cared to regard it. And as she, daughter of the head of the minority religious community, who seemed to be losing her commitment in a heterosexual love relationship, reached up for that necklace, hesitantly, not sure that she really wanted it any more, and Antonio, head of the majority religious community but the loser in a homosexual love relationship, withheld it, not sure whether he should give it to her; and as they stood, poised in a religious and sexual uncertainty that encapsulated much of what the production had been about, the lights went down.

SYLVAN BARNET

The Merchant of Venice on Stage and Screen

This is the Jew
That Shakespeare drew.
> (doggerel lines, attributed to Alexander Pope,
> on Charles Macklin's performance)

Probably most actors who play the role of Shylock believe that they are true to the text, and yet we have reports of a wide range of Shylocks. Moreover, exactly what does one mean when one says that a certain portrayal renders the figure "that Shakespeare drew"? In the absence of any explicit statement by Shakespeare about his intention, how can we tell? And even if we had some sort of explicit statement, how could we be certain that we should trust it? If Shakespeare had told his fellow actors that Shylock proposes the bond only "in a merry sport" (as Shylock says at 1.3.142), would we be compelled to believe him, any more than if he told them that some of his best friends were Jews? (There was indeed a colony of Jews in Shakespeare's London, though outwardly they professed Christianity.) Would we not protest that earlier in the scene, in an aside, Shylock says of Antonio, "If I can catch him once upon the hip, / I will feed fat the ancient grudge I bear him"? (43–44)

Such a passage pretty clearly suggests that Shylock is waiting for his chance to destroy Antonio, in fact, it reveals Shylock in so unpleasant a light that it is usually cut from modern performances which tend to present Shylock sympathetically. Still, in trying to find "the Jew / That Shakespeare drew" we can only look at this passage and all of the other passages that go to make up the whole of *The Merchant of Venice*. If we look at the whole play, we will find many passages that suggest a villainous Shylock. And yet we will also find this:

> I am a Jew. Hath not a Jew eyes? Hath not a Jew hands, organs, dimensions, senses, affections, passions?—fed with the same food, hurt with the same weapons, subject to the same diseases, healed by the same means, warmed and cooled by the same winter and summer as a Christian is? If you prick us, do we not bleed? If you tickle us, do we not laugh? If you poison us, do we not die? And if you wrong us, shall we not revenge? If we are like you in the rest, we will resemble you in that.
>
> (3.1.55–65)

Different actors have emphasized different passages in the play, and thus have arrived at different interpretations. Moreover, different ages inevitably must see the play in different ways. *The Merchant of Venice* said or meant something when it left Shakespeare's hand at the end of the sixteenth century, but today, in the light of the murder of six million Jews in our time, it says or means something else. One school of scholarship protests that we will get the most out of the play if we try to see it in its Elizabethan context, but to argue that "the Elizabethans" thought thus-and-so about Jews is scarcely convincing, for although Shakespeare certainly was an Elizabethan, he certainly was not a typical Elizabethan, and he need not have held all of the commonplace views. Moreover, the Shakespeare that interests us is the playwright, not the Elizabethan man who (perhaps) in his routine hours held the prejudices of the period. As Proust said, a work of art "is the product of a different *self* from the self we manifest in our habits, in our social life, in our vices."

Broadly, actors have given us four kinds of Shylocks: (1) a comic villain, frightening but finally ridiculous, something like a wicked stepmother or witch in a fairy tale; (2) a titanic, diabolic figure; (3) a tragic figure, a hero brought low, a man "more sinned against than sinning" (to use words from *King Lear*); (4) a composite figure, at times menacing, at times pathetic, and at times absurd. Despite much disagreement about how the role should be interpreted, and despite the fact that Shylock appears in only five of the play's twenty scenes, and not at all in the fifth act, everyone agrees that the play belongs to Shylock.

Nothing is known surely about how Shylock was played in the earliest productions, but the first published version of the play, the Quarto of 1600, says that the play deals with "the extreme cruelty of Shylock the Jew," thereby implying that the role is one of a villain. In the First Folio (1623) the play is called a "comical history," but these words do not prove beyond all doubt that Shylock was portrayed comically, since a comedy was a play with a happy ending. In 1664—some three quarters of a century after the play was first performed—a poem was published describing Shylock:

> His beard was red, his face was made
>   Not much unlike a witch's.
> His habit was a Jewish gown
>   That would defend all weather.
> His chin turned up, his nose hung down,
>   And both ends met together.

A long-nosed, redheaded Shylock doubtless would have been a comic figure, and quite possibly that is what Shylock was in the earliest productions, but there can be no certainty about this.

The Merchant of Venice was done twice at court in 1605, but judging from the absence of further references, it seems not to have been a great favorite in the first half of the seventeenth century, and it seems not to have been done at all in the second half. In 1701, however, George Granville's adaptation, *The Jew of Venice*, was staged and published in London, with the eminent Thomas Betterton as Bassanio and Thomas Doggett as Shylock. Doggett was known chiefly as a comic actor, so it is likely that he interpreted Shylock comically. But the comedy in the play was somewhat reduced (two comic figures, the Gobbos, were deleted), and Shylock's part was somewhat cut, apparently in an effort to put the emphasis on Bassanio, the romantic hero. Other changes were the alteration of some of Shakespeare's prose to verse, chiefly by breaking it into lines of approximately equal length, and the addition of a scene in Act 2 (the original 2.1–4 were deleted) showing Bassanio, Antonio, Shylock, and others drinking. Antonio offers a toast to friendship. After Bassanio toasts Portia, and Gratiano toasts all women ("be she black, or brown, or fair"), Shylock says,

> I have a mistress that outshines 'em all—
> Commanding yours—and yours though the whole sex—
> O, may her charms increase and multiply.
> My money is my mistress! Here's to
> Interest upon interest.

While there is nothing in this speech that is contrary to Shakespeare's Shylock, there is nothing in it of merit either.

Nicholas Rowe, the editor of the first critical edition of Shakespeare's plays (1709), must have had Granville's version in mind when he wrote that although he had seen *The Merchant of Venice*

> received and acted as a comedy, and the part of the Jew performed by an excellent comedian, yet I cannot but think it was designed tragically by the author. There appears in it such a deadly spirit of revenge, such a savage fierceness and fellness, and such a bloody designation of cruelty and mischief, as cannot agree either with the style or characters of comedy.

Despite Rowe's interpretation of the play, Granville's adaptation, presumably with a buffoonish Shylock, held the stage until 1741, when Charles Macklin presented at Drury Lane (and continued to present until 1789) a Shylock who, far from being comic, was genuinely terrifying. It is said that Macklin had some difficulty persuading the management to allow him to introduce this new conception of an ominous Shylock, but Drury Lane had fallen on bad times, and apparently in desperation, it took the chance and succeeded. The performance was hailed, and Macklin's reputation was made. The mid-eighteenth-century Shylock was Macklin's, for David Garrick never played the part. It is not certainly known exactly what text Macklin used, but probably his text was close to Shakespeare's, with only minor cuts. What is certainly known is that Macklin was immensely successful in portraying a monster who was to be taken seriously. For instance, Francis Gentleman spoke of his "terrifying ferocity," and Georg Lichtenberg, a German who visited England, wrote that Macklin's Shylock

> is more than sufficient to arouse once again in the mature man all the prejudices of his childhood against this race. Shylock is . . . heavy, and silent in his unfathomable cunning. . . . [When Shylock speaks of "three thousand ducats"] he lisps as lickerishly as if he were savoring the ducats and all they would buy. . . . Three such words uttered thus at the outset give the keynote of his whole character.

J. T. Kirkman, Macklin's early biographer, reported that Macklin's Shylock exhibited "the malevolence, the villainy, the diabolical atrocity of the character." "Malevolence" seems to be the word most used, and if one gets the impression that Macklin presented not a man but a monster, at least the figure was to be taken seriously. In view of later interpretations of the role, which inevitably attempt to justify Shylock's behavior by pointing out that he is responding to persecution, it is interesting to notice that the behavior of Macklin's Shylock was in no way excused. Quite the contrary: Francis Gentleman, commenting on the moral of the play, says that "from the Jew's fate may be learned that persevering cruelty is very capable of drawing ruin on itself."

Although one reads that John Philip Kemble (in the late eighteenth century) and George Frederick Cooke (in the first decade of the nineteenth) were impressive as Shylock, it is not until Edmund Kean interpreted the role that one reaches something radically new. Kean, a minor actor who had achieved some reputation in the provinces, made his London debut on 26 January 1814 at Drury Lane. As in Macklin's day, Drury Lane was experiencing difficulties, and was therefore willing to resort to taking chances in order to regain its popularity. Nothing prepared the audience for what it experienced that day. The essayist William Hazlitt gives us an idea of what was expected (i.e., the Macklin tradition) before Kean presented his shattering interpretation:

> When we first went to see Mr. Kean in Shylock, we expected to see a decrepit old man bent with age and ugly with mental deformity, grinning with deadly malice, with the venom of his heart congealed in the expression of his countenance, sullen, morose, gloom, inflexible, brooding over one idea, that of his hatred, and fixed on one unalterable purpose, that of his revenge.

What Kean revealed to Hazlitt was a man who,

> if he carries his revenge too far, yet he has strong grounds. . . . There is a strong, quick, and deep sense of justice mixed up with the gall and bitterness of his resentment. . . . We can hardly help sympathizing with the proud spirit, hid beneath his Jewish gaberdine, stung to madness by repeated undeserved provocations.

Kean rejected what we can call the monstrous interpretation, and made Shylock more human, less mythic. He wore a black wig and black beard (perhaps unprecedented), and evoked not simply terror but pity, especially in the court scene, where his horrified look at the thought of enforced Christianity evoked sympathy in the audience. His general conception was that Shylock is not a repulsive beast but a man who has been so unjustly treated that his resentment quite understandably drives him to acts of destruction. Kean's Shylock was highly passionate, but not diabolic or monstrous or repulsive. Thus, in the scene with Tubal (3.1), when Shylock says, "I would that my daughter were dead at my foot" (83–84), according to a viewer, Kean

> startled back, as with a revulsion of paternal feeling from the horrible image his avarice had conjured up, and borrowing a negative from the next inquiry ["no news of them?"], gasped an agonizing "No, no, no."

Kean made his reputation, and Shylock's, with the production in 1814. Shylock could no longer be considered a simple comic or monstrous figure. When William Charles Macready took up the role in 1823, he was often harsh, but he also conveyed a sense of restraint and sometimes even of tenderness.

The next step, soon taken, was to sentimentalize Shylock. Here is Heinrich Heine reporting on a visit to Drury Lane in 1839:

> When I saw a performance of this play at Drury Lane, a beautiful pale-faced English woman stood behind me in the box and wept profusely at the end of the fourth act, and called out repeatedly, "The poor man is wronged."
> . . . Thinking of those tears I must count *The Merchant of Venice* among the tragedies, although the framework of the play is ornamented with the gayest masks, satires, and love episodes, and the author's real intention was to write a comedy. Perhaps Shakespeare had in mind to create, for the entertainment of the masses, a trained werewolf, a loathsome fabulous monster thirsting for blood, and thereby losing his daughter and his ducats, and becoming a laughingstock. But the genius of the poet, the universal spirit which inspires him, is always above his individual will, and so it happened that he expressed in Shylock, in spite of all his glaring grotesqueness, the vindication of an ill-fortuned sect.

Along with the elevation of Shylock to the role of sympathetic tragic hero goes the deprecation of at least some of the Christians in the play. Thus, for Heine, Lorenzo is "the receiver of stolen ducats and jewels" (true, of course), and Antonio's companions are persons who are quite as fond of money as is Shylock. In short, Heine says, "However much we must hate Shylock, we cannot blame even him if he despises those people a little." This is a far cry from, say, Francis Gentleman, who found even the jibes of Gratiano "admirably pleasant."

There was no turning back from a serious and sympathetic Shylock. In the productions of Edwin Booth, in the 1860s, when Shylock learned in the trial scene that he must become a Christian, he uttered a groan, staggered backward, gave a despairing look, and collapsed. By the way, like many others in the nineteenth century, Booth omitted the fifth act of the play, in which Shylock makes no appearance, and thus put a further emphasis on a tragic Shylock.

Henry Irving restored the fifth act in 1879, went yet further in depicting a sympathetic and tragic figure, and became the great Shylock of the second half of the century. His interpretation was enormously popular, and the production ran for two hundred and fifty nights; during his career Irving played Shylock more than a thousand times. His *Merchant of Venice* was especially famous for three things: its charming Portia (played by Ellen Terry), its illusionistic sets, and its moving Shylock. The sets, esteemed for their beauty and authenticity, included a practicable bridge over the canal. The first scene was especially rich in local color, revealing a ship moored at the right, fruit vendors, a water carrier, and Arab laborers.

Although he restored the fifth act, Irving made some serious alterations in the text. Because his sets were elaborate, it was not worth taking the time to change sets for a short scene located in Belmont that in the text appears between two scenes set in Venice, so a few scenes, such as 2.9, showing the wooing of Aragon in Belmont, were cut. A very few other scenes were cut for different reasons, probably because they included material Irving found distasteful, such as 2.3, in which Jessica says such things as "Our house is hell," and "Though I am a daughter to his blood, / I am not to his manners," and 2.5, in which Jessica says, "I shall be saved by my husband. He hath made me a Christian." Other cuts, such as the great reduction in Bassanio's casket scene, also show Irving's emphasis on Shylock. And Irving cut the bawdry.

Irving's Shylock used a cane—he appeared a trifle infirm—and wore a brown gaberdine. A gray wispy beard, an Oriental shawl, and a black cap with a yellow line across it marked him as a Jew, an outsider, but he was a sober figure, not a grotesque one. One bit of business became especially famous. After Jessica elopes, there was the sound of a barcarolle, some laughing maskers crossed over the

bridge, the curtain fell for a moment and then rose on
the same scene to show Shylock, lantern in hand, entering
the stage and approaching the door of his house. (Later
actors, as we shall see, amplified the business by having
Shylock enter, perceive Jessica's absence, and scream. But
Irving was content to lower the curtain as Shylock
approached his empty house.) In some later scenes he
showed considerable passion, but on the whole, even though
agonized by Jessica's betrayal, Irving's Shylock acted with
considerable restraint. One reviewer, for instance, says of
the passage beginning "No ill luck stirring" (3.1.90),

> Mr. Irving ... is now less vehèment than might have been
> expected; the Jew's passion seems to have exhausted him. ... He
> is overweighted with trouble, and the delivery of the words "no ill
> luck stirring, but what light's o' my shoulders; no sighs, but o' my
> breathing; no tears, but o' my shedding," is charged with the
> pathos of the heaviest grief.

Ellen Terry reports that in the trial scene Irving for the most
part played the role of an "heroic saint," a man no longer
furious but coldly vengeful. True, in this scene he lost some
sympathy when he fawned on Portia while she seemed to be
taking his side, but his contemptuous look of dismissal when
Gratiano meanly jibed at him regained for Shylock the audience's sympathy.

Enter William Poel, the founder of the Elizabethan Stage
Society and a man who made heroic efforts to produce
Shakespeare's plays in circumstances resembling what he
took to be Elizabethan stage conditions. Poel assumed that
the Elizabethan stage was bare, and that because it was not
encumbered with sets that had to be changed, the action
could flow without interruption. Thus the highly praised,
elaborate illusionistic sets of Irving's productions were to
Poel an abomination. In 1898 he staged his version of *The
Merchant of Venice* as a response to Irving's. Poel assumed
that the Elizabethan Shylock was not Irving's gray-bearded
dignified figure but was a red-wigged comic figure, a caricature rather like the comic stage Irishman of the late-
nineteenth-century English theater. The idea, again, was to

get back to the original conception of the play—"the Jew that Shakespeare drew"—and not to see the play in modern terms. Poel accepted the tradition that the Elizabethan Shylock wore a red wig, and was comic in his rage, and was even comic in the trial scene, since (Poel argued) the audience's sympathy in the trial scene should be with Portia, not with Shylock. At the end of the trial scene, when Shylock departs with "I am not well" (4.1.395)—where Irving went out slowly, with dignity—Poel rushed from the stage. He explained: "Only by Shylock being 'in a great rage' as he rushes off the stage, can the audience be greatly pleased, and in a fit humor to be interested in the further doings of Portia." In 1907 Poel again staged *The Merchant of Venice*, this time seeking an even closer approximation to an Elizabethan production by not dimming the house lights and by giving the performance without intermissions. The comedy apparently was more slapstick, with Shylock something of a comic maniac seeking revenge. But the tradition of Irving was too strong to be overcome, and Poel's version was not well received. Perhaps, too, social conditions had so changed by the early twentieth century that even without Irving a strictly comic production could not be acceptable.

Although in his stagecraft Poel anticipated the future, at least insofar as modern productions are relatively swift-moving and tend to preserve Shakespeare's sequence of scenes, the spectacular and illusionistic tradition of Irving, which required deleting or rearranging short scenes, persisted for several decades, notably in productions by Herbert Beerbohm Tree and Frank Benson. Thus, although Shakespeare follows Jessica's elopement with a scene of Morocco wooing Portia in Belmont, and then gives us Shylock reacting to the elopement, Tree in his 1908 production ran the two Venetian scenes together. Jessica departed with her Christian friends, Shylock entered onto the stage (as Irving's Shylock had done), knocked at the empty house, called "Jessica," raged through the house, emerged, hurled himself to the ground, tore his clothes, and poured ashes over his head. In a program note Tree explained that he had improved the play:

In the present arrangement of the play, I have placed the second act entirely in the Ghetto, in order to bring the story of Shylock into greater cohesion. This I believe, has not been done before. It enables us to see much of the life of the Jews and the customs and manners of the day. For many of the details of this scene I am indebted to the courteous assistance of high Jewish authorities.

In speaking of "the life of the Jews and the customs and manners of the day," Tree is referring to his much-praised representation on the stage of Jews hanging out the laundry, engaging in conversation, and praying.

In 1932 John Gielgud, determined to alter the by now traditional serious Shylock, directed a performance that treated the play as a fairy tale. Gielgud explained that he wished "to keep the play from being the tragedy of the Jew," and he succeeded, as he again did when he played Shylock in 1938, but the most interesting production between the wars was staged by the Russian émigré Theodore Komisarjevsky, who served as guest director at the Shakespeare Memorial Theatre in Stratford-upon-Avon from 1932 to 1939. His first production at Stratford, in 1932 (and repeated in the following year) was *The Merchant of Venice*, done in a highly theatrical (which is to say anti-illusionist) style. There was no need to group the Belmont scenes together, as Irving, Tree, and Benson had done, since Komisarjevsky's elaborate set for Venice simply divided down the middle and glided off to the sides, revealing Belmont. The play began with a masque of Pierrots, and the commedia dell'arte motif was continued in Old Gobbo, who was the pantaloon of Italian comedy. Shylock was a comic figure, to be hooted at and dismissed from the stage without a twinge. But if the production marked the rejection of Irving's illusionism and his tragic (or sentimental?) view, it also marked the rejection of Poel's insistence that Shakespeare's plays make the most sense, and provide the most enjoyment, when they are performed on a bare stage.

The two most notable interpretations of Shylock since World War II were those by Morris Carnovsky (1957 and 1967) and Laurence Olivier (1969). In 1957, when Carnovsky performed at the American Shakespeare Festival in

Stratford, Connecticut, his Shylock was a highly sympathetic figure. Carnovsky had read Harold C. Goddard's *The Meaning of Shakespeare*, which argued that Shylock proposed the bond as "a sincere wish to wipe out the past and be friends." According to Goddard, Shylock is like the lead coffin, ugly on the outside but holding something precious within. Carnovsky, in an essay of his own, published in *Tulane Drama Review* (1958) and also in an edition of the play, said that he fully believed Shylock was sincere when he said that he was proposing the forfeit of a pound of flesh merely as a "merry bond." In any case, the Goddard–Carnovsky view (and it has had considerable influence) is that the Christians are a thoroughly despicable lot. The usual charges are that Jessica is a thief and an apostate, Lorenzo is a receiver of stolen goods, and Portia and the rest of the Christians are spoiled darlings who think that money can buy anything. Only after the Christians corrupt his daughter and take from him the one creature whom he loves, does Shylock become (in Carnovksy's words) "the sad, sick, lonely wolf." The 1957 production, with Katharine Hepburn as Portia, was well received, partly because of Carnovsky's dignified acting, partly because of Hepburn's engaging manner, and partly because of a delightful fairy-tale setting. In 1967, again at Stratford, Connecticut, Carnovsky's Shylock seemed a less sympathetic figure. He was not grotesquely comic, and certainly he was not hateful, but his emphasis on revenge made him unsympathetic, and twice in the court scene he became hysterical, pounding on the judge's bench. Still, he never lost his hold on the audience, and since Bassanio and Lorenzo were vacant fools, and Portia a petulant young lady, he remained the most interesting figure and really the only figure for whom the audience could feel some respect.

In 1969 Jonathan Miller directed a production of *The Merchant of Venice* at the National Theatre, with Laurence Olivier as a businesslike Shylock and Joan Plowright as a rather prissy Portia. The play was set in the late nineteenth century, with Victorian furniture for the interior scenes and, for the exterior scenes, a square that evoked not Venice but the financial district of London. The trial took place in what looked like a boardroom, the participants seated around a table. (Curiously, Olivier in *On Acting* says that the idea to set the play in the nineteenth century was his, but Miller in *Subsequent Performances* says it was *his* idea.) There was little comedy, except in the absurd Morocco and the equally absurd Aragon. This Shylock—beardless, by the way—was equipped with a pince-nez, a frock coat, and a top hat. Only the skullcap which he revealed when he took off his top hat indicated that this Shylock was a Jew. For the Gentiles—secure, elegant, arrogant young people, and silk-hatted elders, all insiders, old boys, persons of inherited wealth—the world was a comfortable club, a club to which Shylock (however English he sought to be) did not belong. If one listened closely one could somehow hear that like a Disraeli or a Rothschild, he just didn't belong. Perhaps it was in the very fastidiousness of his speech that one heard an outsider and detected disdain for the in-group. Betrayed by his daughter, however, and pestered by Christians, he lashed out. (It is pretty clear that this Shylock decided to hold Antonio to the bond, not because Shylock had always hated Christians, but because his daughter has betrayed him and is in league with his Christian enemies.) "Hath not a Jew eyes" (3.1.55ff.) was delivered bitingly, the speaker seeking not to evoke pathos but to taunt. In the trial scene, dressed in his frock coat and seated on the edge of his chair, he attentively listened to Portia's legal reasoning, only to find that the law is an instrument of oppression, always available to be used against outsiders. "I am content," he shouted as he left the courtroom; and then, from offstage, came the sound of someone falling, and a cry of pain. Portia, who earlier had spoken of mercy, was utterly unmoved by the cry. The play ended, however, on a strange and somewhat pathetic (and puzzling) note. In an added epilogue, a messenger arrives from Venice with letters for Jessica and Antonio. As they read the messages, in the distance is heard the *kaddish*, the Jewish prayer of mourning. Possibly it is Shylock wailing, or another Jew lamenting the death of Shylock. And at the very end, Jessica is alone, perhaps absorbing the fact that, like her father, she will always be an outsider.

In other postwar productions some emphasis has been put

on Antonio as an outsider, and thus a parallel to Shylock. Both are merchants, are middle-aged, are pensive, and—most important—both stand apart from the general merriment. Some versions, suggesting that what makes Antonio an outsider is that he is a latent homosexual who is in love with the imperceptive Bassanio, emphasize Antonio's isolation by showing him left alone, at the end of the play, after the nicely matched couples joyfully depart without a thought for Antonio.

The BBC television version (1980), released in the United States in 1981, did not emphasize a homosexual love, but it called attention to the superficiality and even cruelty of the supposedly sophisticated Venetian society. Portia (Gemma Jones) seemed at times a spoiled girl; by contrast, Shylock (Warren Mitchell), though scarcely amiable, seemed a man of deep integrity. Such a man, who threatens to expose the corruption beneath the superficially attractive Christian Venetian society, must be crushed if the shallow people of Venice are to preserve their pleasures. The ugliness of the Christians is especially evident in the scene where Shylock is forced to convert. Gratiano threatens him with a knife, and Salerio then places a necklace with cross around Shylock's neck—it might as well be a noose—and forces Shylock to kiss the cross.

"The Jew that Shakespeare drew" is still the subject of scholarly dispute, but the theater today gives us, in various forms, the Jew—and the Christians—that we must see in the light of the history of the twentieth century. That is, our view is quite properly conditioned at least as much by Nazi Germany as it is by Renaissance England.

Bibliographic note: In the following list of Suggested References, for stage history see especially James C. Bulman, *Shakespeare in Performance: "The Merchant of Venice"* (a survey from the beginning), and Bill Overton, *"The Merchant of Venice": Text and Performance* (on selected modern performances).

Suggested References

The number of possible references is vast and grows alarmingly. (The *Shakespeare Quarterly* devotes one issue each year to a list of the previous year's work, and *Shakespeare Survey*—an annual publication—includes a substantial review of biographical, critical, and textual studies, as well as a survey of performances.) The vast bibliography is best approached through James Harner, *The World Shakespeare Bibliography on CD-Rom: 1900–Present*. The first release, in 1996, included more than 12,000 annotated items from 1990–93, plus references to several thousand book reviews, productions, films, and audio recordings. The plan is to update the publication annually, moving forward one year and backward three years. Thus, the second issue (1997), with 24,700 entries, and another 35,000 or so references to reviews, newspaper pieces, and so on, covered 1987–94.

Though no works are indispensable, those listed below have been found especially helpful. The arrangement is as follows:

1. Shakespeare's Times
2. Shakespeare's Life
3. Shakespeare's Theater
4. Shakespeare on Stage and Screen
5. Miscellaneous Reference Works
6. Shakespeare's Plays: General Studies
7. The Comedies
8. The Romances
9. The Tragedies
10. The Histories
11. *The Merchant of Venice*

The titles in the first five sections are accompanied by brief explanatory annotations.

1. Shakespeare's Times

Andrews, John F., ed. *William Shakespeare: His World, His Work, His Influence,* 3 vols. (1985). Sixty articles, dealing not only with such subjects as "The State," "The Church," "Law," "Science, Magic, and Folklore," but also with the plays and poems themselves and Shakespeare's influence (e.g., translations, films, reputation)

Byrne, Muriel St. Clare. *Elizabethan Life in Town and Country* (8th ed., 1970). Chapters on manners, beliefs, education, etc., with illustrations.

Dollimore, John, and Alan Sinfield, eds. *Political Shakespeare: New Essays in Cultural Materialism* (1985). Essays on such topics as the subordination of women and colonialism, presented in connection with some of Shakespeare's plays.

Greenblatt, Stephen. *Representing the English Renaissance* (1988). New Historicist essays, especially on connections between political and aesthetic matters, statecraft and stagecraft.

Joseph, B. L. *Shakespeare's Eden: the Commonwealth of England 1558–1629* (1971). An account of the social, political, economic, and cultural life of England.

Kernan, Alvin. *Shakespeare, the King's Playwright: Theater in the Stuart Court 1603–1613* (1995). The social setting and the politics of the court of James I, in relation to *Hamlet, Measure for Measure, Macbeth, King Lear, Antony and Cleopatra, Coriolanus,* and *The Tempest.*

Montrose, Louis. *The Purpose of Playing: Shakespeare and the Cultural Politics of the Elizabethan Theatre* (1996). A poststructuralist view, discussing the professional theater "within the ideological and material frameworks of Elizabethan culture and society," with an extended analysis of *A Midsummer Night's Dream.*

Mullaney, Steven. *The Place of the Stage: License, Play, and Power in Renaissance England* (1988). New Historicist analysis, arguing that popular drama became a cultural institution "only by . . . taking up a place on the margins of society."

Schoenbaum, S. *Shakespeare: The Globe and the World*

(1979). A readable, abundantly illustrated introductory book on the world of the Elizabethans.

Shakespeare's England, 2 vols. (1916). A large collection of scholarly essays on a wide variety of topics, e.g., astrology, costume, gardening, horsemanship, with special attention to Shakespeare's references to these topics.

2. Shakespeare's Life

Andrews, John F., ed. *William Shakespeare: His World, His Work, His Influence,* 3 vols. (1985). See the description above.

Bentley, Gerald E. *Shakespeare: A Biographical Handbook* (1961). The facts about Shakespeare, with virtually no conjecture intermingled.

Chambers, E. K. *William Shakespeare: A Study of Facts and Problems,* 2 vols. (1930). The fullest collection of data.

Fraser, Russell. *Young Shakespeare* (1988). A highly readable account that simultaneously considers Shakespeare's life and Shakespeare's art.

———. *Shakespeare: The Later Years* (1992).

Schoenbaum, S. *Shakespeare's Lives* (1970). A review of the evidence and an examination of many biographies, including those of Baconians and other heretics.

———. *William Shakespeare: A Compact Documentary Life* (1977). An abbreviated version, in a smaller format, of the next title. The compact version reproduces some fifty documents in reduced form. A readable presentation of all that the documents tell us about Shakespeare.

———. *William Shakespeare: A Documentary Life* (1975). A large-format book setting forth the biography with facsimiles of more than two hundred documents, and with transcriptions and commentaries.

3. Shakespeare's Theater

Astington, John H., ed. *The Development of Shakespeare's Theater* (1992). Eight specialized essays on theatrical companies, playing spaces, and performance.

Beckerman, Bernard. *Shakespeare at the Globe, 1599–1609* (1962). On the playhouse and on Elizabethan dramaturgy, acting, and staging.

Bentley, Gerald E. *The Profession of Dramatist in Shakespeare's Time* (1971). An account of the dramatist's status in the Elizabethan period.

———. *The Profession of Player in Shakespeare's Time, 1590–1642* (1984). An account of the status of members of London companies (sharers, hired men, apprentices, managers) and a discussion of conditions when they toured.

Berry, Herbert. *Shakespeare's Playhouses* (1987). Usefully emphasizes how little we know about the construction of Elizabethan theaters.

Brown, John Russell. *Shakespeare's Plays in Performance* (1966). A speculative and practical analysis relevant to all of the plays, but with emphasis on *The Merchant of Venice*, *Richard II*, *Hamlet*, *Romeo and Juliet*, and *Twelfth Night*.

———. *William Shakespeare: Writing for Performance* (1996). A discussion aimed at helping readers to develop theatrically conscious habits of reading.

Chambers, E. K. *The Elizabethan Stage*, 4 vols. (1945). A major reference work on theaters, theatrical companies, and staging at court.

Cook, Ann Jennalie. *The Privileged Playgoers of Shakespeare's London, 1576–1642* (1981). Sees Shakespeare's audience as wealthier, more middle-class, and more intellectual than Harbage (below) does.

Dessen, Alan C. *Elizabethan Drama and the Viewer's Eye* (1977). On how certain scenes may have looked to spectators in an Elizabethan theater.

Gurr, Andrew. *Playgoing in Shakespeare's London* (1987). Something of a middle ground between Cook (above) and Harbage (below).

———. *The Shakespearean Stage, 1579–1642* (2nd ed., 1980). On the acting companies, the actors, the playhouses, the stages, and the audiences.

Harbage, Alfred. *Shakespeare's Audience* (1941). A study of the size and nature of the theatrical public, emphasizing the representativeness of its working class and middle-class audience.

Hodges, C. Walter. *The Globe Restored* (1968). A conjectural restoration, with lucid drawings.

Hosley, Richard. "The Playhouses," in *The Revels History of Drama in English*, vol. 3, general editors Clifford Leech and T. W. Craik (1975). An essay of a hundred pages on the physical aspects of the playhouses.

Howard, Jane E. "Crossdressing, the Theatre, and Gender Struggle in Early Modern England," *Shakespeare Quarterly* 39 (1988): 418–40. Judicious comments on the effects of boys playing female roles.

Orrell, John. *The Human Stage: English Theatre Design, 1567–1640* (1988). Argues that the public, private, and court playhouses are less indebted to popular structures (e.g., innyards and bear-baiting pits) than to banqueting halls and to Renaissance conceptions of Roman amphitheaters.

Slater, Ann Pasternak. *Shakespeare the Director* (1982). An analysis of theatrical effects (e.g., kissing, kneeling) in stage directions and dialogue.

Styan, J. L. *Shakespeare's Stagecraft* (1967). An introduction to Shakespeare's visual and aural stagecraft, with chapters on such topics as acting conventions, stage groupings, and speech.

Thompson, Peter. *Shakespeare's Professional Career* (1992). An examination of patronage and related theatrical conditions.

———. *Shakespeare's Theatre* (1983). A discussion of how plays were staged in Shakespeare's time.

4. Shakespeare on Stage and Screen

Bate, Jonathan, and Russell Jackson, eds. *Shakespeare: An Illustrated Stage History* (1996). Highly readable essays on stage productions from the Renaissance to the present.

Berry, Ralph. *Changing Styles in Shakespeare* (1981). Discusses productions of six plays (*Coriolanus*, *Hamlet*, *Henry V*, *Measure for Measure*, *The Tempest*, and *Twelfth Night*) on the English stage, chiefly 1950–1980.

————. *On Directing Shakespeare: Interviews with Contemporary Directors* (1989). An enlarged edition of a book first published in 1977, this version includes the seven interviews from the early 1970s and adds five interviews conducted in 1988.

Brockbank, Philip, ed. *Players of Shakespeare: Essays in Shakespearean Performance* (1985). Comments by twelve actors, reporting their experiences with roles. See also the entry for Russell Jackson (below).

Bulman, J. C., and H. R. Coursen, eds. *Shakespeare on Television* (1988). An anthology of general and theoretical essays, essays on individual productions, and shorter reviews, with a bibliography and a videography listing cassettes that may be rented.

Coursen, H. P. *Watching Shakespeare on Television* (1993). Analyses not only of TV versions but also of films and videotapes of stage presentations that are shown on television.

Davies, Anthony, and Stanley Wells, eds. *Shakespeare and the Moving Image: The Plays on Film and Television* (1994). General essays (e.g., on the comedies) as well as essays devoted entirely to *Hamlet*, *King Lear*, and *Macbeth*.

Dawson, Anthony B. *Watching Shakespeare: A Playgoer's Guide* (1988). About half of the plays are discussed, chiefly in terms of decisions that actors and directors make in putting the works onto the stage.

Dessen, Alan. *Elizabethan Stage Conventions and Modern Interpretations* (1984). On interpreting conventions such as the representation of light and darkness and stage violence (duels, battles).

Donaldson, Peter. *Shakespearean Films/Shakespearean Directors* (1990). Postmodernist analyses, drawing on Freudianism, Feminism, Deconstruction, and Queer Theory.

Jackson, Russell, and Robert Smallwood, eds. *Players of Shakespeare 2: Further Essays in Shakespearean Performance by Players with the Royal Shakespeare Company* (1988). Fourteen actors discuss their roles in productions between 1982 and 1987.

————. *Players of Shakespeare 3: Further Essays in Shake-*

spearean Performance by Players with the Royal Shakespeare Company (1993). Comments by thirteen performers.

Jorgens, Jack. *Shakespeare on Film* (1977). Fairly detailed studies of eighteen films, preceded by an introductory chapter addressing such issues as music, and whether to "open" the play by including scenes of landscape.

Kennedy, Dennis. *Looking at Shakespeare: A Visual History of Twentieth-Century Performance* (1993). Lucid descriptions (with 170 photographs) of European, British, and American performances.

Leiter, Samuel L. *Shakespeare Around the Globe: A Guide to Notable Postwar Revivals* (1986). For each play there are about two pages of introductory comments, then discussions (about five hundred words per production) of ten or so productions, and finally bibliographic references.

McMurty, Jo. *Shakespeare Films in the Classroom* (1994). Useful evaluations of the chief films most likely to be shown in undergraduate courses.

Rothwell, Kenneth, and Annabelle Henkin Melzer. *Shakespeare on Screen: An International Filmography and Videography* (1990). A reference guide to several hundred films and videos produced between 1899 and 1989, including spinoffs such as musicals and dance versions.

Sprague, Arthur Colby. *Shakespeare and the Actors* (1944). Detailed discussions of stage business (gestures, etc.) over the years.

Willis, Susan. *The BBC Shakespeare Plays: Making the Televised Canon* (1991). A history of the series, with interviews and production diaries for some plays.

5. Miscellaneous Reference Works

Abbott, E. A. *A Shakespearean Grammar* (new edition, 1877). An examination of differences between Elizabethan and modern grammar.

Allen, Michael J. B., and Kenneth Muir, eds. *Shakespeare's Plays in Quarto* (1981). One volume containing facsimiles of the plays issued in small format before they were collected in the First Folio of 1623.

Bevington, David. *Shakespeare* (1978). A short guide to hundreds of important writings on the subject.

Blake, Norman. *Shakespeare's Language: An Introduction* (1983). On vocabulary, parts of speech, and word order.

Bullough, Geoffrey. *Narrative and Dramatic Sources of Shakespeare*, 8 vols. (1957–75). A collection of many of the books Shakespeare drew on, with judicious comments.

Campbell, Oscar James, and Edward G. Quinn, eds. *The Reader's Encyclopedia of Shakespeare* (1966). Old, but still the most useful single reference work on Shakespeare.

Cercignani, Fausto. *Shakespeare's Works and Elizabethan Pronunciation* (1981). Considered the best work on the topic, but remains controversial.

Dent, R. W. *Shakespeare's Proverbial Language: An Index* (1981). An index of proverbs, with an introduction concerning a form Shakespeare frequently drew on.

Greg, W. W. *The Shakespeare First Folio* (1955). A detailed yet readable history of the first collection (1623) of Shakespeare's plays.

Harner, James. *The World Shakespeare Bibliography*. See headnote to Suggested References.

Hosley, Richard. *Shakespeare's Holinshed* (1968). Valuable presentation of one of Shakespeare's major sources.

Kökeritz, Helge. *Shakespeare's Names* (1959). A guide to pronouncing some 1,800 names appearing in Shakespeare.

———. *Shakespeare's Pronunciation* (1953). Contains much information about puns and rhymes, but see Cercignani (above).

Muir, Kenneth. *The Sources of Shakespeare's Plays* (1978). An account of Shakespeare's use of his reading. It covers all the plays, in chronological order.

Miriam Joseph, Sister. *Shakespeare's Use of the Arts of Language* (1947). A study of Shakespeare's use of rhetorical devices, reprinted in part as *Rhetoric in Shakespeare's Time* (1962).

The Norton Facsimile: The First Folio of Shakespeare's Plays (1968). A handsome and accurate facsimile of the first collection (1623) of Shakespeare's plays, with a valuable introduction by Charlton Hinman.

Onions, C. T. *A Shakespeare Glossary*, rev. and enlarged by

R. D. Eagleson (1986). Definitions of words (or senses of words) now obsolete.

Partridge, Eric. *Shakespeare's Bawdy*, rev. ed. (1955). Relatively brief dictionary of bawdy words; useful, but see Williams, below.

Shakespeare Quarterly. See headnote to Suggested References.

Shakespeare Survey. See headnote to Suggested References.

Spevack, Marvin. *The Harvard Concordance to Shakespeare* (1973). An index to Shakespeare's words.

Vickers, Brian. *Appropriating Shakespeare: Contemporary Critical Quarrels* (1993). A survey—chiefly hostile—of recent schools of criticism.

Wells, Stanley, ed. *Shakespeare: A Bibliographical Guide* (new edition, 1990). Nineteen chapters (some devoted to single plays, others devoted to groups of related plays) on recent scholarship on the life and all of the works.

Williams, Gordon. *A Dictionary of Sexual Language and Imagery in Shakespearean and Stuart Literature*, 3 vols. (1994). Extended discussions of words and passages; much fuller than Partridge, cited above.

6. Shakespeare's Plays: General Studies

Bamber, Linda. *Comic Women, Tragic Men: A Study of Gender and Genre in Shakespeare* (1982).

Barnet, Sylvan. *A Short Guide to Shakespeare* (1974).

Callaghan, Dympna, Lorraine Helms, and Jyotsna Singh. *The Weyward Sisters: Shakespeare and Feminist Politics* (1994).

Clemen, Wolfgang H. *The Development of Shakespeare's Imagery* (1951).

Cook, Ann Jennalie. *Making a Match: Courtship in Shakespeare and His Society* (1991).

Dollimore, Jonathan, and Alan Sinfield. *Political Shakespeare: New Essays in Cultural Materialism* (1985).

Dusinberre, Juliet. *Shakespeare and the Nature of Women* (1975).

Granville-Barker, Harley. *Prefaces to Shakespeare*, 2 vols. (1946–47; volume 1 contains essays on *Hamlet, King*

Lear, Merchant of Venice, Antony and Cleopatra, and *Cymbeline*; volume 2 contains essays on *Othello, Coriolanus, Julius Caesar, Romeo and Juliet, Love's Labor's Lost*).

———. *More Prefaces to Shakespeare* (1974; essays on *Twelfth Night, A Midsummer Night's Dream, The Winter's Tale, Macbeth*).

Harbage, Alfred. *William Shakespeare: A Reader's Guide* (1963).

Howard, Jean E. *Shakespeare's Art of Orchestration: Stage Technique and Audience Response* (1984).

Jones, Emrys. *Scenic Form in Shakespeare* (1971).

Lenz, Carolyn Ruth Swift, Gayle Greene, and Carol Thomas Neely, eds. *The Woman's Part: Feminist Criticism of Shakespeare* (1980).

Novy, Marianne. *Love's Argument: Gender Relations in Shakespeare* (1984).

Rose, Mark. *Shakespearean Design* (1972).

Scragg, Leah. *Discovering Shakespeare's Meaning* (1994).

———. *Shakespeare's "Mouldy Tales": Recurrent Plot Motifs in Shakespearean Drama* (1992).

Traub, Valerie. *Desire and Anxiety: Circulations of Sexuality in Shakespearean Drama* (1992).

Traversi, D. A. *An Approach to Shakespeare,* 2 vols. (3rd rev. ed, 1968–69).

Vickers, Brian. *The Artistry of Shakespeare's Prose* (1968).

Wells, Stanley. *Shakespeare: A Dramatic Life* (1994).

Wright, George T. *Shakespeare's Metrical Art* (1988).

7. The Comedies

Barber, C. L. *Shakespeare's Festive Comedy* (1959; discusses *Love's Labor's Lost, A Midsummer Night's Dream, The Merchant of Venice, As You Like It, Twelfth Night*).

Barton, Anne. *The Names of Comedy* (1990).

Berry, Ralph. *Shakespeare's Comedy: Explorations in Form* (1972).

Bradbury, Malcolm, and David Palmer, eds. *Shakespearean Comedy* (1972).

Bryant, J. A., Jr. *Shakespeare and the Uses of Comedy* (1986).

Carroll, William. *The Metamorphoses of Shakespearean Comedy* (1985).

Champion, Larry S. *The Evolution of Shakespeare's Comedy* (1970).

Evans, Bertrand. *Shakespeare's Comedies* (1960).

Frye, Northrop. *Shakespearean Comedy and Romance* (1965).

Leggatt, Alexander. *Shakespeare's Comedy of Love* (1974).

Miola, Robert S. *Shakespeare and Classical Comedy: The Influence of Plautus and Terence* (1994).

Nevo, Ruth. *Comic Transformations in Shakespeare* (1980).

Ornstein, Robert. *Shakespeare's Comedies: From Roman Farce to Romantic Mystery* (1986).

Richman, David. *Laughter, Pain, and Wonder: Shakespeare's Comedies and the Audience in the Theater* (1990).

Salingar, Leo. *Shakespeare and the Traditions of Comedy* (1974).

Slights, Camille Wells. *Shakespeare's Comic Commonwealths* (1993).

Waller, Gary, ed. *Shakespeare's Comedies* (1991).

Westlund, Joseph. *Shakespeare's Reparative Comedies: A Psychoanalytic View of the Middle Plays* (1984).

Williamson, Marilyn. *The Patriarchy of Shakespeare's Comedies* (1986).

8. The Romances (*Pericles, Cymbeline, The Winter's Tale, The Tempest, The Two Noble Kinsmen*)

Adams, Robert M. *Shakespeare: The Four Romances* (1989).

Felperin, Howard. *Shakespearean Romance* (1972).

Frye, Northrop. *A Natural Perspective: The Development of Shakespearean Comedy and Romance* (1965).

Mowat, Barbara. *The Dramaturgy of Shakespeare's Romances* (1976).

Warren, Roger. *Staging Shakespeare's Late Plays* (1990).

Young, David. *The Heart's Forest: A Study of Shakespeare's Pastoral Plays* (1972).

9. The Tragedies

Bradley, A. C. *Shakespearean Tragedy* (1904).

Brooke, Nicholas. *Shakespeare's Early Tragedies* (1968).

Champion, Larry. *Shakespeare's Tragic Perspective* (1976).

Drakakis, John, ed. *Shakespearean Tragedy* (1992).

Evans, Bertrand. *Shakespeare's Tragic Practice* (1979).

Everett, Barbara. *Young Hamlet: Essays on Shakespeare's Tragedies* (1989).

Foakes, R. A. *Hamlet versus Lear: Cultural Politics and Shakespeare's Art* (1993).

Frye, Northrop. *Fools of Time: Studies in Shakespearean Tragedy* (1967).

Harbage, Alfred, ed. *Shakespeare: The Tragedies* (1964).

Mack, Maynard. *Everybody's Shakespeare: Reflections Chiefly on the Tragedies* (1993).

McAlindon, T. *Shakespeare's Tragic Cosmos* (1991).

Miola, Robert S. *Shakespeare and Classical Tragedy: The Influence of Seneca* (1992).

———. *Shakespeare's Rome* (1983).

Nevo, Ruth. *Tragic Form in Shakespeare* (1972).

Rackin, Phyllis. *Shakespeare's Tragedies* (1978).

Rose, Mark, ed. *Shakespeare's Early Tragedies: A Collection of Critical Essays* (1995).

Rosen, William. *Shakespeare and the Craft of Tragedy* (1960).

Snyder, Susan. *The Comic Matrix of Shakespeare's Tragedies* (1979).

Wofford, Susanne. *Shakespeare's Late Tragedies: A Collection of Critical Essays* (1996).

Young, David. *The Action to the Word: Structure and Style in Shakespearean Tragedy* (1990).

———. *Shakespeare's Middle Tragedies: A Collection of Critical Essays* (1993).

10. The Histories

Blanpied, John W. *Time and the Artist in Shakespeare's English Histories* (1983).

Campbell, Lily B. *Shakespeare's "Histories": Mirrors of Elizabethan Policy* (1947).

Champion, Larry S. *Perspective in Shakespeare's English Histories* (1980).

Hodgdon, Barbara. *The End Crowns All: Closure and Contradiction in Shakespeare's History* (1991).

Holderness, Graham. *Shakespeare Recycled: The Making of Historical Drama* (1992).

————, ed. *Shakespeare's History Plays: "Richard II" to "Henry V"* (1992).

Leggatt, Alexander. *Shakespeare's Political Drama: The History Plays and the Roman Plays* (1988).

Ornstein, Robert. *A Kingdom for a Stage: The Achievement of Shakespeare's History Plays* (1972).

Rackin, Phyllis. *Stages of History: Shakespeare's English Chronicles* (1990).

Saccio, Peter. *Shakespeare's English Kings: History, Chronicle, and Drama* (1977).

Tillyard, E. M. W. *Shakespeare's History Plays* (1944).

Velz, John W., ed. *Shakespeare's English Histories: A Quest for Form and Genre* (1996).

11. *The Merchant of Venice*

In addition to the titles listed above in Section 7, The Comedies, see the following:

Barnet, Sylvan, ed. *Twentieth Century Interpretations of "The Merchant of Venice"* (1970).

————. "Prodigality and Time in *The Merchant of Venice*." *PMLA* 87 (1972): 26–30.

Brown, John Russell. "The Realization of Shylock: A Theatrical Criticism." *Stratford-upon-Avon Studies 3: Early Shakespeare,* ed. John Russell Brown and Bernard Harris (1961): 187–209.

Bulman, James C. *The Merchant of Venice* [*Shakespeare in Performance*] (1991).

Danson, Lawrence. *The Harmonies of "The Merchant of Venice"* (1978).

Geary, Keith. "The Nature of Portia's Victory: Turning to

Men in *The Merchant of Venice.*" *Shakespeare Survey* 37 (1984): 55–68.

Gross, John. *Shylock: Four Hundred Years in the Life of a Legend* (1992).

Holderness, Graham. *William Shakespeare: "The Merchant of Venice"* (1993).

Holmer, Joan Ozark. *"The Merchant of Venice": Choice, Hazard and Consequence* (1995).

Kahn, Coppélia. "The Cuckoo's Note: Male Friendship and Cuckoldry in *The Merchant of Venice.*" *Shakespeare's "Rough Magic,"* ed. Peter Erickson and Coppélia Kahn. (1985): 104–12.

Leventen, Carol. "Patrimony and Patriarchy in *The Merchant of Venice.*" *The Matter of Difference: Materialist Feminist Criticism of Shakespeare,* ed. Valerie Wayne (1991): 59–79.

Lewalski, Barbara. "Biblical Allusion and Allegory in *The Merchant of Venice.*" *Shakespeare Quarterly* 13 (1962): 327–43.

Newman, Karen. "Portia's Ring: Unruly Women and Structures of Exchange in *The Merchant of Venice.*" *Shakespeare Quarterly* 38 (1987): 10–33.

Novy, Marianne. *Love's Argument: Gender Relations in Shakespeare* (1984).

Overton, Bill. *"The Merchant of Venice": Text and Performance* (1987).

Rabkin, Norman. *Shakespeare and the Problem of Meaning* (1980).

Shapiro, James. *Shakespeare and the Jews* (1996).

Stoll, E. E. *Shakespeare Studies* (1927).

Wheeler, Thomas. *"The Merchant of Venice": An Annotated Bibliography* (1985).

The Signet Classic
Shakespeare Series:

The Histories

extensively revised and updated to provide
more enjoyment through a greater
understanding of the texts

HENRY IV: PART I, *Maynard Mack, ed.*   (527119)

HENRY IV: PART II, *Norman Holland, ed.* (522532)

HENRY V, *John Russell Brown, ed.*   (526902)

HENRY VI: PARTS I, II, & III,
Lawrence V. Ryan, Arthur Freeman, &
Milton Crane, ed.   (523121)

RICHARD II, *Kenneth Muir, ed.*   (527194)

RICHARD III, *Mark Eccles, ed.*   (526953)

To order call: 1-800-788-6262

Signet Classic   (0451)

The Signet Classic Shakespeare Series: The Tragedies

extensively revised and updated expert commentary provides more
enjoyment through a greater understanding of the texts

ANTONY AND CLEOPATRA, Barbara Everett, ed.   (527135)

CORIOLANUS, Ruben Brower, ed.   (528433)

HAMLET, Sylvan Barnet, ed.   (526929)

JULIUS CAESAR, William and Barbara Rosen, ed.   (526899)

KING LEAR, Russell Fraser, ed.   (526937)

MACBETH, Sylvan Barnet, ed.   (526775)

OTHELLO, Alvin Kernan, ed.   (526856)

ROMEO AND JULIET, J. A. Bryant, Jr., ed.   (526864)

TROILUS AND CRESSIDA, Daniel Seltzer, ed.   (522974)

Available wherever books are sold, or
to order call: 1-800-788-6262

S363